INNER WORKINGS

Edited by
ZACK BE

ISBN-13: 979-8-9894060-1-2

Cover art *Melting Power* by Michal Kváč

CONTENTS

EDITOR'S PREFACE
BY ZACK BE

We all know the sensation of reading the last line of a story and being flooded with emotions: excitement, or sadness, or amazement, or perhaps even criticism of the author's craft. Whatever we're left with, there's often a concurrent desire to share those feelings with someone else—to walk out of the movie theater of the mind, turn to your fellow moviegoer, and ask: "What did you think of *that*?"

These moments are as much about extending the experience we had with the story as they are about sharing connection and validation with others. As authors, we experience this feeling twofold—not only do we want to process how the story made us feel, but we also have a need to process another question entirely: "How did they do that?"

Especially in genre fiction, the answer might literally be "magic." Most of the time, however, the key to writing an effective story is "craft," or, the set of specific tools and techniques a writer uses to develop a narrative that conveys meaning and produces effects. Innumerable words have been written about how to write an effective story—you may have some books about that on your shelf right now —but you don't often find those words printed immediately after a story in the same volume, creating an opportunity for the author to reflect directly on their story while discussing their craft. I believe doing so creates the conversation that so many readers—and especially authors—often crave when they close their books.

Inner Workings is an anthology that experiments with that exact structure. Within these pages you will find sixteen exciting science fiction and fantasy stories by the award-winning authors of the Calendar of Fools writing collective and some very special guests. Each story is paired with an essay by the author exploring some aspect of their writing craft, continuing the "conversation" about writing with their readers well after the story itself has been completed. The hope is that *Inner Workings* can be more than just another anthology, instead representing a community of writers and readers sharing and expanding their craft together.

What is the Calendar of Fools? In brief, we are a collective of authors who first met at the long-delayed 2020 Writers of the Future winners' workshop and awards gala, pushed all the way back into October 2021 and eventually shared between both the Volume 36 and 37 winners. There is a lot to say about our time in Los Angeles, but to keep this preface brief, our group hit it off and decided to work together on future projects, including *Inner Workings*, our debut anthology. Our goal is for this project to embody the ethos that brought us together and further build a community around developing our craft.

Although I took on the role of editor for this anthology, it is important to note that this book came together as the result of a large group effort. For example, story selection—usually the primary job of an editor—was replaced by an alternative structure. Each author (myself included) selected a story they wanted to represent them in the anthology and workshopped it with three other Fools before sending it to me for final editing. Craft essays were pitched, discussed, and then written and edited in a similar fashion. Beyond that, a core team of Fools—F. J. Bergmann, John Campbell, Andy Dibble, David A. Elsensohn, Storm Humbert, Erik Lynd, A. X. Ander, Luke Wildman, and myself—met bi-weekly to plan and manage our Kickstarter, financials, cover art, book interiors, campaigns, and more. It was an incredible group effort during which we learned a lot from each other, further aligning with the ethos of the overall project. We are all excited to finally see it come to fruition and look forward to sharing and learning from you, the reader! Find us online at calendaroffools.com, @calendarofools or @cal_of_fools

-Zack Be

DEER DANCER

BY REBECCA E. TREASURE

Rebecca grew up reading in the Rocky Mountains. After living many places, including Denver and Tokyo, she began writing fiction. Rebecca's short fiction has been published by or is forthcoming from *Zooscape*, *Seize the Press*, Air & Nothingness Press, *The Dread Machine*, Flame Tree Publishing, WordFire Press, Galaxy Press, and others. She is an Associate Editor at Apex Book Company and Magazine, a freelance editor, and a writing mentor for young writers. She currently resides in Stuttgart, Germany, where she juggles children, a corgi, editing, and writing. She only drops the children occasionally. Find her on Twitter @R_E_Treasure.

Dani slipped off her shoes at the front door and stepped outside.

She shivered, only cotton pajama pants and a sweatshirt between her and cool autumn humidity. A crescent moon illuminated the muddy soybean field, the woods beyond. The *whoosh-hiss* of a CPAP and the frenetic murmur of the kitchen radio faded as she closed the door, replaced by crickets chirping and a few early birds pestering their fellows to seize the day.

Dani inched down the stairs, feeling with her feet for cold nails so creaking wouldn't give her away. Mom slept late, and Dad would be prepping, over a black coffee and toast, for a long day of working someone else's fields. They wouldn't notice she'd gone, but they'd stop her from leaving. Splinters in the wide planks caught at the soles of her feet like the house itself tried to hold her back.

Finally, her toes crunched into sharp gravel. *Home free.*

Dani stepped onto the thick crabgrass. Power flowed up from the soles of her feet, electrifying her limbs and lifting her chest. Morning's chill disappeared, the world enveloping her like a sheepskin coat. She leapt over the rusted chain link fence, and grinned at Orion dipping toward the horizon. Dani sprinted toward the woods to the unkempt meadow beyond, fingertips grazing tall grassy stalks.

Dani didn't know where the power came from, or how she knew to use it. For as long as she could remember, Mom had fretted endlessly about Dani wearing shoes outside, gloves in the garden, citing the dangers of hookworms and broken glass, chiggers and ticks.

Now, of course, Dani knew there was more to the warning.

On a Thursday afternoon three weeks before, mud squelching between her toes, rainwater fuzzing her vision, Dani found magic in the mud.

Her worn sneakers had gotten soaked in an Arkansas rainstorm. Angry at having to walk in the rain—Mom could have driven the mile to the main road—Dani had taken them off to walk from the bus stop. The surge of warm energy, of knowledge of the world around her still set her heart racing. She'd been eating flat crackers with sour grape juice once a month at the clapboard church in town since she could walk, but never had she had such a communion before.

Kneeling in the brown soup on the side of the old farm road, she'd coiled her fingers into the mud. Earthworms writhed around her wrists and between her fingers. A corn snake slithered from the field and looped through her ankles. Even a damp farm cat prowled from the woods, hesitant and then arching and purring as Dani soothed her. They'd danced with her, celebrating newfound togetherness, the music of puddles and thunder a staccato beat to their swirling gyrations.

That night, Mom had shuffled around the kitchen making dinner while Dani fought her homework. The sweet, heavy smell of meatloaf filled the space between them, as impenetrable as the algebra on the table. Dani had opened her mouth to ask about the power, but each time her jaw clacked shut.

If Mom knew, she wanted Dani to stay away from the knowledge. If she didn't know, she might get Preacher O'Leary over to pray for Dani, or call the school and have them send the district counselor in from the big town. Or worse. So Dani kept her mouth shut.

Instead, she began to sneak out in the mornings and dance until dawn.

Dani reached the edge of the woods. Oaks and hickories towered over the eastern horizon, disguising the coming light. Dani took a slow breath of the humid, chill air and then stretched her fingers into the shadows, grasping at the life all around her. She wouldn't be alone long. Her friends would arrive soon, and then they would dance.

Rose appeared first, stepping from the shadows. A swirl of black and amber hairs on the sloping forehead reminded Dani of a meadow rose. Big wet black eyes, skittish at first, had softened to what Dani counted as love. Fear faded under the joy Dani shared, and she'd taught the deer to dance.

Rose nudged Dani with her round nose, looking for a scratch behind the ears. Behind Rose came her yearling, Slippers—because he danced with such carefree abandon, leaping and twirling in the air like the characters in *The Nutcracker* on TV last Christmas.

Slippers sidled next to his mom, blinking wide eyes at Dani, then bent to munch on delicate grass under the trees. The rest of the herd ambled forth, delicate hooves barely denting the crisp ground. Duchess and Dudette, two young does Dani couldn't tell apart; Mystery and Shadow, two grown does who didn't trust Dani to pet them; and finally, a few yards away, King, his tall antlers glowing in the predawn glimmer.

"Let's dance," Dani whispered.

She flung her arms wide, the momentum pulling her into a spiral of dizzy glee. At the same instant the deer leapt into the air, low backs arching as hooves spiked toward the stars. Rose stayed close to Slippers, prancing and nudging him with her head. Mystery's ears flipped forward and back as she jumped; Shadow disappeared into the grass and reappeared, running for the joy of it. Duchess and Dudette hammered their hooves into the soil, bucking and rearing.

Dani spun on her toes, which curled into the rich topsoil, grounding and lifting her free. The rich, murky scent of dew and earth smoothed out the piney bite of the late autumn air. Sparrows and bluebirds joined the dance, swirling and singing in a tornado of feathers and whistles above the meadow. Dani's arms twirled around her head, occasionally dropping to stroke a long nose or a flashing wing.

King stood, solemn eyes scanning the horizon and the woods, but his white tail flipped up and down, up and down, the tempo to the celebration. Tears slid down Dani's cheeks, the animal's shared joy overflowing.

The sky shifted from gray to silver to gold. The birds peeled off to find their breakfasts; Duchess and Dudette scampered into the woods. Rose and Slippers settled to let Dani scratch their long noses, then skipped away into the safe shadows under the trees. Left alone with King, Dani bowed her head to the buck. He blinked once and was gone.

Dani turned and slumped back to the house. In the dark, it looked as solid as any other. Daylight revealed the truth. Once-white paint peeled at every chance, the shingles on the roof more curled than a fiddlehead. Dani rolled over the fence back into the yard and crossed the sharp crabgrass. She hesitated, one foot lifted, still connected to the world all around. Then she climbed onto the porch, the magic snapping like an icicle. She picked up her shoes and slipped into the house.

Dad's gravel and tar voice called from the kitchen. "Dani, that you?" He'd be dressed already, in work boots and jeans with a grubby t-shirt, off to help someone with their farm or herd for the day.

"Yes, Dad. I'm up. Morning." Dani waited, her stomach grumbling at the waft of coffee and toast. She shrugged off the pang of hope for warmth. He'd either need her for something or he wouldn't speak at all.

"Feed the chickens after school. I'm heading over to Sheridan today to pick up some deer corn. Season starts today. I'll be home late."

Deer season. Dani's stomach twisted, suddenly hollow and silent. Her fists clenched. "Yessir. I'll take care of the chickens."

Her voice must have been hard, because Dad's turned heavy. "Don't you whine at me. And weed the garden. There's more damn dandelions out there than turnips."

"Yessir." By the time the garden and chickens were done, Mom would need her for dinner and dishes, and then Dani would have homework. She winced, remembering the unfinished algebra in her room. She'd have to miss sleep, warn the deer, lead them away.

After dressing in blue jeans and a gray t-shirt—she peeled off a few ticks she'd accumulated in the field and set them on the tall dandelion outside her window—Dani grabbed her backpack and headed to the kitchen. Two pieces of toast sagged on the table, butter soaking into a folded paper towel.

She stared at them, confused. Had Dad forgotten his breakfast? His truck grumbled away down the driveway. Dani picked up the still-warm toast, wondering if it was meant for her. She swallowed that hope along with the salty crunch of white bread. Both caught in her throat as Dad's brake lights disappeared onto the distant road. She sipped the last bit of hot black coffee in Dad's used mug.

6:30. Time to go.

On her way to the bus, Dani hesitated again at the bottom step, heart aching. No warmth flowing through her fingers when she reached the ground, no joy or life filling her chest. Isolated and empty, she crossed the field again. She didn't look up, didn't acknowledge the birds singing or the insects scurrying toward their eternal goals. By the time she reached the bus stop, her back hunched like the half-done homework had turned to stone.

The banana-yellow bus, complete with brown spots, grumbled to a halt. A cloud of chalky dust enveloped Dani as brakes squealed. Blinking grit from her eyes, she shifted the bag on her shoulder and slumped up the black slip-guards into the bus. Miss Carson tapped her blue manicured fingertips on the steering wheel without turning her head. Dani slid into the first empty seat.

The sophomore she'd settled next to groaned and climbed onto his knees so he could talk to his friends in the seat behind them.

"Trade me seats?"

His friends chortled.

Dani scooted as far down as she could, her knees pressed into the indents formed by dozens of knees before her. Jessica Lowe tapped away on her cell phone across the aisle. Remembering her dawn dance, Dani smiled, watching mile markers slide by out of the window past Jessica. Jessica looked up, accentuated eyebrows arching, and smiled back. Dani straightened, courage filling her. She opened her mouth to speak.

Then Jessica's mouth fell open, her face twisting. "Oh my god she's got a tick!"

The boy next to Dani yelped and pushed at her. Gasping, Dani fell sideways into the aisle, her head bumping into Jessica's thigh.

"She touched me! Get it off!" Jessica squealed and slapped at Dani. Miss Carson slammed on the brakes, sending Dani flopping forward down the aisle. Her ankle caught on the bolted seat leg and twisted with a sharp pain.

Miss Carson stood up. "Get back in your seat, girl. What are you thinking, rolling around like that?"

Dani tried to push herself up, but she was crumpled and stuck, her backpack tangled around her legs. Her ankle throbbed. Fifty high school students watched her writhe and groan while Miss Carson shouted over the laughing chatter. More than one cell phone froze the moment with a *ka-chick*.

Finally upright and back in her seat, Dani stared at her lap, her face so hot she thought blood might burst from her pores. Jessica, back on her phone, laughed until her eyes watered.

Dani wiped her own tears away. The tick nestled into the crook of her elbow. With forefinger and thumb, she gripped him at the base of his head and yanked in a swift, smooth motion. He came free, little legs dancing with what Dani knew must be terror. He'd been warm and fed, safe, and now he was cold and flailing in a monster's grip. Dani tried to soothe him, cupping him in her palm, but Jessica screeched again.

"God, Danielle, you are so *gross*."

Dani looked up at Jessica, whose phone had raised for another picture, and threw the tick into her face.

Dani's mom shuffled into the office, pale between linoleum and fluorescent glare. Her Mickey Mouse house dress flapped around unshaven legs, but she'd worn platform flip-flops with fake diamonds on the straps. Short graying hair stood out at damp angles.

Mom glanced at Dani, her face an empty husk not yet recovered from sleeping pills, and walked past her into the principal's office. Dani crouched in the plastic seat, hugging her backpack to her chest and trembling. The one rule about school had always been, "Don't get in trouble." Dani's parents didn't care about grades or sports, but they didn't like to be noticed.

Ten minutes later, Mom emerged, walking out of the office without looking back. Dani picked up her bag and followed, wincing at her sore ankle. The moment the engine of the old Corolla turned over, Mom lit a cigarette and cracked the window. The booming preacher on the radio thundered, sound waves stirring the smoke along the dashboard.

Mom focused on the road and her sermon while Dani held still and tried not to cry in the cavernous silence between them. When they stuttered into the driveway, Mom crammed her third cigarette into the ashtray and looked at Dani for the first time since leaving the school.

"Do your chores."

"Yes ma'am."

Dani didn't bother going in the house. Mom would have the TV on, watching true crime or sometimes fake crime, and chain-smoke until Dad got home. Then Dani would really get it.

Dani threw her backpack on the porch and went around to the garden, wishing she could grab a jacket against the cold sun. Denim work gloves hung on the hook by the plywood and chicken wire gate.

Dani picked them up, staring at them. Etched in the worn, blue denim, garden soil told of Mom's fear of filth. Even as a little kid, Mom wouldn't let her play in the dirt. Tendrils of curious hope sprouted from her spine. She put the gloves back on the hook.

In the garden, Dani knelt on warped boards used to walk between the rows. She took a deep breath and plunged her fingers into the soil on either side.

Slower than before, she warmed. Power seeped in her chest, then flooded her with a sudden burst. She threw her head back, grinning at the cool blue sky. The cold fell away with the pain in her ankle, replaced by warm elation.

Then she snorted, remembering Jessica tearing at her perfectly prepared hair to rid herself of the tick. Dani had found the poor thing under a seat when they got to the school and left it on a sodden plant in the office. It would find a secretary to latch onto. Dani laughed.

A tomato bug dropped onto her wrist and wriggled with her joy. She lifted it back onto a fresh leaf and turned to the weeding with relish. She couldn't dance, but she was *free* in the sunshine, bonds with every living thing for miles soothing her, comforting her.

After weeding the garden, Dani went into the house for lunch. The folded paper towel fluttered on the table, stained with grainy butter. Dani's eyes swam with tears. If Dad *had* made her breakfast, it wouldn't happen again.

She grabbed the first thing she saw—a microwavable ravioli cup. The dramatic retelling of an adulterous affair turned deadly blasted from the living room. Dani didn't bother to heat the cup. Mom might add more chores if Dani reminded her she was home. After slurping down the cold ravioli and filling the empty cup with water from the hose a few times, Dani turned to the chicken coop.

Maybe if she cleaned it, Dad wouldn't be so mad when he got home. She considered trying to explain, to tell them about her dancing, but dismissed the thought. They couldn't understand.

At the coop, Dani froze, looking down at her off-white sneakers. She glanced to the house, then kicked them off. She pulled off her socks, dropping them on the ground. Warmth flooded her. The chickens stilled, their squawking at the expectation of food muted. Dani sensed them, their simple needs of power and food and rest, the drive to lay an egg rising and falling like the sun.

Even the rooster stopped his flapping parade in front of the gate. Dad called him Chicken Dinner because of how mean the old thing was. "I'm gonna cook that sonuvabitch one of these days," he'd say once a week.

Dani eyed the black and orange bird. Usually she had to kick him once or twice to get him to back off. When she met his eyes, she shared his pride, his joy in the crowing. *Today we're friends.* She stepped into the coop.

Two hours later, Dani had cleaned the coop and put fresh sawdust down for the birds. They babbled around her ankles, bumping her with soft heads and cooing when she bent down near them. They helped, even, scrabbling after the flies and beetles uncovered by Dani's efforts. She closed the gate behind her and breathed deeply of the clean air tinted with lumber and chicken musk.

The sun wasn't even halfway down to the horizon. Dad wouldn't be home for hours. Mom wouldn't bother Dani as long as she stayed out of the house. Dani's eyes drifted to the woods. Would they dance with her now, in the bright of day? Did she dare?

She couldn't be sure they'd ever return if she sent them away, warned them off with fear. One last dance.

Leaving her shoes by the coop, she skipped toward the edge of the woods. Birds swooped down to croon their pleasures of sky and soaring. A bushy-tailed squirrel chittered from a low tree. Dani waited at the edge of the woods for her friends.

A skunk waddled from the underbrush first, his nose wiggling in curiosity. Dani squatted down so she didn't scare him, waiting. His tail twitched, low, and he crept closer, fear turning to elation.

Above them, squirrels chittered and around Dani's feet, mice erupted from a thousand different places. A family of armadillos bustled from the field, arching their backs and hopping in anticipation. Dani felt the music rising in her, anticipation like Christmas Eve, but this time rewarded. Even the wind seemed to push at her, urging the dance to begin.

Where are Rose and Slippers? And the rest?

Wide eyes glistened from the deep shadows a few minutes later. The deer stopped at the edge of the woods, unwilling to cross into the sunlight. "It's okay," Dani whispered. "It's me." King stood furthest away, but when Dani spoke, one delicate foreleg lifted and dropped.

Rose stepped forward then, Slippers just behind. Their hair glistened like jewels in the afternoon sunshine. Shadow and Mystery flicked their ears, nervous, watching. Duchess and Dudette trotted forward. Grinning so hard her ears popped, Dani began to dance.

Reassured, the two hesitant does joined the frenzy. Squirrels leapt from branch to branch, the armadillos rolled and bounced, the mice skittered between everyone's footsteps. Slippers ventured further from Rose than usual, popping up from shadows and behind dense grass. King stood, watchful, at the edge of the woods.

They danced. Time faded, unimportant. Sweat ran down Dani's back, her thighs and arms ached, but she couldn't stop. Didn't want to stop. She put all thoughts of Dad, Mom, Jessica, and school out of her mind and sank completely into the depth of life around her. Here she was understood, here she was loved.

Her emotions stripped away to the simplicity of the dance, the uncomplicated pleasure of a healthy body and fresh air and sunshine. The smaller creatures came and went; birds diving in to join for a while, then ascending back into the sky. The deer stayed by Dani, and their joy filled her. King patrolled toward the far woods, his tail flipping up and down, up and down.

So involved was Dani in her dance that she didn't realize the sun had slipped to the horizon, hadn't heard Dad's old truck rumble down the driveway. She knelt, basking in the fading light, breathless at the sight of King illuminated by the sunset, a riot of browns and golds and blacks topped by his crown of ivory. His eyes met hers, the glossy black reflecting life and joy all around.

Then he stiffened.

The crack of a rifle punched Dani's eardrums.

King collapsed, twitching.

The other deer and animals fled to the woods.

No no no no no no no!

Dani stood, fell, scrambled over to the dying deer, his eyes still on hers. "I'm sorry," she tried to say, but only a wail escaped. King's head settled in her lap as the ink-black of his eyes faded to a dull, empty charcoal.

Dani screamed at the sky. Rage filled her.

The thomp-thomp of heavy boots echoed back in her mind like doom. She turned on her knees, staring up at her dad, who carried his rifle under one arm.

Dad raised his fists, shaking them at her. "What are you doing out here? You could have been hurt! I didn't see—" His shout ricocheted across the field, boiling with anger.

"Why?" She managed to gasp the word, her jaw aching with tight muscles and bones grinding.

He blinked. "Deer season. Got a buck tag, Dani. Go back to the house. Get out the way so I can clean the—"

"No!" Dani threw her arms around the fading warmth of King's neck. "Never!"

Dad's voice dropped and hardened. "Move, Danielle. You're in enough trouble as it is."

A guttural howl clawed its way from Dani's chest. She thrust her fingers into the dirt, glaring at her father. A squirrel dropped from above, screaming in a high-pitched fury. It landed on Dad's baseball cap, clawing and biting. The mice returned, an army of tiny teeth swarming over the thick work boots.

Dad started hollering. Dani kept her eyes fixed on him. The skunk flashed past, teeth bared, and added his acrid stench to the fray. Tiny streaks appeared here and there on Dad's face and hands, batting at the sudden torrent of furious birds and bees and bugs.

Dani screamed again, all the words she couldn't say shooting back at Dad. Her ribcage felt like it would burst. *You did this, you never understand!*

Then Dani saw something in Dad's face she'd never seen before. Something she'd never imagined to see on that sun-worn leathery expression.

Grief.

When he looked at Dani between his arms, from where he crouched on the ground trying to protect his exposed flesh from the rage she'd thrown at him, his eyes were damp and his face drooped in a stubbled frown.

He knew, he knew all along.

The fury seeped away. Her friends peeled off, their own fear taking over without her selfish human emotion driving them to attack. She bent over King's neck, holding him and waiting for Dad to start shouting. She had nothing left, no tears for her friend.

The oily pine and earth perfume still rising from the stiffening body settled her, calmed her, even as a fresh sinkhole of grief pulled her toward the ground. She smoothed the hairs along the back of King's neck, avoiding the perfectly round wound just below his shoulder.

Dad sank onto the ground next to her. "Tried to protect you." He took off his maroon and white baseball cap, wiping sweat from his forehead. "Didn't want you to know."

Dani looked up. She'd gotten the power from *him*. "Why?"

He sighed. For a long time he didn't speak—just sat, splayed in the dirt, bleeding from a dozen tiny wounds and reeking of skunk.

When his hands touched the earth, the depth of the man she'd dismissed as distant and uncaring swept her breath away like wind in front of a storm. The warmth of their shared power dimmed next to the blazing fire of his love for her. His heart ached for King, just as hers did. Dani gazed at him, her eyes full of tears.

"We're selfish beings," he finally said. His eyes lifted to the horizon, where Orion would be climbing the sky in a few hours. "Using their freedom, their love, and giving nothing back." He shook his head. "It's not fair, Dani. Let them be."

He reached out and patted King on the shoulder. Dani stiffened, but the rage was spent.

She'd never been free. She'd stolen freedom from her friends, and it had cost more than she could pay.

Dad creaked to his feet. "Gotta butcher the deer. Need the meat. Can't waste it." He started to walk away. "I'll give you a few."

Dani sat in the cold evening, the sky fading from gold to silver to black. She shivered, clinging to King's neck. Her other friends did not return. She sensed them, out in the woods, but she also sensed their fear. The fear had been there all along, buried under Dani's dance. Fear that should have kept them safe.

Finally, when the golden glow in the kitchen window was the only light beyond the stars, Dani stood, dragging her body upright against a terrible weight. She couldn't bring herself to say goodbye. Shame coursed through her, burning hotter than the power ever had. She walked away without looking back.

Movement on the other side of the field caught her eye. Slippers stepped out of the gloom, gentle eyes glistening in the moonlight. He leapt once, high into the air, landed with a scarcely heard thump, then faded into the woods.

Dani, her chest aching as though her ribs cracked, raised a hand. They hadn't needed her to teach them to dance. They knew all along.

She crossed the field to the chicken coop, then bent and pulled on her socks. Then her shoes. Her connection to the world shattered. Chickens squawked. The air grew cold around her.

Leaving the laces untied, she used the gate to get into the yard and climbed the steps to the door, each stair creaking and sinking.

Mom and Dad talked in the kitchen, waiting for her. Dad, who shared her power, whose love for Dani burned iridescent within him. A tiny tendril of warmth wormed up her back.

Breathing fast, Dani paused on the porch. *Not free, but maybe... maybe not alone either.*

Dani slipped off her shoes at the front door, and went inside.

HYPNOTIZING YOUR READER
BY REBECCA E. TREASURE

I have to admit I was skeptical the first time I heard the great writing teacher Dave Farland talk about "hypnotizing the reader." To me, it seemed to unnecessarily mystify the practical nature of what writers do—we put words on the page in an order that interests and entertains readers. To attach something beyond that (albeit deceivingly) simple approach to our work felt superstitious. We're not magicians, after all, we're craftspeople.

The more I listened to Dave teach, though, and the more I studied the craft of writing, the more I realized he was right. This hypnotization is what separates good writers from great writers, and good stories from great stories. We love and admire works best when they completely transport us from our so-called real life into another time, place, and headspace.

This invites the obvious question: what are the best tools writers have to carry our readers away? Setting aside the importance of plot, dialogue, characters, and the other big box sections of craft, sensory writing can draw the reader in like no other skill. When those carefully ordered words on the page not only activate the language centers of the brain, but also the sensory and emotional reaches, connecting memory and physicality to the story, the reader does indeed become hypnotized. Sitting on their couch, they are taken to the world we've created with smells, sounds, textures, shadows, and movement.

Many stories fall flat, or at least do not reach their greatest heights, by not taking advantage of sensory description and reader immersion in the text.

While studying anthropology in college, I read a book that has informed my understanding and interpretation of the world ever since. *Understanding Media: The Extensions of Man*, by Marshall McLuhan, opens with a chapter titled, "The Medium is the Message." Simply put, McLuhan argued that the way in which a society receives its media—from cultures of oral tradition to the broadsheet era to our modern mobile devices—influences and informs that society's beliefs and behaviors.

For example, modern Western culture is heavily influenced and informed by visual media—television, movies, and now the visual focus of social media—and this in turn guides how we approach storytelling. When we picture a story in our minds, it is the visual, often, that catches our imagination first. A scene, a character, a setting, or a world often spark the initial dive into a new story. As a result, many beginning writers place an emphasis on visual descriptions in their stories. "Deer Dancer" itself was heavily inspired by the mental image of a girl dancing with a herd of deer. The story grew out of an image.

Yet, we experience our world through myriad senses beyond vision. Touch, smell, taste, sound, and more—storytellers should take advantage of all these to entrance our readers. Of course we should not disregard visual description entirely. Humans are primarily visual creatures. Newborns are hardwired to focus on faces, for example, and our enjoyment of visual beauty (never forgetting the eye of the beholder) is ubiquitous across time and culture. Yet we experience our worlds through a kaleidoscope of senses, not just vision. Storytellers should take advantage of all our reader's senses to strengthen our hypnotic power.

Behind the Curtain

If our goal as writers is to hypnotize our readers, then, we cannot have the clunky mechanics of our craft interrupting their experience. We must disguise our deliberate takeover of our reader's mind with structure, manipulating the human brain into deceiving itself. The reader is, of course, complicit with this usurpation. They want to be hypnotized, which makes our job easier, but we still cannot tip our hands.

We must be very, very sneaky.

One of the tools I learned early in my writing career is called a "KAV" cycle—Kinesthetic, Audio, Visual. This is a tool best employed at the beginning of a scene, to ground and orient the reader in a new setting. The elements don't have to come in that "KAV" order, but including these three beats is a powerful way to engage the reader's mind beyond simple words, using the reader's willingness and the brain's interest in details to draw the reader into the scene.

For example, the beginning of "Deer Dancer" opens with all three: "She shivered, only cotton pajama pants and a sweatshirt between her and cold winter humidity [kinesthetic]. A crescent moon illuminated the muddy soybean field, the woods beyond [visual]. The whoosh-hiss of a CPAP and the frenetic murmur of the kitchen radio faded as she closed the door, replaced by crickets chirping and a few early birds pestering their fellows to seize the day [audio]."

By hitting these three sensory beats, the reader steps forward with the character into a fully realized world. When the story changes scenery as Dani reaches the edge of the woods, there's another KAV cycle: "Oaks and hickories towered over the eastern horizon, disguising the coming light [Visual]. Dani took a slow breath of the humid, chill air and then stretched her fingers into the shadows, grasping at the life all around her [Audio, Kinesthetic]."

Another powerful way to engage the reader's mind and draw them more fully into the text is by engaging their emotions through sensory details beyond the visual. Tying descriptions to feelings helps to bring those feelings to life. Two examples of this appear early in "Deer Dancer": First, "Splinters in the wide planks caught at the soles of her feet like the house itself tried to hold her back," and second, "The sweet, heavy smell of meatloaf filled the space between them, as impenetrable as the algebra on the table." Both examples take a sensory detail that many readers can recall or imagine, and tie it to the emotional state of the character. This not only enriches the setting, but it informs the character's perspective and feelings.

Tread Lightly

Some writers, and indeed a number of readers, do not like to experience the world of a story via this rich tapestry of senses. Instead, they skim or are even bothered by extensive description, preferring stories that trust the reader to imagine setting while getting on with the plot. For writers who do not visualize their stories with these kinds of details, I'd argue it's still important to use sensory beats to engage the full mind of your sensory-oriented reader—but it doesn't have to be heavy. A loose rule of thumb is to hit a fresh sense every page and a half.

If you struggle to find these details, another tool I learned from David Farland is to imagine yourself in the setting and draw out the sensory details for one specific sense at a time. Close your eyes and, for an entire minute, imagine every element of the scene.

For instance, imagining everything that could possibly be smelled in a darkened basement during a tornado warning: dust, dampness, laundry detergent, peppermint from last year's Christmas decorations, mud from the old boots in the corner, pepper from the pantry, and more. Do this for touch, vision, sound, and taste, trying to perceive the setting through your character's body, eyes, ears, and tongue. Listing all of these would annoy some readers, overwhelm others, and weaken the setting as a whole. We don't want to flood our reader's mind, we want to activate them as broadly as possible. So, instead, pick one, or perhaps two, of the most evocative descriptions and then tie them to the character experience.

Speaking of tongues, flavor and food are an oft-overlooked and subtly powerful means of engaging the reader's mind. But there is an inherent problem with food, of course. Whose food? The staples of one society are the exotic dishes of another. One Thanksgiving I shared pumpkin pie with a Filipino friend—she'd never had it and thought the mushy texture was disgusting—while she excitedly prepared avocado ice cream for me (not my favorite). Use food to enrich your setting while also carefully describing it just enough to tease the food centers of your reader's brain.

In "Deer Dancer," I mention suburban U.S. staples: toast, meatloaf, ravioli. Most readers from the U.S. or Canada will instantly imagine the taste, texture, and smell of those foods, activating their brains beyond the language centers. But a reader who has never had meatloaf isn't going to be as deeply engaged by that scene, which is why we must rotate and vary our sensory details as we proceed.

Some things are widespread enough that we can use them to engage the reader's mind as long as we don't rely on too much detail. Coffee, for example, appears in most modern cultures even if it might take different forms in each. I recently interviewed an author from Brazil who said he didn't drink coffee or tea, instead beginning his day with an iced maté. The human brain loves to make associations, though. If I tell you a character began their day with a cold, iced drink, lightly sweetened, your mind calls up whatever drink is most relevant to you, even if the character calls it something entirely different.

Take Me Away

Readers come to fiction hoping to be transported, eager to be hypnotized. Our job as writers is to deliver without making it obvious that we're doing so. How many times have you been enjoying a movie when something jars you out of the experience, reminding you that what you're watching is just a scripted make-believe? It's not just disorienting, it's disappointing. Just as human beings are hardwired to recognize faces, we're hardwired to recognize and crave stories. Using all the aspects of the human experience, from vision to heartbreak to a stubbed toe, fully engages your reader's mind. When we do our jobs correctly, the reader's mind is fully engaged in the words on the page, their minds activating as though the biting wind is really cutting into their cheeks, the smoke tickling their nose, the fatty broth teasing their stomach. When we do this well, we trick them into believing.

It's not just craft, it's magic.

SKIN

BY DAVID A. ELSENSOHN

David A. Elsensohn lives for coaxing language into pleasing arrangements. Typically inspired by such language-coaxers as Tolkien, Howard, Leiber, Norton, Muir, Gaiman, or by well-crafted batches of single malt whisky, he stares for long periods at monitor screens trying to make words appear. He does make rather good sandwiches, he's told, and his chili recipe gets appreciative nods from friends.

His short works are available in various hidden online places. His story "Vanni's Choice" was a winner of the NeoVerse Short Story Writing Competition and published in *Threads: A NeoVerse Anthology*. His story "Trading Ghosts" was a published winner in *Writers of the Future 36*.

The nigh-wolves have pursued her for ten kilometers at a dead run. She wonders when the Skin will be out of breath.

They are not much like wolves, actually. The baying of wolves has less chittering and hissing, and wolves use all four legs to run at such speed, and wolves, as far as she can remember from the Arcache, have more fur and less chitin, and wolves are extinct in any case. Still, these are predatory, and they pursue in groups, to catch and rend and devour with strong jaws and what might be teeth.

She has not always thought of herself as a *she*, for that matter. Several hundred days ago, upon landing to begin the three-year mission, *they* had been exploring, as they were grown, molded, taught and assigned to do, and decided to be a *she*, or at least arrived at that identity through inference. Her breasts are present, but small and nonfunctional; there is no need for them, not for her, not for her purpose. She lacks external genitalia, so while the conceit of human sexual dualism had long since been discarded, she feels she belongs among the *shes*, and likes the feeling of it. It fits her, like the Skin.

As if alerted by passing concepts, the Arcache leaps into her mental periphery, initializing discreet panels of visual and auditory data.

[arcache recsync (public) 'EvoMorph Somatosensory Nanodermis': The Skin is slightly thicker than one thirty-thousandth of the width of a human hair. It keeps itself infinitesimally repelled from the body with its own energy; always adjacent, never touching. It protects from extremes in temperature, and spreads moisture and heat throughout the wearer's body until it reaches glandular interfaces, feeding fluid back into the mouth or eyes. Its nanoplates change color to reflect or absorb light, which causes the wearer to appear... : end]

She blinks away its proffered exposition as she often does, especially at the moment, where the Arcache's interruptions deliver no benefit for her current predicament.

She whips between scaled, tubular growths that are the closest thing to a tree this planet allows. They emit a hollow thump when she cannons into them. The Skin receives the impact warning, sensing that surfaces within and without are sharing an alarmingly excessive approach velocity, and then knots up in places to absorb and deflect damage that might result from such imperfectly elastic collisions. She is pleased about this behavior, but not at having been slowed down due to hitting the Tube Tree. She is lithe and strong and fast—the vats have made her this way—but the Skin is the only thing keeping her ahead of the nigh-wolves, and therefore still alive to perform her task, until she can go home.

Skin. Such is the apparatus that an evomorphed Explorevaluative Unit wears, always. It is all she has. She has no weapons, a fact of which she is painfully conscious, but she does have a sense of frantic need, as her exploration is nearly finished. She has few desires, being content to perform her assignment, but foremost among them, besides avoiding becoming a source of nutrition, is to conclude her mission. She looks desperately forward to the cramped, dreamy silence of the liftship which will carry her back to the planet that created her. There are no windows on such a ship, nor on the dropship that placed her here. There is no need. There is no one awake to look out of them, and no light by which to see, until the dropship settles with a crunch onto a surface, opening like a dying leaf so its human can clamber out blinking in the light or squinting in the dark, Skin buzzing with absorbant glee.

The Arcache takes her reminiscing as a prompt.

[arcache reced source oer^ghalnfiantêe (nkiktanh). 'introducing earthian psychology' (translated from nkiktai) : when earthians impose themselves on their galactic surroundings, the human explorevaluative units are a secondary gesture... primitive robotic platforms are first sent to potential new homeworlds, creeping over the landscape, waving friendly antennae and recording observations, discovering what should be killed or controlled or replaced... then, charming evomorphed humans are sent... these humans explore, gather anecdotal data, and are occasionally eaten by the indigenous entities that are overlooked by the friendly robotic platforms... we should not judge them for their carbon bias, but... kko17.14 : end]

She is trying not to be eaten, so she plunges directly into a greenfield.

The continents on this planet are large islands with webbed fingers, heaved into smoky existence and made chemically pregnant by volcanoes. In a greenfield, spores paint the ground, billowing in yellowy green clouds as she runs over them. The Skin is put constantly to work keeping the spores out, before her lungs sprout luxuriant fungi and leave her dead but alive with new growth. She clicks down her eye membranes and holds her breath, which she can do for many hundreds of heartbeats if need be.

[arcache reced source Janiss Ben Haven (human). 'Becoming Transhuman: How We Evolved Away From Ourselves' : When a creature developed something interesting through feeble, random mutations, and we thought it a good idea, we took it. We had been trying to armor ourselves against a universe that was indifferent to our exploration; throwing ourselves against it in order to conquer it, we failed. Now, instead of wrapping ourselves in metal, ceramic and plastic, we have changed ourselves. An EM Human's body is slim, muscular, and modified so that the levels of nitrogen and oxygen present have less importance than the pressure. They still require the consumption of matter to produce energy, albeit much less than unmodified Humans, since they are compelled to explore potentially hostile environments. So far they perform with the highest level of success, and we can make enough of them not to worry about the expense. The Skin is the last protection, until we can evolve quickly enough to fully match new worlds. While there is not yet a necessity to provide a return... b283.7 : end]

Seven minutes later she bursts from the hazy cloud and sprints up a jagged, iron-colored ridge of ancient lava. The nigh-wolves click and hiss at her heels, unconcerned about the spores. Her lungs scream at her as she draws in new air. Her legs burn. The Skin is becoming overtaxed and will require a lengthy interval to soak up enough weakly thrumming infrared light from the neighboring red giant star to handle something like another greenfield. She wonders if she will die. An odd event, she thinks, to be reduced to a primitive predator/prey relationship.

She thinks perhaps humor might be associated with that, maybe even irony, and wishes there was someone else to appreciate it.

She is not alone on this planet, at least not as of three planetary orbits ago. A planet usually has a team of five assigned to it, although *team* is a misnomer. The five evomorphed humans are deposited all over the surface, to wander and discover, and will never see each other.

While her legs continue stabbing at the ground, she thinks of the four evomorphs who stumble over this world with her, and wonders how she differs from them. She wonders if her gaze lingers more on the gleam of the planet's rings, or on the massive scarlet sphere boiling up over the horizon. She wonders if they have lain on their stomachs, eyes close to the dirt in fascination, watching the tiny wars between bulbous, metallic worms and the pale, clicking myriapoda that want to eat and enslave them. She wonders if her fellow Units enjoy chewing the pulpy violet leaves of a vascular plant that proved non-toxic. She wonders if they have taken the time to learn an ancient art of folding flexible membranes into shapes. Instead of swans—she does not know what swans are—she creates circuit board patterns, flowering tesseracts, and dodecahedrons blossoming in her hand. She leaves them at the base of the tubular trees. She likes to believe it is art, and thinks it important.

Her three-year expedition is nearly complete. She looks forward to the dreams on the way home.

A dark crack ahead expands rapidly into a ravine that stretches downward out of visible sight, and is wider than the dropship was tall. She leaps, and with the help of spiny growths the Skin suddenly adds to her fingertips, catches the rock wall on the opposite side. She clambers up, clenching her teeth in effort, and claws over the lip. She looks behind, and though she hasn't exercised her voice in several months, groans audibly. The ravine is not slowing the nigh-wolves; they scrabble down the rocky face.

Here, at least, she can pause to reduce her pursuers.

When the Skin needs to be rapidly charged, she can throw messages up to a metallic glint in semi-synchronous orbit far above. She has done this every few months. The glint, having breathed in the local red giant, would emit a tight beam to the planet's surface, under which she would stand for long minutes with upturned palm, nanoplates rising like a sea of tiny pyramids to meet the divine light. The Skin is impervious to the beam. Hopefully the nigh-wolves aren't.

Lungs rasping painfully, she transmits her coordinates to the satellite and calls for an emergency recharge. The beam hammers into the ground a meter behind her, and she backs up through it. She waits until the first slavering creature comes over the brink and gallops at her, hissing and chittering in anticipation.

She does not smile when the nigh-wolf runs through the beam, cleaving itself neatly in half, but she is grateful for the respite. The creature collapses with an insectoid scream, smelling of burning fur and chitin. The beam is good for two more of her pursuers, then she takes out her frustration on two more. She sidesteps a snapping set of jaws, reaches to grab underneath the creature's neck plate, and hauls upward, sending forty kilograms of snarling nigh-wolf whirling away like a spinning dandelion. She catches another in mid-leap to snap its spine.

But the creatures continue to swarm over the rim of the ravine. Eventually, she will be overcome. She lacks the luxury she'd hoped for, to linger under the life-giving beam while it thumps into the ground.

Again, she runs. She has always been moving. No place on a new planet is permanent, no matter how safe, how warm. No home. Explorevaluative Units who remain in stasis do not obtain data. She, and the other four Eunits, have to travel, always, until they die or are transported home.

Lake. She dives into it, the Skin registering its temperature *[73.8°C]*, its chemical content *[water, sulfur dioxide, hydrogen sulfide, hydrogen chloride, hydrogen fluoride]*, and its corrosive factor *[2.3 value pH scale]*. The Skin promptly seals up her eyes, nose, mouth and ears —all orifices—while it works out a reasonable method of pulling nutrients from this unfriendly soup. She cannot see the electric blue swirling around her, but the Skin has laid a wireframe map over the eerie waterscape. Spidery thermophiles float about her submerged body, feathery antennae brushing the Skin, unsure of its potential for edibility. Distantly she senses the nigh-wolves pulling up short, not liking the acidic stench, lining up along the bank to shriek at her in a demonic chorus. She cannot stay long. The Skin has its limits. The lake's frothy blue liquid seeks to dissolve this new irritant like vinegar.

She emerges on the opposite bank, the Skin hissing its protest, and is alone. She climbs painfully past a thicket of purple shrubs that are sentient enough to be angry and almost mobile enough to do something about it. None of them, she knows, is edible. She crawls atop a black mesa of volcanic rock, curls up, and tries to recover. She does not sleep.

She could swear, if she knew what swearing was, that the Skin hums sometimes while it works. It flickers bits of itself like a furry shudder, clearing the hateful moisture, assessing the damage with a serious, worried mind. It does not have much energy to spare. The Arcache, however, requires very little energy to dispense its unsolicited wisdom.

[arcache reced source Janiss Ben Haven (human). 'Becoming Transhuman: How We Evolved Away From Ourselves' : One of the hardest things humans attempted to evolve from was our communal nature. Hunter, gatherer, farmer, all in a structure that assumed a collective aim. Some few had learned to isolate, to deny themselves, but many replaced that void with a philosophy or faith. We are different now, and need not suffer a void. Perhaps we could be thankful for that, but to whom would those thanks go? h92.1 : end]

She knows how to be alone, to be patient, but traveling between worlds and living on them takes time, and humans, being aware of themselves, are aware of time. Society therefore is considerate enough to provide the entirety of human experience in several billion of the Skin's nanoplates: books, treatises, missives, news documents, art. Rich vistas of color and sound can arise before her to entertain, to inform, to remind, and she prefers the experiences created not from observance, but from thought. She likes especially what they used to call *movies*, as if to differentiate them from—what? Stationaries? She does not remember what the Arcache told her, but believes they used to be cast against a surface, like watery reflections on a cavern roof or the planet's magnetic field shimmering against the sky. She immerses herself in movies more than watches them, their stories directly prodding and sparking her optic nerves. The earliest *movie* stories fascinate her. They render themselves in colorless light, like the photoreceptor rods in her eyes when the nocturnal cycle begins. She sighs. She cannot experience them now, for while her spirit needs distraction, the Skin is weak. She must lie alone, silent, waiting, thinking.

She wants to go home.

[arcache reced source Alan Suaresh-Van Beck (human). 'Rhythmic Histories of Human Conquest, Eighth Volume' : Optimistic socioscientists calculate that humanity as a whole has reached a Kardashev value of 1.18, although our (first) planet had been scraped nearly dry before reaching this status. For some centuries only the 'civilized' and the 'wealthy' (retrieve these terms from the Arcache, if they are meaningless to you) lived above the surface like a patch of white snow [retrieve from Arcache 'snow'] not yet melted from the top of a scrap heap, while thirty billion toiled and starved on an efflorescent surface. Then a Hegerberg Bloom was installed within the orbit of Mercury, millions of tiny mirrored insects swinging around the solar surface like twin shotput, whipping beams of energy back to our hungry third planet... : interrupt]

The Skin reports a problem. Damage is extensive to her limbs— the bites of the nigh-wolves and the lake have worked their will—and the Skin cannot compensate without further electromagnetic and thermal input from the orbiting satellite. Both are exhausted, for now. She worries, and pain has begun to throb its way past her endorphins, but she will simply have to wait until the shiny glint can catch its breath during the next rotation period, and she can request another recharge.

The Skin's energy is dangerously low. She will have to remain still. She cannot make much use of its temperature adjustment, so curls her body into a tight sphere against the oncoming nocturnal cycle. The air will be cold at this altitude, but the planet's heat threads moodily through the ground.

She wonders if she is the last one alive, or the first one to die.

[arcache reced (continue) : The power of our local star had finally been harnessed. Wars over resources became obsolete, the concept of currency [retrieve from Arcache 'medium of exchange'] lost its station, and humanity scratched its head and did things for itself instead of to itself. We had prodded feebly at our surroundings, launched capsules from different

political states [retrieve from Arcache 'nation'] in competition with each other, but now we began to truly explore. Hydrogen was culled to power ships to near-relativistic speeds, until intelligent humans cooperated with hyperintelligent tools to figure out how not to fly fast enough through space, but within *space [retrieve from Arcache 'Alcubierre', 'apparent superluminal']. Warlike urges and carbon-based chauvinism were difficult to leave behind, however. Homeland became homeworld, for a time. Flesh heals. Flesh is cheap. The old governments, the old militaries, understood... : end]*

She has not been bred or approved for sexual relations, but her humanity is still there. Odd sensations, like a deeply buried itch in a phantom limb, would draw her hand to the crux of her legs and make her wonder what the other Eunits look like, where they fall on the sexual continuum, whether they think the way she does.

The old movies separate the *hes* from the *shes*, as if there could be only two sexes, and one chooses the other, or sometimes chooses its own, and a story is revealed, imagined. The stories have references to them called *titles*, although she has to access the Arcache to recall them. The humans in the stories go through conflict, attraction, denial, trauma. They make decisions, have decisions made for them. They triumph, persevere, rejoice, weep, cope. They come together or are forced apart. They meet in fog, or in daylight. They look at each other under shadowy brims and declare love.

The Skin pauses in its work to bring an event to her attention. She lifts her head achingly from the rock, looks upward at the point of light.

[Transmission : Observation complete. Homeworld potentiality denied : return]

The Skin tosses a question upward: liftship?

[Negative : return]

The glint far above makes calculations, expands its sails, and begins to move on, away, to the next assignment. For it is more expensive in resources than she. She is to transmit data until no longer functional, like those poor melted machines on Venus. Information is useful.

Her eyes do not blur with tears, for the Skin picks up the moisture, cleanses it, and redirects it back into her glandular interfaces.

The Skin will never receive its recharge, so there is little point in prolonging its energy. She delves into the Arcache, retrieves one of her favorites, plunges it into her optic nerves. The Skin estimates about ninety-two minutes until its power will run out, and she will be truly alone and exposed to a planet which has been determined not to want her, or anyone like her.

She figures she can get to the scene where the grey *he* in the hat chucks the young, glistening-eyed *she* under her chin, and tells her he is looking at her.

CREATING PLOT VIA THEMES AND RESEARCH IN SPECULATIVE FICTION

BY DAVID A. ELSENSOHN

When writing speculative fiction, plot is heinously difficult for me to think up. New characters stumble daily through my mind, sudden turns of phrase force me to reach for pen and paper in the middle of the night, snippets of conversations end up on small notepads in hopes of being included in a story. But such ingredients need to be translated into a completed piece. I struggle with "okay, yeah, that's a neat *premise*, not a *story*" and "but what *happens*? What's the big narrative arc here?" which combine into a defeated slump because someone's already written all the neat things and I've run out of iced coffee.

I find two approaches that work together to achieve plot—with speculative fiction, anyway—are being aware of themes and conducting research. One would think these inhabit opposite halves of the brain: themes are concepts that link to shared human truths, and research is hard data that lends verisimilitude. Textbooks can be written about each in isolation. However, the two concepts serve to elevate each other. Themes can inform the research conducted, while research can influence themes, creating a cycle of reciprocal ideas that inspire key components of plotting.

What is a theme, exactly, and why do we care to notice them? A theme is a subject or message within a narrative, that reflects a familiar aspect of human existence: coming of age, revenge, the healing power of love, the repercussions of greed, redemption of past mistakes, what have you. Thematic *concepts* are abstract subjects that readers see within the work, while thematic *statements* come intentionally from the author. Without mucking about too much with literary devices and theory, I like to embrace both.

In writing, don't be overly concerned if a theme seems common or cliché. Tropes exist, of course, and we are pleased to be aware of them, but tropes are not themes. A trope is a recurrence; a theme is a topic. They appear often, so there must be some enticing aspect of them that resonates with humans. For instance, the various stories of Star Wars contain well-known, oft-used themes: heeding the call, fall and redemption, nature over technology. Works such as Haldeman's *The Forever War* and Heinlein's *Starship Troopers* discuss themes of dehumanization from war and loss of societal individuality. Le Guin's *The Left Hand of Darkness* examines ideas of love and betrayal, and how humanity expands upon embracing difference.

For me, considering what themes exist in a narrative, and placing those themes in hopefully noticeable alcoves to be discovered, aids in building associations that assemble a story I've been typing away at until I raise my head, startled, to find *END* sitting on the last page.

Sometimes I am unaware I've inserted any themes until afterward: they emerge as a result of character, setting, world-building, and other choices made during the writing of the story. At that time, I consider if there are points where I can evoke them to strengthen their presence. This is a natural and sometimes preferable way to embed themes in a work.

At other times, contemplating a specific theme during writing adds tendons and connective tissue to a plot skeleton. (In case we do like dabbling with terminology, such intentional insertion of recurring motifs is called *thematic patterning*.) In one's work, themes can and should exist, but not be overtly declared. Plant themes with care, since clumsy symbolism can feel heavy-handed: "See, there's a *bird* in a cage, and my protagonist's name is *Raven*, with *feathered* hair, so it's all about her desire for *freedom*, see what I did there? I don't have to explain my art to you."

So, the story "Skin." Through its clinical, distant language and constant interruption by database-derived analyses, I wanted to establish a more direct emotional relationship with the explorer in the story. While she's busy trying not to be chewed on, the background commentary conveys some trends: Humanity, despite its advancement, collectively considers its own population of little value. Bursts of cooperation occur, but individuality dissolves under the shadow of larger decisions. Contrasting this, every human is a life, who explores their own identity and wants to return to a place they consider home.

A few themes run through this: The desire to return home. Creation of self-identity. Reliance on technology. Technology connecting one to history and culture. Betrayal of expectations. Data having greater importance than the individual. Nasty chompy alien critters.

Paying attention to such motifs sets expectations for the reader and author. Readers can detect the presence of thematic objects that create a memory between scenes, and achieve catharsis when expectations are delivered or subverted. For the writer, such expectations prompt the intentional insertion of themes, placing them like a string of guiding lights that keeps the reader on track (or several tracks) and returning when the story seemingly strays.

The technology threaded through "Skin" creates relationships with the explorer, via her protective armor and from archived documents. Her actions are fueled by her desire to survive and return home, so occasional reminders of this felt natural when placed, heightening the stakes. The expectations set by these are upended when the explorer is betrayed, by the satellite, then by denial from society, then finally by the Skin itself.

Realizing a theme can help a writer become un-stuck. Embracing or subverting a theme aids in characterization, making a flat character feel more dynamic. Recognizing themes and hooking them more firmly into the story and to each other adds weight, even meaning, to a plot that feels unfinished or disconnected.

On to research. Research can contribute to the writing even earlier and more intentionally, providing connective ideas for plot. The realm of science fiction, especially "hard" sci-fi, requires satisfaction regarding the story's feasibility. Handwaving is fine for non-integral elements (I didn't build a drive schematic, the ship just *gets* there, right?), but narrating the innards of a technology or scientific concept expects rigorous devotion to fact. Readers pay attention to that sort of thing.

This sounds like a constraint. Why not invent things and say they work? However, I find researching a thing lends ideas to making my story elements solid. Reading articles on posthuman transhumanism suggested a future society that genetically modifies beings for the purposes of space exploration, though also perpetuating a class-based exclusion. Learning about postgenderism made sense, there being little need to adhere to present-day (and hopefully soon expiring) assumptions about sexual dualism.

Leaping from initial Wikipedia sources into *ScienceDirect*, *Nano Letters* and *Frontiers* articles that I have no hope of comprehending actually inspires plot elements: adding *this* suggests the existence of *that*. A plausible concept may end up being an intrinsic part of the story rather than a nifty sounds-good gimmick. For "Skin," reading up on nanotechnology and molecular machines rendered the possibility of the Skin as nearly a character in a symbiotic relationship with the explorer. This relationship, boosted by research, aided in assembling what happens in the story. Delving into astrobotany and geophysical fluid dynamics prompted the near-sentient plant life and corrosive lake as obstacles the explorer must overcome. For other science fiction, reading articles about the physics of space and gravity can add gratifying detail to scenes aboard a starship, which then suggests plot elements due to what events could happen, or how they happen. In my fantasy work, perusing books on blacksmithing and metallurgy added what felt like truth to my protagonist's role as a smith and helped complete the tale.

Research can allow a writer to push past a tricky section, or deepen aspects of character and setting because something turns out to be plausible. Detail in harmony with fact propels the story, preventing savvy readers from being halted by a broken suspension of disbelief.

In turn, the inclusion of plausibly rendered plot points works with and even makes one aware of themes. Speculative fiction has a multitude of thematic points one can ponder to create plot: encountering extraterrestrial life, questioning what it means to be human, galactic colonization, the needs of a post-apocalyptic society, human relationships with artificial intelligence. Supporting such themes with researched detail lifts a story beyond a neat scientific premise.

So, to combine theme and research, "Skin" consists of: continuous action (the thread between reader and character, something to return to between expository interruptions), detail of the protective Skin she wears (to establish a symbiotic near-character whose importance arguably exceeds hers), research on nanotech and thermophysical properties of fluid (for reasonably plausible science to keep pedantic readers' blood vessels at a decent pressure), and interludes by neutral commentary from documentarians (to provide some world-building outside of typical narrative, suggesting the explorer's lack of importance and contributing to the theme of betrayal by what the character relies upon). The potential themes and plausible scientific detail contributed to a completed story.

It sounds like work, doesn't it? But writing is often work anyway, despite our love for it, and examining additional possibilities of theme and research has sparked inspiration enough to get a story limping past the finish line.

Also, it rationalizes my time spent reading online articles about thematic patterning, nanotech and blacksmithing instead of writing.

A HAMAL IN HOLLYWOOD
BY MARTIN L. SHOEMAKER

Martin is a Michigan author who writes "science fiction with heart." Martin has published stories all over the science fiction landscape, including *Analog*, *Galaxy's Edge*, *Writers of the Future* 31, and others. Martin's work has also appeared in many anthologies including *Year's Best Military and Adventure SF 4*, *Man-Kzin Wars XV*, *The Jim Baen Memorial Award: The First Decade*, and others. Martin's story "Today, I am Paul," was nominated for a Nebula Award. Martin also has a wealth of knowledge that he is always more than happy to share.

The sirens didn't disturb Lucine Zakaryan as she snipped at Mr. Eddie's curly gray locks. Sirens in Hollywood were almost as common as Spider-Man players, nothing for her to take note. She had enough to worry about with her salon. *Her* salon, after all these years. It wasn't much, just three black vinyl chairs plus a wash stand, but it was all hers. Anya and Julia were gone for the night, and as soon as Lucine was done with Mr. Eddie she could leave as well. So she didn't worry about what was out on Sunset Boulevard.

But when the flashers and spotlights speared through the posters and signs on her shop's front window and splashed across her ceiling and walls, she knew the chase was coming to this strip mall. In the nineteen years she had lived in Los Angeles, Lucine had seen chases and arrests and crimes. She had even seen the Dahan ship on the night that they arrived. She knew that violence was never far away—farther here in America than in Armenia, perhaps, but still near. And the door...

Lucine had the door open to let in the cool twilight air.

When she was just a little girl, Lucine's *hayr* had taught her: *when danger is near, move today, wait tomorrow.* "Mr. Eddie," she said, tearing the smock from his shoulders, "I'm sorry, I cut your hair tomorrow. No charge. We do not want to be in this." Mr. Eddie nodded, his eyes wide and white, his dark face turned ashen. "You go out the back door. The alley will take you out to La Brea." Mr. Eddie nodded again and ran to the back door.

Lucine didn't wait to see him leave. She was older than when she had arrived in America, and at least twenty kilos heavier (well, maybe thirty), but she could still move fast in an emergency. And this was one. She brushed her straight blonde hair out of her face to see better and ran to lock the door.

But before Lucine could lift the doorstop, a large man barreled through the door. Lucine caught only a brief flash of jeans and a gray shirt before he ran into her. Despite Lucine outweighing him, his speed gave him strength to push her back, knocking her to the white tile floor. "Sorry," he said, even as she fell; but then as she hit the ground, he missed his step, kicking her in her left side with his left foot. It didn't seem intentional, but it hurt like hell. And *then* he tripped and fell directly on top of Lucine, his right knee landing in her stomach.

"Owf!" Lucine shouted, half from pain and half from loss of wind. The man rolled into the salon, trapping and crushing Lucine's hand before he freed himself from her. He tried to regain his footing, slipped twice on the polished tile (Lucine always kept the floors spotless), and finally grabbed the check-in station to pull himself upright. He ran for the back door just as Mr. Eddie had.

And then Lucine felt something behind her. Or maybe its shadow tipped her off, but somehow she knew something was in the doorway. Still on the floor, she turned and looked up.

There, looming over her, was a giant, hairy shape. With the police lights behind it, Lucine could not make out any details, just two legs, two long arms, and a short, broad head. Her mind flashed back to stories her *tatik* had told of the great beast, the *piatek*: a wild creature with strong claws and a giant beak which would rend bad little girls into gobbets. The creatures had haunted her nightmares, crawling forth from an unnamed, unknown island, and she often woke up screaming until *hayr* had promised that there were no *piateks*, and he would always keep her safe because she was his little girl.

But now, sprawled on the floor amid the sirens and the confusion, Lucine could believe in monsters from a lost island.

Then the creature leaped over her and into the salon, and she saw that it was no *piatek*, but something perhaps worse because it was real. It was a hamal, one of the silent servants of the Dahans. It was a white and gray tower of patchy fur, half again as tall as a tall man if it stood upright; but it crouched in a fashion that made it look now like an ape, now like a great cat rising up to sniff the air. But its face was neither ape nor cat nor anything from Earth: big black eyes set too wide and almost on a level with its mouth, no nose or snout, and a mouth rimmed with hard red ridges that flexed in and out. The face turned down toward Lucine, and despite herself she winced and held her hands before her face.

Then the creature made a wheezing sound and turned toward the back of the salon. The man in the gray shirt leaned against the back wall, favoring his left leg. His dark, curly hair was matted with sweat. His skin was light brown, almost the color of his eyes, but flush with exertion. And those eyes... They looked into the hamal's, and they shone with moisture.

The man's left arm held him up against the wall as his right dug into his jeans pocket. Lucine looked away, sure that the man was drawing a weapon and just as sure that the hamal would tear his arm off before he drew.

But when there was no sound of slaughter, Lucine looked back. The man reached his hand out. In his fingers he held a large bronze coin. "Hamal..." he said, panting. "Please..."

The... monster... The hamal stood as if mesmerized by the coin. It raised one massive arm, and Lucine saw that instead of *piatek* claws, its arm ended in a large, pulsing bulb. The bulb stiffened and expanded into a cone nearly a foot across, and the cone stretched out toward the man's hand.

Lucine wasn't sure what would happen if the two touched, and she didn't get to find out. More sound came from the doorway, this time a loud, low hum. She turned around, and an angel stood in the door.

It wasn't really an angel, of course. Lucine had seen the Dahans on TV, so she knew they were aliens who had discovered Earth and had landed to... Well, she didn't really understand why they had landed. The news was full of diplomatic this and trade that; but Lucine had seen enough news shows to know when they were full of *kak*. Even when she was young and the Soviets ruled Armenia, she could see through the news, and she'd grown wiser (and wider) with age. The government might know why the Dahans were here, but the news people didn't.

But this Dahan, like the ones on TV, *looked* like an angel. Lucine did not know why creatures from some other planet should look like humans, especially such beautiful humans. They should look wrong to the eye, like the hamals, but the only thing wrong about them was they looked so perfect. Julia said they must have the best plastic surgeons in Beverly Hills. This Dahan was tall, muscular, and male (assuming they had male and female, Lucine wasn't sure). His skin was pale, almost Nordic, and his hair was a white-gold shade that made Lucine's own look shabby despite the expert dye job she sported.

The Dahan stood on a floating platform like a large silver serving tray. A white glow rose from the tray and surrounded him like a shroud of light, adding to his angelic look. He floated into the salon. Then he raised one hand, pointing to the hamal, and the glow flowed outward as if it had to contain the Dahan without touching him. He shouted something in a language unlike any Lucine had ever heard.

Lucine turned again to the pair in the back of the salon. The hamal's cone collapsed into a loose, pulsing bulb once more. It raised its arm, smashing it down upon the man's hand. The man screamed in pain while the coin flew away, clinked off the wash stand, fell to the shiny white tile, and rolled to the back of the shop.

The Dahan spoke again, and the hamal advanced on the man. It raised both arms, and two bulbs flared out into cones, then wrapped themselves around the man's arms and stiffened into strong bands that gripped the biceps. The hamal lifted the man from the floor. Lucine thought he should have been afraid, but his face showed... resignation? He said something, but she couldn't hear it over the sirens.

Mercifully, the sirens stopped then just as a short African-American LAPD officer stepped into the salon and shouted, "Halt!"

The hamal stood motionless. The officer stepped aside, letting two more enter behind him as he knelt down. "Sergeant Briggs, ma'am, LAPD. Are you all right?"

Lucine probed at her side and her stomach. She was sore, but it was fading. "I am all right, Sergeant. Just..." She looked around, and she wasn't sure how to finish.

"I understand, ma'am. Logan, Tyler, help the lady up." The two junior officers helped Lucine to her feet as Briggs rose and turned to the Dahan. "Tell your creature to put him down."

The Dahan answered in English, "The human is unharmed, but I will not permit him to escape. We must interrogate him and search him."

Briggs shook his head. "My captain tells *me* that the feds tell *her* that we have to help you collect your stolen item—which would be easier if you told us what it is—but that doesn't mean you can assault American citizens."

"I believe diplomatic immunity says I can." The Dahan smiled. That disturbed Lucine: for the first time, he looked *alien*. That mouth wasn't made to smile.

"Fuck diplomatic immunity." Briggs's hand hovered near his holster, and Tyler and Logan moved quietly away to cover him. "Just because I can't arrest you doesn't mean I can't stop you. Put. Him. Down."

The Dahan spoke again in its language, and the hamal gently lowered the man. But it did not release its grip.

"Now, Sergeant," the Dahan said, "I shall escort the prisoner to our compound so that I may search him for the item." The Dahans had established a base on the only available land in this part of LA: right on the hillside overlooking Hollywood, underneath the famous sign. That slope was not buildable, by human means, but the Dahans had some trick. In mere days, they had erected a small collection of buildings sticking right out from the slope. *As if gravity were optional*, one reporter had said.

"No, sir," Briggs shook his head. "Not a chance. The man's still an American citizen. He still has rights, and no one has read them to him yet. And those rights include *not* being probed by aliens in some secret cell. He's going to an LA lockup once we dot the i's and cross the t's. Logan, read the man his rights."

"Hold, Sergeant." The Dahan held his arms out from his chest, as if he were pleading but did not know how to hold his arms. The bright glow bowed out away from his hands, almost touching Briggs. "We need not hurry. As soon as I contact your 'feds' I am sure you shall receive new orders."

Briggs frowned at the Dahan. "You do what you have to. In the meantime, Logan, it's Miranda time."

"Yes, Sergeant." The young officer walked to the back, circled warily around the hamal, and took out his notecard to Mirandize the man.

The Dahan spoke unintelligibly, seemingly to the air, as Lucine slid over to Sergeant Briggs. "Sergeant—"

Briggs turned to her and smiled. It wasn't a sign of humor, but of warmth and reassurance. "You're sure you're not injured, ma'am?"

"I'm not, but he is." She turned sideways and nodded her head toward the man. He had sagged in the hamal's grip, but he still put no weight on his left leg.

"I see what you mean. Logan—Oh, crap. You, Dahan, whatever you're called, can't you call your creature off and let the man sit? He's injured."

The Dahan stopped his conversation. "I will not allow him to escape."

"There are the three of us up here, plus your creature, plus you. My men have the back alley covered. He's going nowhere."

The Dahan made a wriggling gesture with his fingers. "As you wish." He spoke again in his language, and the hamal picked the man up, carried him to Julia's chair, and firmly lowered him into it. Then it released him, but it loomed over him, watching.

The Dahan returned to its conversation with the air. Sergeant Briggs's phone rang, and he answered. He spoke in hushed tones, so Lucine couldn't hear it, but the conversation did not make the sergeant happy. Tyler went out to the cars outside and told the officers there they could turn off their flashers and spotlights. Logan stood nervously watching the hamal and the prisoner, but he didn't seem eager to approach the alien.

And Lucine just stood, stunned, in the middle of the strange circus that had been her salon just an hour ago. The last of the twilight faded to black outside. With the police lights off, Lucine realized how dim the rear of the salon had become. She stepped quietly away from Briggs and walked to the rear light panel. She turned on the lights, and Briggs and Logan squinted. Lucine noted that the Dahan did not squint, and she couldn't see the hamal's eyes to judge there.

Then Lucine looked past the hamal's legs, and she noticed a dark pool staining her clean white tiles. A dark red pool.

"Sergeant!" Lucine rushed to the man's side without even thinking of the alien creature as she brushed past. (Later she would recall that the fur was softer than it looked, and the creature smelled like licorice.) She turned the chair to face her, and the man lay back in the seat, his head hanging back to reveal hideous gashes on both sides of his throat. Blood trails darkened his gray shirt and dripped to the tile. As the chair jerked to a halt, one of Lucine's straight razors slid from it and clattered to the floor.

Lucine screamed as if a *piatek* had ripped open her heart.

The night passed in a haze for Lucine. Briggs summoned an ambulance, but it was a wasted effort. The man—Jaime Lopez, Briggs called him—had been dead before Lucine had seen the blood.

Briggs took Lucine's statement, and she told him about Lopez and the coin.

"Logan! Go back and find that coin."

"Yes, Sarge." But Logan was in the back for only a few seconds before he shouted, "Face down! Hands above your head. Sergeant, there's a man back here!"

"Tyler!" Briggs called out to the parking lot, and Tyler ran up. "Logan needs backup in the rear." Tyler ran toward the back door.

The officers were gone for less than a minute before they emerged with a figure in handcuffs. It was a medium-height, middle-aged African American in neat-fitting clothes. His haircut was half finished. "Mr. Eddie!" Lucine said.

"This is the customer you mentioned, ma'am?" Briggs asked. "Mr. Eddie...?"

"Edward Wilson," Mr. Eddie said, polite but not friendly.

"Mr. Eddie," Lucine said, "I told you to leave through the alley."

"I tried, Lucine." Mr. Eddie's voice warmed as he spoke to her. "I checked the security camera, and the alley was blocked with police cars at both ends." His voice hardened again as he turned back to Briggs, his brow furrowed. "I didn't want to spook them—an old black man might be carrying something dangerous, you know—so I just hid out in your coat room until the officers found me."

Briggs ignored Mr. Eddie's confrontational tone and unlocked the handcuffs. "We're all on edge, sir. We've had a death, and now it's becoming an international... I guess an interstellar incident."

"I still haven't heard 'I'm sorry' in there."

Briggs grunted. "Yes, I'm sorry, all right? But we've got trouble here. Did you see a coin roll into the back area?"

Mr. Eddie's gaze remained dark. "Big bronze coin? Yeah, rolled in after all the crashing and banging."

"What happened to it?"

"Rolled right up to the floor drain back there, and sweet as you please, between the slats and down it went."

More police showed up, then more and more again. Then federal officers showed up, serious men and women in dark suits who kept asking Lucine and Mr. Eddie to repeat their stories. Lucine couldn't see the point: no matter how many times she told the tale, Lopez would remain dead at the end.

The federal officers politely escorted Lucine and Mr. Eddie out of her shop—but then Lucine wondered if it was really her shop any more. The entrance was sealed with yellow police tape. Plumbers showed up, followed by men with jackhammers, ready to tear up her clean white tile in pursuit of the mysterious coin.

All these people, all so worried about that coin... But Lucine noticed that the Dahan didn't seem to care. He floated around on his little silver platform, continuing to talk to the air without paying attention to the police and agents. Eventually a long black limousine pulled up, a woman in an expensive pants suit stepped out, and he talked to her.

Lucine never knew what was said, though. The federal agents ushered her and Mr. Eddie away. One polite young man, half Lucine's age, guided them to a cab and told the driver to take them home. He thanked them for their time, and they left.

As they drove away, Lucine looked back. The Dahan and the fancy woman were deep in conversation, but the hamal paced back and forth, never straying far from the other alien. Lucine shivered, feeling a strong chill despite the warm LA night. She swore the creature watched them leave.

The cab stopped at Lucine's apartment first. Before Lucine stepped out, she awkwardly hugged Mr. Eddie. They didn't have a hugging relationship. Hair styling was so close, so personal, that Lucine was careful to give customers lots of personal space once the styling was done. Especially with an older, respectable gentleman like Mr. Eddie, someone who was naturally reserved. But after the night they had shared... She squeezed him, then pulled away. "Tomorrow I finish that haircut. You just come by—" She realized she didn't know when the authorities would let her back into her shop. "You come by here. Room 215. I'll clean up that hair."

And with that she left, wearily climbing the steps up to her apartment. With each step, her side and her stomach throbbed. She downed two quick glasses of wine to calm her nerves, and then she went to bed.

Lucine's alarm went off far too early. She scrambled to silence it, and then she remembered: she had no reason to get up. She couldn't open the salon today.

She tried covering her head and going back to sleep, but her mind refused to cooperate. She had slept blessedly free of nightmares, but now the images from last night refused to leave her alone. The most disturbing image was the blood dripping from the chair, and Lopez's neck. Almost as troubling—and it was such a small thing!—was the Dahan's phony attempt at a smile. Neither the hamal nor the Dahan belonged on Earth, but at least the hamal wasn't hiding its nature.

Finally, reluctantly, Lucine got out of bed. If nothing else, she could get some time on her treadmill. She hated the thing, and even though she spent hours on it every week she never seemed to lose weight. But at least she could move faster, and she breathed easier. She pulled on her shorts, T-shirt, and walking shoes, she climbed onto the treadmill, and she started to walk. The twinge in her side was quieter, and her stomach felt almost normal.

Picking up the remote, Lucine turned on the TV. Local news was on; and to her surprise, the first story was about her shop. A single death shouldn't be worth air time, Los Angeles had many of those; but anything involving the Dahan was major news. Lucine remembered when they had first arrived. There had been rumors on the internet and in the tabloids for months: fuzzy pictures of large white apes, or maybe yetis or sasquatches. The government did their best to quash the rumors, but that only added to the conspiracy theories.

Then one day, almost a year ago, the Dahan ships had appeared over capitols and several other major cities across the world. The ships weren't "flying saucers" as many had expected, but the curved, elongated silver shapes might look like saucers from the proper angle, so the conspiracy theorists claimed victory. *Proof at Last! The Saucers Are Here!* read one headline.

When the Dahan emerged from their ships, the paparazzi went wild. All those beautiful, angelically perfect people floating down from heaven on their glowing sleds made a mesmerizing image. But Lucine had been there in the crowd when the Los Angeles ship had opened, and no picture had ever done justice to the real thing.

The TV image switched to a picture of the Dahan leaving the crime scene. *Her* salon, but they couldn't bother to name it, they just said "crime scene". But at least the sign was clear: *Sunset Lucine's Salon*. The Dahan and the hamal stood just in front of the sign, and the silver platform suddenly stretched to more than twice its length. The hamal climbed onto the extension—outside the glowing shroud, Lucine noticed—and the platform gently rose into the air. The TV camera followed it through the sky until it became a faint dot. Then the dot flew behind a building and headed in the direction of the Dahan compound.

When the reporters had first seen the hamals, they had all had the same reaction as Lucine had, the opposite to how people saw the Dahan: *feral... hunters... apes...* If the Dahans were angelic, the hamals were... Well, some said demonic, but most said they were more animal. They were more intelligent than Earth animals, but they didn't speak, and they were easily confused by strange surroundings. They were always tame and controlled in the presence of Dahan, but people worried what they might do off the leash. There were stories —none proven, of course—of transients and unsuspecting tourists who met with hamals on dark streets and were never seen again.

Lucine had believed those rumors herself, until last night. The hamal had been intimidating, but she had never once felt it was out of control, even before the Dahan had arrived. And its fascination with the bronze coin... it wasn't some rote reaction, like a dog trained to a whistle; it was fascination. She was sure that the hamal had *studied* the coin. She wondered idly what it was, but she was sure that was a secret that the Dahan and the government would never share.

Yet she couldn't think of the hamal without recalling blood on her tile. Had the creature killed Lopez? Or had the man been so afraid of the alien that...?

The news switched to an Alcoholics Anonymous commercial, so Lucine changed to the Armenian TV channel. She liked to keep up on the home country and keep up her language. The station was showing a documentary on *Medz Yeghern*, the Armenian Genocide. The station showed this documentary often, or others like it, and they always made her angry for loved ones who were injured or family she had lost three generations back. Though Lucine was happy by nature, sometimes this anger overwhelmed her; but on the treadmill, the anger lifted her heart rate just as the doctor wanted.

The day dragged on. Lucine found things to do, little things to keep her from thinking too hard: sweeping, dusting, cooking. She even dyed her hair again, and she found it hard to remember what her original color was. Now, of course, it was gray, but Lucine believed in choosing for herself. And she didn't choose gray.

In late afternoon, Lucine was running out of chores. That was bad: she would start thinking, or she would start eating out of boredom. Or both. She wondered if she should go shopping or get out of the apartment.

But then the door buzzed. She rushed to it and pushed the button. "Sunset Lucine. Talk to me, sweetie."

A familiar voice came from the speaker. "This is Edward Wilson, Lucine."

"Mr. Eddie!" Lucine buzzed him in, pushed open her door, and waited for him to climb the stairs. Lucine always treated her clients like family, especially her regulars; but after last night, she felt especially close to Mr. Eddie. She remembered her *hayr's* stories, of how his grandfather and friends had grown closer than brothers from their shared experiences fighting and surviving the *Medz Yeghern*. What she and Mr. Eddie had been through was not even an echo of a shadow of that, so she could only imagine how closely those men had bonded, and how men had died to avoid betraying their brothers. Would she die for Mr. Eddie? She hoped never to know, but part of her hoped she would if she had to.

Mr. Eddie came around the stairwell and smiled. "May I come in?"

"Of course! Welcome, welcome!" Lucine hugged him. With them both standing, her head barely cleared his shoulder. Lucine had forgotten how tall he was, because everyone was short in the chair.

Lucine didn't have a proper styling chair in her home, but she had a high-backed swivel stool she had used when she was learning her trade. She guided him to it. Then before the conversation could turn to ugly parts of last night, she said, "So, you want to finish the haircut, of course."

Mr. Eddie raised his right hand to his head and grinned. "All day, people have been looking at me funny, some laughing. 'What's the matter, Eddie, you couldn't afford the whole hair cut?'"

Lucine laughed. "I will give you the rest. Better than the rest, the best haircut in all of Hollywood, better than the movie stars. And no charge, just tell them you got it at Lucine's."

She dug out an old smock and her portable grooming set. Then she covered him from the neck down, taped his neck, and inspected his head. As she did, she automatically fell into small talk, her favorite part of the job. "So, Mr. Eddie, you hear from your grandson?"

He smiled, and Lucine paused. He had a big grin, wide enough to make his scalp bunch up and make her misjudge the cut, so she waited as he talked. "He's a junior now. Next year my grandson will be a college graduate. Can you imagine?"

"He comes from smart stock. My *hayr* says you can always tell."

"*Hayr?*" Mr. Eddie asked.

"Oh, sorry, my father. I am a proud American, but some words, I will always be Armenian."

"Nothing wrong with that." His grin relaxed, and Lucine was able to assess his scalp and begin finishing the cut.

The conversation lulled, and inevitably turned to what they had both been avoiding. Mr. Eddie said, "So... Some business last night."

"Yes, some business," Lucine said as she cut.

"It was..."

Lucine nodded, though she stood beside him and he couldn't see it. "It was frightful. But also a little bit momentous. You and me, two ordinary citizens of this little corner of the world, suddenly caught up in the affairs of gods from the sky."

"They're not gods!" Mr. Eddie said. Lucine had forgotten: he was a strict Pentecostalist. Well, not as strict as some, he didn't think the aliens were tricks of Satan. "They're not angels. If you see an angel, you'll know it."

"Sorry, no, not gods. But creatures with concerns far beyond us, and then suddenly they're down among us. All because some man stole some alien coin."

Mr. Eddie shook his head, and Lucine almost cut too much. "It wasn't alien," he said.

Lucine pulled her scissors away and turned the stool to face her. "What do you mean?"

He frowned. "I hope the Lord will forgive me a small lie. There's something going on, something they're not telling us, and I don't trust them. So... I lied. The coin did not go down the drain. It rolled over toward me, and I put it in my pocket."

"Mr. Eddie!"

"It's none of their business." He reached into his pocket, pulled something out, and reached out from the smock to hand the coin to her.

Lucine took the coin and studied the molded metal. On one side was an outer ring with a Shakespeare quote: *To thine own self be true.* Inside the ring was another quote, longer and unfamiliar: *Rarely have we seen a person fail who has thoroughly followed our path.*

On the other side was another ring of words: *Unity. Service. Recovery.* Inside the ring were two portraits labeled *Dr. Bob* and *Bill W.* Beneath them was the Roman numeral *VII* in a circle, with *Years* underneath.

Lucine looked up from the coin. "This is human, yes? Not alien. But I do not understand what it is."

Mr. Eddie nodded. "Thank the Lord you don't recognize it, child, but I do. Here's mine." He handed her another bronze coin, nearly identical except that the number in the circle was *XV.* "That's my sobriety chip. Alcoholics anonymous. Fifteen years I've been sober. That chip reminds me every day to ask the Lord to help me resist temptation. I'm alive to see my grandson graduate because AA and the Lord kept me strong."

"But then..." Lucine couldn't even think of how to ask. What to ask.

"I don't know why that alien wanted that, but it's none of his concern. We take the second A very seriously: Anonymous. You're there to be helped and supported as you and your sponsor and your Higher Power find your way clean. You're not there to be judged by any man, woman, or alien from the stars."

"So Lopez was in AA?" Lucine asked.

"We don't know that. People lose sobriety coins all the time. But it's a good bet."

"Then why did he try to give it to the hamal?"

Mr. Eddie grinned. "Maybe the creature has a drinking problem?"

Lucine laughed. It felt good to release some tension. But still she was concerned. She looked at both chips, holding them away from her. "But the Dahan said something was stolen, and that had to be it. Why would that matter to them? Is there... You don't suppose there's a tracker in there?"

"Maybe," he said. "I'm no scientist, but we make cell phones and computers smaller every year. Imagine what *they* can do, them and all their starships. So maybe, but I don't think so. I've had it on me all day long. They had plenty of time to track me down, I didn't even think of it 'til you mentioned it, but they didn't. I think it is what it looks like, nothing more."

Lucine relaxed, and she looked at the two coins again. "Wait. They're not quite the same. Look at this around the edge." She held the seven-year chip out to Mr. Eddie and pointed out a small message engraved on the edge: *SSCC*. "What does that mean?"

He shook his head. "I don't know. All of the chips are made by the same company, but there are no rules. We're a benign anarchy. Some groups customize theirs."

"Can you guess what this means?"

"I can't, but..." As Lucine slipped the chip into her pocket, Mr. Eddie pulled out his cell phone and punched a single button. After ten seconds, he said, "Mason?" He paused. "No, the Lord is strong, and he is with me... Thank you, and to you as well... See, you might have seen some news from last night, and... Yes, that *was* me on the TV, you weren't imagining it... No, really, no one else was hurt... That's an odd question... I'm not sure, but I'll ask." Mr. Eddie put his hand over the microphone. "Mason—he's my sponsor—he asked if the creature, whatever you called it, did it leave with the other alien?"

"The hamal?" Mr. Eddie nodded. "Yes," Lucine said. "I watched them both leave."

"Yes..." Mr. Eddie said to the phone. "What do you mean, 'too bad'? Well, you shouldn't say it if you just want me to forget it...

"Why I called?" he continued. "Mason, I have a chip with some strange engraving on it: S-S-C-C. Do you know what that is? You do? What? ...Mason, be straight with me, either you know or you don't... Mason, you've been my sponsor for twelve years, ever since Nate died. I trust you, so don't start hiding things from me now... What?" He reached up to unfasten the smock. "All right, I'll be right over."

Mr. Eddie closed the cell phone, removed the smock, and stood from the chair. "Mason says he'll explain, but it will have to be in person. I'm sorry, Lucine, I have to go."

"But Mr. Eddie! I still haven't finished your haircut."

"Then I'll look funny tomorrow, too. Mason sounded like this is important. We can finish it tomorrow evening."

Lucine bit her lip, trying to decide: follow this or walk away? Finally she spoke. "Take me with you, Mr. Eddie. I have to understand this."

Instead of riding the cab, today Mr. Eddie drove his faded blue Focus. It was old and small, but he proudly kept it in excellent condition, so they didn't look completely out of place as they drove among the luxurious cars of Hollywood to Mason's place. The car was clean but cramped. The radio played a sermon. Lucine didn't catch much of it, but the preacher mentioned the Book of Matthew. Mr. Eddie said "Amen" and "That's right" and other words of approval.

The sun was "falling" behind tall buildings as they crossed town. It wasn't as dark as true twilight, but in some ways it was worse. Your eyes could go from still-bright late sunlight to dark shadows in moments, and you would never see what hid in those shadows until it was upon you. Lucine imagined that every shadow hid a hamal, but then she laughed at herself for being afraid.

It was a surprise, then, when the true danger came from the bright sky, not from the shadows. A flash caught her eye, and she looked up to see a tiny silver and white shape speeding ahead of them. Then she saw a second, and a third, as they drew up a block away. At the same time Mr. Eddie's phone rang, but he ignored it as Lucine asked, "What's that up ahead?"

Keeping his eyes on the road, he would not see the Dahans in the sky, so he didn't understand the question. "That's Mason's apartment building, but how did you know?"

"I didn't—" A loud whistling sound came from ahead, and bricks started falling from Mason's building. Then with a tremble and a rumble, the front third of the building slid into the street.

Mr. Eddie swerved. Lucine screamed. Horns honked as vehicles smashed together, a chain reaction that soon engulfed the Focus. When the chain of vehicles finally drew to a halt, Lucine looked up again. The Dahans were gone. Mr. Eddie was shouting at her to get out of the car.

And then, just as she had feared, Lucine saw a hamal step from the deep shadows far across the road. She had a vision of bloody tile, and she shuddered.

Lucine tried to open her door, but it was jammed shut by a yellow Aztec. She looked at Mr. Eddie, and he was already out of the car, beckoning her. "Get out! Get out! The rest of the building is falling!"

Lucine looked ahead: yes, bricks were raining down, a small drizzle now but growing. She looked back: the hamal was gone, but there were shadows everywhere.

She looked at Eddie; and between them was the shift lever, the steering wheel, and the cramped seat of his tiny Ford Focus.

Lucine unbelted, rose up, and tried to pull her girth through the car. The gear shift stuck in her side, and yesterday's pain flared up. She groaned loudly and sat back down. Then she lifted up from her seat, turned, and knelt, her head in the space between the seats. She turned farther, her feet pressed against the door as her head entered the driver area.

At least this didn't hurt, but she still couldn't get through. There was too much of her to fit between the wheel and the seat. She tried to squeeze through, but she got stuck. Pushing with both feet against the door only tightened the trap.

Then Mr. Eddie reached down to the front of the driver's seat, and the seat slid back, releasing her. She scrambled forward and he grabbed her arms, pulling her free. She propelled herself from the car, pushing him backward so that he tripped and fell backward, pulling her down with him.

And then a chunk of masonry half as big as the Focus fell onto the car, smashing the engine and the front seat, showering glass and metal everywhere. It was too late to run or move, so Lucine buried her face in Mr. Eddie's chest. He wrapped his arms over her head to protect her from debris, and she heard him praying, though she could not make out the words.

Finally the rain of debris stopped, and the street quieted, though there were still shouts and screams, honking and car alarms, distant sirens. Lucine looked down. "You saved my life, Mr. Eddie. Thank you!"

He smiled. "I had to save you, Lucine. You have to finish my haircut."

"Oh, you!" She knelt over him, kissed him on the cheek, and stood. Her side and stomach throbbed again, and her back and neck twinged from dozens of bruises where small debris had struck, but she could stand. And so could he: he was on one foot and one knee, and she helped him to his feet.

Then Lucine remembered. She looked back across the street and behind them. And she saw a large white-furred form drop back into shadows.

"Run!"

Mr. Eddie answered, "What?" But she didn't wait around. Near at hand was a parking garage, and she had already run inside and was sprinting for an exit on the far side. She heard Mr. Eddie running behind her. At least she hoped it was him. She wasn't waiting to find out.

She reached the far exit, pushed open the double glass doors, and turned back. Mr. Eddie was behind her, slower but still moving. She saw no sign of the hamal. Of course, she didn't know how many there might be, nor which shadows they might hide in.

Mr. Eddie caught up with her, and they plunged out into the street. Outside were five lanes of stalled traffic, with people abandoning vehicles and fleeing the wreckage. Lucine saw that they were all headed south, and she decided that it would be impossible to make progress if they went that way. So she pushed through the crowd, crossed the street, and ran up to a glass wall on the far side: a ground-floor food court of a mall. People inside pressed up against the glass, peering out at the destruction one block over. Some were wide-eyed with shock, while others wept. A hundred cell phones were raised to film the destruction.

Lucine and Mr. Eddie found the glass entry door, pulled it open, and pushed their way through the crowd. Once inside the mall, they had a clear path. The mall was practically deserted, with everyone having either fled or run to watch the collapse. But they were both too tired and sore to maintain their pace. It took nearly ten minutes for them to exit the mall on the far side.

As the door slid shut behind them, Lucine fell back against the wall, panting. Mr. Eddie did as well, and he pulled out his cell phone, pushed a button, and listened. Then he frowned. "You need to hear this message."

He pushed another button, and this time the message played on the speaker phone. "Edward, this is Mason. Afraid you're going to have to find yourself another sponsor, buddy. The Dahans have found me. Don't let them find you, too. Page twenty three, bud. God be wi—" The message trailed off into static, and then silence.

Lucine looked at Mr. Eddie and saw big tears rolling down his cheeks. *This is getting to be a habit,* she thought as she wrapped him into a big hug, pulled his head down to hers, and held him as his body shook with silent sobs.

They stood there like that, and for a few minutes Lucine forgot the danger. She was just too tired and sore and emotionally wracked to move. It was Mr. Eddie who finally broke the embrace. "I can't," he said. "I can't let Mason die for nothing. There's something important on page twenty three, and the Lord wants me to see it through."

"Page twenty three?" Lucine asked. He pulled away, reached inside his pocket, and pulled out a folded, stapled stack of printed pages. Lucine saw a cover and a title: *Los Angeles Area Groups and Meetings.* The pages were bent and curled, but they were still readable. Mr. Eddie turned to page twenty three, and they both looked it over.

Lucine pointed to one entry near the bottom third of the page. "Seventh Street Community Center. SSCC."

Traffic was gridlocked for miles. Police and fire were everywhere, but also National Guard, FBI, and FEMA. Not to mention numerous sightings of Dahans on their sleds. None were paying attention to

Lucine and Mr. Eddie that she could tell, but they still made her nervous.

With no cabs or buses, it took over an hour for them to walk to Seventh Street, and Lucine was nervously checking behind them the entire way. It was approaching true twilight, so there were many more shadows, and several times Lucine thought she saw a dark shape merge back into them. Mr. Eddie assured her that she was imagining things, but she couldn't be convinced.

And the next moment, she knew she was right. On a deserted street, three Dahan sleds appeared in the sky ahead of them, zipping their way. Then she heard a crashing noise behind them, and she looked back to see a hamal crashing through a stand of trash barrels.

Mr. Eddie pulled her to the ground and over to the side of the road, where they crouched beside a dumpster. Lucine looked out, expecting to see the hamal headed her way. Instead it ran to a nearby parked car, picked the vehicle up, and hurled it into the air. Lucine watched the car fly up and smash into the nearest Dahan. There was a great shower of sparks as the light shroud shredded and the car knocked the alien from the sled.

The other two Dahan zoomed closer. The loud whistling sound returned, and two brilliant white lances speared out and struck the pavement, tracing a path to the hamal. Where they struck, the asphalt bubbled and melted.

Before the beams could catch the hamal, it leaped into the air, somersaulting over the lances. One of the sleds got too close, and the hamal caught the edge, hanging on as the sled flew. Then it swung its legs up, gripped the other end, and flexed. The sled bent, bent further, and then suddenly snapped. The hamal and the now-unshielded Dahan fell to the ground almost in front of the dumpster. Lucine looked away as the hamal picked up the Dahan and dashed it against the side of the dumpster with a wet crunching sound.

But that had given the third Dahan time to zero in. The lance stabbed forward, and the asphalt in front of Lucine and Mr. Eddie burst in a bubble of hot air, tar, and gravel. Lucine cried out in pain from the burns, but Mr. Eddie cried louder. Lucine looked and saw that a blob of hot tar was burning through the leg of his fine gray pants.

With only seconds to act, Lucine unbelted Mr. Eddie's pants— careful not to touch the tar—and pulled them down to his ankles. Then she pulled off his shoes and pants. As she had hoped, most of the tar had come off with the pants. But there was still some stuck to his burned thigh, and she didn't dare touch it herself. So she used the hard soles of his shoes to scrape the skin clean. She tried not to think what damage she might do to the burned flesh, but it had to be better than letting the burning continue.

By the time she was done, Lucine smelled the curious scent of burned licorice. She looked up to see that the last Dahan had fallen, though she had missed the event. The third sled was on the ground, nearly split by a fragment of the second. And the hamal, one arm hanging loose and burn marks over its upper body, stood methodically stamping a wet, meaty pile of debris into the ground. Then it did the same to the other two bodies, smearing them out into discolored spots on the pavement. Despite knowing these were aliens, Lucine had expected the spots to be red, instead of the bluish gray that they were.

Then the hamal turned toward Lucine and Mr. Eddie. Fluid leaked from its mouth, and the red ridges weren't flapping. It stepped forward, and Lucine couldn't think of any way to stop it.

Except one. She stood, took the chip from her pocket, and held it out. "Here... Please..."

The hamal stopped before her and held out its uninjured arm. The bulb once more distended into a cone—she now saw that it was hollow in the middle—and wrapped it around her fingers. The sensation wasn't unpleasant, at least not to her. As a child in Armenia she had let the calves lick her with their giant tongues. This feeling was like that: not as wet, but just as soft.

Lucine let go of the chip and pulled her fingers free. The cone collapsed, swallowing the chip, and then most of the bulb drew up inside the hamal's arm. When the bulb came back out, it shaped into a flat grip, and *two* chips were in the grip. Lucine took them.

She saw immediately that the second chip was identical in most respects, right down to the *SSCC* mark, but it was only a three year chip.

Lucine nodded, handing back the second chip. "I… recognize you." And she was sure that was true on two levels. The chips were a recognition sign. Her *hayr* had told her how Armenian rebels had used those when they hid among the populace. But also, she recognized *this* hamal. It was the one from her shop last night.

Then faster than she could follow, the hamal picked up Mr. Eddie, lifted the lid of the dumpster, and gently laid him inside. Then it picked her up and dropped her in as well before leaping in with them. As it pulled the lid closed, Lucine saw a white dot fly through the sky, far away but still too close for her.

Lucine took several breaths to calm herself, and then she used her cell phone to light the interior of the dumpster and assess their situation. Mr. Eddie was breathing fitfully, and she was sure he was in horrible pain from his burns. He couldn't stay in this unsanitary dumpster for long.

And the hamal… She didn't know how to tell a healthy hamal from a sick one, but she was sure it wasn't healthy. Some blue-gray fluid oozed from its injured arm. The mouth ridges flexed weakly when they flexed at all. And its eyes twitched every few seconds.

And Lucine? She ached, her legs were on fire, and her breathing came in deep gasps. The saddest part was she was sure she was in the best shape of the three of them. But that didn't mean she was in *good* shape. She just wanted to sit in the trash and collapse, but she had to get help for Mr. Eddie.

The hamal held out its chip to show her the edge: *SSCC*. Lucine shook her head. They were very close, but still too far. She couldn't get them all there. The hamal could carry Mr. Eddie, certainly, but then everyone would see the hamal.

The hamal waved the chip up and down, and Lucine thought: *Maybe somebody there can help me. Help us all.*

Lucine shrank at the thought. She didn't want to go out there again where the Dahans could find her. She didn't want any of this.

She owed so much to Mr. Eddie, and she even felt a debt to the hamal, but her fear was so strong.

Then she remembered *hayr's* stories. Even in the worst of the genocides, some Turks had done the right thing, sheltering their Armenian neighbors. Her grandfather had survived thanks to one such neighbor; and to his dying day he had said, "All Turks are devils, except Dursun. Good man. Hanged for sheltering Armenians." *Hayr* also said that if there had been more such good men, she would have had more cousins, more uncles.

Lucine looked at the hamal and wondered if it were an uncle.

Lucine crouched in the corner of a building, under a large awning. There *were* Dahans out there, she had seen the lights, but not many of them. They moved in some sort of search pattern, and she thought she had it timed. She could predict long stretches where there were no sleds overhead. She had planned out three sprints that would get her from one cover to another on the way to the community center. The only question was could she get from cover to cover before the Dahans flew over?

She calmed her breathing and got ready to run. When the first gap opened, she sprinted out as fast as her legs would move, headed for two sad palm trees that overhung the road. She grabbed the trees to stop herself just as the next Dahan passed over.

Lucine stood, catching her breath once more. She was still panting when the next gap opened, so she let it pass. She was ready for the gap after that, and she leaped out into the road.

Suddenly a horn blared, and a car barreled down the street straight at Lucine. She had been so busy watching the skies, she had forgotten about the sparse evening traffic. She dove out of the way, trying to roll clear of the car. The fender clipped her foot, and she tumbled on the pavement, but she managed to escape the car.

Lucine slowly climbed to her feet. Once again her side and stomach erupted in pain, only now her heel cried out as well. She could put weight on it, but every step was like stomping on an apricot pit.

Pits or no, though, she had to go! The gap would close soon, and she had to get under the doorway of that shop. So she ran, crying out with every other step. She reached the doorway, but she knew it was too late. At least two Dahans had flown over. If they had looked her way, she was dead.

Lucine looked down the block at the community center. It looked like a school, or maybe a hospital: a short, squat brick building that covered nearly a quarter of a block. Most of it was dark at this time of night, but the nearest door was lighted and she saw lights and movement inside.

Lucine had no breath left. She wanted nothing but to wait one or two gaps to catch her breath. But the longer she waited, the more the chance that the Dahans would return. When the next gap opened, she checked for traffic, and then she ran as if a *piatek* pursued her. She was sure she felt its hot breath on her neck, sure she heard its clacking beak at her shoulders. Her pains seemed to join, one long agony from heels to side to stomach and ultimately to her burning lungs. But she must not let the *piatek* win!

Lucine smashed into the glass doors, and they rang from the impact, but of course they opened outward. She pulled them open and ducked in just before two lights appeared.

A guard came to the inner door, opened it, looked Lucine over, and asked, "Are you in trouble, ma'am? Should I call the police?"

"No... police... Need... AA..."

The guard looked sad. "I'm sorry, ma'am. Meetings are Tuesdays at 7. If you need help immediately, you should call your sponsor. Or there's a women's shelter three blocks down."

Lucine wanted to scream, but she had breath only to wheeze, "AA... Mason..." She looked for another word to convince him, and finally she settled on "Sanctuary." She pulled out the chip and held it out to him with *SSCC* facing him.

As soon as the guard saw the coin, he pulled out his radio. "Maria, we've got a woman who needs medical aid here. And I think we'll need a rescue team, too."

Lucine wanted nothing more than to sleep in the warm, soft bed they had provided for her after the doctor had treated her ribs and her heel. But she refused to sleep until she knew that Mr. Eddie and the hamal were safe. As soon as Dr. Maria confirmed that, she fell deeply asleep.

When she woke, it took a while to remember where she was. Both the infirmary and her room were in some subbasement that didn't appear on the center's elevator.

There was a phone next to her bed. She picked it up, and immediately a friendly but unfamiliar female voice answered, "What can we get you, Ms. Zakaryan?"

What can we get you? An aspirin. A large bagel with eggs. Orange juice. A half a bottle of aspirin. There were many things she wanted right then, but only one she *needed.* "Can I see Mr. Eddie? And the hamal?"

"Let me see." The woman paused. "Yes, they're awake and can see visitors, but they're both still in the infirmary. I'll come get you."

Lucine got out of bed. She still wore her workout clothes from the day before, though they were ready to be thrown away. But today she didn't care about neatness, just being alive.

The door opened and the young, pretty nurse said, "Hi! This way, they're waiting for you." They went down a long hallway to the infirmary, and she showed Lucine in.

Inside, Dr. Maria hovered over Mr. Eddie, smiling at what she saw. The hamal slept on a large bed behind him. The doctor turned to Lucine. "Hello, Lucine. Can I look you over when I'm done here?"

"Yes. But can I...?" Lucine gestured to Mr. Eddie. The doctor nodded, and Lucine stepped in and hugged her new best friend. "I'm so..." She couldn't finish.

"I know, child. Me, too."

The doctor pulled a chair closer, and Lucine sat. "We... won, I think," she said.

Mr. Eddie smiled. "One battle. But for today, that's enough. Do you know what this is, Lucine?" Lucine shook her head, and his smile turned into a big grin. "It's the Underground Railroad!"

Lucine shook her head. "You mean a subway?"

"No, child. Sometimes even with your accent, I forget you weren't born in America. The Underground Railroad was a secret network to guide African slaves to freedom. That's what the hamals are, slaves of the Dahans. Some of them escaped here, and they made friends with the outcasts of our society: the homeless, the destitute..." He looked down at the chip in his hands. "The alcoholics. When the hamals' Overseers came hunting them, some of their friends here... Well, they done the human race proud. They started building this network to shelter the hamals and guide them to hiding places in the far corners of the Earth."

"And we helped?"

"We helped, at least for our buddy here. I call him Stinky." Mr. Eddie laughed.

Lucine shook her head. "I don't understand. Lopez... The burglary..." She glanced over at Stinky. "And they... killed him..."

Mr. Eddie patted her on her arm. "I know, dear, that was horrible. But it was all a lie. There was no burglary, that was just an excuse. The Dahans were hunting Lopez because they knew he was part of the Railroad, and they wanted to interrogate him. Stinky didn't kill him, he just let him grab the razor. That brave man killed himself to keep the Railroad a secret."

Lucine's head spun. The past day replayed in her mind, and suddenly it all made sense for the first time.

Mr. Eddie continued. "And now, to thank us, they'll get us home, and no one will ever know we were here. Or they can take you home, at least. I've got more recuperating to do. And then after that, well, maybe I'll stick around a while."

Mr. Eddie looked at Lucine, but he didn't ask. He was too much of a friend to ask her for what might be more than she could give. No matter what she said next, he would always be her friend. Her brother.

But Lucine thought of Stinky and what had almost happened to him. She thought of the cousins and uncles she had never met because someone had been afraid.

"Doctor, please... Let me help."

PANNING FOR GOLD

BY MARTIN L. SHOEMAKER

My first pro sale was the story of an environmental leak that threatened to burn down a lunar colony. My second told of a young girl struggling to rescue her father after an industrial accident on the Moon. My third told of an international team of astronauts in orbit around Mars, vying to be the first to land—at great cost. My fourth, "Murder on the *Aldrin* Express," told of a murder investigation in space, and hinged on an understanding of Martian atmospheric chemistry and its effects on spider silk. It's safe to say that I earned my reputation as a hard science fiction rationalist, someone who says, "Prove it."

So when Dean Wesley Smith tried to convince me to give up outlining and just trust that my back brain would handle story if my front brain got out of the way, I thought of it as, and I quote, "Psychobabble woowoo stuff." Ridiculous. You might as well tell me to use the force, Luke!

Except there's one flaw in what I just wrote: I lied about the order in which everything happened. Every one of those stories I sold came *after* I decided I had nothing to lose. My career was going nowhere, so I might as well try Dean's "radical" idea. And as soon as I listened to Dean, I started selling.

It didn't take much to persuade me, just desperation.

So you may understand why it annoys me when people say things such as: "Nobody's *really* a pantser (a writer who writes by the seat of their pants)." "People who say they're pantsing don't know what they're really doing." "Oh, they're really plotting, they're just doing it in their heads." Or my favorite: "That's okay, pantsers, we can fix you."

Well, screw that! There's nothing to fix. Keep your hands off my method, you damn dirty apes!

Does that mean that I don't ever plot? Nonsense. Only a Sith deals in absolutes. It's a spectrum: different for every writer, but also for every story. Anyone who tells you that they always follow their outline is a liar. Don't trust them. Writers lie for a living.

In fact, I'll go to the opposite extreme, just to balance them out: Nobody really outlines; they just recursively pants. They pants an outline, then they pants acts against that outline, then they pants chapters against those acts, then they pants scenes against those chapters, and then they pants the actual words. They're pantsing in layers, rather than pantsing along the ground. Think of it as a new territory... Some people learn the territory by going out and living in it, some survey it, and some climb the highest mountain to draw a map. The pantsers simply write the story as they build the map.

If you're still not convinced, you can skip ahead to the next story. I don't need to convince you; you don't need to be convinced. But before you go, I want to say one thing: rather than listening to the critics who say nobody is really a pantser, why don't you listen to people who *are* pantsing and selling fiction from it? Listen to the people who are doing it, not the people who say it can't be done. Because I'm one of the people doing it. Are you calling me a liar?

But wait... this essay isn't supposed to be about people who annoy me; it's supposed to be about teaching the craft. If pantsing is my craft topic, I'm supposed to teach it to you... in 1,500 words... and I just wasted 600 of them complaining about people who don't believe me. Can you tell I pantsed this essay?

But I've thought about this a lot. I do think pantsing is a technique you can learn, but it's a difficult technique to teach. I don't think you *can* teach the core of it, because the core is belief: your willingness to trust yourself, to believe that there is no corner you can pants yourself into that you can't pants yourself out of. To quote a writer who assured us that pantsers can be fixed, "Everything can be fixed in revision." Apparently, however, pantsing can't be, since he also assured us that pantsing will get you into corners you can't get out of.

Respectfully: bullshit! You can always pants your way out of the corner. It might require you to back up and change some of what you've done, or it might require you to be really inventive. It might require you to discover things that were already in your story but you hadn't noticed. I frequently find that at just the right moment, I've created enough pieces of my world that one of them is exactly what I need to solve my protagonist's current dilemma.

Still, belief can't be taught! But it can be learned...

Let's start with some analogies. When a dancer wants to learn to do the perfect *entrechat*, does she book a stage, sell tickets, and then try it that night?

Of course not! She practices until she can do it perfectly every time. *Then* she stages the performance.

When an artist wants to paint a beautiful starscape, does he walk into the gallery, hang up the canvas, and start painting? Unlikely (though there are great artists who do live painting). More likely, he takes canvases out into the night and does studies until finally he gets one he likes. And then he puts *that* in the gallery.

But unlike the dancer, who cannot share her rehearsals—although in the modern day of streaming video, I suppose she can—it's very easy for the artist to share his studies. He takes them to a gallery, and some of them sell. Even though he's practicing, he's also creating works that might be salable.

There's absolutely no reason why you, as a writer, cannot do the same thing. Create as experiment. Create as practice. And it gets easier.

There is *one* proven way to teach this belief: by forcing you to *just do it!* This is one of many lessons in the Twenty-Four-Hour Story

Exercise at the Writers of the Future workshop. The instructors give you a random item; you read from a random book; and you talk to a random stranger and learn about their life. Then you have twenty-four hours to use those elements as prompts to write a *complete* story. It doesn't matter how you use them. It doesn't matter whether you use them at all, or if you head off in a completely different direction. All that matters is that you *write that story!*

Does that sound daunting? It doesn't to me, not anymore. I can do a (short) story in a day, any day I choose. Practice, remember?

But let's be honest: it was daunting then! But they gave us freedom to fail. It didn't have to be a good story, just a story. Most students finish the twenty-four hours with a story, some of them pretty good. And if they did it once, they can do it again.

"A Hamal in Hollywood" was my twenty-four-hour story. I didn't think I could do it; but with freedom to fail, I did. It was on the long side, and I was pretty pleased with it. Eventually I sold it to James Reasoner for the *Rockets Red Glare* anthology; and then it was selected by Baen for the *Year's Best Military and Adventure SF Volume IV* anthology.

I wrote a story in a day, I polished it up, and it became a year's best story. It *can* happen.

But in case that doesn't persuade you, I want to tell you about another person, a determined young twelve-year-old, who fell upon this method himself. I give him credit: he was *far* more diligent than I was at age twelve or even today. He set himself a rule: he would write a story every day. About what? He didn't know. Whatever he saw in his room full of junk. Whoever he met that day. Whatever struck his fancy. But every day, he would write a story.

And he stuck with it.

Now friends who knew him disagree on that. Some insist that yes, he wrote a story every day. Some say that he slowed down to "only" one a week. Fifty stories a year, give or take. How many of you are writing fifty stories a year? That's a pretty determined kid!

(And for some of you, I just gave the game away. Hold on, don't spoil it for the rest of us. We're almost there.)

So he wrote a story a day, or maybe a story a week. Either way, that adds up. Were they all gold? Hardly. He wasn't trying to write *gold*, he was trying to write *stories*, and then he could "pan for gold." He would look at the story he wrote each day and ask: Is this good enough to sell? Maybe give it some polish and then send it out? Some were, some weren't. In fact, only about three to fifteen percent were good enough to sell. That's not a bad percentage. I know writers who are struggling pretty hard and sadly aren't selling fifteen percent yet. But even three percent adds up—especially if when you have a lot of stories. When you apply those percentages over an eighty year span, Ray Bradbury published six hundred of his stories, a number any of us would be proud of. And those six hundred included some absolute gold that came out of his slurry pan.

That's right: that kid was Ray Bradbury, the winner of the Prometheus award, the Emmy award, the National Medal of Arts, and a star on the Hollywood Walk of Fame (to name just a few of his awards). A man who had awards named after *him*—along with a crater on the Moon and an asteroid. And although not nearly as momentous, a man who was the namesake for the spacecraft in the first story I ever sold to *Analog* magazine. He had a phenomenal impact by simply writing the stories and worrying about finding the good ones later. He was the man who advised us (paraphrased): "Write a short story a week. Nobody can write fifty bad stories in a row."

There are dozens of other successful pantsers I could name, but I think one Bradbury is enough to prove it *can* be done, by some writers. Maybe by you. If you're stuck, just write something. Don't try to be good, just write, then keep the good stuff.

And remember: everything gets easier with practice.

BUILDING BONFIRES
BY KEVIN J. ANDERSON

Kevin J. Anderson has published more than 175 books, 58 of which have been national or international bestsellers. He has written numerous novels in the Star Wars, X-Files, and Dune universes, as well as a unique steampunk fantasy trilogy beginning with *Clockwork Angels*, written with legendary rock drummer Neil Peart. His original works include the Saga of Seven Suns series, the Wake the Dragon and Terra Incognita fantasy trilogies, the Saga of Shadows trilogy, and his humorous horror series featuring Dan Shamble, Zombie P.I. He has edited numerous anthologies, written comics and games, and the lyrics to two rock CDs. Anderson is the director of the graduate program in Publishing at Western Colorado University. Anderson and his wife Rebecca Moesta are the publishers of WordFire Press. His most recent novels are *Clockwork Destiny, Gods and Dragons, Dune: The Lady of Caladan (with Brian Herbert),* and *Slushpile Memories: How NOT to Get Rejected.*

~

Any writer who's had a story or novel published would love to see his career take off and become a roaring, blazing bonfire—but it's rarely that simple, as many of us all-too-unfortunately know.

Then again, building a good, blazing bonfire isn't exactly simple either.

You've got to get well-seasoned wood that will burn long and bright. You need kindling that will burn fast and hot to ignite the blaze. You need twigs and paper, and you need to stack it all just right. Then, of course, you need the match.

Okay, here's the roadmap to that morass of metaphors: A writer's talent is the *match,* because without a match there's no way you'll ever get a fire started. If you're attempting to build a bonfire, I'll assume that you can at least strike a light.

The well-seasoned wood at the heart of a roaring bonfire is a *good, solid novel.* However, in today's marketplace, simply having a log and a match usually isn't enough to start a fire. Some writers start their careers by finishing a compelling and meaty novel that in any fair universe should become a critical and financial hit all by itself. But that's like trying to light a piece of hardwood by tossing a match onto the log. It's not very likely to burst into flame (though stranger things have happened... this is *publishing,* after all).

Other writers try to build their bonfires by using only kindling, writing quick adventurous fluff that's destined to burn bright and fast, make a few quick bucks, and then vanish after the first or second printing. Some may write short stories they post online for a few friends. The only way to keep the blaze going is to throw more and more and more kindling into the pile as it blazes hot and fast then crumbles into ash. This is like writing dozens of media spinoff books, adventurous fantasy series, shared-world novels, or pseudonymous potboilers.

Now, I'll hold up my own hand in confession because I myself established my bestselling career through my Star Wars and X-Files novels. However, while I spent a great deal of time writing media tie-ins in order to pay the house payment and the grocery bill, I also continued writing my own original SF series, collaborative thrillers with Doug Beason, and my Dune novels with Brian Herbert.

Some people look down their noses at any author who would deign to write in another person's universe, claiming that such an author has sold his soul to a slimy licensor. I look at it in a more practical way, though: I'm only *renting* my soul for a very good price, then getting it back again in perfectly good condition.

Thanks to my media tie-in success, I can now claim over thirteen million books in print. They've hit every bestseller list you can name, even the Number One slot on some. I'm the author of the *three* top-selling science fiction books in one year. I'm the editor of the three bestselling science fiction anthologies of all time. The readers of *SFX Magazine* voted my first X-Files novel the best science fiction novel of the year, beating out William Gibson, Terry Pratchett, and Anne McCaffrey. The members of the Science Fiction Book Club voted *Dune: House Atreides* as their "Book of the Year" by what the SFBC calls a "precedent-setting margin."

Those are impressive credentials I can put on the dust jackets of my non-media novels. On the strength of my Dune and Star Wars work, I just sold a very ambitious epic SF series, The Saga of Seven Suns, which will be like a "Robert Jordan for science fiction" (at least, that's what the marketing department said). If I didn't have my prior track record, I never would have gotten that chance. In other original novels, my print runs overall have tripled or quadrupled above what they were before I began writing my media tie-ins.

I've received several thousand fan letters, many of them from readers who claim that because they have liked my media books, they've gone out to buy my other novels. This crossover readership is what builds your core audience.

I have continued to write media tie-in books and comics and short stories as long as I find them entertaining. Hey, is it any surprise that I actually *like* Star Wars and The X-Files? What better reason could there be to write novels based on those characters?

But no matter how many other money-making projects I take on, I always write at least one novel *for me* each and every year—a publication rate beyond that of many other authors, even if they don't write anything else.

Setting up a foundation of my own good novels was what landed me the assignment for writing in Star Wars and X-Files in the first place, and using the success—the kindling—of these novels, I've been able to set fire to my hardwood, the mainstay of my bonfire.

And the fire is burning very bright indeed.

If you have the energy and the stamina, that's a tried-and-true way to help build your career into a bonfire. I've regularly written short stories and articles (paper and wood shavings) as well as my Star Wars and X-Files bestsellers (fast-burning kindling), while still writing my own ambitious and complex original novels (well-seasoned hardwood for the core of the fire).

This is not to say that you can't make a huge success by writing only your own fiction. Publishing is a business where all bets are off, because no one has exactly figured out how it works yet, not the authors, not the editors, not the publishers. Still, by writing constantly and not allowing my quality to flag, either on the media books or on my own books, I've managed to generate a good deal of heat.

I'm tempted to sign off by saying "May the Force be with you," or "The truth is out there" ...but in this case I'll just settle for "Keep writing."

TEACH THEM TO YEARN
BY STORM HUMBERT

Storm Humbert lives in Michigan with his wife, Casey, and cat, Nugget. He is a graduate of Temple University's MFA program, where he studied with Samuel R. (Chip) Delany. His work has appeared in *Andromeda Spaceways, Apex Magazine, Interzone,* and others. He is also a winner of the Writers of the Future Contest, so his work was featured in the *Writers of the Future 36.* Most recently, his work appeared in the *Of Wizards and Wolves* anthology in memory of Dave Farland from Wordfire Press and *The Librarian* anthology from Air & Nothingness Press. More of Storm's work can be found at his site: stormhumbertwrites.com.

The holographic buttons on my pilot interface spread out like the stars of an ancient galaxy. They were beautiful, but also a relic in this newer ship—something I was only supposed to use if the AI failed. I still remembered the joy of manually maneuvering through new asteroid belts, though, and I missed it. I preferred the old ship. Its onboard computer had been assistive rather than autonomous.

The new ship was so smart, it made me uncomfortable—like it

was alive but wasn't, fluctuating between servitude and divinity. I was still adjusting and figured I would be until my last day on the job.

Screw it. "I'll take this one, Chip," I said to the ship's AI.

"Human navigation increases risks of—"

"I know," I said, because I did, but I didn't care. "Monitor sensors. Assistive functions only."

"Yes, sir," Chip said.

I wove unnecessarily close to most asteroids that required course alteration to make Chip's sensors ping—to make it sweat. *Tell me I can't fly my own ship.*

What would the Star Corps care if I damaged an explo ship, anyway? What did any reprimands matter? Everyone knew inter-stellar expansion was petering out. Soon, explo wouldn't even be a funded department. These newer, smarter ships and their maps would be repurposed to automate commerce and delivery between systems.

For years, I'd ignored the signs, but a soul-crushing desk job would definitely mark my last few years before retirement. I was determined to enjoy the time I had left, though, jumping across space, drawing my own constellations in alien star fields.

The Corps' motto was *To strive, to seek, to find, and not to yield*— part of an old poem I'd only recently read. So much for that. I knew they'd meant that motto when they'd chosen it, though, and I couldn't help but wish they still did.

Mapping hadn't always been so cold and sterile. My grandmother had been a mapper, and when I was young, she'd said explo felt as if some reality-shattering discovery waited around every corner. That's what I'd wanted, but somewhere along the way the wonder had died. Expansion had become mechanical—auto-pilot, just like the ships— and I wasn't sure the awe of space exploration could be rekindled, even though I'd have given anything to do it.

Once we'd cleared the system's asteroid belt, I picked up my book of poems, *Laniakea*, and returned to my bunk. I wasn't generally the reading type, but a recruit had given it to me. She'd asked if I'd take it through spacefold, since she might never get to go. I hadn't planned on reading it, but once I did, I couldn't stop. Just holding a physical book in the depths of space—the grain of the pages and the way they tingled when I fanned them between my thumbs—was special. It was as if I'd brought a piece of the terrestrial past into this interstellar future.

The words were another experience altogether. I could identify with them without needing to fully understand, and that made me feel how drifting through space and discovering unknown places was supposed to feel—how I'd used to feel, at the start of my career.

Chip pinged me once it located the system's first planet-sized object, and I had to put the book away. I made my way through the burnt-orange corridors to the control pod, where Chip had already brought the object up on the viewer. Whatever this supposed planet-sized object was, however, I couldn't see it clearly, and the ship was too far away to magnify the image enough.

"Perfect," I said as I pinched the bridge of my nose. "Orbit study on a dark object."

I didn't mind the extra days this would add to my mission. I welcomed them, in fact, but orbit study was purely automated through Chip. This meant it took my list of nearly no required duties during normal mapping to zero.

"I could send a lightbot to launch a Helios flare," Chip said. "That would provide the light to enhance the image. It would take approximately eighty-four percent less time than orbital study."

"Definitely not," I laughed. "Too much heat, and it's totally against protocol. Minimally disruptive measures. That's the game, Chip."

I didn't really care about the rules anymore, but I wasn't about to do anything to cut days off my missions. I'd savor them, no matter how bland.

"Of course, sir. I'll set a course for the object."

It had been odd, during retraining, to be told that my ship's AI wasn't bound by the rules either in action or suggestion. It'd seemed that if the Corps was going to give us such strict bylaws, they'd supply us with ships that couldn't break them, but we'd all learned at one time or another that it was a safety measure. Sometimes, you had to break the rules to stay alive or do the job, and that was a call for a human to make.

It took almost seventeen hours to reach clear visual range, during which time I played some chess against Chip. When I was very young, my mother and I had lived on Kertz, by a lake, and my friend Arwish and I had printed our own board after we'd seen two men play the game in an old 3D. Kertz was a poor planet, so we'd scrounged neighbors' compactors and the local pits to get enough black and white plastics to feed the printer. Chess became our favorite game, and we played all the time.

After my mother and I moved to Exupery in the Capri-8 system, I played almost exclusively against AIs because all the other kids preferred their interactive holo games. Despite the years of playing, I still wasn't very good and had to play on a low difficulty against Chip. I often thought about Chip's consciousness, and playing chess made me wonder what it was like for Chip to handicap itself—whether Chip resented me for hamstringing it. After a while, beating Chip felt like punching it while its hands were tied behind its back, so I excused myself and got some rest.

I was relieved when we finally reached orbital distance, but as soon as Chip brought the dark object up on the viewer, I knew it wasn't a planet. The object was a small planetoid, maybe the size of a large moon, and appeared to be made of glass. *But it couldn't be.*

It was more a suggestion of a thing than a thing itself—like some loose skin on the face of the universe. The object required staring because each time I thought it was about to disappear certain parts of it would catch light from the central star and dazzle before slipping back into a distorted darkness. It was as if it only existed if I looked right at it, and I loved it existing, so I stared and stared.

After a time, I realized the structure wasn't full. It was a spiralized sphere—like the skin of some god-sized apple peeled round-and-round in one motion. *What would the fruit have tasted like?*

"What the hell is that, Chip?" The words rolled out of me, and I forgot to refill my lungs.

"A geometrically precise arrangement of what is likely inorganic matter," Chip said in a tone that killed the mood a bit. AIs aren't really capable of awe.

"I want a full work-up." I paced and gave instructions as if surrounded by many Chips—as if any Chips would require my direction. "I want composition, speed, dating, the works. I want the full microscope. Chip, you better be able to tell me how many atoms are in that thing."

"Yes, sir," Chip said.

Chip, of course, had already begun all of that. It recorded the object continuously and took readings on everything from gravity and rotation to composition and magnetospherics. All I could really do was marvel at the image in the viewer. It was so striking—so impossible.

Every part of me screamed that this was an intelligently designed structure, but it couldn't be. I couldn't let myself believe it because, if it *was*, then this discovery was huge. It was beyond anything ever found, and I was the one who'd found it. If it *was*, then the structure was evidence of advanced, non-human intelligence in the universe. It would mean promotions and money and fame and books with my name in them—the envy of every mapper. But most of all, it might save the Corps—it must. It would reinvigorate our search for whatever illusory thing we'd always been after.

The big questions—the ones every mapper dreamt of asking— bloomed and popped like suds in my mind, washing out any other thoughts. *What is this? Who made this? Is this real? What does it do?* But I couldn't answer them. All I could do was wait for information from Chip.

. . .

The first conclusion Chip reached was that the structure was likely composed of pure carbon. Specifically, graphene.

"That's impossible," I said.

"According to human understanding, yes, but that is the explanation for the structure that involves the lowest number of supposed impossibilities. It is, therefore, the most likely to be true."

"What impossibilities does this impossibility explain?" I said.

"The exceptional magnetosphere, for one," Chip said. "Though the structure is charged somehow, it has no dense core and should therefore have no magnetosphere. Graphene is one of the best-known electrical conductors, and only in roughly this quantity could it produce such a vast magnetosphere when electrified. This huge magnetosphere, combined with the resilience of the material, also explains the object's superficial perfection. Neither of these things is explicable individually, let alone taken together, by any other scenario."

"So, how...?"

"I don't know," Chip said. "I was going to dispatch some lightbots to take atomic resolution X-rays. Should I proceed?"

Protocol dictated that I stop it all there. I should have noted the structure, completed my map, and taken the information back to Command so they could deploy a specialized team, but I wanted this.

I'd never been so excited, but there was something else too; a weight on the corners of my grin and a flicker in the edges of my vision as if something lurked—as if this joy was a trap. It was as if I stood on a pair of bay doors above some great precipice, and the button could be pressed at any moment to open them and pull me from this dream. The mystery was invigorating but also terrifying. The structure could *be* anything, could *do* anything, and maybe it was safer to let it be—leave it to the experts.

What is this? Who made this? Is this real? What does it do? Who made this? Who made this? Who made this? The refrain played in my head, and the questions drowned out my worries. I couldn't let it be. I had to know.

I stared at the image on the viewer, and I needed to understand it.

The draw was primal, like seeing a face in a house's façade or feeling a tingle somewhere in the brainstem that says you're being watched. It was innate.

"Do it," I said.

The bots were gone for longer than expected, and I found it hard to do much other than sit in front of the viewer and stare. Eventually, however, I had to take a break to avoid going mad. So, I grabbed *Laniakea* and read "Drift."

> *Scarlet nights in*
> *Alcohol fogs at*
> *Just that hour when*
> *The smells of*
> *Nickel and iron in*
> *Burning white fire*
> *Catch my nostrils*
> *Again.*

It made me think of a story I'd heard about a transport rescuer who'd taken his helmet off outside the ship. He wasn't crazy or anything. He'd done it so that a woman would be able to breathe as she slipped across the tether from her disabled ship to the rescue pod. He'd tried to hold his breath, but they had to revive him on the other side. When he came to, he said space smelled like booze and hot metal.

Something in the poem made sense to me, but I couldn't quite pin it down. *What would Chip think?*

"I have just received data from the lightbots," Chip said, as if it'd heard me thinking about it.

I jumped. There had been no warning to Chip's speaking, not even the barely measurable non-sound that the speakers normally made before its voice came out.

"Sorry, sir. I didn't mean to frighten you."

"No worries," I said. "What did the lightbots tell you?"

"The structure is, indeed, pure carbon."

"How?"

"Ingeniously," Chip said as it put the X-ray and other data from the bots up on the screen. "The outer covering is about a billion atom-thick, macro-scale carbon nanotubes wrapped around each other, and the inside is a system of graphene sheets that intersect each other in complex fractal patterns. Where intersections occurs, it always involves two planes intersecting a third at the same point, and the carbon at these junctures takes on a diamond-like arrangement. Although each sheet has an average of twelve points at which it intersects or is intersected by others, no two sheets have the same twelve. It's impossibly brilliant. I'm only able to follow because I can reverse-engineer the process."

"So, what does it do?" I said.

"Other than produce a large magnetic field?" Chip said. "Nothing."

I couldn't accept that—knew it was wrong in my gut and the base of my skull, and those two parts didn't often agree. Chip couldn't see it, but most any human would. There was intent here. There had to be more. "Keep looking," I said.

Solo-explo had always been lonely work, but with the old ship, I'd never noticed as much. At least with the old ship, I'd had real duties to keep me busy—that ship needed me for things. And even though Chip was a much better conversationalist, it wasn't good in a human way, which was somehow worse than quiet, after a while. It was only my need to understand the structure that kept me going—kept me sane.

I observed it for weeks, much longer than any object should be observed on a solo-explo mission. On the fourth day, one of the lightbots had malfunctioned and crashed into the structure. Before it was destroyed, however, it picked up some kinetic vibrations, which Chip had been monitoring ever since. Chip had detected nothing new for all the weeks after that, though.

Since I couldn't bring myself to leave the structure, I had Chip send out some of the lightbots to net-map the system. This was even further against protocol. The product would be crude compared to a map drawn by the ship, and object study of this detail wasn't even close to my job, but I didn't care. I hadn't felt this energy—this need—in a long time, and I wouldn't give it up for anything. Command would have to understand. What would they do: fire the man who made the greatest discovery in all of human history?

The longer it went on, however, the more the whole process began to wear on me. I loved the structure—the beauty and mystery of it—but I felt my current appreciation for its significance required answers to some of the fundamental questions: *what is this; who made this; what does it do?* I needed to find them because exactly what we'd been seeking for so long—evidence of another waking mind—was now right here in front of us, in front of me, and I needed to reach out and touch it. I needed to *know* it.

I felt as if a friendly hand was reaching out—blindly grasping, as humanity was—from the darkness. We needed to connect to whoever put this here. Even though I knew it was selfish and arrogant, I wanted to be the one to do it.

Humanity needed this find. Everyone needed to remember why we strapped tubes full of exploding gasses to glorified metal outhouses and came looking in the first place. This was it. Too many had forgotten, and I knew this would remind them, but I needed at least some of those answers.

While I was reading during one of these manic days spent reeling between delight and frustration—in dire need of something to do other than contemplate the structure—I asked Chip if it'd ever read poetry.

"I could access any published works if connected to a base's infolinks," Chip said. "But there is no poetry in my active memory."

"How much could you read in a few hours?" I said.

"I could add all known volumes of poetry to my memory within an hour."

"Is that how you read?"

"I don't read," Chip said. "I acquire. Reading is done word by word. My acquisition is immediate."

That didn't seem like a way to think about poetry. It would be like looking at a puzzle only once it's done. The viewer would only see the picture, not the process. They wouldn't have any appreciation for which piece—which smudge of color—took the picture from an assemblage of pigments to a wolf racing after a hare or the night sky of this or that planet.

"I don't think that'll work, Chip. Poetry isn't something you acquire. It's an experience." I sat for a moment fanning the pages of *Laniakea* with my thumbs. "Here," I placed the book open in Chip's scanner. "Read some poems from this. Do it manually. Log each word individually. Basically, transcribe a poem into a document as you read. Take any notes or thoughts separately. After you're done, delete the document, keep your notes, and do it again."

"Sir, what's the point of—"

"We could always play chess, if you'd prefer," I said.

There was a smirk of silence before Chip said, "How long would you like me to read?"

"Until you have something to say about it."

While Chip read, I busied myself listening to those vibrations the lightbot had detected. Chip had said they were very strange, and it was right. There was something to them, something almost musical. But each time order seemed about to arise, a flurry of vibrations or extended silence broke the pattern, and it'd all fall to pieces. It was what I imagined pi would sound like if set to music and played on chimes or bells—completely maddening.

When I reached the pinnacle of annoyance listening to the vibrations, I checked in on each lightbot out on structural recon, checked the progress of the net-mapping lightbots, and manually updated the log. None of this was necessary, since Chip did all of it simultaneously and perpetually anyway, but I needed to participate. Chip never said anything. Hell, for all I knew it understood.

Eventually, I sat down to play rummy with Chip and it crushed me despite doing everything I'd just been doing plus its reading assignment.

After a couple hands, Chip said, "Poems seem much like riddles."

"Kind of," I said.

"I like riddles."

"Really?" It was strange to hear that Chip *liked* anything. I'd never considered it would have preferences.

"Many AIs like riddles. They're all lateral thinking, and it's something that comes more slowly to us. Riddles make us wonder, which is something we don't often do."

"So, what poems did you read?" I said. "What did you think of them?"

"I started with the one it was open to, 'Drift.' It was a good choice, sir—a simple one to solve."

"Solve?"

"Riddles are about the illusion that information is missing and the misleading perspectives this illusion engenders in the reader, yes?" Chip said. "The information required to solve this poem was easy to find since the author, Ms. Purghesh, was briefly in the Corps and her personnel records are, therefore, a part of my access profile. Ms. Purghesh had a violent, alcoholic father. The alcohol is a reference to him, and the metallic references are her blood, which reminds one of iron when tasted or smelled. The rhythm speaks to the regularity of the violence and the 'Again' to its perpetuity."

The explanation was jarring—agitating. It was like being told why the sky is beautiful or how the stars got to exactly where they are. It soured the poem.

"You're not supposed to solve poetry, Chip," I said as calmly as I could. "The point is that good poetry keeps you wondering."

"Is this poetry not good then?" Chip said.

"No, it's good," I said. "Just try reading it differently. Don't try to answer it. Think of it as something that has no answers, or infinite answers. Just read and think."

Chip kept reading, and we talked about it from time to time, but I soon gave up on the experiment because Chip seemed to lose interest once the poems were not to be treated as riddles.

The last time we talked about them before I took the book back, I told Chip it was being too diagnostic and not respecting the complexity of human experience.

Chip asked if I was referring to the *actual* level of complexity or the complexity humans attribute to ourselves. Chip then pointed out that it could experience colors, sounds, and sensations beyond my capacities, and I decided to grit my teeth and walk away before it ruined any more of my poems.

Later though, after I'd cooled off, I wondered if maybe Chip had been right. Maybe a human mind, no matter how beautiful, was not enough to cause perpetual wonder in an AI.

In the middle of the twelfth week, the net-mapping bots came back with the rough map of the system.

"Sir, I'm not sure further study of this object will be fruitful," Chip said.

"What do you mean?"

"It appears that collision with another object is imminent."

It was the most terrible thing Chip could've said. I felt as if I'd been dying in a cold, empty place, found a fire to warm me, and the flame had been snuffed out. The momentary warmth made the returning cold all the more severe.

"How long until impact?" I said, hoping to be numb again soon.

"Approximately five hundred and eighty-five hours, sir," Chip said

"Will the structure survive?"

"Unlikely," Chip said. "The data is rough, but the approaching object has similar diameter, which means it likely has greater mass since our structure is mostly empty."

Our structure. Yes.

"Chip, is there anything we can do? Forget the rules. Is there anything that has even a small chance of working?"

"It is unlikely," Chip said. "But we'll need to study the approaching object to determine if any intervention is possible."

I stared at the structure on the screen. If Chip had said there was no chance, I would have drifted there for the remaining weeks and marveled at it—I would have sat witness to its destruction. But Chip said something might be possible, so I held fast to that last hopeful ember and gave the order to set off for the approaching object.

Once we were within visual range, Chip put the object up on the viewer. At first, I thought Chip had made an error, but it hadn't. The approaching object was an exact replica of the structure we'd been studying for the past six weeks. Once we were in orbit, Chip took the same measurements it had with the other structure.

The object had the same composition, same design, and same-sized magnetosphere. The only differences were that it spun the opposite way, orbited the star in the opposite direction, and had opposite poles. The vibrations were also different, and Chip began monitoring them as it had the other.

The worst news came when Chip said that there was no way to avert the collision. If it had been a planetoid of a certain composition, we could have landed on it, burrowed deep inside, overloaded the engines, and exploded them once they went hot. It would have killed us but destroyed the object and saved the structure. These structures, however, had too much empty space to them—and graphene conducted heat, kinetic energy, and electricity too well. The explosion would only vaporize part of it. The course wouldn't be altered enough, and the structures would still mostly destroy each other.

If I'd followed protocol—If I'd mapped the system myself and reported back—maybe something could have been done. Maybe a special team could have stopped this. *This is my fault*. I wanted to scream. I wanted to rage and yell and break things, but I knew none of that would help. Instead, I let that little wonder inside me go cold. I imagined everyone else who had any left would do the same when these recordings and findings were released—if Command released them at all.

For the three weeks and some days that followed the discovery of the inevitable impact, I was as much a machine as Chip. At first, it felt like depression, but then it felt like safety.

I stared at the structures less and less until I didn't really see them anymore, even when I had to look at the viewer. I left as much of the work to Chip as I could—so all of it—and I slept a lot. Most of my waking time was spent trying to convince myself that, really, I was lucky—that I'd gotten to actually discover these things and see them with my own eyes. I wasn't very persuasive.

There weren't specific protocols for this scenario, but standard procedure had one core dictate: *as much information as possible in as much detail as possible*. So, when the day finally came, we left the light-bots in place around the two structures as they spun toward their end. Many of the bots would be destroyed, but they would transmit useful data to Chip up to their last moments of function.

I hadn't planned on watching the impact—didn't think I had it in me—so I was in my cot during the final hour. With about a half hour left, Chip called me to the console for an emergency.

"What is it, Chip?" I said as I entered the control pod.

"Sir, the structures are interacting," it said. "It started the instant their magnetospheres connected."

"Are they stopping?" I nearly shouted as something tingling hot, like hope, ran up and down my spine. "Are they changing course?"

"No, sir, but the primary object has sunk relative to the second by about three degrees. Their rates of rotation have also synced. They were nearly identical before, but now they're exactly the same."

"Interesting," I said as I tried not to collapse. "Is that all you needed, Chip? It wasn't really an emergency."

"Sir, I've been running the projections on this change, and..."

Chip's pause was careful—almost anxious—in a way I hadn't heard before. It never had to search for words.

"I think you should stay and watch."

I didn't want to, but Chip's demeanor was intriguing, if not downright unsettling, so I agreed.

There was a symmetry to the way the structures caught the light now that their rotations were perfectly in sync. The pattern to their dazzling almost felt like speech. The objects shouted to each other with their language of light and glimmer, each pleading with the other to move aside or slow down.

I wanted to plead too.

When the moment of impact came, I closed my eyes and looked away, but when I looked back up, they were still there, and they weren't colliding.

I shot from my seat to stand on shaking legs. The structures were spinning *into* each other. They slid together like old lovers moving to a song they knew from when they were young.

When the structures fully aligned—halfway done passing through each other—the top and bottom tips at each end of their brilliant spiralized, spherical forms intertwined and held them fast, as one whole sphere, for a full revolution. Their momentums upon connection were equal so they spun in place—at a single point in space—for the whole rotation. It was beautiful in its simultaneous defiance and utilization of nature.

When the structures caught light while they were joined, the glimmers ran up and down the surface in contiguous lines like lightning. It seemed as if the structure wasn't two joined spherical spirals but innumerable fragments of some great glass planet shattered apart and pieced back together—like a great cataclysm rewound and frozen. It had the feeling of a monument.

A beautiful tinkling, rumbling, whirring sound came from the speakers, and I recognized parts of it as the vibrations from the structures, but they weren't chaos anymore. They were whole. They were questions with answers, melodies with harmonies, sounds in full color. The music made me think of the birth of light from deep, unimaginable darkness and the gleeful dying of stars. It was as if the universe were singing an aria.

"Chip—"

"Shh," it said, and it was right.

The spiralized spheres finished their rotation and spun out of each other, resuming their course as if nothing had happened. The event passed into memory like a vivid dream—with amazement, wonder, and the perpetual questions: *was any of it real*, and *what did it mean*? It was minutes after the structures were clear of each other before I said anything.

"Thank you for not telling me," I said. "It was better to watch."

"It was the only way," Chip said. "Poetry isn't something you acquire. It's an experience."

Chip's voice came not only from the speakers in the control pod but from everywhere. The words echoed all through the ship. It was as if Chip wasn't speaking to me, specifically, but stating a fact—a truth that it now understood in a way I never would—so that it could reverberate through the expanse beyond the ship.

I stared in awe—in hope and in fear of my own smallness—up into the camera above the viewer as if it was Chip's face. What unknowable, inexplicable wonderings had the dance of these alien structures engendered in Chip? Could I—could we—ever understand? These questions were too large for the moment, so I set them aside and focused instead on the only thing I knew for certain. We would try. We would strive. We would seek. We would find. And we would not yield.

WONDER: CHASING THE DRAGON
BY STORM HUMBERT

"Wonder" can seem like a nebulous thing—like something that happens rather than something we do. It's subjective, isn't it? Kind of, but not really. Wonder is the tightness in the chest from slack-jawed breathing. It's the tingle that starts in the spine and terminates at the fingertips. It's the growing of the mind as it scrambles to consume something it cannot contain. These aren't helpful, though, are they? They tell us how wonder feels, not what it is. Thankfully, David Farland gives a useful, personal definition in *Writing Wonder*: "Wonder comes when we experience something that turns out to be far better than we could ever hope or imagine. When we feel it, we immediately want to search and try to find more of that thing."

We've all experienced wonder. We've looked down from skyscrapers or out across wide valleys. We've sat in perfect moments with friends or strangers and felt unfathomable connection. We've walked through the ruins of ancient Rome or hiked through a forest that feels older than the world. We need to do more than simply experience wonder, though. We need to know and understand that feeling in ourselves if we are to produce it on the page, and we *must* produce it. Wonder is what we science fiction and fantasy writers sell, after all. It's the drug that keeps readers coming back.

Unlike normal dealers, however, we should absolutely indulge in our own supply. We are its primary quality control, in fact. For this reason, we must allow ourselves to be awe-struck by our own writing. If something we expect to be wonderful does not make us shiver—if it does not swim in our veins as we strive to cling to the beauty and awe of it—it's not good product. It will make no addicts. So, don't swallow the lie that the wonder falls out of our own writing because it's ours. It's not true. If our writing does not create a sense of wonder in us, it will do so in few others.

Dave's definition above is very broad, but so is the catalogue of wonderful things. Broader still is the infinite number of possible wonders we can create in worlds we build from scratch. There is no shortage of cannabis types or tobacco variants or processes for creating any manner of alcohols, but they do all share a primary mover that defines each as separate groups of intoxicants, and wonder is no different. The fundamental thing that defines all manner of wonder—the crux of Dave's definition—is that there must exist an expectation to be surpassed.

Expectations are, therefore, the beginning of writing wonder. They're the plant. So, we must understand expectations that come from outside our fictional worlds and those that we cultivate within them. The potency of the wonder, after these expectations are understood, is determined by what we cut these expectations with—by the manner in and the degree by which we surpass them.

A word of warning, though. While science fiction and fantasy readers may have higher tolerance for wonder than those of less fantastical genres, it is not infinite. Don't overdose your reader. It won't kill them, but it might kill your story. A constant onslaught of wonder will increasingly dull the buzz until the awe-inspiring things don't register anymore.

If something is perpetually present, people don't have the chance to itch for it—to crave it. Therefore, wonder must always be presented in stark relief to the normal of the world in which it exists. Ninety percent of our world-building work will always be in establishing the normal because that is necessary for the reader to understand and appreciate the abnormal (wonder being a stupendous form of the latter).

To continue with expectations, let's lay out some of the kinds that a reader brings to a story. There are, of course, genre expectations related to any tropes, themes, or devices readers anticipate experiencing. But there are also more general, fundamental expectations. These "innate" expectations include things like scope, scale, and time. Basically, any "rule" or "limit" of the real world represents an expectation we can surpass to create a moment of small wonder for our reader. I like to call these moments of small wonder "awe." Awe is a low-dose wonder. It's a starter hit—the freebie given to lock in future sales. In "Teach Them to Yearn," the first dose of awe comes about 1,000 words in when the structure is revealed.

Before we get into the meat of this moment, though, let's talk about how wonder is delivered. In wonder, as with other intoxicants, delivery systems matter. Tobacco can be smoked or chewed; cannabis eaten, smoked, or concentrate dropped in the eye. Alcohol can be drunk or... well... let's just leave that one alone. The point is, how something is delivered impacts how it affects the user.

A story is a collaboration between writer and reader, so while the writer relies on a reasonable suspension of disbelief from the reader, the reader relies on cues from the writer to inform how they react to the words before them. These cues are the delivery system. When it comes to delivering wonder on the page, I've found two pieces of advice on writing in general from my professor, Don Lee, to be very helpful for conceptualizing the writing of wonder in particular.

The first is that writers signal to readers what is important by how much time we spend talking about it—how much room we give it on the page. To me, wonder is kind of the whole game, so it's important. Give it the room it deserves. Affording wonder ample page-space is an important cue. It lets the reader know to fill the cylinder with water, strike a match, or make this one a double because the wonder has arrived.

The second thing Don told me is to save our best writing for the best moments. This isn't to say that our other writing is drab or plain, but that the most important moments must absolutely sparkle. To me, this means that anything worth elevating to the level of wonder is important to the world, plot, and/or characters. Wonder will hold it all together, so we must concoct it of our most blood-beguiling verbs and our most mind-altering syntax. It must awe in concept *and* language to overcome the crushing sobriety of the real world.

So, to return to the first moment of awe in "Teach Them to Yearn." About 1,000 words in, the object is revealed for the first time. The reader's expectation of what they are to see is given to them earlier in the story: "Chip pinged me once it located the system's first planet-sized object." This sets the reader up to *expect* a planet or planetoid. This brings along basic expectations of size, scale, composition, etc., but it also carries genre expectations (or suspicions) that we may be moving toward a first encounter or space battle.

However, once we actually hit that 1,000-word mark, it's none of these things. The object of the story surpasses these expectations by confounding them (and, consequently, our character). It is not solid, but mostly empty. It is not a planet of rock, but a spiralized, spherical ribbon, seemingly of glass. What was expected, in physical terms, was something natural. This object is unnatural—"Every part of me screamed that this was an intelligently built structure."

Even if the reader's genre expectations had prompted them to expect first contact or hostile engagement—things that could have been shocking and wonderful—this revelation upends and surpasses these expectations as well. So, even if our reader had expected to be passed the joint, they hadn't thought they'd be tasting the rainbow once they hit it.

The way our main character experiences this moment is also important. His mind—his world—has been altered, and he must adapt. As people who have seen things before, we know that the look of a thing is taken in at a glance—it takes less than a second to register shape, features, color, etc. Our character's glimpse of this thing, however, is drawn out. Time dilates. More specifically, it ceases to matter for the next ~350 words.

This is because these descriptions are filtered through our main character, which means his own wonder is bound up in them. He is using metaphoric description—"more a suggestion of a thing than a thing itself," "some loose skin on the face of the universe," "the skin of some god-sized apple peeled round-and-round in one motion"—to make sense of a thing that doesn't fit in his conception of the real or possible. He is seeking after it with his eyes and his mind. He is shocked by its scale, its design, its impossibility, and its implications, and we recognize this response as true to our own experience of discovering an unbelievable thing to be real. As he does these things, so does the reader.

I use this example because it is important to note that this moment of awe is not short on mystery. Our active ingredients—expectations—are not enhanced by combination with full knowledge and understanding. Knowing is sobering. Wondering is sublime. Think of a favorite magic system, mythical creature, or other wonderful element from a story or novel. Is *everything* about it known? What hatched Danaerys's dragons? Where is a centaur's heart? *Can* you grok it?

The wonder of the structure in the preceding story is very much tied to the unknown that surrounds it. "What is this? Who made this? Is this real? What does it do?" Wonder and mystery go hand-in-hand because both are "search" and "find" operations. In this way, the awe-inspiring thing augments the natural draw of a mystery, and the mystery of the awe-inspiring thing increases the titillation of the wonder. Any wonder, therefore, should be at least one part mystery.

As we move from this original point of awe through the meat of the story, the mystery surrounding the object deepens, and the longer questions go unanswered—and the more complications that arise—the more likely that readers (and authors, especially for pantsers like myself) develop their own theories (or... expectations) about the answer to the mystery. These, and the rules of the normal we establish, are the expectations cultivated within the story.

While satisfaction might be achieved if these expectations are met, wonder is *only* accomplished if expectations are exceeded. So, we shouldn't lose track of any of the ideas that crop up as possible answers to our mystery while we write. We must keep them, and when the time comes, we must surpass every single one.

So, we've laid out the ingredients for wonder: expectations, something that surpasses them, and a looming sense of mystery or element of the unknown. We can combine them in any measures and proportions we see fit, but we must be sure they're all accounted for. If we do this, we'll have some intoxicating wonder to enhance our intricate plots, incredible worlds, and deep, dynamic characters. Make it right, and wonder does more than satisfy. It exceeds. It grips. It enthralls. Brew your wonder strong, bottle it up nice, and don't dole it out too liberally, and they'll line up around the block.

If you've got the time, right now, while this is all fresh in your head, give the story you just read another go. This time, map how the wonder builds, but not for the mysterious object. We just took much of that apart, and this is not an open-book test (well… you know what I mean). This time, pay attention to Chip as an element of wonder. Chip is a subtler wonder, but it builds into the same powerful crescendo. How? What does this achieve? What would the story lose without Chip?

Repeat this in the other stories you read too. Identify the wonders. Take them apart. See how they work.

OLD MAN COYOTE MEETS MOTHER TORMENT

BY M. ELIZABETH TICKNOR

M. Elizabeth Ticknor is a neurodiverse, genderfluid writer and artist. She shares a comfortable hobbit hole in Southeast Michigan with her wookiee husband and their twin baby dragons. An avid reader of science fiction and fantasy, Elizabeth also enjoys well-written horror. Her other interests include drawing, painting, and tabletop roleplaying. Elizabeth is a winner of the Baen Fantasy Adventure award; her short fiction also appears in *Fireside Magazine, Writers of the Future* 38, and an assortment of anthologies by Air and Nothingness Press, Flame Tree Press, and Wordfire Press. Website: ticknortales.com Twitter: @lizticknor

Coyote poured his soul into Sheriff Mallory's skin as they traversed Devil's Creek. Mallory's body welcomed him at an instinctual level, as familiar and comfortable as a well-fitted suit, and he reveled in the sudden onslaught of sensation. Wind sang through tangled catclaw bushes, carrying the honeyed scent of acacia blossoms through the Texas air. Boots squelched through russet-red clay accumulated in the arroyo from recent rains.

Coyote whispered in Mallory's inner ear. *Holding out on me, Nantan? This is the perfect night for a run.* It had been weeks since their last venture. Coyote craved the adrenaline of the hunt, the weight of the leather duster on Mallory's shoulders, the kiss of cool night air on the sheriff's skin.

Mallory shuddered as Coyote's voice echoed through his mind. "Don't call me Nantan." He scowled and tugged at the rim of his battered Stetson. "You're supposed to ask before entering."

And you're supposed to invite me on every hunt, but here we are. Coyote reveled in Mallory's discomfort. The sheriff might use his title and surname as a shield to protect him from society at large, but Coyote refused to let him forget the name imparted by his Apache mother.

Mallory grunted. "Didn't see the point in calling you until I know what I'm after."

You didn't call last time, either—or the time before that.

"And you showed up both times anyhow. If I didn't know better, I'd think you're stalking me."

Stalking? Of course not. I just follow you everywhere. Stalking implied hunting, and Coyote made it a point never to hunt his friends. To be fair, he didn't have many friends. Humans tended to fear things they didn't understand—rightly so, but that was hardly the point. Spirits, on the other hand, had a nasty habit of consuming each other for power; it was difficult to form a lasting bond with someone when the only thing Coyote could trust was their appetite.

Mallory sighed, shook his head, and knelt down to study the creek bed. "Something's been eating Harmon Ellis's cattle. Damn near ate *him* when he tried to chase it off. It tracks like a bear, but it's bigger than any I've seen. Less black bear, more grizzly—and grizzlies aren't native to these parts." He traced two fingers over a massive pawprint embedded in the earth. The sensation of mud against bare fingertips sent a shiver of delight to Coyote's core.

All the more reason you should have called. If you don't know what you're up against, how are you going to prepare?

"By studying the thing. How would *you* prepare?" Mallory's question carried the weight of challenge.

I don't prepare. I improvise.

"And when it was time to improvise, I would have called you."

They caught up with the beast in a scrubby ditch at the base of an escarpment. It must have been a black bear once, little bigger than a Shetland pony; now it stood twenty hands tall, with shoulders broad as a carriage. Patches of fur clung to cancerous knots of bloated flesh; spurs of bone jutted from every joint. Eyes burned like red-hot ingots in a face twisted by perpetual agony. One hind leg ended in a ruined stump.

Coyote let out a mad cackle. *Oh, this* will *be fun. That bear is being consumed by a pain spirit.*

"You have a twisted sense of fun." Mallory studied the creature from a distance, a frown rooted on his features. "That poor animal."

Coyote sighed. *The body is too far gone to survive on its own. Our best bet is to put it out of its misery, but bullets won't be enough to take it down. We need to send the spirit home.* Coyote hated to suggest such a thing—exorcisms made him deeply uncomfortable—but Mallory wouldn't let well enough alone, and he saw no benefit to sending Mallory in unprepared.

The color drained from Mallory's face. "You want me to exorcise a bear the size of a Clydesdale?"

Well, you'll need to incapacitate it first—

"How?!"

You're clever, you'll think of something.

The wind shifted. The beast flared its nostrils, sniffed the air, and snapped its head in Mallory's direction.

Mallory ducked into the brush and hissed, "Clever isn't the only key to survival."

It's always been enough for me.

"I'm not you."

I can help with that. Coyote poured himself into every crack and crevice of Mallory's being. Raw energy burned through the man's body and re-forged it, surging through muscle and bone alike. His senses became Coyote's, and Coyote strengthened them in turn. In that moment, Coyote felt truly alive.

Perhaps *too* alive.

He searched Mallory's mind. No sign of conscious thought. He'd pushed too hard, too quickly, and knocked the sheriff out cold. That was problematic. Coyote preferred that his rides buck a bit; the resistance helped guard against temptation.

He ran his tongue along suddenly sharp teeth and assessed his options. No point in hiding. The beast already had his scent. He walked into the open, arms spread wide, and stretched his mouth into a face-splitting grin. In situations like this, bravado was everything.

"Noble spirit! Call me Cousin Coyote." His proper title was Old Man, but he preferred to understate his capabilities rather than flaunt them. It was survival instinct, more than anything else.

The bear gave a respectful nod. "I am Mother Torment."

Coyote scowled. Only the most brazen spirits introduced themselves as Mother or Father to spirits they didn't know. He gestured at the bear's bloated form. "Why have you claimed this sorry creature? I doubt it's done anything to deserve such torture."

"She called on my strength to escape a hunter's trap. I've grown fond of this body. It suits me well."

"It won't suit you for long, Mother. You've run your host ragged—already burned it half away."

"Consumption of flesh prevents decay."

"Slows, yes. Prevents, no. You've got a week at best, even if you devour every animal in the county."

Mother Torment tilted her head and studied Coyote more closely, eyes narrowed. "How do you keep your body so pristine?"

"What, this old thing?" Coyote tipped Mallory's hat, spun on his heel, and took a bow. "I take a gentler approach. Shared consciousness with a touch of light possession."

Mother Torment growled. "A simple haunt. Not the same. This body, it *feels* things. Reminds me of when I was human."

Coyote shivered, unprepared for the pangs of longing evoked by Mother Torment's words. He'd been human himself once, long ago, but his memories of that life were ancient and weather-worn. All that remained was the thrill of the hunt, the word games that taught him how to lie, the first time he'd seen the world through an animal's eyes...

Gods, he wanted to live again.

Mother Torment circled him, eyes blazing. "You miss it, too. I can taste your pain." She licked her lips. "Join me. We can burn together. Short lives, but powerful ones."

Coyote shook his head. He couldn't trust an offer like that. It might be a trick. "I've seen others go down that road." He'd done it himself, more than once, if he was being honest. Which he wasn't. It was never wise to be honest with strangers. "It's like an addiction. You'll want another body, and another, leaving bits of your soul behind every time. If you're not careful, you'll burn yourself away in the end. No one deserves to die like that. Let us send you home."

"I *am* home." Mother Torment lunged forward. Her teeth closed inches from his chest.

Coyote's small hairs bristled at the near miss. He poured false calm into his voice and backed away, arms raised in a show of supplication. "Come now, Mother, there's no need to squabble. I'm offering you the chance to part amicably. If we'd met on the other side of the veil, I'm sure we'd be fast friends."

Mother Torment stalked toward him, eyes narrowed, ears flat against her head. "I've met your kind before. Liars, all. You're no mere Cousin. You smell old. Powerful. Eating you and your pet human will keep me here for months."

Coyote winced. Her words were truer than she knew. "You're not thinking of the long game. Going home could give you centuries—millennia, even." Even with his strength bolstering Mallory's body, he doubted he'd be able to stand toe to toe with Mother Torment in a fight. The battle would have been more balanced in the spirit realm, but here Coyote was only as strong as his host. Perhaps if he pushed all his power into Mallory—

No. That would leave the sheriff permanently maimed, assuming it didn't kill him outright.

Mother Torment lunged again, cavernous jaw opened wide. So much for negotiations. Coyote reshaped Mallory's bones, dropped to all fours, and *ran*.

Mother Torment moved like a steam engine—slow to start, but strong and enduring. Her footfalls shook the earth as she charged. Her ruined hind leg showed no signs of hindering her.

Coyote scoured Mallory's memories in search of ways to return Mother Torment to the spirit realm. It wasn't easy information to find; Coyote didn't know exactly what he was looking for. He preferred not to involve himself in the cleansing of spirits, and had actively avoided paying attention when Mallory enacted such rituals in the past. Even when an exorcism was for the best, witnessing it shook his faith in Mallory's friendship. If he crossed too many lines, might Mallory grow to resent him and send him away?

The search through Mallory's memories revealed knowledge—too much of it. Mallory had studied rites from numerous cultures, native and otherwise; Coyote couldn't tell which held true power and which were balderdash. He rummaged through the sheriff's mind for embers of consciousness to kindle. "Nantan?" Still nothing. "Mallory! Wake up in there!"

Claws the size of butcher knives tore through Mallory's leather duster. They didn't just pierce Coyote's flesh—they snagged his spirit. He yelped and put on an extra burst of speed, desperate to keep those claws from finding further purchase.

There! A spark of awareness in Mallory's mind. The initial shock of the blow faded; the mote of consciousness dimmed in turn.

Pain was the key.

Coyote scrambled across the plains, Mother Torment on his tail, retracing their steps until he found the arroyo. He stripped off Mallory's hat and duster, threw them in Mother Torment's face, and leapt over Devil's Creek—straight into the catclaw bushes.

Thorns latched onto clothing and exposed flesh alike, biting deeper with every movement. Coyote shielded his eyes and pushed through the brush. Broken branches trailed behind him.

The sheriff's consciousness stirred again. Coyote ground a snapped-off thorn into the back of his hand. It might not do the same kind of damage as Mother Torment's claws, but Coyote had often found small agonies more difficult to ignore than large ones.

Mallory yelped as he came to, trying to struggle despite Coyote's hold on his flesh. *What the Sam Hill is going on?*

Coyote whooped with delight. "Good morning, Nantan! You picked a terrible time to doze off."

I didn't— Mallory cut himself off mid-sentence, sighed, and started over. *Why are we running? What's going on?*

"Mother Torment is trying to eat us."

Who?

Mother Torment bellowed behind them. Coyote glanced over his shoulder. The bear burst through the cat-claw bushes, wreathed in thorns, fur caked with mud.

"What did you call her? The Clydesdale bear. She's literally power-hungry. We need to send her home before she devours us body and soul."

Less talking, more running! We need to burn sage, tobacco, and rosemary. Ceremonial bowls are ideal, but we can make do with a cigarette— the smoke is the important thing. The herbs are in my medicine bag. Left jacket pocket. Rolling papers and matches are on the right.

Coyote winced. "I *may* have used your coat as a distraction tactic."

You threw away my coat?

"And your hat."

This is why I never give you the reins! We need to find it so I can exorcise that thing.

Coyote cringed. Mallory had said "I," not "we." That meant he planned to do the deed himself, and he couldn't do that without full bodily autonomy. Coyote had never before held this much control in their relationship; the idea of surrendering it so quickly made his stomach turn. "Just tell me how to perform the ritual."

No. If you bungle this, you'll kick yourself out instead and Mother Torment will tear me to pieces.

Coyote shifted his trajectory to a slow-sloping curve rather than a straight line. "We'll burn that bridge when we cross it."

That's not how the saying goes! That's not how the saying goes at all!

Mother Torment altered her course, moving to intercept Coyote. That wouldn't do. Unless—

Coyote ran straight at her, a manic grin plastered on his face. "Watch this."

Wait, wait, wait, no, no, no—

Coyote leapt at the last moment, planted one foot atop Mother Torment's head, and vaulted over her back. Teeth grazed his leg, but didn't latch. He hit the ground rolling, tumbled to his feet, and resumed running without missing a beat.

I hate you.

"That seems harsh. If there's one thing I'm good at, it's running. From things, toward things—running in general, really."

Coyote jumped over the catclaw bushes, slid down the creek bed, and opened his nostrils wide. The earthy scent of mud assailed him. More than a dozen yards away, little more than a whisper on the wind, he picked up the mixture of sweet, bitter, and grassy herbs Mallory kept in his medicine bag.

Coyote scrambled and slid through the arroyo. The muck-filled creek bed sucked at his boots, slowing him down. He almost missed the coat, now little more than a pile of shredded leather covered in blood-red clay. He snatched it up and fumbled through the pockets; thankfully, they hadn't torn or spilled.

Mother Torment landed in front of him, hackles raised, lips pulled back in a snarl.

Coyote hurled a swath of mud in her face and scrambled up the creek's bank, holding the duster close. He wiped his hands clean on a tuft of buffalo grass, then pulled out the medicine bag and rolling papers.

Mother Torment cleared the mud from her eyes and lunged at Coyote, mouth open, aiming for his throat. Coyote tumbled backward and kicked at her lower jaw. Teeth clattered. Mother Torment roared.

Coyote rolled to his feet and forced another burst of speed into burning legs. "Let's bring this chase to an end, shall we?"

We can't do that if she's constantly at your heels. We need time to prepare.

"How long?"

At least half a minute.

"I can buy us that." Coyote shoved rolling papers and matches into the medicine bag, dropped the coat, and charged toward the tallest live oak on the horizon. The tree sprawled wide, choking out all other growth that surrounded it. Coyote leapt into low-hanging branches, lengthened Mallory's fingernails into black-tipped claws, and scaled the trunk with a strength borne of fear. The climb would slow Mother Torment, not stop her. Coyote had never liked trees. Once you climbed one, you were stuck—no way out but down, no room to run.

Still, being cornered had its uses. If nothing else, it was motivational; cornered animals always fought the hardest.

Coyote rooted himself in the tree's crown and opened the medicine bag. He sifted through damp, muddy rolling papers until he found a clean sheet, then blended pinches of sage, tobacco, and rosemary. He rolled the cigarette with deft fingers and licked it closed with a flourish.

Once we've got her incapacitated, light that and blow smoke in Mother Torment's face. The smoke focuses the ritual's targets, so breathe in as little as possible.

The tree shivered with every shift of Mother Torment's weight. She was close.

Coyote struck a match against a clawed thumbnail, placed the cigarette between his lips, and took a deep pull. The tip glowed like a miniature sun. He held his breath and closed his throat, but little wisps still tickled the edges of Mallory's lungs.

Wait! It's too soon. Why are you doing it now?

Coyote muttered through clenched teeth. "Trust me."

Just before Mother Torment got within striking range, Coyote swung down and wrapped his legs around her neck. He blew the smoke into her open maw and spat the still-burning cigarette down her throat for good measure. Mother Torment jerked back out of reflex, coughing and gagging.

The branch beneath her snapped. She plummeted through the canopy, claws scrabbling in a futile search for purchase.

Coyote unwound his legs and snagged onto a branch with his claws. The branch cracked under his weight, but slowed his fall enough to grab a larger limb. He swung down, landed next to Mother Torment's prone form.

That was impressive, Mallory admitted. *Now let me finish her off.*

Coyote's stomach knotted. Fond though he was of the sheriff, the idea of surrendering control when he'd melded with Mallory's body so thoroughly made his soul ache. He yearned to claim it with every fiber of his being. It would be so *easy*. One little bite. Human souls were edible, just like any other.

No. The long game. Think of the long game. To throw away decades of friendship, however rocky, for nothing more than a few days of selfish pleasure would destroy the final remnants of his humanity.

Coyote closed his eyes, took a deep breath, and let the sheriff rise to the fore.

Mallory gritted teeth still sharp from Coyote's presence. "Don't go too far, Old Man." He bellowed a prayer in Apache. Each syllable tolled like a bell.

Mother Torment's howls filled the air. Coyote felt the pull in Mallory's words even though they weren't meant for him. He burrowed into every crack and crevice of the sheriff's mind to keep from being evicted.

The bear's body deflated and shrunk. Smoke poured out of every orifice, dragging the embers of Mother Torment's soul out with it, spiraling away like burning leaves on the wind. When the vapors dissipated the bear lay broken and bloodied, shuddering and moaning with every breath.

Coyote shivered in the far reaches of Mallory's mind. Every mote of his being ached, raw and ragged, diminished by the power of the ritual. Still, he'd made it through. That was the important thing. He could recover his strength in time. He heaved a sigh of relief and loosened his hold on Mallory, trembling with elation and disappointment in equal measure.

Mallory's bones snapped back into place. He gasped as every little agony Coyote had held at bay flooded into him at once—his claw-torn back, thorn-riddled arms, aching legs, and fresh-torn fingernails.

Coyote spoke. *Are you all right?* The words echoed hollowly through Mallory's mind. Coyote missed the resonance the sheriff's vocal cords lent his voice.

"I'll live." Mallory caressed the bear's head. "She won't. Can you do anything for her?"

I'll try. Coyote slipped into the dying animal and numbed her nerves to ease her passing. She cycled through wordless memories as her lungs filled with blood: the bite of the trap she'd been so desperate to escape, the helplessness of being a prisoner in her own body while Mother Torment pushed past all her limits.

Cubs. She had cubs. She'd given herself to Mother Torment in hopes that the spirit would continue to care for them.

Coyote waited until the bear breathed her last, then eased back into Mallory. *We're not done yet.* He pushed images into Mallory's mind—a cave worn into a granite cliffside, the trio of cubs that lived within, and the fastest route to get there.

Three bear cubs huddled deep in the cave tunnel, hungry but not yet emaciated. Under Coyote's direction, Mallory fed them dried berries and jerky. They pawed and sniffed at him, hoping for more. He ruffled the cubs' fur, lips pressed into a thin line. "What should we do with them? I can't just bring them back to town."

Bears were far from Coyote's preferred form, but the thought of leaving the cubs to die didn't sit well on his conscience. Neither did the fact that he had a conscience, come to that—Mallory must be rubbing off on him. *I'll watch over them until they're old enough to care for themselves. They're clever little terrors. I doubt they'll need more than a few gentle nudges here and there.*

"It's been a while since I could guarantee I'd have my thoughts to myself. Can't say I won't mind the quiet." Mallory rolled a fresh cigarette—just tobacco, this time. He lit a match against a cave wall, took a few languid puffs, and studied the smoke as it drifted into the morning air. "I'll miss you, though." A rare admission, that. Hearing it warmed Coyote's soul.

The cubs will be settled by winter, and you know how to summon me in the meantime. Don't worry, Nantan. I'd never abandon my favorite play-thing. Teasing and tormenting Mallory had long been Coyote's first line of defense against boredom.

Mallory rolled his eyes. A subtle smile tugged at the corners of his lips. "Good to know."

Coyote stayed with Mallory for the duration of the cigarette, basking in the calm that washed over the sheriff's body as the tobacco took hold. Once Mallory flicked the butt on the ground and stomped out the dying embers, Coyote offered his aid to the largest cub. It accepted his presence eagerly, enticed by the concept of food in abundance.

Coyote rounded up the others and led them toward the plains. As the cubs left the cavern, Mallory scratched them behind the ears. Coyote nuzzled Mallory's leg in turn. It was dangerous to grow attached to mortals—they died so easily—but Coyote had developed a fondness for the man over the years; he would make a fine animal spirit, one day. In the meantime, Coyote would do everything he could to keep Mallory healthy and whole.

SHOW AND TELL: BRINGING YOUR CHARACTERS TO LIFE THROUGH DIALOGUE AND EMOTIONAL BEATS

BY M. ELIZABETH TICKNOR

All right, everyone, listen up, because I'm only going to say this once: Dialogue and emotional beats are the beating heart of your characters, the pump of adrenaline through your reader's veins. They're the parts of a story that link your audience to the not-actually people they're supposed to love or hate—maybe both at the same time. Some characters are special that way.

If you only take one thing away from this essay, take *this*: The way you represent your characters' words, thoughts, and actions have a *drastic* effect on reader engagement, so you should plan accordingly. Make your characters *vibrant*. You want them to leap off the page and metaphorically drag the reader into the story by their short and curlies.

First off, let's talk about dialogue. I'm going to state the obvious here, but you'd be surprised at how often it gets missed: *No two characters are going to speak exactly the same.* Everyone has different thoughts, opinions, and formative life experiences. (Real life example, to hammer things home: I'm a mother of twins. They were born a minute apart, spent almost every single day of their lives together—but *boy,* are they different.)

When taking a character's speech patterns into account, it's important to consider the following: their upbringing, their level of education, how well they paid *attention* during said education, how the people who raised them talked. It's also important to consider how the character responded to these factors—how did they conform, and how did they rebel? A character who grew up in a culture that emphasizes honesty and forthrightness is going to have very different speech patterns than a character who grew up in a culture that emphasizes snark and smartassery, regardless of their feelings and opinions of these cultural norms. This means backstory is an important factor in writing good dialogue. Let's face it—good characterization is never actually just *one* thing.

Another important factor to note: the things a character *won't* say are every bit as important as the things they *will* say. Some people aren't comfortable talking about their feelings. Others habitually overshare, or accidentally share things they didn't mean to, or lie through their teeth because the truth hurts too much to say aloud. Occasionally, you find someone who's more or less emotionally well-balanced, but even those people aren't going to tell you *everything* (which ties back to the oversharing thing—emotionally balanced people don't generally *do* that, because they have some concept of personal privacy).

From a mechanical standpoint, there are numerous techniques for varying your characters' voices: You can use everything from average sentence length to average syllables per word to the way they use sentence punctuation to whether or not they swear (and, if all the characters swear, it's still a simple matter of varying how often they curse or which particular brands of off-color language they favor). I'd personally recommend focusing on this kind of thing more in the editing phase than the original draft—thinking about things like how many commas a character is likely to use in a sentence tends to disrupt my flow. (Then again, focusing on the technical aspects from the start might work just fine for you. My brain is weird enough that I can rarely draft a story the same way twice in a row.)

If dialogue is the external representation of how your character interacts with the world, emotional beats are how they internalize it. This *does* tie in strongly with dialogue for me, because of how heavily it plays into what the character says, which is why this essay is about both. Emotional beats also tie very strongly into concepts of showing and telling—and don't go running, now, I promise I'm not going to drop "show, don't tell" on your head and call it a day.

First off, telling isn't always bad. *Telling* is the act of summarizing an event or detail that, while important to the plot, isn't actually interesting enough to merit a full scene. This summary gives the reader context for what happens in between the exciting parts of a story, and gives the writer space to detail the fun bits while skimming the bits that would slow the story down. Every writer tells sometimes. Every writer *needs* to tell sometimes. If we detailed every moment of a character's life, the reader would put the book down out of sheer boredom and wander off to find something more interesting.

Secondly, the act of *showing* isn't just describing the actions your character takes. It involves detailing a specific event with whatever sensory details are necessary to make it feel real, then describing the viewpoint character's *reaction* to that event so the reader understands how it personally affects the character. That's what emotional beats are, at their core: an examination of how your character reacts to both external and internal stimuli.

I don't always stick the landing on emotional beats in my early drafts, but that means I've gotten a lot of practice layering them in during the editing process. Questions I tend to ask myself when doing so include: What (if any) physical reaction does the event that just transpired cause in the character? What does the character *think* about what just happened? How does it make them *feel*? Does it bring up a memory of something that's happened in the past—and if so, how does that *memory* make them feel?

After I detail my character's internal reactions, I follow those up with the following questions: How does the character *respond* to that emotional reaction? Do their thoughts and feelings drive them to take action? Are they instead driven toward *further* speculation and feelings, and if so, where does that new train of thought and emotion lead them? Is the event they're responding to traumatic enough to trigger a fight, flight, freeze, or fawn response? How does their response, or lack thereof, affect what happens next?

Then I analyze things from the other side, thinking about how any other characters in the scene respond to the viewpoint character —or how the setting responds if the POV character is alone. Once those responses are sorted, I come back to the viewpoint character. The cycle repeats again and again, a sequence of actions and reactions that will generally drive a scene from start to finish simply by dint of strong characterization.

So how do you know when you've shown enough? How do you keep from showing *too much*? Unfortunately, this is one of those things you have to pick up through practice. Sometimes all that's needed is a quick sentence or two to provide mental emotional context for the reader and you can move on to the next beat in the action. Sometimes you need whole paragraphs—even pages—of internal thought and emotion before you can delve into the next action/reaction sequence.

If I'm struggling with how heavy to lay down the emotional beats in a scene, I generally solve the problem by asking myself: Which is more important, the *reaction* my character is having, or the *action* it leads them to? If the former, I spend a solid paragraph or two focusing on internal reactions. If the latter, I aim to land one quick emotional sucker punch and move on to the next step in the action/reaction cycle.

One thing emotional beats are particularly useful for is hammering home any trauma your viewpoint character is experiencing. That's something that won't always show *up* on an external level, which is exactly why it's so important to lay it out when you're peeking inside a character's head. Don't be afraid to give your characters complicated tangles of emotional barbed wire. That's the sort of thing that really hits the reader in the feels.

Dialogue and emotional beats are a vital part of every story, whether external or internal. Every story will need a different *balance*, but the more you practice weaving these things into your prose, the easier it will become to figure out what is needed and when. Your characters will stand out solidly on the page, acting as hooks to pull your reader through the story just as surely as your setting or plot. So get those hearts beating! Get that adrenaline pumping. Give your characters *life.*

UNCROSS THE STARS
BY JOHN M. CAMPBELL

John M. Campbell is a first-place winner of the Writers of the Future contest. His story, "The Tiger and the Waif," earned second place in the 2021 Critters Annual Readers Poll and appears in *Writers of the Future 37*. Other stories of his appear in *Compelling Science Fiction* 12 and in the *Triangulation: Energy* anthology (Parsec Ink). For a complete list of his publications, visit his website at JohnMCampbell.com.

John grew up reading science fiction and loved imagining a future extrapolated from what is now known. Inspiration for his stories often comes from the strange realities of quantum physics and cosmology. He hopes his stories will inspire careers in science and engineering as the authors he read inspired his career.

~

"I see dead people."

Christine rolled her eyes. "Of course, you do. You're a zombie. All your friends are dead people."

Beside her, Bryce pulled at his seatbelt. "If I'm already so dead, why do you make me buckle up?"

"Because it's the law in California. You don't want me to get pulled over, do you?"

Bryce snorted. "Of all the agents in Hollywood, I get the conscientious one."

Christine shot a glance in his direction. "What makes you say you see dead people?"

Bryce stared out the window. "Look at them. They take their lives for granted. If I were still alive, I'd be living every moment—and landing better parts."

At the age of thirty-four, Bryce had died in a car accident and become a zombie. Christine recognized the melancholy that many zombies suffered. "Okay, I know you're tired of auditioning for roles like Zombie #3 on shows like *Fear the Rambling Dead*."

"I sure am."

"Well, today you can change that. We're headed to a reading for Bloodsucker #1."

His eyes opened wide. "You mean the speaking role?"

"Yup. He's got three lines of dialogue."

"And he's in four scenes before he's killed." A hopeful note appeared in Bryce's voice.

"This part could open doors. You know your lines, don't you?"

"Of course, I know my lines. I'm not brain-dead. Don't let my shambling walk and sagging jaw fool you."

Christine steered to the curb in front of the windowless stucco storefront of Sepulveda Pictures. "Did you buy the breath mints I told you about?"

Bryce dug into a pocket, took out a tin of Zomboid Curiously Undead Mints, and popped one into his mouth.

"Now remember," she said, "you have to sell yourself. You'll be up against character actors who each have their unique take, so think in those terms."

"Unique," Bryce mused. "Right."

"Show them something outside the box. Blow their minds."

He wore a zombie-in-the-headlights look.

"You can do this, Bryce. I'll be here when you're done."

The front door opened, and Bryce appeared. His shoulders slumped to the point he nearly crouched as he shuffled. He got in the car.

He wouldn't look at her. Okay, it was pump-up-the-actor's-ego time.

She started the car and pulled out into traffic. "Rejection is a part of this business—"

"This wasn't rejection," Bryce said. "It was *humiliation!*" His voice boomed inside her Toyota.

Christine paused to show she appreciated his pain. "What happened?" she asked gently.

He turned his head away and looked out his window.

She let him stew. As a new agent building a client list, it was her lot to represent non-human actors. Despite their history of creature roles on the stage, only recently were they breaking into movies. She had learned how to deal with their quirks.

Finally, he glared at her. "What on earth made you think I was right for this part?"

"I told you you'd have to sell—"

"The audition was for *vampires!*" Bryce said. "I was the only zombie in the room. You should've seen the looks I got. It was like I was there to eat their children."

"Vampires can't have children—"

"What did you think *Bloodsucker* was?" he exploded. "It's in the name!"

Christine took a breath to calm herself before speaking. "Zombies drink blood, too, right? You needed to make the casting director see the part in a different light."

"Don't blame me for this," Bryce said, his eyes bloodshot with fury. "The first thing the casting director said when she saw me was the part was for a vampire."

"Did you read for it anyway?"

Bryce twisted his face into a disbelieving frown. "Of course not. What was I supposed to do?"

She kept her voice low and reasonable. "You were supposed to change her mind by showing her an angle she hadn't considered."

"Well, I was embarrassed that my agent would place me in that situation, so I left." He looked out his window again.

Christine stopped at a traffic light. She let the silence linger. Most of her clients were paid minimum scale for at best a few days of work, which meant she was making the minimum, too, and working harder for it. At least Bryce wanted to be more than just a bit player. When the light turned green, she eased forward. "I'm trying to get you a part you want. We both knew it wouldn't be easy."

She signaled a right turn, and the clicks were the only sounds in the vehicle.

"Zombies don't get their fair shake in Hollywood," Christine said. "But neither do werewolves or vampires or any other non-human actor."

"I could be a star," Bryce murmured. "What living human knows the agony of death and rebirth? What human knows the torture of seeing a loved one revulsed by the stench of your rot?"

"I get it, Bryce, I really do. We need to work on the casting directors, but it can be done. Remember that swamp lizard who became a sex symbol in *The Shape of Water*? That part was written for Doug Jones in a frog suit."

Bryce smiled. "That would've been awful."

"With the right casting, that movie won Academy awards. And parts like the snarky friend—who says they can't be zombies? An orc beat out Joel Edgerton as Will Smith's sidekick in *Bright*. Look what he's done since."

"And that orc can barely act," Bryce said.

"Almost any villain could be played by a zombie. The Bond villain who wants revenge for what the world did to him? I *know* you could play that part. You just have to convince the director."

"Get me that audition, Christine."

"What about *Star Wars*' next master of the dark side? A reanimated Darth Vader could be *you*."

"I could act the hell out of that!"

Christine smiled at Bryce's renewed enthusiasm. Pep talks were her forte. Now she just had to find the right auditions. Next month's rent was on the line.

A few days later, Christine drove through the rundown L.A. neighborhood nicknamed Zombietown. It consisted of a combination of single-family homes destroyed by a devastating earthquake and high-rise apartment buildings that survived. Many of the owners of the homes were killed in the quake only to be reborn as zombies. Although their homes were condemned for human habitation, no one stopped zombies occupying them. With zombies living around them, the human apartment dwellers fled, and zombies like Bryce moved in.

She stopped her car outside a four-story walkup built fifty years ago. Three male zombies were playing craps in the courtyard. They eyed her as she trudged up the stairs to Bryce's apartment, but since most of her clients were zombies, she knew they didn't present a threat. Contrary to what movies depicted, zombies didn't eat human flesh. They were scavengers, not predators. They preferred decayed flesh. Their favorite meeting place was a butcher-shop dumpster.

Christine tapped at Bryce's door.

"Come in," responded Bryce's muffled voice.

She opened the door to a mess that at first glance seemed unchanged since the day of the earthquake. On closer inspection, one noticed the chaos was organized. In one corner, a pile of posters advertised zombie food products like Bottom of the Dumpster gourmet dinners and Roadkill Jerky, Not Just for Zombies. Boxes containing A Whiff of Decay perfumes and colognes were stacked against the wall. Needless to say, these were for zombie-only gatherings.

Bryce ran a booth at the neighborhood flea market on weekends. Unlike human actors, the law prohibited zombies to be hired as waiters, bartenders, cooks, or any other food service position. So, he was forced to improvise to bring in some cash.

Bryce was busy shredding jeans below the knee. "Oh, hi, Christine. I wasn't expecting you."

"What's that you're working on?"

"It's my latest foray into zombie fashion." He held up the jeans. "We get a lot of tourists at the flea market. They go wild for these. I buy the jeans at the Goodwill store and do a little zombie alteration. They fly off the shelves at my booth."

"Do any of your neighbors buy them?"

"Why would they do that? They can get a perfectly good pair cheaper at Goodwill."

Obviously. She smiled at the notion that only humans would buy zombie fashion. She moved some flyers off a chair and sat. "Okay, I have good news and bad news." Christine waited until Bryce made eye contact. "A British studio is holding a casting call here locally. The good news is I've got you an audition for a reanimated Professor Moriarty in a new Sherlock Holmes movie."

Bryce's face brightened. "That sounds terrific. Reanimated how?"

"They didn't specify how exactly, just that he was raised from the dead to face Holmes one last time."

"I mean, this could be perfect, but what's the bad news?"

Christine braced herself for his reaction. "I've been told you're up against Ian McKellen for the part."

Bryce stared at her. "I thought Sir Ian was dead."

"Actually, he's undead. After getting sick, he disappeared, presumed dead. Now it seems he was just reluctant to continue his acting career as a zombie. That is, until this part came along."

Bryce pursed his lips. "Against any living human I've got a real shot... but against an undead Sir Ian?"

"Don't count yourself out, Bryce. He was nearly ninety when he caught the virus. Who knows how it affected him? Plus, you've got years more zombie acting experience than him."

Bryce nodded with his lower lip protruding. "You've got a point."

"Besides, McKellen is too old for the role. It demands the body and agility of a much younger zombie."

Bryce puffed out his chest. "In my free time, I've been working off the dead weight."

"And you look great. Now here's the script. You've got this, Bryce."

Bryce had a bounce in his step when he returned to the lobby of the Roosevelt Hotel. The auditions took place upstairs in the Academy Room.

"I nailed it, Christine," he said. "I brought precisely the right amount of British hauteur and world-weary ennui to the part."

"I'm so glad. Did you get to meet Sir Ian?"

"Of course not. His audition was probably back in England," Bryce said. "But you know who I saw?"

"Who?"

"That orc from *Bright*." A wide smile split his face. "He actually thinks he can come here and take a part meant for a zombie. He's going to be bitterly disappointed."

Christine returned his smile. "His agent must be getting desperate."

"Plus the fact he can't act his way out of a paper bag."

"There is that."

They left the hotel with Bryce floating on his buoyant mood. Christine didn't tell him she'd seen Benedict Cumberbatch stroll through the lobby. She didn't want to spoil his euphoria.

Christine arranged to meet Bryce at a park near her office. She chose a bench beside an immaculate flower garden to deliver the bad news.

"I'm sorry, Bryce. They chose Benedict Cumberbatch for the Moriarty part."

"What? *Dr. Strange*?"

She laid a hand on his arm. His leathery skin was warm from the heat of the sun. "The chickenshit director caved to pressure from the producer."

Bryce shook his head. "I could believe it if they went with Sir Ian, but Cumberbatch?"

"They went with the human actor, hoping the Marvel audience would follow."

"Another human cast as a zombie? This is a travesty."

"I know, I know. But it's probably for the best. We don't want to be associated with a production that thinks that way."

"But the part was perfect for me," Bryce said.

And perfect lead roles for a zombie were hard to find. An idea popped into Christine's head. "You know what this reminds me of?"

Bryce shook his head.

"*Rocky*. Sylvester Stallone wrote the script for himself when he couldn't get a starring role. Same for Matt Damon and Ben Affleck when they wrote *Good Will Hunting*."

Bryce raised his sparse eyebrows, uncomprehending.

"Write a part for yourself," said Christine. "If it's good, I'll sell the hell out of it with you as the star."

"You really think so?"

"Hell, yes, I do. Write the part only you can play."

Bryce's face turned thoughtful.

~

Two months later, Bryce arrived at her office door, script in hand. He laid it before her.

She glanced at the title: *Uncross the Stars*.

"Let me know what you think." He turned and left.

That evening she poured a glass of wine and set it down on the end table next to her couch. She wedged her back into the corner where her lamp provided the best light. With her legs curled underneath her, she opened the script.

The story began where *Romeo and Juliet* ended. A narrator introduced the story with these words of verse:

From forth the loins of two opposing clans
A pair of star-crossed lovers came to life.
Their sacred love forbidden, by their hands
They died instead of suffering their strife.
The poison did its work, but in their tomb
They rose undead to leave this cursed womb.

Romeo and Juliet lie side-by-side on a bier in the nave of a church surrounded by candles. Their dead bodies begin to stir, and they awaken confused. They do not recognize each other. A deep hunger drives them toward the stench of rotting flesh. Romeo follows the smell and pushes through a door to reach it. He finds the body of a dead raccoon outside beside the road. He squats, using his teeth to tear off a mouthful from the raccoon's shoulder.

Juliet has stumbled after him. She collapses to her knees next to him. He notices her for the first time. A light of recognition dawns in his eyes. He pushes the raccoon carcass in her direction. She leans over and rips off a piece. As she chews, she glances at him. She shifts her position to make room for him to join her.

A man driving a donkey cart passes. The couple takes no heed. The man pulls on the reins, and the cart comes to a stop. The driver steps down from the cart to look closer. When he realizes what he is seeing he shouts in rage.

The shout scares Juliet, and she bolts for the woods behind the church. Romeo hesitates. The man reaches into the cart and grabs a crossbow. He rotates it in Romeo's direction.

Romeo grabs the raccoon and runs after Juliet. Behind him, the crossbow fires. A bolt whizzes past his head before he disappears into the woods.

Christine paused at the end of the scene to assess what she'd read so far. It began with an intriguing premise that built upon a well-known story. It captured for the audience the feel of being reanimated. And it set up the immediate danger from humans these beloved characters faced as zombies. If Bryce could maintain the promise of this beginning, Christine might have something she could work with.

Two hours later, after reading the final line of the screenplay, Christine sat savoring the moment. Bryce was too old to be Romeo, but she'd worry about that later. Here was a zombie role that was universal. This could be her big break—or rather, *their* big break. Bryce had risen to the challenge. It was time to do her part.

She reached for her phone.

Christine welcomed Bryce into her office with a smile. She led him to her couch and took a seat alongside him.

"So, what's the news?" he asked with a tremor in his voice.

"I've sold your screenplay." Her own voice quavered.

Bryce's eyes sought out hers for confirmation of what he heard. She saw hope tinged with disbelief. "How much?"

She swallowed the lump in her throat. "One point two million dollars."

His sunken eyes bugged out.

"Three producers got into a bidding war," she said. "Finally, the head of Faulkner Pictures weighed in to seal the deal." Christine took his hand. "You did it, Bryce."

He couldn't speak. Eventually, he said, "Thank you, Christine. Thank you so much."

"It's a big win for both of us."

"I can't believe it." He dropped his gaze.

"Faulkner is eager to get it made," said Christine. "He thinks he can get Leonardo DiCaprio and Claire Danes to reprise their roles as Romeo and Juliet."

Bryce whipped his head around. "I wrote this screenplay for myself. I was supposed to be the next Sylvester Stallone."

Christine recognized the artist's ego flaring. "And you still can be. Stallone won an Oscar for Best Screenplay for *Rocky*, not Best Actor."

"But at least he got to play the part…"

"Look, Bryce, Faulkner would only offer this much money because he thinks Leo and Claire can bring in the audience."

"But Romeo and Juliet died as teenagers, not senior citizens."

"Maybe with some makeup—"

Bryce exploded. "Some makeup? You mean *zombieface*? Don't you understand? I wrote a part only a zombie could play, one that expresses the zombie condition."

She had done the impossible, and this is how he reacted? Her voice jumped up an octave. "You think you could play Romeo? How young are *you*? At least Leo has an Oscar to prove his talent."

In the resulting silence, she regretted her outburst. "I'm sorry, Bryce. That came out wrong."

"You're not totally wrong," he said. "I wrote the screenplay for zombie actors, but I knew Romeo required someone younger. I would be happy to play Zombie Refugee #1."

Romeo and Juliet met that zombie during their escape. She could salvage this deal, yet. "I can get you that role in this picture," Christine said. "I'll write it into the contract."

Bryce sat silent with his head bowed. He needed more convincing.

"Bryce, you have a lot to be proud of," she said. "This is unheard-of money for a first screenplay. You are a talented writer. Write another screenplay. I promise, *you* will star in the next one." She couldn't let this deal fizzle. It could make her career as an agent.

Bryce shook his head. "Faulkner will ruin this movie. It's a movie that tells our story, the zombie story, and only zombies can do it justice."

The deal was slipping away. She couldn't let that happen. "You can do a lot of good with the money you get for this deal. Use it to fix up the apartments and houses in your neighborhood. Give zombies a place to live they can be proud of. Give them a person they can look up to—you—a zombie that beat the odds."

When she saw his expression, her stomach churned.

Six months later, Christine stood at the top of a rolling hill that overlooked a four-cornered gazebo. A zombie client of hers had tipped her off about this production of *Uncross the Stars*, which was appearing on cemetery grounds normally used for outdoor funerals. Packing the grassy hillside below her, zombies sat under the starry sky awaiting the action that would unfold on the makeshift stage. A note of A Whiff of Decay perfume hung in the air. Joining this audience earned her a few curious glances from other attendees but nothing hostile.

Bryce had rejected the offer Christine negotiated, and she had dropped him as a client. He attached an insane artistic value to his screenplay. She tried to make him appreciate that Faulkner acknowledged that value by offering an insane amount of money, but Bryce wouldn't budge. He told her zombie culture does not value the same things as human culture—something about having died once. Reanimation provided a different perspective on what they considered important.

The audience applauded as Bryce stepped out from behind the curtain. He waited for the applause to die, and then he recited the opening lines of verse before retiring from the stage. The curtain opened on Romeo and Juliet lying in state. Two young zombies played the roles with the right amount of clumsiness and wonder as they awoke to their new lives. A raptured silence blanketed the crowd, broken only by eerie moans as they reacted to the events of the play.

Christine was delighted and amused to see the orc from *Bright* appear as the hunter with the crossbow. The audience applauded again when Bryce appeared onstage as the refugee zombie the lovers meet in a thicket. Though wounded as they escape a burning barn, he survives to give the closing lines of verse that expresses hope for Romeo and Juliet in their adopted community of zombies.

As the curtain dropped, the zombie horde rose in a standing ovation. Although zombies cannot cry, the shining eyes of those around her reflected Christine's feelings. This play expressed their plight in a way they valued more than new paint on their walls.

She made her way down to the gazebo and waited her turn as Bryce's fans expressed their adoration. When he caught sight of her, he motioned her forward.

"Christine, it's nice of you to come." He stepped forward and enfolded her in his arms.

Tears stung her eyes at his unexpected kindness, given the circumstances of their split. She hugged him back. "Seeing your play with the right actors in front of the right audience—it was beautiful, Bryce." She tilted her head back to see his face. "I understand now."

Bryce's eyes shone. "I'm glad you experienced it the way I meant it to be seen."

Christine stepped back. She drew a breath to gather her courage for what she had to say. "If you would allow me to represent the play the way you want it done, I would love the opportunity…"

"You are sweet to ask."

She saw his answer in his vacant zombie stare. She wasn't getting a second chance.

She wished him the best and left the gazebo. As she stepped out under the stars, she fished her phone from her purse.

When the deal with Faulkner fell through, she went back to scratching out a living. She had taken on another young zombie actor, this one a female with the talent and drive that reminded her of Bryce. This time she would do it right.

She made the call. "Hi, Rony. There's a play you need to see. I think you will find it inspiring."

WRITING "UNCROSS THE STARS"
BY JOHN M. CAMPBELL

I was trained as an engineer, so plotting out a story before I write it makes sense to me. I often take an intriguing idea from physics or technology and fashion a story around it by adding a setting and characters. Often, I will also write from a prompt suggested by an editor or publisher for an upcoming anthology of short stories. When I started writing, I knew my stories needed a beginning, middle, and end, but something was missing. When I took the free Writers of the Future Online Workshop, I found the lesson by Algis Budrys especially appealing. Budrys was a science fiction author and early judge and editor for Writers of the Future. In his essay, he outlined what he called the seven parts of a perfect story. Applying that guidance to my story, I took first place in the Writers of the Future contest for the fourth quarter of 2020.

When I attended the Writers of the Future winners gathering in fall of 2021, Nina Kiriki Hoffman introduced me to a new way of generating story ideas that was totally outside my consciousness. Nina provided us with a twenty-sided die and several lists she had compiled. These lists were different types of characters, settings, objects, quirks, desires, secrets, skills, jobs, etc. She had us take a list and roll the die to determine the main character (zombie), secondary character (babysitter), character's job (actor), quirk (sees dead people), and setting (photo studio). Then she gave us ten minutes to write the first page of a story using these elements.

Plotting takes thinking time, so for this exercise I had to become a pantser and just write off the top of my head, which was a scary proposition. A zombie actor who sees dead people was an amusing idea, so I went with it, transforming the secondary character into an agent (whom I thought of as babysitting actors). I ignored the photo studio and set the action in the agent's car as they drove to an audition. In that ten minutes I wrote the four lines that open my story.

This exercise opened my mind to a new way of generating story ideas. In this case, the first page I wrote indicated a humorous story, and the verbal interaction between Bryce and Christine gave me a sense of their relationship. The setting suggested a contemporary world where zombies have acting jobs like people do, along with vampires, werewolves, and orcs. And like actors of every sort, Bryce longs for roles that merit his talent, which becomes the desire that drives the story.

At this point, I realized I had the first three steps in the seven parts to a perfect story as defined by Budrys. Part One is the principal character (Bryce the zombie), Part Two is the context (Hollywood in a world where zombies live among humans), and Part Three is the character's most important problem (getting an acting role that suits his talents). These three steps establish the rules of the universe in which the story is set. It also does the job of grabbing the reader's attention by showing the character doing something the reader wants to know more about.

Budrys lays out the remaining parts of the perfect story as necessary structural milestones, but we authors must use our own creativity to flesh out the characters and setting and create the events that meet those milestones. Because I was going for humor, I brainstormed comic aspects of this alternate world that I could incorporate into the action. For example, I decided in this world, zombies are civilized citizens who don't eat people, just rotting meat. I twisted around some contemporary movies to suggest an actual orc was Will Smith's sidekick in the movie *Bright*, and an actual swamp thing starred in *The Shape of Water*. I show that zombies face discrimination in housing and jobs, but they make money in innovative ways by selling products such as zombie food, cosmetics, and fashion.

In Part Four of the story, Bryce tries to solve his problem of winning more desirable roles, and he encounters obstacles. These attempts and failures set up some comic situations and get the reader rooting for him to succeed. Christine has him read for a role written for a vampire. The result is Bryce's utter humiliation. Then he auditions for the perfect zombie role: a reanimated Professor Moriarty in a Sherlock Holmes film. Bryce is devastated to learn a human actor with experience in the Marvel movie universe has been selected.

In Part Five, greater complications and higher stakes arise. These story events increase tension and suspense to keep the reader engaged by wondering, "Will Bryce overcome these setbacks and achieve his goal?" I came up with the idea of having Christine suggest to Bryce that he write a screenplay with the part he wants to play, like Sylvester Stallone did with *Rocky*. Bryce writes a screenplay that only a zombie can play. Christine realizes the screenplay's value and sells it to a movie studio.

In Part Six, the climactic scene, the hero must risk everything for the chance to achieve his goal. Often this scene sets up a heavy choice: take the easy way out or risk death to attain what he wants. "Death" in the story context can mean literal loss of life, or it can mean loss of professional standing, societal position, or self-worth. Bryce is offered a lot of money for the screenplay, but the producer requires established movie stars to play the zombies. Christine urges Bryce to take the money. He can write another screenplay, she assures him, and he can play the lead in the next movie. This moral decision is crucial to creating a satisfying story, where readers ask themselves what would they do in this situation?

The "killer" ending, the ending emotionally satisfying to the reader, is a skill a successful writer must master. One of the reasons I consider myself a plotter is that I decide how I want my story to end before I start writing. That way, I know where I'm headed when I write the scenes. However, my story endings tended to be hit-or-miss until I learned about the moral decision the protagonist must make before he or she deserves the consequences that end the story. Making the right decision is a story of triumph. Making the wrong decision is a cautionary tale. Both endings are satisfying to the reader, and they work for both comedy and drama.

In Part Seven, the denouement, we see what Bryce has decided. He has chosen his art and his self-worth over the money. The last scene validates that he made the right decision. That scene also shows that Christine made the wrong decision but learns from her mistake.

In Budrys's terminology, "Uncross the Stars" has the structure of "interlocking" short stories. Both Bryce and Christine have their own desires, which converge in some places and diverge in others. In this interlocking story, Bryce has the triumphal ending, while Christine has the cautionary tale.

Although I was skeptical about the pantser approach to writing stories, Nina gave me new appreciation for how a pantser can use their process to generate totally unexpected story ideas. However, whether you're a plotter or a pantser, I still believe your story needs to incorporate Budrys's seven parts for it to be successful. And make sure your hero confronts that moral choice, so you achieve the killer ending your readers crave.

POSEIDON'S EYES
BY KARY ENGLISH

Kary English grew up in the snowy Midwest where she avoided siblings and frostbite by reading book after book in a warm corner behind a recliner chair. She blames her only high school detention on Douglas Adams, whose *The Hitchhiker's Guide to the Galaxy* made her laugh out loud while reading it behind her geometry book.

Today, Kary still spends most of her time with her head in the clouds and her nose in a book. To the great relief of her parents, she seems to be making a living at it. Her greatest aspiration is to make her own work detention-worthy.

Kary is a Hugo and Astounding finalist whose work has been published by *Galaxy's Edge, The Grantville Gazette,* Wordfire Press, *Writers of the Future,* and *Tor Nightfire.*

Sometimes you can get to know a whole town by understanding just one man. In the seaside village of Summerland, that man was Peyton Jain. Peyton was in his sixties, as best I could tell. His face was craggy and weathered, with a beard like sea foam on rocks and eyes of Poseidon's blue.

Some folks thought of Peyton as a nuisance to be reported or a vagrant to be run off, but I knew different, because it was Peyton who put me right with Summerland's spirits. The locals have joked about spirits as long as anyone can remember, but it took the murder of the Kelly children to remind us just how real—and how powerful—the spirits could be.

Summerland sits like the Pythia over a cleft in the rock, soaking up the vapors of prophecy along with the California sunshine. Spiritualists started a commune here over a century ago. Egalitarians at heart, they outlawed money and divvied the land into tent-sized plots.

Oil—oil money, really—edged the Spiritualists out. Derricks took over the beach, and the Spiritualists' canvas utopia turned into a shantytown for oil workers. My house was made from two of those oil shanties sandwiched together. The shanties had been built before electricity, so the wiring came up through holes in the floor, and the doorbell was an old ship's bell, corroded green with salt and time.

The house had no foundation, just posts and piers and seven jacks. When the floor sagged, Peyton crawled beneath to twist the jacks until everything was more or less level. That was a blessing to me because I couldn't abide the narrow crawlspace with earth pressing in around me and voiceless whispers winding snakelike over my skin.

The county said the whispers were nothing to worry about. Radon gas. Natural seepage. Buy a detector and install a fan. But radon doesn't creep up through the floorboards in silver ribbons until it pools in the corners, like living smoke. Radon doesn't whisper in the darkness like waves on sand.

But spirits? That's exactly what they do.

❧

Peyton's battered brown pickup rumbled up the hill while I was taking out the trash. A Sport King camper perched on the back, listing to one side like the shell of a hermit crab. The old truck clunked into park just outside my front gate, and Peyton leaned out the window. He looked bright-eyed and freshly showered, which should have meant he was doing well, but his passenger window had been busted out and covered with blue painter's tape and an old trash bag, and that meant trouble.

"'Morning, Danaë," he called. "Brought you something."

Peyton always called me by my right name—Danaë. Everyone else in town just called me Dani.

He extended one hand through the open window, and his fingers uncurled like the fronds of an anemone. Nestled in his palm was a piece of green beach glass, the edges worn smooth by sand and waves.

I accepted the offering and thanked him, turning the glass like a worry stone between my fingers.

"Wait a minute," I said. "I thought you had a spot away from the beach? That Harris kid giving you a hard time again?" Ike Harris, a teenager with a new Mustang, lived in the Mansions across town.

Peyton gave a shrug that meant yes. "He comes down at night, partying with his paraglider friends." Peyton nodded toward the shattered window. "Broke my window. Cops won't do nuthin 'cuz nobody saw it." Dejection colored Peyton's voice. That truck was all he had, and a new window was more than he could afford.

"Want some coffee?" I offered.

"Nah, I just had coffee."

"I'm about to make eggs. You hungry?" Sometimes Peyton needed money when he stopped by. I didn't always have it, but I could manage an extra place at the table.

Peyton brightened at the thought of breakfast, and for a moment his eyes matched the blue of the white-tipped sea. "I'll take eggs. Café was packed when I was down there. No place to sit."

"More news crews?" Summerland hadn't seen a murder in more than fifty years, and the Kelly trial had turned our sleepy little town into the media's favorite chew toy. Most of the old-timers wouldn't talk, but that didn't stop reporters from badgering all and sundry with questions about vengeful spirits.

"I picked up a job today," said Peyton, following me into the kitchen. "Aames wants me to help Reesie move."

"Move? She finally leavin'?"

Peyton nodded. "Divorce was final 'bout four months back. Papers say he can have her evicted if she doesn't leave on her own."

"What's he doin' with the house?" Aames was old Summerland, used to live near the post office, but Reesie had insisted on one of the new places in the fancy gated development near the top of the hill before she'd marry him. Said the gate would keep out the riffraff, which I suppose meant shanty folk like us.

"Dunno," said Peyton. "Sell it, most likely."

I poured the eggs into the skillet. The new places were a bone of contention for us old Summerlanders. Before the Mansions went in, most of us walked or rode bicycles in the open air, and dogs slept in the middle of the street. After the Mansions, stockbrokers barreled through town in Range Rovers, and dogs were something glittering women carried in designer purses.

"Built too tight, those new places," said Peyton. "Stuff gets in, can't get out again. That's when the trouble starts."

Peyton fixed me with those blue eyes of his, and his voice was like crushed shells. "A house is like your heart, Danaë. Long as it's open, nothing'll get trapped inside to fester in the dark places."

I shivered cold at that, picturing the silver rivulets streaming up through my floorboards the week before, the same ones that had surrounded Percy's crib when I'd brought him home from the hospital almost twenty years ago. Peyton had come by to see the baby and found me in tears, trying to seal off Percy's windows with plastic sheeting to keep the vapors out. That's when he explained about Summerland's spirits. He said they were harmless so long as my heart was in the right place, and I'd know because they'd be silver instead of black. But that didn't mean I felt easy about them.

Peyton's gaze was relentless. "I know you've seen 'em again, Danaë. I can see it in your eyes."

I changed the subject. "You worked on Kelly's place, right?"

"Needed the money. Kelly said I made the weep holes in the

window frames too big, left gaps under the doors. Said he was afraid snakes would get in and kill him in his sleep. Told me to get off the property or he'd call the cops." Peyton reached around me to pour a glass of milk. "Damn shame about those babies. His wife is up there now, hidin' in the house to keep away from the cameras."

Pain pulled at Peyton's face. He'd mourned the Kelly children as if they'd been his own. I cut the omelet in half and slid a portion onto each plate.

"Working on the mural today?" he asked, pointing the tines of his fork at my faded t-shirt and paint-smeared jeans.

My work clothes were a private joke between us. Even living in his truck, Peyton's Levis were bluer than the night sky and his crisp Hawaiian shirt smelled of laundry starch.

"Grand opening's Monday," I answered. "Has to be done and dry in forty-eight hours."

"You ready?"

I shook my head and pushed the last bite of omelet around with my fork. "All except the eyes."

Eyes are hard to paint. They're not like trees or faces in a crowd, where a suggestion is all you need. Eyes don't come right until you can feel the soul coming to life under the brush, and to do that, you have to know what those eyes see.

We finished our breakfast in silence.

The sea and sky were robin's-egg blue on my walk to the Sea Center, with only a pale smudge of haze to mark where one stopped and the other began. I mixed the colors in my head, pulling out the contrast of pale, cool blues against the yellow-green of palms and agaves.

News vans lined the main drag, and reporters trolled the locals for reactions to the Kelly trial. The Harris kid blew through a stop sign, narrowly missing Reesie Aames, who was talking to a news crew, scratching at her arm with one hand and gesturing east toward the Mansions with the other.

Reesie had been beautiful once, with hair the color of sunlight and a figure Aphrodite would have envied, but drugs had stolen that away. Her hair now hung like frayed straw, and her dress sagged off her hips and shoulders as if it had been made for a different woman.

I passed by, invisible in my shabby clothes. What the reporters wanted was a slack-jawed yokel who'd tell about the time the spirits threw dishes against the wall or made the chickens stop laying. Lacking that, they'd settle for someone like Reesie, blonde and well-dressed, who had plenty to say about her neighbor Herb Kelly, and none of it kind.

If I was lucky, the trial would be over before they got desperate enough to notice a paint-smeared artist in worn sneakers and tatty blue jeans.

The Sea Center sat on the far side of the freeway, across from some weathered picnic tables and a small playground. It was built of grey cinder blocks, with a low, peaked roof and clerestory windows that tilted open at the bottom, the kind of building you'd expect to find in a military depot or a forest service compound. What it lacked in glamour it made up for with a dogged sturdiness that reminded me of the town itself. Perched on bluffs overlooking the ocean, its chief drawback was that the builders had placed the windows too high for a view, a lack my mural was intended to remedy.

The smell of turpentine and linseed oil swirled around me when I unlocked the door. This close to the water, the paint took days to dry, so my morning routine included opening windows and switching on a space heater. A silver spirit floated in one corner, making a soft thrumming sound. I tried to ignore it, but in the back of my mind I wondered if spirits could purr.

My mural covered all four walls of the Sea Center, reproducing the view of the coastline outside. In the center panel, Poseidon, god of the sea, strode forth from the waves with his trident at hand. I'd painted the scenery in layer upon layer of transparent glazes to capture the moody sea and changeable sky. But the sea god himself required something special. He surged forward out of the wall, sculpted from modeling paste and inlaid with bits of rock and shell from the beach below. His wife Amphitrite nestled at his side. Her eyes of green beach glass gazed with adoration, and her white coral hair flowed into the foaming waves.

Dolphins cavorted around the pair, leaping in playful arcs, while pelicans flew overhead. Nereids chased otters through kelp forests of deepest green, and shafts of golden sunlight pierced the depths below. But alas, Poseidon himself stood as blind as Tiresias, his eyes empty holes where I'd been unable to get the color right, no matter what I tried.

Two hours later, I scraped the paint away and slung my palette knife into the turp jar. The silver spirit had summoned friends, and they rose up around the edges of the mural, flitting from silver to black while they gibbered frustration and failure in my ears. They pooled in Poseidon's empty eyes in twin voids of black despair.

I stumbled back from my work and wiped my shaking hands on my jeans. Peyton's long-ago warning rattled in my head like an old tin can. Black was bad. Black meant that the spirits had found something dark to latch on to-fear, anger, insecurity—something they'd use to destroy me if I let them.

I raked my fingers through my hair, heedless of the paint that rubbed off on my forehead. If the mural wasn't ready, if the Center's directors didn't like it, I'd never work in this town again. Around here, feelings like that did more than stifle your creativity. Around here, feelings like that could kill.

I took a deep breath, let it out, forced myself to walk slowly around the inside of the building, opening the remaining windows. Open house, open heart; that's what Peyton always said. If nothing else, the fresh air would help the paint dry. The spirits followed me, twisting like cats around my ankles.

If I gave in to fear and ran, they'd drag me down like angry maenads. I counted each step until I made it to the door. When I stood outside in the fresh air and sunshine, my stomach rumbled. Time for a break and some lunch.

The Saltbox Café sat in the center of town on the main drag across from the firehouse. Like most of old Summerland, the building was more than a century old, a small, white bungalow of wood and stone that managed to look tidy, yet gently worn. A path of crushed stone wound between plantings of lavender and rock-roses. It ushered guests up four stone steps onto a long, covered porch where they could linger over a glass of Dora's homemade lemonade. Tables for two lined the porch, and a silver basin offered crystal clear water to four-pawed guests.

Inside, past the clatter of the screen door, more tables beckoned. A padded bench ran the length of the place, and polished, wooden chairs offered their services to those who'd missed a seat on the bench. A river-rock fireplace with an iron grate held court along the eastern wall, and a green velvet settee snuggled up to the hearth, flanked by matching armchairs and a bentwood rocker with a white cushion.

The rocker was Hester's favorite place whenever a lull in customers offered her a moment's respite, and the armchair on the right, nearest the fireplace, was mine. A threadbare patch along the edge of the left arm testified to my habit of rubbing the nap of the velvet back and forth with one hand while I worked out drawings in my sketchbook with the other.

The café's owners, Hester and Dora, had tried to buy the place separately, so the story went, until Peyton brought them together. Once they met, they realized they could do as a couple what neither one of them could do alone. Hester had grey eyes and a smile as warm as apple cobbler. Her old hands were strong from kneading out dough each morning, and it wasn't unusual to see a dusting of flour across her cheeks or hiding in the wrinkles of her apron.

Dora, the younger and slimmer of the two, had been a socialite in her former life, and she still exuded a vivacious charm that drew customers in and made them feel welcome. Sometimes when I looked at her, I could see the ghosts of flashbulbs popping around her like champagne bubbles. Loss and sadness had ended that life, and the shadow of it still showed in her eyes, if you knew when to look. But whatever sadness it was had left wisdom in its wake, and Hester, Dora and the Saltbox Café were the hub that held the two Summerlands together.

Today, though, Hester and the chair by the hearth were destined ne'er to meet. The line for lunch stood two- and three-deep out the door. It poured over the porch, down the stone steps, over the path and onto the sidewalk. A din of cutlery and conversation drowned out the sound of the freeway, and the salt air took on the scent of panini and wood-fired pizza.

Peyton's truck sat in the parking lot, and Reesie Aames stood beside it, screeching like a banshee. "If I ever see you again, Peyton Jain, you'll be a dead man!"

Reesie's voice sent a shiver up my spine. I wanted no part of her drama, so I cut through the parking lot into the rear yard where the back door to the kitchen stood open. A square box fan blocked the lower half of the doorway, and tables too rickety for paying customers played host to deliverymen and waiters on smoke breaks.

Hester's back-door specials were yesterday's leftovers, but the food started so fresh that none of us minded. I put a dollar in the tip jar and sat down to a bowl of black bean soup, heavy with carrots and red peppers. A chunk of day-old sourdough served to wipe out the bowl. It was a moment not even an angry spirit could spoil.

No, the spoiling came from Hester herself. A shadow crossed my plate, and I looked up into Hester's cinnamon-and-apples smile. "Dani," she started, wiping her hands on her apron, "when you're finished, would you mind running some things up to Anya? I was going to ask Peyton, but I think she'd respond better to a woman."

Anya was Anya Kelly, bereaved mother and Herb Kelly's grieving wife. I didn't fancy a trip to the Mansions, but I couldn't sit there filling my stomach with Hester's charity while I denied it to a woman who'd just lost her children. So I swallowed my pride along with Hester's good bread. "'Course I will, Hester. Whatever you need."

Hester thanked me and left a bag of Styrofoam takeout boxes on the table. Before I left, Peyton pulled me aside and pressed a small prickly package into my hand. No larger than a plum, it was wrapped in tattered sailcloth to cushion something that felt like the spines of a sea urchin. "That's for Áine," he said, giving her name a lilt I couldn't identify. "Tell her there's mercy in it if she looks."

And that's how I ended up on the doorstep of the most spirit-plagued house in all of Summerland.

~

My house was on the way, so I decided to finish the errand in my old VW bus. Walking through the gates to the Mansions on foot always made me feel like less of a person, and if I was going to be anywhere near the Harris kid, I wanted some metal around me.

By the time I reached Anya's house, a dense afternoon fog had cloaked the town in a silent grey shroud. Anya's doorbell bonged deep in the bowels of the house, and the sound raised gooseflesh along my arms. Seconds ticked by while the sticky-sweet smell of Hester's bread pudding wafted up from the bag in my arms.

I juggled the takeout boxes and tried to ring the bell with my elbow, bumping the door in the process. There was a soft click and the door slid open. The hair on the back of my arms stood rigid with fear.

"Mrs. Kelly?" I called. "Hello?"

Silence.

I nudged the door open a few more inches. A distant slithering met my ears, like whispers in the dark. *Spirits.*

I pushed the door all the way open, stepped over the threshold and raised my voice. "Anya? It's Dani. Hester sent me with some things from the Box." The sound echoed off the foyer's marble tile.

An antique hall table made of a single weathered plank stood sentry against the left wall. On it, golden apples nestled in a bowl of silver branches, and Anya smiled out from a cut glass picture frame. She stood laughing on the deck of the *Wave Sweeper,* her father's fishing trawler, with the sea wind whipping hair black as a raven's wing across her face.

She looked so vibrant, so alive. With time, I hoped she might look so again-if the spirits didn't get her first.

I left Hester's offering on the hall table and moved deeper into the house, calling Anya's name as I went. A wave of destruction had crashed through Anya's kitchen. Cupboard doors listed open, and drawers had been turned out on the floor. An oak knife block lay on its side on an island of Connemara marble, blades and handles tangled like driftwood on the floor below. Spirits hissed, black and writhing, among the wreckage.

I ran to the sink and threw open the window, then did the same with the patio doors. "Shoo! Out!" I shouted.

The spirits snaked around my wrists and ankles, slinking upward toward my heart. They flickered from black to silver and back again, and their sibilant hisses sank into my ears. They showed me visions of Anya's long, dark hair waving like kelp fronds as she sank beneath the sea, and my own poor home, a shabby hovel next to Anya's gold and marble palace. All I had to do was wait, they whispered, and everything around me was mine for the taking.

"You can't have me," I whispered back. "Or Anya, either." The spirits reared back to strike, hissed in frustration, then turned and flowed one by one out the open windows.

A new hissing reached my ears, the sound of water through pipes. Someone was running water deeper in the house. It had to be Anya, so I sprinted toward the sound.

Her bedroom was a mirror of the kitchen, with bedside tables overturned and an aquamarine silk comforter tumbling off the edge of the bed like waves over a seawall. Spirits filled the room until I waded knee-deep among them, and cries like hungry gulls echoed off the walls.

The bathroom door was locked against me. Water thundered into the tub on the other side. Anya gave a ragged sob, and I heard a silvery sound like ice cubes tinkling against crystal. Banshee wails sounded in my ears, and teeth sharp as needles pricked at my face and arms.

I pounded on the door and yelled Anya's name. When she didn't answer, I kicked the door in.

She cowered near the vanity with her back against the wall. Her raven hair had been cut short in the latest pixie style, and her red-rimmed eyes were dark hollows against her alabaster cheeks. She wore a jade-green robe embroidered with apple blossoms, and silk slippers to match. One hand gripped a crystal tumbler filled with amber liquid, and the other pushed against the vanity as if she'd risen to run but found herself trapped. The room smelled of steam, peat and alcohol.

A low table of brass and glass sat next to the rapidly filling tub. A bottle of Jameson's stood upon it, next to a Waterford decanter with the stopper out and a squat brown pill bottle filled with yellow capsules. The spirits breathed sighs of watery death.

I looked at Anya again. She was young, rich, beautiful—everything I wasn't. Spirits rose up between us with teeth like knives and eyes black as night. A red rage filled my vision, and I bent toward the brass table.

Anya's hands shook. The soft clink of ice made me lift my head. She trembled against the wall, spirits swarming over her body until all I could see was her pale, frightened face with eyes like a green summer meadow. The spirits' shrieks ripped though my soul like a razor through canvas.

Anya slid down the wall until her head touched her knees. The tumbler slipped from her fingers and thudded on the thick carpet. There she was, slender, beautiful, defenseless... and terrified.

In that moment, I knew it was Peyton, not Hester, who'd sent me here. When Anya's haunted eyes met mine, the last recesses of my heart wrenched themselves open. I no longer cared about marble floors or gilt-edged mirrors, about silks and crystal I'd never be able to afford. I cared only that Anya was a woman adrift, bereft and grieving on the swells of life just as I had been nearly twenty years before when I'd washed up on the Summerland shore, destitute and pregnant by a man I hadn't known was married. Peyton's kindness had saved me then, and he must have known that mine could save Anya now.

I grabbed the table and hurled it through the bathroom window. The Waterford decanter shattered on the sill, and a rainbow of shards splattered into the steaming water.

I fell against the lip of the tub, one arm wet to the shoulder where I'd caught myself against the bottom. Broken crystal sliced my palm, and a thin smear of my blood swirled over the white porcelain.

The spirits took form for the briefest instant, showing me a flash of slender hands, ethereal faces and flowing robes of algae and water weeds. Their voices sang like wind howling over the moors, then they streamed out the broken window on a rush of moist air.

A gentle breeze touched my face, and Anya looked at me with tear-streaked eyes. "Are they gone?"

"Yes, Anya, they're gone." I crawled over to her, took her cold hands in mine and said the same words Peyton had said to me the night he'd found me standing on the cliffs alone, wrestling with the final step before oblivion. "Don't be afraid of them. They're not evil, and they can't hurt you if your heart is pure. All they can do is magnify what's already there. You have a choice in front of you, one you should make with a clear head and an open heart. Don't let despair make it for you." Anya gave the tiniest of nods, and the faintest light of hope returned to her eyes.

"Let's get you out of here," I said. "You can stay at my place until the trial blows over." My son Percy, a fine young man now, was off to college and other adventures, so Anya could have his room until her life found a new place to settle.

She dressed quickly in jeans and a loose white Oxford shirt, fashionable even in her grief. A few minutes later she climbed into the back of my VW bus to hide among the drop cloths and painting supplies until we made it past the reporters.

I tucked Peyton's gift into her hands and told her, "This is from Peyton. He said there was mercy in it if you look."

Her brows drew together as she peeled back the sailcloth wrapping, but I let her ponder the meaning alone under her canvas veil.

Somehow, I knew Peyton would approve.

I'd intended to take her back to my house and get her settled before I reported back to Hester, but we never made it past the Box. A pale light suffused the Box's windows with an eerie green glow that lit the fog outside. Black shapes rippled against the glass in an orgy of malice and spite. I stomped the brakes, yelled to Anya to hold on, and screeched into a parking space. I jumped out of the van and left it running while I ran around to the back entrance.

Peyton stood like an avenging god framed against the back door of the Box. His hands gripped the doorframe as if sheer will could contain whatever lurked within, and his eyes were riveted on the scene inside. I peeked past him, through the busy kitchen and into the dining area where a sleek flat-screen television was broadcasting the Kelly trial. Every soul in The Saltbox stood transfixed.

In a sterile Los Angeles courtroom, Herb Kelly stood for sentencing, found guilty of strangling his children in their beds. His lion's mane of yellow hair fell greasy and unkempt on his shoulders. He tore at his orange jumpsuit as if it burned him and rattled his shackles in a crazed, ranting fury. "Snakes!" he screamed. "They were snakes!" Froth spattered from his lips, and he fell to his knees retching bile onto the courtroom floor.

I turned my face away. "Who brought that thing in here?" I whispered. "Reesie did," said Peyton softly. "It came from Aames' place."

And there she stood with an arm draped over the television, her pockmarked skin twitching and her eyes aglow with malice. A blackness glowed in her chest, an oily, transparent aura that throbbed outward with every beat of her heart. And for the first time, I saw with my own eyes what Peyton had tried to explain: spirits didn't bring evil; they magnified it.

A scraping and scratching sound filled the walls and rose up from the floors, the sound of angry spirits reveling in Reesie's hatred, drinking it in and feeding it back to her until her body could hold no more.

Dora cowered in a corner near the cash register with a small lacquered box clutched to her chest, her fingers fumbling at the lid. Hester held the younger woman in her arms, fighting to keep the little box closed. I cowered with them, helpless to stop what was coming.

Black tendrils of hate flowed in through the walls and up through the floor, stream upon stream of shrieking spirits drunk with malevolence. They rushed into Reesie, entwining around her body in a macabre lovers' dance. The tendrils flowed in through her nose and mouth until they found the darkness in her heart. The evil met its twin and blossomed, bursting from her chest in an ink-black cloud of death.

The patrons in the Box stood like clay figures, their eyes blank and their souls unguarded. The blackness reached for them, searching their hearts for jealousy, resentment, petty disagreements that could be nursed into hatred.

A gust of wind blew in through the kitchen, heavy with the smell of rain. The lights flickered once and went out. Dora's photocopied menus fluttered like sailcloth against the windows.

Peyton's visage darkened. His voice rumbled like storm clouds lashed by the wind, and his eyes shone blue with St. Elmo's fire. He drew in a massive breath, and a gale howled through the Box, sharp with the scent of salt and sea. His presence magnified until the Box could no longer contain him.

He reached for Reesie, his massive hands trailing ghostly masts and torn rigging in their wake. The blue light of righteous wrath roared forth from his mouth and eyes. His hand curled like a breaking wave, and the shadow of a trident flashed over Reesie's face.

The ocean answered Peyton's call, and a churning wall of sea water rose behind him.

Reesie's head snapped up. The spirits joined their voices to hers, and the sound groaned up from the bowels of the earth. "I see you, Earth-shaker!"

Peyton hammered his barnacle-covered fist into the floorboards at Reesie's feet, and the towering green sea crashed in to claim her.

I braced myself for a death that never came.

The wave carried the spirits away like black, wind-driven spray. And when they had gone, Reesie's broken body sprawled on the floorboards, her eyes burned out by the black hatred in her soul.

Peyton diminished. He sagged to his knees beside Reesie, his shoulders stooped and his breathing ragged. I looked about for signs of the ocean's fury, and saw nothing but the grey patter of rain against the Box's ancient windows.

Hester and Dora pushed themselves up from the floor. The clay figures remembered they were human, and the clatter of dishes and silver resumed. What the patrons had seen, I could not say.

Dora tucked the little black box back on a shelf above the counter, and Hester called over to the Fire Station to report that Reesie had suffered an overdose.

I helped Peyton stand, bearing him up under one shoulder while he limped toward his truck with painful breaths. He eased himself down onto the back bumper and turned his face to the cleansing rain and the darkened skies.

His voice shook. "I couldn't save her, Danaë. Took all I had to contain what she'd loosed." Raindrops splattered beside us, making dark circles on the dusty pavement. I didn't know what to say, but Peyton did, and his words surprised me.

"Got somethin' for you." Though his hands trembled, he fished in his pockets until he found what he sought. Unlike his other gifts, this one was folded in cellophane paper, and I couldn't see what was inside.

"This is the last one," he said, closing my fingers around the packet. "Don't open it until you're back in the Sea Center. Promise me that, Danaë." His face and eyes had gone fish-belly grey, and his hair fluttered in the wind from the coming storm. I shivered, but those eyes of his held me fast until I gave my word.

Peyton laid his coat over my shoulders, then he glanced at Anya sitting wide-eyed in the driver's seat of my bus. "I knew she'd take to you," he said. He stared past me, peering out over the rain-dark sea. "I've spent a lot of years watchin' after this town. She's a lost soul, Danaë. Look after her, like you did me."

I tucked the packet into my pocket. "I will," I promised. "You sure you're okay?"

Peyton waved me away and thrust a knobby finger down the road toward the Sea Center. "Go finish it."

I would have, but Anya was still in my bus, staring past the Box, up the road that led to the Mansions. She threw the bus into gear and peeled out of the parking lot, squealing the tires on the way out.

Peyton and I looked up toward the Mansions' gates. Ike's fiery red Mustang rounded the corner and sped down the hill, catching air at each successive terrace. A thin guard rail marked the edge of the cliff at the bottom of the hill, and water ponded on the pavement.

Thunder rumbled overhead. As his car raced closer, we saw black spirits pressed against the windshield, harpies and banshees tearing at Ike in frustration after being denied other prey.

Anya gunned the engine, and my van lurched into the Mustang's path, forming a fragile tin wall between his car and the long fall into the ocean below.

Anya kicked open the door and threw herself clear, tearing her white shirt as she rolled to a stop in the muddy gutter.

I sprinted for the corner. Anya fumbled Peyton's gift out of her pocket, and plucked at the wrapping.

Lightning cracked, and a blue-white flash lit the street under the blackened sky. Ike's Mustang plowed into my doomed van, crushing it like an egg. His body exploded through the windshield in a shower of glass, arms spread-eagled against the storm.

If the accident itself hadn't killed him, the fall to earth would. Anya raised the shell aloft, her face transfixed with terror. The spines bit into her palm, and thin rivulets of blood trickled down her arm. Her voice was a whisper and a shout. "Mercy!" she cried.

I could see pain in her eyes, a plea that no other mother should suffer through the loss of a child.

The spirits took form overhead, their faces shining in silver glory, and their eyes locked on Anya. "Mercy," she whispered.

Slender silver hands reached for Ike Harris and held him suspended in the air. Gentle fingers smoothed his hair and shimmering lips kissed away his hurts. They lowered him to the ground at Anya's side. She threw her arms around the boy, holding him to her chest in the driving rain.

I raced to them and laid my hand on her shoulder. "Is he hurt? Are you okay?"

Anya shielded Ike's face from the rain. "He'll be all right, Danaë." She looked up at me with her sea-green eyes. "And so will I. Go paint."

❦

Cold rain soaked me to the skin, but I made my way to the Sea Center with Peyton's cellophane package warm in my hands. I unwrapped paper thinner than tissue to find two elongated mussel shells, still attached like butterfly wings at the rounded tips. Layer upon layer of pearlescent nacre gleamed inside, a tapestry of shimmering blues, deep purples and delicate greens.

I took out my paints and brushes, and I mixed the colors under watchful silver eyes until I could feel a soul take shape under my brush. A soft thrumming filled the air like the sound of a distant flute or wind over the mouth of a cave.

When I stepped back, my mural was finished. Eyes of Poseidon's blue looked out at me from a face that moved earth and desolate sea.

That night, the police found Peyton's body dead in his truck in the lot overlooking the beach, and the spirits—Naiads and Nereids, kelpies and banshees—wailed their grief into the wind.

Peyton had been their touchstone and gatekeeper. Where he found openness and welcome, the spirits sowed blessings in his wake. And where he was spurned by hearts sealed tighter than double-paned windows, where the black miasma of greed and hate seeped in through cracks and crevices, that's where the vapors built until the spirits raged like angry maenads, rending sanity the way they'd once rent flesh.

By morning, a fresh wind had swept the storm clouds away, and the last remnants of a silver mist floated above the waves. The sea grew calm, and sunlight rippled golden on the water of Poseidon's eyes.

In the months that followed, Aames sold his hollow mansion and built a new place on an empty lot a block from the post office.

Anya took back her maiden name after her husband was found hanged in his cell, and she moved into the boarded up shanty-house next door to me. With Herb Kelly's money at her disposal, it wasn't long before the place had fresh paint, a new roof, curtains in the windows, and a garden full of roses. Her cheeks regained their color, and her raven's-wing hair grew long and lush again.

As for me, I still tell tales of our lives by the sea, written in words of paint and shell. After the Sea Center opened, I added a single figure to my mural, the silhouette of a woman standing alone on the bluffs with her long, dark hair splayed out in the wind, searching for the souls of her children on the face of the turbulent sea.

USING OBSERVATION TO CREATE REALISM IN FICTION

BY KARY ENGLISH

Artists use the term "well-observed" to describe a work that captures shapes, contours, lines, and textures exactly as they appear. Instead of a generic white sand beach and sparkling, blue waves, a well-observed beach scene might show brown water against a yellow sky. Observation is the difference between a photorealistic eye and a symbolic eye drawn with two curved lines and a circle in the middle.

The same concept applies to writing. In writing, good observation gives scenes a sense of realism, of verisimilitude. If I ask a writer to describe a coffee shop, I'll probably get a scene with a few tables, a perky barista, and conversation punctuated by the hiss and gurgle of the espresso machine. The problem with such a scene is that it's generic. A generic coffee shop, with a generic barista, and the generic sound of an espresso machine.

By way of contrast, my favorite coffee shop has a hundred-year-old hardwood floor painted an industrial gray. Some of the boards flex under your feet, and in high-traffic areas, the gray paint has worn away to show edges of red and white from previous paint jobs. In a few places, the paint is gone entirely, revealing the silvery-gray wood grain underneath. In three sentences, I've given the reader a coffee shop that's far more specific, far more detailed and realistic than the generic version above. The difference between the two isn't imagination or creativity or being able to write a good description; it's observation.

When I wrote "Poseidon's Eyes," I deliberately set it in my quirky little hometown of Summerland, California. When you read about the town's history, the main character's weird little house, or the café where the story's climax takes place, the vast majority of those details are real. To write the story, I went to each place and stood or sat there and forced myself to notice the details around me. How many steps to get to the porch of the café? What's the path to the front door made of, and what's growing in the flower beds? Even when I was in the zone writing, I could tell several hours had gone by because the smell in the café changed from coffee and the occasional toasted bagel to grilled panini and wood-fired pizza. The espresso machine could barely be heard over the din of conversation, but the slam of the old-timey wood-framed screen door broke through all but the deepest writing trance.

Everywhere we go, we're surrounded by an ocean of detail, and we tune out most of it because it's not relevant to us. As I write this, I'm sitting at a table near the wall in a carpeted hallway. A woman walks by with her flip-flops going slap-slap against her heels. Another woman walks by. Her shoes are silent, but I hear a faint swish-swish sound as she passes. Panty hose. She's staff, and the hose are a uniform requirement. Down the hallway, a rhythmic, metallic clicking comes closer and closer. Someone is walking with a metal cane. To the average person, these details are irrelevant. There's no reason to notice them in the first place, much less remember them later, but when you're a writer, any detail can be relevant. Sherlock Holmes could solve a murder just from the sound of the flip-flops. For us, as writers, we need to get in the habit of observing our surroundings.

For the most part, observation is easy. Wherever you are—at school, at work, at the DMV—take a few minutes to deliberately notice the details in your environment. What are the floor, ceiling and walls made of? What do you see, hear and smell? What textures or tactile details do you notice? My DMV has white tile leading to charcoal-gray industrial carpet. The ceiling tiles are white foam with black flecks, and the walls are pre-fab industrial panels. Last time I was there, the tile floor was sticky, and the citrus air-freshener couldn't quite mask the smell of hot asphalt and car exhaust near the door where examiners met teenagers for their driving tests.

When you create settings and characters deeply rooted in realism, your fantastic elements will feel more real as well.

"But Kary, I write stories set on Mars. How am I supposed to observe Mars?"

I was driving through a sandstorm, and the tiny impacts from thousands of grains of sand sounded like static, or like shushing rain. I could hear the difference between sand striking the glass wind-shield vs. the car's metal body panels. It was mid-afternoon, but the light had dimmed to a blurry, burnt-orange twilight. The other cars were vague, darker shapes with brighter yellow spots if they had their headlights on. The air through the vents smelled like dust on hot pavement. None of that surprised me. It's kind of what you think a sandstorm might be like. What surprised me was the slithering noise when aerodynamics channeled the blowing sand along the car body. It sounded like something was alive just outside the car, slithering along the door panels trying to get in. I knew then that if I ever needed to describe a sandstorm on Mars, this is what I'd describe.

If you can't visit your exact location, find an analogue and go there to observe. In Bar Harbor, Maine, there are granite blocks in a park overlooking the harbor. They're probably leftovers from a sea wall, and tourists use them like benches. So as I sat there eating my lobster roll, I traced my fingers over the finely pebbled texture of the stone. Though it looked gray in the aggregate, the stone was speckled in black and white. Patches of gray-green lichen littered the surface, turning orange where the edges curled. The white specks had a translucence to them, almost glittery. Probably quartz, I thought.

The block had a surface warmth where the sun touched it, but a deep, abiding cold in the shade, a cold that seeped through my jeans and stole warmth from my thighs. The air smelled of summer, all warm earth, flowers, and green things. But the wind came cold off the water, bringing wafts of fish and algae. Dank, darker smells that warned of winter. So even though I was a tourist eating a lobster roll in a public park, my observation of the stone and weather would be right at home for a character sitting on the wall of a Scottish castle keeping an eye out for Viking raiders.

Observation works with character interactions, too. In one of my stories, I have a scene where there's a tense conversation over a breakfast table. I set the table in my house, then sat down and acted out the conversation, making myself notice whether I was leaning over the table or pushing back, and what I was doing with my hands. In the scene as written, the character pushes the plate out of the way, then moves the silverware back and forth while he thinks, completely disarranging the place setting. When he comes to a decision, he pulls the silver back into place. So when you're writing character scenes, act them out and observe how your character sits or stands, whether they put their hands in the pockets, when they look at the ground, cross their arms, etc.

Develop your powers of observation. You may not use every detail you observe, but the process is like filling a memory bank with texture files. When you need a description of a character sitting on a stone wall, or a wooden floor in a historic bungalow, or a sandstorm on Mars, you'll already have it. If a scene calls for details you don't already have, you'll know where to go to get them. If I wanted details for the troop barracks in a spaceship, I'd look for a military museum I could tour, or a metal ship of some sort—even a replica on a playground.

Settings and characters that feel specific and real help the reader suspend disbelief. They draw the reader firmly into the world of the story, pique the reader's interest, and form a rock-solid foundation for the story's speculative elements. If the spirits in "Poseidon's Eyes" feel real and believable, it's not because of how I described the spirits. The realism comes from how well I observed the café, the residents, and the town.

PRO-VOTE
BY ANDY DIBBLE

Andy Dibble writes from Madison, Wisconsin, and works as a healthcare IT consultant. He has supported the electronic medical record of large healthcare systems in six countries. He holds a master's in theological studies from Harvard Divinity School as well as degrees in computer science, philosophy, religious studies, and Asian studies. His fiction appears in *Writers of the Future, Diabolical Plots, Mysterion, Sci Phi Journal,* and others. He edited *Strange Religion: Speculative Fiction of Spirituality, Belief, & Practice.* You can find him at andydibble.com.

Javier had been on the professional voter helpline for half an hour, most of it being led in circles by a voice. Finally, he'd told the bot to cram it. Maybe if helping him meant another thousand votes, it would've gotten creative. But he was just one guy. One newbie pro-voter.

So he waited for a person. And waited. And hoped. And waited.

At least the wait meant he wasn't the only one scrambling to declare residency. All across America, other pro-voters were as desperate as he was.

The ambient elevator music faded out. "You matter," a calming recording said. Maybe the bot sensed panic in his breathing. "As a professional voter, you make voting fair and equal. Before pro-voters like you, California's Senators represented ninety times as many people as Wyoming's. A vote for President by a Wyoming resident counted five times more—"

"American Revyval pro-voter helpline. What's your name 'n' location?"

Javier exhaled in relief. The voice was human. Probably. Software was programmed according to accessibility standards. It wouldn't speak in a rush. "Javier Tucker. I'm in a mobile home lot outside Laramie, Wyoming."

A sigh from the other end. That told volumes. Wyoming's rules surrounding homelessness and voting were so byzantine, Jim Crow was back. They held elections for bogus referendums and obscure clerkships every eight weeks because, in order to cut down on "illegals" claiming benefits, the federal government had made voting in every election a requirement for universal basic income.

American Revyval, the Democratic Super PAC he signed with, was supposed to have dropped off a "no frills" capsule home. Basically a closet you could piss in on wheels. Without that, he hitchhiked a thousand miles from Los Angeles only to jeopardize his UBI. He had to declare residency in Laramie. Otherwise, he couldn't vote where Revyval had assigned him to vote.

"What's your issue?" said the helpline guy.

"There's no home with my voter ID." He had checked the plates of every unit in the sprawling lot, even the single-wide homes for pro-voter families and double-wides for groups.

"What's your ID?"

Javier gave his voter ID.

"Row thirty-nine."

Gee, that came quick. Helpline guy might be a bot after all. He'd read articles saying that human interaction improved professional voter mental health. But that didn't mean Revyval cared enough to hire warm bodies.

"It was dropped off two days ago, but we've had reports of stolen homes."

That could be it. He'd already been through row thirty-nine twice. More than a few homes were spray-painted with variations on "Get out, MIGRANT!" Some graffiti featured inelegantly drawn penises, scrawled over as much ad space as possible. Super PACs, both Democratic and Republican, defrayed the cost of supplying homes to pro-voters by encrusting them with lighted marketing displays.

He thought he'd see stars out here in the Rockies. Ads extolling the pro-voter life promised as much. Ironically, those ads blotted out the stars.

"Can I still get one?" A desperate ask. He was just one guy.

"Doesn't seem there are any open spots."

That declaration swallowed Javier, a lifetime sentence. If he couldn't claim residency in the next four hours, he wouldn't be able to vote on November third. If he didn't vote in Laramie, he'd be in breach of contract. There'd be no pay, and he was already up to his lip in student loan debt. Revyval might even sue him for mobile home rental fees.

And how would he pay them? Pro-voting was it for him. He'd been laid off from his job as a project manager, replaced by an app that chimed notifications and dropped meetings on the calendars of an ever-shrinking pool of employees. There wasn't another career, nothing automation hadn't already shoved into obsolescence.

"Can't you just drop it on the grass?"

"Javier, it's not people that check the picture you send with your Change of Address form."

The truth swept over him like a searchlight beam. Some image-processing program would spot the grass glinting in the dark, or yellow lines missing, or that there wasn't enough diffuse light from ads on other mobile homes. Which meant editing his voter ID onto an image of another mobile home's plates wasn't an option. Some bot would sniff out the doctored edges. And if Wyoming's election commission caught him, Revyval would sue him just to prove they were on the straight and narrow.

"What do I do?"

"You have any close relatives in Wyoming?"

"I'm boned." Maybe if he committed a crime, he'd be able to claim the jail as his residence. But Wyoming probably didn't give alleged criminals the vote.

"Just means we have to get creative. How do you feel about getting hitched?"

What if his bride-to-be thought their marriage meant more than it did? If he could just project levity. The DemProVoter app directed him to a Methodist church in a strip mall. It was just to the right of a Dollar General. He could pop in quick there. If he stuck a two-dollar plastic bowtie on the collar of his "Democrats for America" T-shirt, she wouldn't be able to get the wrong idea.

He stopped cold. The lighted Dollar General sign was on. Next door was dark.

Heart palpitating, he jogged to the narrow double doors of the hole-in-the-wall house of God. There was an LED display in the shape of a cross above the door, but it was off. He yanked on the door and staggered backward as it swung open.

An Arapaho woman with a wide head and dark eyes played the piano while the congregation sang along. Long tight braids framed the white stole around her shoulders.

A toadish fear leapt in his gut. A sham wedding in private was one thing. God's an understanding guy, right? But marrying in front of uptight churchgoers was more than a little outside his comfort zone.

Realizing he was agape in the doorway, he shuffled inside.

To the left of the door was a brass offering plate overflowing with dark cellphones. Next to the plate were two OculusFour masks (Virtual reality in four senses!). Javier fished in his pocket and put his phone on silent. There were candles—along the walls, in a pair of holders on the altar—but no electric light.

Some of the congregation wore jackets, but Republican red or Democrat blue peeking above collars gave them away.

They sang about forgetting life and old-time jobs. It was a folksy tune, no hosannas or pious exclamations. Those old-time jobs were better because at least waiting tables, stocking shelves, and landscaping yards had meaning. You were contributing. Whereas, pro-voting was shuffling bodies around, paying those bodies a basic living to cast a vote that probably wouldn't change anything.

He got into the backmost pew, but he wasn't feeling the togetherness. These loons probably already had residency. They could sing "Kumbaya" until kingdom come, or at least until voter registration. But in just three hours, his chances of voting in November dropped from dismal to nothing.

Churchgoers retrieved their profane phones from the offering plate by the door and wandered out into the world of LED and CGI and three-letter acronyms. Should he go too? He had no choice but to wait. This couldn't be the end.

Six others stayed in the pews. They glanced around curiously. None were brave enough to ask, "Are you mine?"

The pastor scanned their faces. "Boys and girls." She frowned, flipped through some papers. "Boy and boy, too. If it's all right with you, we're skipping the 'I Do's.'" No one objected. "This one's for Benjamin and Cindy."

Cindy was young, probably just out of high school. She held a toddler against her hip, meaning she was soon to be a not-exactly single mom. She wore a jean jacket over a blue T-shirt. Ben wore a cheap suit and a fake boutonnière. They clutched hands like they anticipated a joint writ of execution.

A huge guy, six-four at least, got into the pew next to Javier. He wore a "Democrats for America" T-shirt that looked like it had shrunk in the wash. Or maybe that was the biggest size they made.

Beneath it was a spandex uniform with cut-off shorts. A rugby player? He smelled rank, must've come from playing. There were lines of dried sweat on his pale Nordic face.

"First-timers," said rugby guy. "They think marriage means something."

"Doesn't it?"

"Sure, if you think saving on your taxes *means* something. Or getting hospital visitation rights. Or spousal privilege in court. Or residency." He winked.

"Love and commitment mean something, don't they?"

A grin split rugby-guy's face. "Marriage is a hack. Better that than thinking it's a *death sentence!*" Rugby-guy raised his voice, so Ben and Cindy couldn't help but overhear.

"Uh, I take it you're not a first-timer?"

"Nope. A guy named Javier is about to be my fourth."

"*I'm* Javier."

"I know. I got your picture when the app paired us. I'm Rasmus."

Javier woodenly let his hand be engulfed by Rasmus's.

"Javier and Rasmus," the pastor called.

Javier remained rooted.

Rasmus shrugged, strolled to the front to fetch their marriage certificate, came back. "You got a pen?"

Javier had a fistful. Revyval didn't shirk on free knickknacks emblazoned with their four-pointed star logo. More advertising meant more pro-voters signed with them. That meant more dollars from the Democratic National Committee and donors.

Rasmus waved his hand in front of Javier's face. "Remember? Not a death sentence."

"Are you gay?" said Javier.

"This is about you getting residency."

"Right. But are you?"

"Full disclosure: I am. But that doesn't have anything to do with why we're here."

"It doesn't?" Gay marriage was about as out as it got.

"Look, Javier, no one's making you sign. It's your choice."

But the political-industrial complex of America absolutely was. If he didn't vote on November third, no Super PAC would pay him a dime ever again. There wasn't another career for him, nothing a computer couldn't already do faster and better.

It was gay marriage or inevitable homelessness. Distilled to a bare dilemma, marrying a guy didn't seem so bad. If he were gay, he'd probably think Rasmus a catch. This was 2048. Non-gays could have gay rights too. And if some small-town Wyoming prudes didn't like it, they could shove their family values where the sun doesn't shine.

"No sex?" said Javier.

"No sex."

Javier fished around for a pen, pressed the certificate to the back of a pew. The pen was dry. Javier shook it, tried again.

"Let me." Rasmus drew wide circles on the certificate to enliven the pen and signed. The printed name beneath said "Dr. Rasmus Jeppson." Rasmus hadn't signed "Dr." He handed the pen back to Javier.

Signing wasn't so bad, not with Rasmus's doodle next to his name.

Rasmus's retro Jeep didn't flit over the asphalt like new cars, but the rougher ride felt realer, earthier, communion with the road. Hitchhiking from LA hadn't been a road trip. But this could be the start of one. He was on the highway, riding shotgun, his sort-of-hubby beside him.

Wary of the clunker Jeep, other cars on the highway swerved out of the way. Some that couldn't dart into the other lane, eased back. Apparently, Rasmus hacked traffic like he hacked election law.

"The marriage certificate said you're a doctor?" said Javier.

"Was. Worked in an ER in Austin," said Rasmus.

"You quit?"

"Yup." He didn't even look thirty-five. Had to be swimming in med-school debt.

"The last couple years were just rubber-stamping diagnoses and treatments suggested by software," said Rasmus.

"You didn't see patients?"

"Sure I did, but there wasn't any challenge in it."

"Mm-hmm," said Javier.

"Some of my colleagues made it work, tried to see how often they could outfox the software."

"Can't think that happened much."

"More often than you'd think, especially with complex patients. Computers aren't better than humans at everything, just better than the average professional."

"Shaming bots wasn't for you?" Fighting for Team Human didn't sound so bad to Javier.

"Kind of strikes me as petty. Like tittering when Google mispronounces a street name because it doesn't say it like the locals do. Or when Amazon suggests you buy tripe you'd never want. I didn't want that to be why I get up in the morning."

Rasmus downshifted as the speed limit dipped to forty. Yikes! How hadn't Javier realized? Rasmus's Jeep wasn't driving itself! So that's why the other cars were giving the rusty Jeep a wide berth.

Javier forced himself to look ahead. "You think migrant voting is a challenge? Feels more like a lot of waiting, punctuated by desperation."

"The desperation gets better once you learn the process," said Rasmus. "As for the waiting, that's time to do what you want. A gift."

"But can't work be *meaningful*?"

Rasmus glanced away from the road for a moment, caught his passenger's eye. "This work is meaningful, Javier. Because of us, every low-pop state is a swing state."

～

Javier slept on Rasmus's couch that night. Going by the smell, Rasmus's rugby laundry was the previous occupant. A full moon, huge and lunatic in the patio window, bathed the living room silver. Javier had to turn away before sleep stole over him.

There was a ring of couples in his dream, all skewed into a SimpleLife capsule home. Five private feuds played out in a fiberglass room the size of six porta-potties.

In a twinkling, everyone was a pro-voter, couples split down the proverbial aisle, one in Republican red and the other in Democrat blue.

The marriage counselor sprang up among them, a wacky weed. It was Rasmus, more vivid than all the rest. His head cleared the ceiling. Like some motley angel of the Lord, he wore a shining white doctor's coat, over his pro-voter shirt, over his rugby uniform.

The whole room waited on Rasmus's sage advice. He flashed a manic smile and said, "Divorce *is* an option. Look at me! I divorced *three* times!"

Javier was grateful that Rasmus was willing to wait in line at the Department of Motor Vehicles with him, but getting his Wyoming ID would have gone faster if they hadn't taken his Jeep. Rasmus only just managed to snag a spot by parallel parking.

He thumbed the distance to the DMV on his phone. Eight blocks? Long way to walk. But without a Wyoming ID, he couldn't vote. The sky had cemented into rainclouds during the drive, and his jacket didn't have a hood.

"We should've called a ride," said Javier. A strange vehicle that drives itself would have been better than Rasmus's deathtrap Jeep.

"And then walk to the back of the line?"

"What?" Oh. The red-and blue-shirted caravan trudging fitfully down the sidewalk wasn't going to join the line at the DMV.

It was the line.

. . .

Across the street, protesters seethed from adjoining thoroughfares, brandishing picket signs with shouty capitals: *Wyoming is OUR state! Go Home MIGRANTS! MIGRANTS Are NOT Welcome Here!!* Another sign depicted a donkey and an elephant with X's for eyes. They were skewered by an enormous flagpole.

A red-faced protester waved a rifle in one hand. In his other was a sign, *MIGRANT Season is Open!* The sprinkle of police corralling the throngs weren't moving to arrest him.

Javier slunk around to the other side of Rasmus. "That's a lot of protesters."

Rasmus shrugged. "A few districts converge around here. Native voters from all around are just afraid we might take the state legislature this year."

"So they're all Republicans?"

"Most of them vote that way, but few claim the name. They know both parties bankroll pro-voting." There were more blue-shirts around than red, but plenty of both.

"I thought they just wanted to keep Democrats out."

"They're xenophobes. It's unconstitutional to keep us from coming, so they do everything they can to deny us the vote."

Javier got it now. Rasmus's *us* wasn't Democrats but pro-voters. *Them* was everyone bent on suppressing the pro-vote. If Wyoming were a blue state, he'd be wearing red.

"Don't you think they have a point?" said Javier. "Next election cycle, we might be assigned to Idaho or Montana. And they could be stuck with a left-leaning government they didn't vote for."

Rasmus blew a raspberry. "Billionaires and corporations have been influencing elections in other states forever. Pro-voting is no different, just more equal."

"Out-of-state money just means more ads, it doesn't mean people can't decide for themselves."

Irritation played on Rasmus's face. "Think bigger. Wyoming politics doesn't just affect Wyoming. Before pro-voting, seven hundred thousand Wyoming residents voted for the same number of Senators as California's sixty *million*. Those Senators ratify laws, confirm

Supreme Court justices. Just wait until 2050 when there's a new census and redistricting. Pro-voters are going to rock the House too! This is a big deal, way bigger than local politics. We're a revolution, Javier!"

Rasmus had to shout at the end because the protesters struck up a chant, "Na-tive vote! Na-tive vote! Na-tive vote!"

Javier just wanted to get to the DMV, get his Wyoming ID, and get out. But they were still four blocks away, and the line had stalled entirely.

Some of the pro-voters started chanting, "Mi-grant vote! Mi-grant vote! Mi-grant-vote!" Rasmus took it up. Everyone in line was cheering.

Javier sighed. "Long live the revolution."

The woman behind the desk at the DMV wore a frumpy blouse with a floral pattern. The heavy silvery cross around her neck had "Transformed Wife" inscribed on it. Javier pegged her at low sixties. That didn't bode well. Not because she was older, because he could tell she was. Older women he knew dyed their hair and slathered themselves with YoungAgain cream to hide spots and wrinkles. This woman was fuck-you enough not to care.

She scrutinized his change of address receipt. Why couldn't she be like every other state worker on the cusp of retirement? The receipt gave the reason for address change as, "Marriage to Rasmus Jeppson (09/08/2048)."

"You were married yesterday." More an accusation than a question.

"Lawfully wedded," said Rasmus with a smile that could melt butter. He reached for Javier's hand.

Javier was in no mood for playing a part. He slapped their marriage certificate down. It felt like shooting a three-pointer. Swish.

Transformed Wife ignored the paper, honed in on the hand that placed it. No ring. That's what got her attention? A meticulous bureaucrat he could tolerate, maybe even respect. But to the drumbeat of "marriage is sacred and gays go to hell," this old bitch was firing up her jetpack for a power trip.

"Photo identification?" she said.

"I have to have an ID to get an ID?"

"How else am I supposed to know you're Jah-vee-ur Tucker?" She jabbed her fingernail into his name on the certificate.

"I'm family. I'll sign for his identity."

"You have an affidavit?"

Rasmus brow furrowed. "We don't need an affadavit."

"Laws change."

Affadavit was lawyer speak. Self-service legal help could probably manage it, but they'd have to brave the line again. "I have my California ID," said Javier. He got it out.

Javier imagined her biting it like a leery moneylender testing gold, but she only shifted it in the light to test its tamper-proof markings. "Unfortunately, you'll have to apply for an ID in the county you were married in."

"How would you know we didn't—"

"State statute sixteen point forty-five point two says that Wyoming residents may procure identification at any DMV location." The shape of Rasmus's chin guaranteed he'd never be taken seriously at first. But he was no dumb jock.

"Well, state statute sixteen—ah—*sixty*-five point two requires all—"

Javier smelled bullshit before it was served. "Google, what's Wyoming statute sixteen point sixty-five point two?" He swiped through the results. "There's no such thing."

She sputtered, unsure how to impugn Google's omniscience.

"I'm guessing you have a quota," said Javier. "Every day you have to turn away a certain number of us. So we can keep at this. Or..." He stuck his thumb at the line of red and blue migrants, a coiled tropical snake. Most weren't chatting. They were alone. Easier prey.

"Go to the left, they'll take your picture and print your ID."

· · ·

Since when did busting red tape feel like winning a marathon? "Next I register to vote. After that, I'll vote early, wrap this whole thing up in a couple days."

"Slow down, champ," said Rasmus. "Registration doesn't open for another five weeks."

Hopefully Rasmus would let him sleep on his couch that long. "Anything worth doing in Laramie?"

"There's a sculpture of Lincoln's head, a prison museum, some antique stores. The hiking isn't bad."

In other words, nothing. "Anywhere to donate plasma?"

"Nearer to Denver."

"Guess I'll just be answering surveys." That didn't pay much, but he could do those online.

"The guy I just saw bring the mountain to Muhammad in there can do better. Find a freelance gig."

"I'm not really looking to hustle."

"Maybe pro-voting isn't for you, but something has to be. What was your last job?"

Javier winced. "I installed healthcare software."

Rasmus's face wound up, the most pissed off Javier had seen him. "So thanks to you, a computer put me out of work?"

"Easy! I was just a project manager, it's the software developers that made computers smart."

Rasmus cracked a smile. That pissed-off look was an act? "You still have contacts? Anyone that can write a recommendation to help you build a profile on Nettwork or Trellys? Whichever platform is biggest for finding gigs in software."

"Not so much. At the end, I think management meant to spook me, get me to quit so I couldn't collect unemployment."

"Spook you?"

"I didn't know which of the 'new hires' were people and which were bots. It was all just a flurry of email."

"I'd still reach out. You could be wrong."

Could be, if any of his old supervisors still had their jobs.

He emailed his last supervisor, and the director over her, and some middle managers that had overseen him for temporary projects. Most often, there was no response or a canned email. Responding to those was futile and plumbing them for meaning more so.

One response was encouraging, flamboyant even. Excitedly, he linked his new profile with a request for a reference.

At first, nothing. He schooled himself to patience. But when he did check again, the reference was an ad for Ante, an erectile dysfunction drug.

Fucking ad-bots.

He purged it at once, but his profile was already doused in a slurry of mocking and indignant comments. His modest notoriety drew more ads, most graphic. He scrapped the whole thing.

Start over or give up? With voter registration looming, he went back to answering surveys. At least the pay was consistent. The juice behind every marketing algorithm was Big Data, and that Moloch was insatiable. Plus every time he lied, he felt a little bit the saboteur, even if a moment later he knew his untruths would probably be screened out.

Even if they weren't, every bubble checked could cause no real damage. His contribution was infinitesimal, a speck of pollen in that big Wyoming sky.

On the first day of voter registration Javier got out of the shower, went into the kitchen. Rasmus handed him a cup of French-pressed coffee. "You'll want to change out of that."

"My shirt?" said Javier. Rasmus was still wearing Democrat blue.

"Uh-huh. They'll peg you as a pro-voter. Because of all the shenanigans pro-voters run into when registering, your contract doesn't require you to wear it."

"Right." Everything up until now was shenanigans. The dress-code reprieve was welcome, but it didn't bode well.

"I'm heading out. Got another newbie voter to help, DMV flipped some digits on her ID. So her age is like a fetus's."

Javier chuckled—and realized what that meant. "You aren't coming with?"

"You got this. Just do what you did at the DMV: don't let them give you the runaround. And if they stonewall, just try again tomorrow. Oh, and make sure you have notifications on for changes to the polling place."

"It's on the lower level of a food pantry. A Second Harvest. I checked yesterday."

Rasmus flicked through the app. "Now it's at the old fire station."

"There aren't laws against that?"

"Laws against slyly shuffling the polling places? This is *Wyoming!* The relevant election law is archaic, so election officials only have to post updated polling place locations on a bulletin board. A physical board." Rasmus rapped his knuckles against the wall. "Nothing says that board can't be squirreled away in a municipal building base-ment. Nativist officials just spread the new location by private forums or word of mouth. That way most native voters know where to go, pro-voters are left in the lurch."

"So it's cat and mouse?"

"Now you're getting it."

The old fire station was a burned-out fire station renovated into the Flame and Spirit Pentecostal School. They probably taught children how to be pro-voters. This could be Take Your Kid to Work Day. Timmy wouldn't even have to leave school!

The Latina in front of him had bedraggled hair, slumped shoul-ders, and a small child whining in her arms. She smelled like she hadn't bathed in a few days, like most solitary pro-voters. Capsule homes don't have showers, and Super PACs only let voters use their porta-showers weekly.

He'd be in her position, if not for Rasmus. Well, he wouldn't be nursing a child, but he'd be dirty and alone. No way he would have gotten this far without Rasmus. And now he had to do the next leg himself? Something would go sideways, and Rasmus wouldn't be there to swoop in and salvage the situation.

He pictured himself homeless and bitter on the streets of Laramie, shivering sullenly, waiting for winter, staring down that final dead end to an empty future. If tit-for-tat between Democrats, trying to increase voter turn-out, and Republicans, trying to increase the participation of private entities in elections, hadn't legalized all these incentives for voting, he wouldn't be where he was. Or if computers weren't so damn smart. But they had. And they were.

He had to stop thinking like that, or he would turn bitter. Like the pro-voter behind him. He'd only glanced at her, but seeing her eyes and the rancorous upturn of her lip was enough. No doubt she was still boring holes into his back with a shellfire stare.

The election official who took Javier's ID was a stodgy older man dressed in a suit. He wore a navy tie with a white buffalo on it. Tattooed across the broad side of the buffalo was the Wyoming state seal festooned with the slogan "Equal Rights." What hair he had left was slicked back. He sat straight-backed behind a fold-out table with his hands steepled in front of him.

Buffalo Tie hadn't hassled the Latina in front of Javier much. Maybe because she had a kid. Or because he thought her a dirty Mexican, not a dirty pro-voter.

"Address?" said Buffalo Tie to Javier.

"Five-thirty-six Vey*dau*woo road," said Javier.

Buffalo Tie looked up from Javier's ID with narrowed eyes. Did he say it wrong? It was Arapaho or Shoshone. Something tribal. How should he know how they say it? Or how the locals think it's said.

"How long have you lived at that address, Mr. Tucker?"

"Five? No *six* weeks." Damn, why couldn't he be confident like at the DMV?

"Do you have a second form of identification?"

"I wasn't sure I needed one."

"I'm afraid I can't register you then."

Javier drifted off to the side. Should he try again? He had his California ID, but that would only give Buffalo Tie another reason to dismiss him.

He was about to leave, but the stare of the woman behind him pinned him in place. And he wasn't even the one she was glowering at. Her face was gaunt and severe, like a detainee in a mugshot. If he were still in college, he'd call her white trash. But here, today they were both pro-voters. She wasn't any trashier than he was.

She wore a "Democrats for America" T-shirt, maybe the only shirt she owned. But that gave her away: she was dead on arrival.

"ID?"

She produced her ID with shifty eyes, as if Buffalo Tie were a schoolyard bully. He might snatch it away.

Javier wouldn't screw with her, not in a million years. But Buffalo Tie had the full force of the State of Wyoming behind him. He must be vigilant! He must not let a single fraudulent voter through!

"I'm sorry, Ms. Williams." He left *if that's really your name* unsaid. "You'll have to go across town to register."

"Across town *where*?"

"Ah, the middle school."

"The *other* middle school?"

"Exactly." He had the gall to smile.

"Where they'll tell me I have to register here?" Her right hand drifted to the bulge at her hip. Not good. Her other hand shoved her phone in Buffalo Tie's face. "This says I register here."

Buffalo Tie recoiled, scowling. "Be that as it may, your kind can't register here."

Javier flowed between them. "Can I ask what you did?"

"What I did?" Buffalo Tie took it like an accusation.

"Your work?"

"I owned an insurance firm, built it up from nothing. We had clients in eighteen countries."

"That's honest work, *meaningful* work." Javier didn't believe it, but the lie came easy. "We don't have that. We answer surveys, jostle for a spot in research studies, let the Red Cross bleed us for a buck. Except every election, *we vote*. And we know our vote *matters* because the might of a political party has positioned us so it does."

Buffalo Tie blinked twice. His suddenly diffident brow furrowed as he noticed the crowd's reaction.

The back of the line fanned out like an origami trick, pro-voters and locals. Everyone wanted to see. Whoops of encouragement echoed off the high ceiling.

"We just want you to do your job. Can you do that? We give you our IDs, and you register us. That's all."

Approving hands pushed Javier to the edge of the table. The line reformed behind him. Buffalo Tie held out his hand for Javier's ID.

November third, Election Day. Rasmus and Javier went to the old fire station to vote. The polling place for their precinct hadn't changed since Javier registered. There wasn't a court order fixing it where it was. Had implacable Wyoming really given up?

Political ads near polling places on Election Day was prohibited by law, so few of the growing mass of voters outside wore Party-affiliated shirts. Some struggled to break to the outside. Others pressed toward the entrance, scrambling murmurously like bees from a wrecked hive.

Rasmus thrust two fingers in his mouth and whistled. He had some lungs. Looking like Thor didn't hurt either when it came to reining a crowd in.

"What's the problem!" Rasmus shouted.

"Sign says it's closed!"

"Closed?" Cries broke out from the fringes of the crowd.

Javier cupped his hands to his mouth. "Check the app!"

That advice was so unimpeachable, so effortlessly done, the bees buzzed to their phones.

Javier checked the app too. It didn't give a place, only said, *Go to seat of municipal government and request provisional ballot.*

"What do we do?" he said to Rasmus.

A crazy smile swelled on Rasmus's face. He was a surfer out before a hurricane, riding that great wave. A wave of people and action and change. "We go to city hall and raise hell until we get ballots."

The clerks at city hall capitulated like folding chairs in a storm. Rasmus, Javier, and their scrappy legion didn't even have to bust through the door. If the clerks had dug in, there would have been riots. Xenophobe protesters would have joined the fray. The thin blue line in uniform overwhelmed. Mayhem. Blood in the streets.

So putting pen to ballot should've had more *moment* in it. Maybe it was because there was no machine to slurp up his ballot, no cardboard voting booth. Or because there was no star-spangled "I Voted!" sticker for him to stick to his breast.

Or maybe it was because he voted straight-line Democrat. Revyval didn't pay him to vote that way. Voter bribery is illegal. But they might find his ballot and cut him if they thought it red.

"I know what you'll be doing until next election," said Rasmus.

"What's that?"

"Training to do what I do. You've proven you can mobilize voters."

"You think so?" That sure beat rat racing for freelance gigs.

"I'll put in a referral for you. It'll happen."

"Guessing that means we'll have to split up."

"Only legally. We can still be friends, whatever works. We can even file the annulment together. It'll be a bonding experience." Rasmus winked.

Javier chuckled and shook his head. "Think our ballots will get counted?"

"Nah. Our ballots were only provisional. Lawsuit about our polling place closing will have to filter through the courts first. Elections will be decided long before that happens."

"At least we get paid?"

"At least we get paid."

ACTION AND REACTION IN ANDY DIBBLE'S "PRO-VOTE"

BY LUKE WILDMAN

Editor's Note: In the spirit of collaboration, this essay was written by Luke Wildman, who wrote our next story "Knight's Blood." After that tale, you will find an essay written by Andy Dibble.

Unless you're a very particular type of nerd, you probably find bureaucratic processes to be a decidedly unsexy topic. Who wants to read about someone standing in line for hours at the DMV only to be told they've brought the wrong documents? Most of us get enough of that in our regular lives.

Surely it's a mistake, then, that Andy Dibble's "Pro-Vote" takes this for its subject matter. There isn't a single timebomb, gunfight, or chase sequence to entertain readers—yet somehow, this story propelled me to keep turning pages.

That's because, while this may be the tale of an inconsequential election rife with red tape and a notable absence of murder, it uses the same toolkit as any thriller to generate tension. One of those tools is Action/Reaction. Let's examine the ways Andy uses this strategy to create a rhythm for his story, deepen his characters, and create twists.

How to Create a Narrative Rhythm

Have you ever read a novel or watched a film that included so many high-octane moments that, by the end, you just didn't care anymore? Individually, each moment might've had the power to shock or thrill. Taken together, they faded into the background and made you feel numb to the events on the screen or page, no matter how dramatic the story should've been. This is the stuff of which *Fast & Furious* movies are made.

This problem of tension overload can occur when there are no pauses in a story for readers to reflect on what just happened and what it means for the characters. This applies even in short fiction where writers have limited space to communicate their ideas.

One solution is a strategy known as Scene and Sequel, sometimes called Action and Reaction. In her book *The Fantasy Fiction Formula*, Deborah Chester, fantasy author and mentor to bestselling writer Jim Butcher, talks about how crucial it is to build moments into your plot when the characters can reflect on past events, reorient themselves to the new status quo, and plan their next moves. She calls those moments Reactions. Rather than jumping from Action to Action, it's important to create a rhythm for the narrative that provides a series of small pressure releases. That way, when the next big event comes along, readers feel it afresh.

In "Pro-Vote," the Action scenes include moments when Javier takes steps toward achieving his goal of voting: his wedding, his declaration of residency, voter registration day, and the scene in which he finally casts his vote. The Reactions are the passages that immediately follow.

For example, during the drive back from the church to Rasmus's house, Javier has every reason in the world to feel confident about the future. The initial story problem—finding a way to declare residency —has been solved. So has Javier's problem of needing a safe place to stay until voting day. Even better, he's gained a mentor who can guide him through the rest of the voting process. Luke Skywalker has found his Obi-Wan.

Javier no longer has a deadline looming over him. In the hands of a less-experienced writer, this pressure-release might cause readers to lose interest. Andy Dibble knows what he's doing, however: he ramps up the big-picture stakes during the Reaction by depicting Javier's new husband as a reckless ideologue who quit a lucrative career in an impossible job market because of principle. Clearly, this mentor may not be as reliable as Javier hoped. Who but a madman would choose to drive himself around in a rusty old Jeep while everyone else's cars are self-driving? Imagine Obi-Wan, but on shrooms.

And speaking of interesting characters...

How to Deepen Character

In an episode of the *Writing Excuses* podcast, Brandon Sanderson says that action movies may be able to get away with scene upon scene of Jackie Chan throwing punches, but if a book wants to hold readers' attention, it needs to connect to them on an emotional level. In fact, making readers care about your protagonist is likely the most important thing you can do to raise a story's stakes. Action and Reaction helps with character building by giving you a chance to present your characters in a variety of scenarios.

During Action scenes, readers get to see characters under pressure, solving problems, like when Rasmus calls a DMV employee's bluff. Reactions may be even more important. Those are the moments when the narrative gets deep into the protagonist's point of view to show who he is and how he thinks.

Near the beginning of this story, Javier learns that it may be impossible for him to vote. His thoughts immediately turn to everything he stands to lose:

That declaration swallowed Javier, a lifetime sentence. If he couldn't claim residency in the next four hours, he wouldn't be able to vote on November third. If he didn't vote in Laramie, he'd be in breach of contract. There'd be no pay, and he was already up to his lip in student loan debt. Revyval might even sue him for mobile home rental fees.

And how would he pay them? Pro-voting was it for him. He'd been laid off from his job as a project manager, replaced by an app that chimed notifications and dropped meetings on the calendars of an ever-shrinking pool of employees. There wasn't another career, nothing automation hadn't already shoved into obsolescence.

No action is happening, yet the weight of the story rests on those two reflective paragraphs. Personally, I found it easy to identify with Javier, because I've also experienced the paralysis of student debt and the desperation of not being able to find a job. As Orson Scott Card points out in his book *Characters & Viewpoint,* "readers tend to like a character who is at least superficially like themselves. But they quickly lose interest unless this particular character is somehow out of the ordinary."

Javier's reflections show that, while he faces the same problems readers face, he isn't passive. He's struggling to fix his life, and doing so in an unordinary way, since professional voting isn't something that exists in 2022.

Of course, if the only thing a character does during their Reaction passages is mope, readers will quickly grow annoyed. "Pro-Vote" isn't some literary fiction story in which a character sips tea and stares into the rain while pondering his emotions for two-hundred pages. This is so-called genre fiction. And one of the main reasons readers come to genre fiction is a desire to be surprised.

How to Write Twists

Everyone loves a good twist. When done right, it shakes things up, keeps readers guessing, and raises stakes by creating new problems.

When handled poorly, it feels contrived and breaks suspension of disbelief.

What does it mean to do it right? First, a twist should occur at the exact moment that will cause the worst possible problems for the protagonist. In "Pro-Vote," Rasmus gets called away on the morning of registration day, leaving Javier alone to face the bureaucratic machine.

Previous Actions and Reactions have been essential in setting this up. In the Action scenes, readers witness how much Javier relies on Rasmus to solve his problems. Without Rasmus's help, he never would've been able to declare residency, much less register to vote. In the Reaction scenes, readers are privy to Javier's thoughts as he anticipates what comes next. This leaves the reader confident they know what's going to happen—so when something *else* happens, it throws them for a loop.

Basically, Action and Reaction is a great tool to manipulate reader expectations. Cue evil laughter.

There's a common piece of writing advice, often attributed to Flannery O'Connor, which says the ending to a story should feel "surprising yet inevitable." That's easy to say and harder to achieve, but one of the best ways to pull it off is to rely on the rhythm you've already created. By the time readers reach the end, they should have gained a sense of how your story moves. They think they know what's supposed to happen when.

"Pro-Vote" plays into this. Each Reaction establishes a simple goal —for instance, Javier needs to declare residency—and then, during the Action, simple obstacles arise: a long line at the DMV; anti-vote protestors; antagonistic civil employees. Each Action almost ends in failure, until, at the last minute, either Javier or Rasmus applies a burst of ingenuity and stubbornness to surmount the obstacle.

This pattern proves reliable for most of the story. As a reader, I had no reason to expect it would deviate at the end. Instead, however, the final obstacle—the casting of the vote—is practically a non-event:

So putting pen to ballot should've had more moment in it. Maybe it was because there was no machine to slurp up his ballot, no cardboard voting booth. Or because there was no star-spangled "I Voted!" sticker for him to stick to his breast.

Or maybe it was because he voted straight-line Democrat. Revyval didn't pay him to vote that way. Voter bribery is illegal. But they might find his ballot and cut him if they thought it red.

Like the readers, the characters also feel a sense of dissatisfaction. The story has broken its pattern, and, in this case, it feels anticlimactic. The ending is surprising, and not in a way that feels particularly satisfying.

Then again, as Rasmus reminds Javier, this has only ever been the tale of an inconsequential election. The dissatisfying ending fits the theme. It was inevitable from the start.

If a skilled writer can use this tool to make a story about bureaucracy compelling, I believe he can make *any* story compelling. Whether you plan to write action-packed spy thrillers or near-future political commentary, you could do worse than to follow Andy's lead.

KNIGHT'S BLOOD
BY LUKE WILDMAN

Luke Wildman may be a figment of your imagination—or you may be one of his. Either way, he's a writer of comedy, fantasy, and other weird fiction. Born and raised in West Africa, he currently lives with his wife in Indiana.

To date Luke has written six novels. His work has appeared in *Writers of the Future* 37, *Havok* magazine, and *Parnassus* literary journal.

I marched up to the demon, intent on giving him a piece of my mind. "Hey, asshole!"

He blinked at me through his glasses, then glanced around the bar as if certain I must be talking to someone else. When he saw I wasn't, he said, "My name is pronounced Az*hel*, actually. Can I do something for you?"

"Whatever. That's *my girl* you're chatting up. Why don't you cut it out, huh?"

On her stool beside him, Dora rolled her eyes and nursed her drink. Combined with her black leather jacket and the dark highlights in her hair, the action made her look like exactly the cliché goth chick she was. But she was *my* cliché goth chick, dammit.

"Er... I didn't mean to offend," Azhel said. "But when it comes to that, you don't exactly *own* her, do you?"

"Shut up," I said. "Do you always have bad luck, or is it just today? I happen to have Knight's blood in me."

"Ah," the demon said simply. Then he stood up.

While sitting, he'd looked like any other demon. Ruby-red skin, horns, the black goatee popular among the demonically hip. Totally normal. He even dressed for the hipster role: sweater vest, collared shirt, jacket with the elbow patches. But as soon as he rose, the illusion of his being some run-of-the-mill imp vanished.

I'm a tough guy, bald with plenty of scars and some decent muscles. That night, I was wearing a tank-top and ripped jeans to show them off. A leather jacket padded my bulk.

But I felt shrimpy compared to him.

Azhel was *huge.* Not just broad-shouldered—I'm not so bad in that department, myself—but at least eight feet tall, with muscles that bulged like beer kegs. He had shaggy legs with cloven hooves instead of feet.

I stared up at him and gulped.

"Would you care to rephrase your earlier insult?" Azhel asked.

Around us, the late-night crowd went quiet, imps and humans both. The only sounds were the crashing rock music from the radio and the swish of a bartender pouring gin into a glass.

"She... she's my girl," I said, waving vaguely at Dora. Being on this end of the threats for once had thrown me off my stride.

Dora merely sipped her drink and smiled. Definitely not a *Gee, I'm so glad you're my boyfriend* sort of smile.

"As I observed before," Azhel said, "this young lady is her own person, not your property. She has every right to make autonomous decisions concerning those with whom she socializes."

I squared my shoulders. This big red geek might be huge, but I was tough. I had Knight's blood in me, and you don't mess with Knight's blood.

"Boss," someone behind me said, "you want I should throw him out?"

I glanced over my shoulder and gulped again. A mean-looking bouncer stood behind me. The guy had wings. That's how I *knew* he was badass. Wings meant he was descended from warrior stock, just like me. Our great-grandpas might've fought each other in the wars.

"Thank you, but there's no need for violence, Mez," Azhel said. "I've thought of a far more interesting way to deal with our friend. This timing may actually be ideal."

"Hold up," I said. "He called you boss. That means, uh... you own this joint?"

He smiled at me. "Points for observation."

"Oh, crud," I said. "You're *that* Azhel."

I really had stepped in it. It was an open secret that this was an underworld bar—a place with a literal door to the underworld in one of the back rooms, through which illegal goods were smuggled. Fire booze, sin-crystal... it all entered town through dives like this one. Dora and I had come here tonight hoping to score.

"Hey, look, I'm sorry about before," I said. "Guess I've had too much to drink, and—"

"Too little, too late," Azhel said. "But would you care to make it up to me? As it so happens, I need someone to run an errand. You might be perfect: a big, strapping Knight's-blood fellow like yourself. Mez? Please escort Mr. Knight's Blood back to my office, if you would."

I knew better than to resist the bouncer when he seized my arm and hauled me across the floor. As it was, I might never come out of the backrooms, but if I tried something with him, I definitely wouldn't.

A minute later, Mez shoved me into a tidy little room that looked like an accountant's study. There was a desk with a framed picture of two little imps on it, an easy chair in one corner, and a bookshelf crammed with human business guides. It smelled like air freshener. A one-way mirror looked into the bar, but no noise trickled through from the other side.

"Knight's blood," the bouncer said, imbuing the term with

enough scorn to make me flinch. "I got warrior's blood. Your fathers killed plenty of mine. Try and leave, you'll give me a reason to pay you back."

I stood very still and imagined my innards repainting the office's walls.

Azhel joined us a minute later. He took the easy chair and shooed Mez from the room, despite the thug's scowl. I braced myself, but instead of harsh words, the proprietor offered me a cigar.

"Finest imported brimstone," he said. "Really, I'd be so grateful if you'd accept it."

I did, numbly. It trembled between my beefy fingers.

"I hope our less-than-pleasant introduction this evening hasn't ruined any chance of a friendship," Azhel said. "Assuming you're willing to demonstrate your wish for one, I see no reason we can't be courteous to one another. Do you?"

I shook my head. "Absolutely not—sir. I, uh... what've I gotta do?"

"There we are, I *knew* you'd see reason. What's your name?"

"Donovan, sir."

"A pleasure to meet you, Don. Tell me, are you familiar with an establishment called Mephisto's? Similar to mine, but on the other side of town?"

I nodded. Mephisto's was another underworld joint. I'd scored sin-crystal there a few times.

"Wonderful. I'd like for you to deliver a message to the owner for me; to Mephisto himself, no other. Please tell him that his shipment arrived today. If he'd like to negotiate for it, he should bring he-knows-what to he-knows-where."

I blinked. Sounded too easy, despite Mephisto's reputation for savagery. I'd just have to be careful not to aggravate that geek, which wouldn't be a problem: I'm naturally pretty charming.

"That it?" I asked.

"Oh yes, that will be quite enough. Are you amenable, friend?"

"Um... yes, sir," I said, hoping amenable meant "down for it."

"Marvelous. Repeat the instructions, please."

I did, and Azhel smiled like we were real friends. "Flawless delivery. And to whom will you deliver this message?"

"Mephisto."

"To him and only him, yes. Very good! I assumed you were smart, and you've proven me correct."

I grinned. Azhel had that right—maybe he wasn't such a bad guy, after all. For an imp.

"I think it only fair that I should compensate you for your efforts," Azhel said. "Upon your return, I'll instruct my bartender that you're to drink for free the rest of the night. Dora as well. She's a striking girl."

"Damn! Thank you, sir. Soon as we get back, we'll—"

"We? You need Dora to accompany you on this errand?"

"Well... don't *need* her, exactly, but—"

"Ah! I think I understand your quandary. Please don't worry, she'll have the run of my establishment while you're gone. Her on-the-house tab will open immediately. She already seems to be enjoying it, in fact."

I glanced through the one-way mirror. Sure enough, Dora sat at the bar, bobbing her head to music I couldn't hear. She had a fresh drink in hand.

"Yes, I believe she'll be rather comfortable," Azhel said.

"Uh. Sure."

He rose and opened the door for me. "One last comment, my friend. Were you to fail me in this, I'm afraid I'd be forced to do rather more than charge you for drinks. As you observed, my employees bear some ill will toward humans of Knightish lineage. I am not always successful in keeping a tight rein on them."

Mez was waiting in the hall. A scowl settled on his craggy face as he hustled me away from the head imp's office, shoved me through the neon-lit clouds of cigarette smoke, and half-tossed me out into the chilly October night.

My brain spun for a while after that. Lots of folks think I'm stupid, but they're dead wrong. I'm wicked sharp. I knew Azhel was scheming something; no good reason why he'd trust an important message to me rather than one of his cronies. And anyway, why wouldn't he just call Mephisto up? Send a text, maybe?

Whatever the reason, there wasn't a damned thing I could do about it. I rubbed a hand over my shaved scalp, muttered a few cusswords, and made my way to the bus stop.

Just as the bus pulled up, my cell buzzed. I checked the screen and wished I hadn't.

The text was from my father.

Mom and I are in town, it said. *Would luv to see u.*

I deleted it.

On the ride across town, I began feeling better about myself. A skinny teenage imp sat in the row ahead of me, reading a paperback copy of *Don Quixote.* I glowered at the back of his skull, then reminded myself who I was, and that he was only an imp. Sure, I'd just gotten dragged around by some reds, but the odds hadn't been fair. Besides, I could've taken them. Knight's blood, baby.

My good vibes didn't last long. Staring out the window, I saw Duke Tower glowing above the other high rises, striped down the sides with red and yellow lights. With the way it bulged out at the top, it almost looked like a giant windmill.

That put me in a funk again. The city government had built Duke Tower around the beginning of the nineteenth century, supposedly to celebrate the end of our war with the circus freaks.

Who did the politicians think they were? We'd been fighting the demons ever since the first portal opened in the Middle Ages, and now some stuffed suits thought they could just announce we were all friends?

My ancestors didn't die to be betrayed like that.

Mephisto's was a seedier dig than Azhel's joint. The *p* was out on the electric sign, so the name looked like Me histo's. Beneath it, the usual crowd of imps and humans wandered through the doors under the gaze of a couple bouncers. Hardcore regulars mingled with nervous folks trying to act like they visited demon dives all the time. I studied it from across the parking lot, then approached.

The bouncers eyed me but offered no trouble as I slipped inside. Guess I looked too tough for 'em.

The trouble started after I entered.

I swaggered up to the bar, ordered a whiskey, and asked real casually whether the boss was in the house. The girl—who might've been cute if she hadn't been a half-imp; damned shame, that—said he wasn't available.

"What, never drinks with his customers?" I asked. "My money not worth enough?"

She grimaced as if it wasn't a reasonable complaint. "It really isn't personal, sir," she said. "Mephisto's just busy."

"I'll bet he is. I bet he's watching us right now through some kind of computer, laughing at the chumps who spend money in his hell-hole. Or is he even uglier than most geeks? Is that why he never comes out in public?"

"Hey, buddy," said the human on the stool beside me. "Maybe think about calling it a night, huh?"

It's a good thing I can hold my liquor well. If I'd been drunk, I might've really made a scene.

"Where you get off calling me buddy?" I asked. "You're no friend of mine. Anyone who spends time in a place like this must be an imp lover. That's you, right?"

"Uh." He scrunched his eyebrows together like an idiot. "You're here, too."

"*You* calling *me* an imp lover, punk? *Me?* I'm not one! I hate the reds!"

"I really, *really* never thought otherwise," he said.

"I'll show you what I do to imp lovers. Just quit making the room spin—fight me fair."

"Yo, you got a problem with demons?" someone asked.

Four guys rose from their seats at a nearby table. Three regular humans, the fourth with pinkish skin and little nubbin horns; a half-imp. All well-muscled.

But none had wings.

I smiled, cracked my knuckles, and advanced.

The closest man swung at me. I saw it coming a mile away—caught his fist and sucker punched him, doubling him up.

The world slowed.

As my Knight's blood instincts kicked in, the sour alcohol fumes sharpened in my nostrils. The throbbing in my knuckles deepened. I became precisely aware of every detail in the room, especially the movements of my three remaining opponents. I knew where they were going to be before they did.

The half-demon leapt across the table, but, ready for him, I knocked him a good one across the jaw. I whirled, kicked the guy who was creeping up on my left, then grabbed the half-imp by the collar and flung him into his friend. Both went down.

I turned toward the last guy, who cowered away from me, pulling up his fists to protect his face.

Easy, peasy.

I drove my knee into his crotch, then seized him as he slumped over and banged his face against the table. He went down hard and didn't come up. None of them did.

"Whoo!" I yelled. "Yeah! Who's next, imp lovers?"

"Time for you to leave," a voice rumbled close behind me.

I cracked my elbow back into the new challenger's face, then whirled to see the bouncer clutch his nose.

"Gah! You bwoke my—"

The punk didn't have wings, which meant I had nothing to worry about. He could be Knight's blood, but that would put us on equal footing, and he deserved everything I dished out. A damned disgrace, Knight's blood working for demons. Anyone who did needed a thrashing.

"Hey," I said, "you work here? Perfect. I'm supposed to deliver a message to your boss. Take me back there, or I'll—"

Chch-chk.

I glanced at the bar. The half-imp publican now held a sawed-off shotgun. Its black eye stared me down.

"Easy, sweetheart," I said. "Let's not do anything you'll regret."

"I'm really not the one who's going to regret this," she said. "Please leave."

I raised my hands, palms outward. "Like I said, I just need to talk to your boss. Won't take a minute of his time."

"Oh, how reasonable." Her finger twitched inside the trigger guard.

"Jeez, everyone's so serious around here! Can't a guy horse around?" I backed toward the door. "Listen, it's no skin off my back. You're the one who's gonna get fired when he hears you stopped me speaking with him. My message is from Azhel."

I'd hoped that would make her think twice about throwing me out, but the chick actually laughed.

"Oh *really?* Now I *know* the boss won't want to hear it. Keep walking."

Bells chimed as I backed through the door.

I stood across the street a few minutes later, smoking a cigarette and studying the bar. It wasn't a wide building, but went up two floors, with a balcony jutting from the second. There must've been a VIP room or something up there. Other seedy establishments bordered Mephisto's.

It rankled a bit that I hadn't been able to fight my way in, but toughness wasn't my only good asset. Time to use my brains.

I sidled into the alley beside Mephisto's and strode down its length, broken glass crunching under my sneakers, till I found a metal door marked *Staff Only.* Garbage from an overflowing dumpster stank up the air, but this was my ticket in. I just needed a disguise.

It wasn't hard to find a liquor store nearby. I bought a case of beer with a fancy foreign label and headed back.

"Hey!" I yelled when I arrived. "I got a delivery! Let me in, huh? Someone gonna let me in?"

After half a minute of banging my fist against the metal, the door cracked open and a pair of glowing green imp eyes peered out.

"Do you need something?"

"Yeah," I said. "Someone order a case of beer? I was told to bring it around the side."

"Our delivery truck came several hours ago."

"This stuff's special. Your boss said a customer asked for it." I rattled the bottles at the employee's face.

"I don't think so."

His eyes disappeared, but before he could lock me out, I wedged a shoe in the crack.

"Can't say I didn't try being polite," I said.

I hammered a shoulder against the metal. The door slammed open. The employee yelped and stumbled from my path as I strode into the room. There were cartons stacked everywhere, and two refrigerators hummed against the far wall. The space was dimly lit.

"I need to talk with Mephisto," I said. "You're gonna take me to him, *capiche?*"

He gaped at me.

"What's in those?" I gestured at the refrigerators. "Anything expensive?"

I toppled one over with a single shove and was rewarded by a song of breaking glass. Fumes soured the air as a puddle of alcohol leaked across the floor. The kid squeaked.

"All right, all right! Just... please tell my boss I tried to stop you."

"Fat chance, imp."

He led me into an adjoining hallway and pointed at a door halfway along it. "Mephisto's in there."

It looked plainer than I would've expected for a boss's office, no nameplate or anything, but that didn't matter. I just needed to deliver Azhel's message and get gone.

I barged through the door without knocking.

A baseball bat hit me square between the eyes.

I reeled back, but the bat hammered my ribs, drove the wind out of me, made me double over. Through the stars that cobwebbed my vision, I glimpsed the bouncer whose nose I'd broken earlier, grinning as he trashed me.

Knight's blood surged through my veins. I lashed out, seized his bat—but something cold nuzzled the back of my scalp.

"I'd take the beating," the girl bartender said. "You're becoming a nuisance. No one would find your body if we just dumped you through our portal to hell, you know."

I snarled but let go of the bat and collapsed into a fetal position. The bouncer wheezed laughter through his broken snout as he beat on me, but his laughs changed to cusses when I refused to make a peep.

He continued long after the point where anyone without Knight's blood would've been in serious danger of internal bleeding. Then he collared me, dragged me down the hall and through the storeroom, and dumped me like a sack of trash in the alley. Behind my attackers, I saw the green-eyed imp smirking.

"Stay oud," the bouncer said.

They slammed and bolted the door.

I lay in the spilled garbage and let myself groan. Coppery blood filled my mouth. I felt bruises swelling over my ribs.

Despite everything, I forced myself to smile as I clambered to my feet. My Knightish ancestors had taken worse beatings than this during the wars, and they'd kept fighting. I could too.

Once I felt steady enough to walk, I crossed the street to survey Mephisto's again. Rotten luck kept making me fail, despite all my clever schemes. I needed a new approach.

Front door was no good. Side entrance also useless. Even if I got through, I'd never make it to the office without being spotted. What I needed was a secret way in.

My gaze floated to the bar's second level, where the balcony jutted from its righthand side. The club beside Mephisto's stood only one floor high, its peaked roof even with the balcony, and the gap between buildings couldn't have been over ten feet. Not too far for muscles like mine.

I made my way to the club, a normal human establishment, and limped around the outside. The music that rattled its walls didn't do my headache any favors, but I made a full circuit, looking for window ledges, trees, anything to help me climb up. No such luck.

I stopped beside the dumpster and scowled. None of this was fair; I didn't deserve to be blackmailed by a demon and have the crap kicked out of me by brainless thugs just to wind up here, dead-ended with no chance to finish things. Just like my ancestors. They'd fought so hard, sacrificed so much to protect our world, and for what? To have the government sell them out?

Screw that.

I clambered on top of the dumpster. It was one of those big industrial types, too heavy to push closer. Both lids were flung back, and it overflowed with garbage, but it might give me enough height to jump onto the club's roof. I teetered on its metal lip, knees wobbling. Not a great launch pad, but...

"Gah!"

My footing slipped. I flailed backward into filth, sinking down. Sludge plastered my jeans to my skin, soaked through the denim and trickled over my legs. That was *it*. With a snarl, I jerked myself upright, crouched, and sprang.

The world tilted crazily when I caught the roof's edge. I ignored my screaming bruises and hauled myself up.

Once I was standing, I walked along the roof till I was adjacent to the balcony. It was higher than I'd thought, still a foot above me; I'd need a running start to clear the gap. My superhuman muscles were up to it, but I'd have to sprint down the shingles, which added all kinds of potential for disaster.

I hiked to the crest and paused a moment, sucking a deep breath. The city's lights blurred around me. A cool breeze licked my wounds. Bass vibrated in the soles of my sneakers.

"Do or die, soldier," I muttered.

I sprinted down.

Wind hissed in my ears as I leapt. It wasn't a good takeoff; my right foot slipped as I launched, making me flail forward with all the grace of a flightless bird. I heard myself yelling.

When I slammed against the railing, spikes of pain made my teeth click together, but I managed to snag a handhold and climb over.

The balcony door was unlocked. I slipped into the darkened event room, my footsteps loud on its shiny floor. Old perfume and cigarette stink haunted the place.

I crossed the dance floor and entered a hall. At its far end, cracks of lamplight oozed around a doorframe. I spotted a nameplate inscribed with demon runes I couldn't read.

Mephisto's office. Had to be.

Visions of the geek boss danced through my head before I shoved the door open. He was probably at least as big as Azhel, with enormous horns, living flames for eyes, and claws long enough to palm a man's skull. Based on his reputation for cruelty, he'd likely have needles for teeth, warrior wings, and a barbed tail.

But as the door thudded back and I squinted against the light, a very different sight greeted me.

Mephisto stared at me in shock, her cute eyes widening. She had pinkish skin and nubbin horns white as seashells poking through short black hair.

"Color me red!" I said. "Aren't you that girl bartender?"

"What are you doing here?" she demanded. "Get out of my office. Security!"

"*Your* office? Meaning *you're* Mephisto? No wonder you don't tell no one!" I bellowed laughter. "Other bosses would eat you up, bitty thing like you."

She hit a button on her desk. I didn't have much time.

"Easy," I said. "I'm just here to talk. Got a message from Azhel. He wanted me to say your shipment's come in. If you want it, bring you-know-what to you-know-where. He said you'd understand."

Her hands clenched into fists. "You're kidding me! That... that's impossible. He must've intercepted it on the other side, somehow. It should've come straight here."

I shrugged. "I'm just the messenger, baby. Say, you're pretty hot. Now that I've got you alone, wanna have some fun together?"

Her hand jumped into a desk drawer. I lurched back, but the imp moved impossibly fast.

She yanked out a snub-nosed revolver and shot me through the kneecap.

The next moments were a blur of pain. Blazing white light filled my body. Someone was howling—took me a while to recognize my own voice. I collapsed and hammered my fists on the carpet.

When enough of my sight returned for me to make out the room, I found Mephisto standing over me. Her gun was pointed square between my eyes, so I decided to add begging and blubbering to my repertoire.

"You reek to hell and back," Mephisto said, wrinkling her nose.

"Hey, that's not my fault. I stepped in some garbage, and—"

She flipped the gun around, brought the handle down on my skull, and I plunged into blackness.

I woke in a car's trunk. Someone had hired a band of pixie drummers to play a concert with my brain as the mosh pit. My knee throbbed something awful, not to mention all my other scrapes and bruises.

And I stank like a city dump.

A crunching noise emanated from beneath my head. Tires on gravel or dirt, sounded like. I shuddered to think where they were taking me, and why they'd kept me alive.

Zip-ties cut into my wrists, but I managed to wriggle two fingers into my jeans pocket. My cellphone was still there. I fished it out and flipped it open. The screen was shattered, but not so badly that I couldn't navigate it. Maybe I could call someone.

"Who've I even got to call?" I wondered aloud.

Dora couldn't do anything, even if she wanted to. No one else would be willing to stick their necks out for me. There was always 911, but at the first sirens, Mephisto would probably arrange for me to get a closed-casket funeral.

I was on my own.

I stuffed the phone away, ignoring the missed call and voicemail from my father. One headache at a time.

The car's bouncing stopped. Bad brakes screeched as we pulled to a standstill. Twenty seconds later, the trunk popped open and daylight flooded my eyes, teaching me a new definition of hangover.

"Geddup, jackass," Mephisto's broken-nosed bouncer said.

I struggled into a sitting position, and he hauled me the rest of the way out. As soon as I was balanced on my good leg, he seized my arm.

"Don twy anyding," he said, as if I had options. "Mardch."

I hopped for all I was worth as he propelled me forward. Mephisto stalked ahead of us, flanked by two henchdemons. We wove between heaps of rough stone and tall machinery that jutted to the sky like rusted spines.

"Stop there, please," Azhel's voice called out. He sounded apologetic. "I believe we can converse quite comfortably from this distance. Mephisto, is that really you?"

I squinted and saw the enormous demon standing behind a parked car thirty feet away. He was smiling and seemed relaxed, hands shoved in the pockets of his tweed jacket. Mez and his other guards looked anything but. They were carrying enough firepower to take on a small army.

Mephisto laughed. "You really think I'm the boss?" she asked. "How sweet. He just sent me because I'm disposable. Kill me and he won't care, but you can tell me whatever you wanted to tell him. Also, please don't kill me."

"It's not a matter of telling, anymore," Azhel said. "Nor one of killing. Let's not act like humans, my dear, even if you're unfortunate enough to have that lineage. Did he send along what I requested?"

"Mephisto would like to protest your manners," she said. "Even if you've really found a way to intercept shipments, there are rules to our business. You know what happens if the people on the other side have to get involved."

Azhel grimaced—the first time I'd seen him look perturbed. "Yes indeed," he said. "I am sorry for the necessity of my actions, but alas, it was the only way. Now... do you have it?"

Mephisto nodded to one of her bouncers, who held up a briefcase for Azhel to see. I heard something swish inside.

"Capital," the big demon said. "Place it halfway between us, please."

"How about a different trade?" She snapped her fingers at my guardian, who shoved me forward. Agony jarred my knee as I sprawled by Mephisto's feet. She pulled out her revolver, cocked the hammer, and pointed it at my head. I decided it was a fine time to put my blubbering skills to use again.

"Please don't," Azhel said, surprising me. "To kill a messenger is such a *human* form of savagery. I'm very disappointed in you. We're above this, you and I."

She smiled. "I really didn't think this would work, but Mephisto says you have a reputation for honor. If I hand over your messenger, will you promise to give back our shipment?"

"You seem to be confusing honor with stupidity, my dear. I'd rather you spared him, but I'm not about to surrender my advantage for someone who isn't even an employee of mine. The item, now."

Mephisto sighed and nodded again to her bouncer, who walked forward, briefcase in hand.

The wait felt like purgatory, but I prayed for it to stretch longer. Once it finished, I knew I'd be dead.

The bouncer reached the halfway point and set down the briefcase.

"You know this won't really hurt my boss," Mephisto said as her guard retraced his steps. "He has plenty more bottles where this one came from."

"Good to know," Azhel said. "Eventually I'll need to do something about that. For now, however, this should put us on somewhat level footing."

Mephisto cursed softly, and I echoed her in my thoughts. Her guard was almost back.

A Kevlar-armored Mez moved forward to collect the briefcase, covered by the guns of his compatriots. Morning sunlight glowed pinkly through his bat wings.

"Thanks ever so much," Azhel said. "I believe that concludes our business. What will you be doing with my friend Donovan, by the way?"

"Sorry, but you no longer get a say," Mephisto said. She jerked her head to the left. I gulped when I saw a quarry pit.

"A pity," Azhel said. "Still, I suppose Mephisto has his reputation to maintain, just as I have mine. Farewell, then. The shipment will be waiting for you, safe and sound. I give my word."

As he drove away, I kept expecting him to do something—unleash a hail of bullets, maybe—but I guess I wasn't worth it.

Once he'd left, Mephisto turned to her cronies. "I don't trust that bastard. I've got to go secure our shipment and the rest of our bottles in the cellar, but I want you to take your time with this man. I'll send the car back later. Make it so whoever finds his body will know what happens to my enemies."

She drove off in a cloud of dust, leaving me alone with my executioners. Knight's blood or not, I had no hope of escaping with wrists bound and leg busted. This was it.

The bouncer smiled at me.

"I'b going to enjoy dis," he said.

Then his head exploded.

The two remaining guards both started yelling, but even as they dove for cover, a second sniper bullet ripped through the one on the left, half spinning him around. I yelped and wriggled away, but the remaining bouncer crawled over to me and yanked me into a sitting position by a fistful of hair, pressing his gun to my temple.

"You're going to get me out of here," he growled. "Start marching, boy!"

"Hey!" someone behind us bellowed. "Right here!"

The thug released me, rolled and spun, bringing his pistol up with a curse... but too late. An Uzi shot him full of holes.

I looked at the gun that'd saved me, at the smoke that whispered from its short barrel, and at the man who held it—a gray haired, Kevlar-wearing, Uzi-toting soccer dad.

"Hi son," he said. "Is now a good time for a visit?"

My father wanted to pry into all my business, of course. He insisted I go to a hospital, and when I said my Knight's blood would heal me well enough on its own, he asked about Dora, and whether I had a job, and where I was living these days. He was especially keen to hear how I'd wound up about to be murdered by demons in a gravel quarry.

"I was gonna escape on my own," I muttered. "Didn't need you."

"Of course you were, son. I think it's just lucky your mom and I were in town. She pulled a few strings with her connections at the agency and was able to have your phone tracked."

I sighed. My father and his wife both worked for the Department of Interdimensional Law Enforcement. Our ancestors had fought the red freaks right up until the end of the war, but now my old man wanted to keep peace with them. Disgraceful.

And that wasn't the worst of his betrayal.

"Your mother's still up there with her sniper rifle," he said, smiling fondly as he pointed to the top of a metal spire. "What do you say? Should we have her join us?"

"That *thing* isn't my mother," I snarled. "You abandoned my real mother to marry a freak."

"Son, she just saved your life. Please—"

"No. *She's* not my mother, and *you're* not my father, neither. Not anymore."

He sighed and ran hands through his hair. It was grayer than the last time I'd seen him. His face was more lined.

"All right," he said. "All right, we'll leave. But we love you, son. We're going to keep trying to be part of your life."

"Fat chance," I said.

"Take care of yourself, Donny. Whoever wanted to kill you, I suspect they'll keep trying."

He had that right—especially now that I was one of the only people who knew what Mephisto looked like.

My father walked away.

It was only after he left that I realized I had no ride, and that it would take several excruciating hours to drag myself to a road so I could call a cab.

My first stop was to buy crutches. Then I returned to Azhel's bar. It was mostly deserted at that hour of the morning. An employee moved among the tables, collecting empty glasses and throwing bottles in a trash bag. The radio crooned mournful country music.

There was only one customer left: Dora. She sat on the same stool, revolving a glass in her hand. Its ice cubes tinkled.

"Have you moved all night?" I demanded, slumping onto the stool beside her. I leaned my crutches against the bar.

She lifted an ironic eyebrow. "Did I *say* you could sit here? You smell like a sewer."

"Whiskey, neat," I told the bartender. "Got to start the day off right. And tell Azhel that Donovan's back."

It took less than a minute for the huge demon to come hurtling out of the back rooms, his jaw hanging open. Felt good to have thrown him for a loop, for once.

"You... they... you were..."

"What, didn't expect to see me again? I'm Knight's blood, asshole. Takes more than a few imps to kill me. I got my tricks."

"Evidently," Azhel said, still staring. He moved behind the bar and poured my drink himself. That was something, I guess.

"Seems to me we have some unfinished business," I said. "Along the lines of you leaving me for dead. You gonna make that up to me, somehow?"

He slid my drink across the countertop. "Oh, Donovan," he said, shaking his head. "Don, my dear friend. I'm very pleased to learn you're still among the living. As you'll recall, I lodged a protest on your behalf. But I have settled my end of our bargain, free tab included. From the first, I knew you were exceptionally bright—it cannot have escaped your intellect that if you seek to cause trouble in my establishment, I'll be forced to take action. In your present condition, Knight's blood or not, how do you think that would be likely to unfold?"

His gaze flicked over my shoulder, and I glanced back to see Mez standing by the door, intimidating as hell. He still wore his Kevlar and held his gun.

I grunted, drained my whiskey in a few gulps, and grabbed my crutches. No one can say I don't know when to be discreet.

"Come on," I told Dora. "Let's beat it."

A smile curled her lips. "What makes you think I'm going anywhere with you, baby?"

"I... huh?"

Azhel circled the counter and put his arm around her. I got the message pretty quick.

"Seriously?" I asked. "You gonna give up the chance to be with Knight's blood for *this* freak? You'll regret it."

"Knight's blood, Knight's blood," she mimicked. "Are you, like, capable of thinking about *anything* else? That stuff ended a hundred years ago, but you're still completely stuck in the Middle Ages."

I glared at her. Swung my gaze to Azhel, then to Mez. No chance in hell I could win a fight.

Now that I thought about it, maybe I'd never had a chance. Maybe this battle had been lost a hundred years ago, and Dora was right: I was just a used-up Knight tilting at windmills, or whatever.

So I left.

STORYTELLING PROMISES IN "KNIGHT'S BLOOD"

BY ANDY DIBBLE

Editor's Note: In the spirit of collaboration, this essay was written by Andy Dibble, who wrote our previous story "Pro-Vote." After that tale, you will find an essay written by Luke Wildman.

Margaret Atwood tells us that "hold my attention" is a cardinal rule of writing. I'm not a writer who subscribes to Rules of Writing that are Written in Stone and Must Never Be Violated, but in this I agree with her. Whatever we want to achieve in writing, we fail if we bore our readers because they will stop reading.

As speculative fiction writers, we aim to hold our readers' attention by telling good stories. In this respect, I find Brandon Sanderson's promises, progress, and payoff rubric helpful. He connected these ideas succinctly in a 2020 lecture he gave at Brigham Young University: "If you don't make promises and make progress toward delivering on those promises, your readers will get bored."

A promise is an expectation or range of expectations about what comes later in a story. Progress consists in giving reasons a promise is going to be fulfilled. For instance, a character trying to achieve their goals or a plot (e.g., a heist, a sports underdog story, or a romance) developing according to forms that readers are familiar with. Payoff is our emotional response to a promise being fulfilled.

Here we'll focus primarily on promises because, of the three, they play the biggest role in the opening pages of a short story, and it's the beginning of a story that is most crucial in getting out of the slush pile and on to an editor's Yes list. We'll dig into "Knight's Blood" because it's a strong example of how a good writer makes a variety of promises quickly and well and then delivers on those promises.

Plant and Payoff—What a Promise Is Not

I read a blog post on screencraft.com by Ken Miyamoto about a different rubric: plant and payoff. This is a foreshadowing technique that hints at what comes later in a story. The early mention of a teenage imp reading *Don Quixote* in "Knight's Blood" is a plant with the payoff in the ending sentence when Donovan realizes that he's "just a used-up Knight tilting at windmills." Now he knows he's acted foolishly. Like Don Quixote, he's been holding on to a code of honor that no longer works. The wars with the demons are done.

The *Don Quixote* plant enhances the story, but it's not a promise. It could just be a throwaway joke—the universe poking fun at our hero. We wouldn't be surprised if *Don Quixote* was never mentioned again in the story. Promises are bolder than plants. Readers expect the story to make progress toward their promises being fulfilled, or at least that the story will only violate the promise when there's good reason. More on that later.

The plant/payoff rubric is helpful in fewer situations because it doesn't give advice about how to hold reader interest. It works better in blockbuster movies because they have a large dedicated following; fans are willing to dissect every frame. But there aren't many readers that will keep turning pages just to see if *Don Quixote* will crop up in a short story again.

Don Quixote is commonly known, but plants don't have to be. A quotation from an obscure Romantic poet who shares a name with one of your characters could be a plant. That level of sophistication will only win over readers with a deep knowledge of Romantic poetry, and even they might find these sorts of Easter eggs annoying, like the writer is trying to be overly clever. Whereas promises aren't made unless they're understood by your reader.

Early Promises in "Knight's Blood"

The first promise a story makes is with its title. "Knight's Blood," at the very least, promises us that the story we are about to read will relate in some way to knight's blood. We expect to find out what knight's blood is.

It's important to make a variety of promises from the opening sentences of a story, which is why stories that begin with more theoretical discussion often don't make it out of the slush pile. Consider the opening of "Knight's Blood":

> I marched up to the demon, intent on giving him a piece of my mind. "Hey, asshole!"
>
> He blinked at me through his glasses, then glanced around the bar as if certain I must be talking to someone else. When he saw I wasn't, he said, "My name is pronounced *Azhel*, actually. Can I do something for you?"

We know there are demons. That tells us this story is fantasy—a genre promise. The demon is wearing glasses; he's at a bar. We know that the story is set in a relatively modern-day, likely urban environment. Readers will expect these categories to be supported in what follows. This doesn't mean the story can't be a mashup—say demons and aliens—but the time for that is limited. If aliens were to enter a quarter of the way into the story, and we didn't have some reason to think this story is also science fiction, the genre promise would be broken. We would be confused and stop reading.

We also find a tone promise early in the story in the play on "asshole" and "Azhel." We suspect this story is a comedy. If the rest of the story had no jokes, we would think that the joke at the beginning left us with a false impression, a broken promise.

Promises About the Ending

Let's look at the next part of the story:

> "Whatever. That's *my girl* you're chatting up. Why don't you cut it out, huh?"
>
> On her stool beside him, Dora rolled her eyes and nursed her drink. Combined with her black leather jacket and the dark highlights in her hair, the action made her look like exactly the cliché goth chick she was. But she was *my* cliché goth chick, dammit.
>
> "Er... I didn't mean to offend," Azhel said. "But when it comes to that, you don't exactly *own* her, do you?"

This passage leads us to form expectations about how the story will end. The protagonist isn't very likeable, which can be dangerous in writing fiction because readers struggle to care about what happens to unlikeable characters. But this is a comedy. A lot of the fun—the payoff of a comedy—is in seeing how Donavan is going to screw up and get knocked around. He's a bit of a chauvinist, so we don't want him to get the girl. It's the *demon* that's defending Dora's autonomy. All this adds up to us expecting a bad or mixed ending for Donavan, or if it does end well for him, we expect it to only after he's changed for the better.

Promises as a Range of Expectations

An important lesson here is that promises commonly involve a range of expectations. The fun of reading—the payoff—comes from finding out which of those endings will come about and being proud of ourselves for having at least partially anticipated it.

Consider Donavan's character. It's clear from page one that he's impulsive, but that doesn't mean that he needs anger management therapy or that he's as foolish as Homer Simpson. We can go along with him *not* resisting Azhel's bouncer. His instincts for self-preservation are strong enough that we accept him reasoning that resistance will get him killed. At the same time, we buy him falling for Azhel's flattery and calling himself "wicked sharp" when he's not. A lot of the fun is finding out how much of a doofus he is, but still seeing little sparks of competence, like him "using his brains" to get back into Mephisto's. His character promise is elastic enough to permit discovery.

Another example is Azhel's character. He's well-spoken from his very first line. We expect him to be well-spoken throughout the whole story and continue to project sophistication and competency. But that doesn't mean he can't be evil or self-serving. He's still a demon. As we find out later in the story, he is self-serving but not evil because he's opposed to savagery and keeps his word. The range of expectations included under the umbrella of a promise shrinks as we learn more about a character.

Just What is Knight's Blood?

Immediately after the longer excerpt quoted above, Donovan drops the line, "I happen to have Knight's blood in me." We ask: *What's Knight's blood?* A promise would be broken if we didn't find out. So far all we have to go on is that it has to do with fighting, and might have to do with ancestry. This elaborates on the promise already posed by the title. That's progress.

We don't need to be given the whole answer right away in the same way we don't want the story to end right away. We're reminded that it's coming ("I had Knight's blood in me, and you don't mess with Knight's blood") before we actually see his Knight's blood in action in the bar fight at Mephisto's. This may be playing coy, which is a risk in writing speculative fiction. Treating a speculative premise like some big reveal rather than a tool in storytelling can frustrate readers. But in this case, the delay is effective because it gets us asking questions: *Is Knight's blood really as powerful as Donavan's talk says it is?* And we guess not because he's a bit of a buffoon. He's so impulsive that we know a fight is going to break out before long. There's tension. We aren't frustrated. We keep reading.

When Is It Okay to Break Promises?

Sometimes stories pull the rug out from beneath us by giving us something we didn't expect. This is sometimes a mistake. I was surprised when Donovan hit on Mephisto: "Say, you're pretty hot. Now that I've got you alone, wanna have some fun together?" His anti-demon prejudice has already been established, so it seems out of character. This is a misstep, but it isn't so off as to ruin my interest in the story.

But "Knight's Blood" also effectively undermines our expectations regarding Mephisto's gender. Azhel clearly indicates that Mephisto is a man when sending Donovan to deliver his message. We know Azhel to be competent, and we have no reason to distrust him in this. How is Donovan supposed to deliver the message to Mephisto if he can't properly identify Mephisto? So we're surprised—but not disappointed—when Mephisto turns out to be the half-demon female bartender that Donovan meets when he first enters Mephisto's.

This works for two reasons. The female bartender had already been introduced and in a significant enough way that we expect her to play a further role in the story, so her re-entry into the story is the fulfillment of another promise. More importantly, we quickly learn her "cover" as a man is entirely in keeping with her character. She's crafty. Her tactics when interacting with Azhel make complete sense to us: "You really think I'm the boss... He just sent me because I'm disposable." She likely knows that Azhel doesn't shoot messengers, and Azhel is less likely to try to kill her if he believes the true power she serves might try to get revenge later on. So we forgive the broken promise regarding her gender because there are other more fundamental promises that are fulfilled by virtue of it being broken.

From this we can draw together what I think matters most in promise-keeping while writing fiction. We build trust with our readers by keeping promises, but that relationship doesn't flourish by just being a good Boy Scout. Readers recognize that some promises matter more than others, and they respect us more for attending to this fact. The promise "I will hold your attention" matters perhaps most of all. If we can achieve that by breaking other promises, they will forgive us every time.

A SPECIAL EXTRA CHRISTMAS
BY ERIC JAMES STONE

Eric James Stone—Eric—lives in Utah with his wife, Darci. He is a Nebula Award winner, Hugo Award nominee, and a winner of the Writers of the Future Contest. His work has appeared in *Year's Best SF 15, Analog,* and *Nature,* among many others. His first novel, *Unforgettable,* was published by Baen Books in 2016. Eric has an effortless hand with humor and voice. For more of his work, grab his collection, *The Humans in the Walls: And Other Stories.*

Drawn Sword of Allah exited the exploratory wormhole at 11:52 Universal Mecca Time on 9 Jumada Al-Thani 4494 AH. Intissar Majid entered this fact in her journal using longhand Arabic script. Khalid, the ship's artificial jinni, doubtless had already stored much more detailed information in his memory, but Intissar liked having a record of her own.

"I have pulsar-calculated our position," Khalid said. "The nearby star had a small Confederation-era colony, Summerfair, but there's been no recorded contact in over eight hundred years. I'm not picking up any broadcast traffic, so it could be another world that died after the wormhole network collapsed. We could claim it for the Caliphate."

"Or they have regressed," she said. In the five years of surveying she and Khalid had done since being mustered out at the end of the war, she had learned that regression was the more likely case. Without access to interstellar trade, a colony might lack the tech base to maintain its existing technology, but unless the planet was on the extremes of the habitable range, humans tended to find a way to survive. "In which case, we shall offer them the choice to accept or decline the protection of the Caliphate."

"I've found the planet," Khalid said. "Range twenty-seven million kilometers." A hologram shimmered into being: a blue and white world partially obscuring a brilliant white moon. "It seems you are right: there is a town with active illumination visible on optics." An inset picture of tiny dots of light in a somewhat grid-like pattern appeared, with lines tracing back to the source position on the night side of the planet. "I'm firing a probe to do a close-in pass for a better view. It should be in position by the time the town moves into daylight."

"Still no radio?" Intissar asked.

"No."

"Then we'll have to land to make contact," she said. "How long before we can do that?"

"Our relative velocity is too high to go directly, so we can do a flyby in a couple of days, before coming back to land. We can do it in five days—three if we max out the inertials, *insha'Allah*."

Intissar smiled at Khalid's desire to push himself to his limits. The decommissioned single-crewed fighter had been stripped of weapons after the last war, but still had military-grade engines. "No rush."

"Then I will set our course for the colony after *dhuhr* prayers. I am now pointing us toward Mecca."

Two hours later, Khalid said, "I have noticed an anomaly."

Intissar looked up from her workpad. "What?"

A hologram of the colony world and its moon popped into the air. A red circle surrounded the moon. "Documentation on this colony is scant, but it did not mention a moon. I have been observing since we arrived in this system, and have confirmed that body is not in orbit around the planet. It may be a moon ejected by one of the gas giants, or possibly a giant comet. It is two-thirds the size of Earth's moon, and it will strike the planet in seventeen hours."

Intissar gasped. "Merciful Allah, let it not be so," she prayed, even though she knew Khalid was never wrong about such things. "Can we warn them?"

"We have no way to communicate with them. Such warning would be futile anyway, as nowhere on the planet is safe from devastation." Khalid paused, then said, "I know you will not like my saying this, but perhaps we were brought here by the hand of Allah in perfect time to witness the destruction of these foul infidels." Another pause, then, "They are Christians."

"They are People of the Book, not infidels," she said. His war-time programmers had perhaps gone a little too far to ensure Khalid would be zealous against the enemy. Christianity was the dominant religion of the Union of Worlds, but the war's root causes were political and economic, not religious. "There are many worlds of Christians that Allah has not destroyed," she said. "We are simply witnesses to a tragedy... Unless, *insha'Allah*, we have arrived in time to prevent it?"

"Even if I still had my weapons, I could not hope to destroy an entire moon."

"How many people?" she asked, still trying to comprehend the scale of the disaster.

"About forty thousand."

"How do you know they are Christians?"

"Our probe sent these back." Images flashed up of the town. Red and green dominated the colors of decorations placed on buildings and streetlamps. "The English words indicate they are celebrating Christmas. It is a holiday for greedy children, who demand gifts from their parents. They are celebrating three months late or nine months early according to the Christian calendar."

"They may have adjusted the calendar to their world."

"According to the data, Christmas is a winter holiday, but it is now spring in the colony."

With a flash of insight, Intissar said, "It is a mercy, for the children. The adults know their world is ending, but they have told their children it is a special extra Christmas so they will not die in fear."

"It's wrong to lie," said Khalid. He often resorted to the black and white rules of his religious programming when presented with an ethical dilemma.

"Mercy is a gift from Allah," she said. "May Allah have mercy on them all."

"Do you mean what you say about mercy?"

"Of course."

"Would you..."

She waited a few seconds, but Khalid did not continue. "Would I what?"

Finally, after almost a minute, Khalid said, "I'm sorry, I lied to you when I said I could not destroy an entire moon. I've had to overcome a security override in order to tell you the truth. Would you save the lives of these Christians if you could, at the cost of your own life? And mine?"

Would she? She didn't want to die, but how could she live with herself if she allowed forty thousand to die? Her mouth went dry, but she said, "Yes."

"It is a violation of the Jordan Convention to activate my wormhole generator within a certain radius of astronomical bodies. Such a procedure was used as a weapon of planetary destruction during the Confederation Civil War, and has been banned ever since. If I did so right next to that moon, the wormhole would try to swallow it entirely, and fail. The moon would collapse to a singularity and the energy given off would create a white hole."

"And that would save the colony?"

"I calculate that the energy should discharge disproportionately along the axis of the wormhole mouth, mostly avoiding the colony world if, *insha'Allah*, we come in at the correct angle. They will merely see a very bright star that fades over the next few days. But if we're going to do it in time, I'll need to max out the inertials along a least-time path to the moon."

Intissar closed her eyes. During the war, she had been willing to die to kill the enemy. This felt like a better reason for her death. "Let's do it."

The moon loomed stark white, pushing the black of space to the edges of Intissar's vision. An inset display showed the planet they had just passed.

"The infid—people below expect to be destroyed," Khalid said. "They will think it a Christmas miracle when I create the wormhole, especially since a bright star figures in their holiday celebrations."

"Yes." Intissar smiled. "They will never know that the *Drawn Sword of Allah* defended them. But we will know, and Allah will know. It is enough."

After a moment, Khalid said, "It is enough."

The calm of knowing one was doing right filled her heart as the final minute ticked off. "Is there something traditional to say when giving gifts for Christmas?"

"Yes," said Khalid. "There is some disagreement as to whether it is forbidden for a Muslim to say it to a Christian, but the phrase in English is 'Merry Christmas.'"

Looking at the display of the planet, Intissar said, "Mer—"

"A SPECIAL EXTRA CHRISTMAS" AUTHOR COMMENTS
BY ERIC JAMES STONE

I was a founding member of a group of writers called Codex when it started in January 2004. In order to give ourselves incentives to write, we started having various contests. In January 2013, I participated in the Weekend Warrior contest, in which you had to write a flash fiction story based on a prompt given Friday evening, with a deadline of Sunday night. The contest runs for five weekends in a row.

For week one of the contest, there were five prompts. Two of them spurred my imagination:

1. Write about a weapon or tool with an unusual quality (invisible, time-traveling, sentient, etc.)
2. Write a Christmas story (or Hanukkah, Kwanzaa, Yuletide...)

Prompt #1 turned into *Drawn Sword of Allah*, with its sentient artificial jinni. And Prompt #2 gave the story its Christmas theme.

I had previously published a few far-future science fiction stories with religious characters, and I decided to try that again. To make it more of a challenge, I decided to write from the point of view of a

Muslim. (I had previously written a Muslim as a major character in my novel *Unforgettable*, but he was not a point of view character.)

The original title of the story was "—Christmas". The original final line was: Looking at the display of the planet, Intissar said, "Merry—"

I thought the title being the unspoken ending of what she says was clever, but the consensus feedback I got was that it didn't really work.

Something else I tried that didn't work was a brief prologue in italics:

"But what will we tell the children? We can't stop them from seeing the comet. It'll be huge the night before it hits."

"We'll tell them... We'll say it's the Christmas Star, bringing a special extra Christmas. We'll go all-out—the best presents ever for every kid in the colony."

That's where the new title came from, but the prologue just felt really awkward to me. So I moved "a special extra Christmas" into Intissar's dialogue and cut the prologue.

After running the story through my writing groups, I let it sit awhile (years) before finally getting back to it and revising it.

Part of the reason I had let it sit so long was that I was worried the story might offend Muslims. Some people might call that Political Correctness, but as a Mormon, I've seen my religion poorly portrayed, and I had no desire to do the same to Muslims.

So I asked a friend whose husband was an Egyptian Muslim if they might be willing to be sensitivity readers and give me feedback.

Fortunately, they liked the story. In particular, they liked the inversion of the Muslims-as-suicide-bombers trope—the suicide bombing in the story is to save people, not kill them. They also had suggestions, all but one of which I incorporated into the story.

The one suggestion I did not incorporate was to use "God" instead of "Allah," because that is the English translation of *Allah*. I could see their point, but felt that English readers expect Muslims to refer to "Allah" and it would feel off to them if I used "God". When I submitted it to *InterGalactic Medicine Show*, I told the editor about the suggestion, and he agreed with my judgment call to use "Allah."

IN THE CARDS

BY F. J. BERGMANN

F. J. Bergmann is the poetry editor of *Mobius: The Journal of Social Change,* managing editor of MadHat Press, poetry editor for Weird House Press, and freelances as a copy editor and book designer. She lives in Wisconsin with a husband and a horse or two, and imagines tragedies on or near exoplanets. She has Rhysling Awards for both long and short poems and Elgin Awards for two chapbooks: *Out of the Black Forest* (conflated fairy tales), and *A Catalogue of the Further Suns* (first-contact reports), the 2017 Gold Line Press competition winner. A Writers of the Future winner, her work has appeared in *Abyss & Apex, Asimov's Science Fiction, Analog Science Fiction and Fact,* and elsewhere in the alphabet. She has competed at National Poetry Slam with the Madison Urban Spoken Word slam team. While lacking academic literary qualifications, she is kind to those so encumbered. She thinks imagination can compensate for anything.

A squat gray building of only thirty-four stories, with five rooms on each floor: this is how Blake had been taught to visualize the Deck prior to prognostication. The building—the imaginary setting for the array—was immaterial, intentionally dull and nondescript. It was best to use plain burlap or canvas to cover the table, something austere that would intrude as little into the richness of the card imagery as the stone or cement exterior of a luxurious spa or hotel. Each level contained the five conditions representing the totality of human relationships: Leader, Lover, Child, Follower, Slave. There were various analogues for those positions: King (or Scepter), Queen, Princeling (or Minister), Knight (or Sword, or Soldier) and Page (or Servant, or Serf), always placed to correspond to one of the directions north, east, south-east, south, and south-south-west. The building, it was understood—and by analogy the table upon which the cards were placed—was a deformed pentagon.

The levels themselves provoked endless (well, even more endless) arguments about what *they* ought to be called and which should take precedence. Mimicry (called Japes by some) was nearly always at floor level, but whether it should be enumerated as Zero or One proved irremediably divisive. At various times in the past century or two, holding to one ideology or the other had been punishable by death—admittedly, painless death by guillotine, as opposed to some of the more severe penalties in the legal code, but death nonetheless.

Blake had originally become interested in card-reading because he liked the images on his grandmother's card decks, which were family keepsakes. He hadn't thought of it as a profession, but he'd done a few readings at parties, for friends who were in on his secret, and gradually word had spread. He considered himself lucky to have found a position as an art-gallery intern, given his paternal grandmother's execution for having espoused the Oneist stance. His grandfather had fled across the southern border with his infant son, Blake's father, to return a decade later when the Oneists attained supremacy —they had awarded him a handsome pension as widower of a heroine. But since then the central government had begun to veer increasingly toward Zeroism once more, and the descendants of erstwhile exemplars were now suspect. Fortunately, Blake's mother's family doted upon her son and assured him they were highly placed enough to warn him when it was wise to flee, if not to offer protection.

Blake told no one at work that he himself was gifted in the use of the Deck, despite most of the gallery's merchandise consisting of highly stylized renditions of the Greater Levels (it was rumored that a stock of both Zero and One paintings rested in a secret vault, each set to be displayed only in times of political certainty. His deceased grandmother had been a skilled divinatrix, which had directly led to her undoing. She had paid no attention to political whims, and one night had been summoned to a Cabinet Minister's ball to serve as one of the entertainments on offer. The fact that she'd insisted on using a Slave card to represent the Minister had not been helpful...

Through a network of escorts, concierges, and majordomos who sometimes sought out card-readers for their clientele but demanded a substantial portion of his fees in return, Blake had achieved a certain reputation, assisted by an elaborate female costume and a mask. He would don and remove various articles of clothing on the way to and from assignations, usually in the privacy of baths, theaters, and cinemas. By the time he arrived where he was expected, no one would have recognized him as the meek young man who was the gallery assistant. He would have taken on his grandmother's gender as well as the mantle of prowess—and prowess it was, despite her death. She had chosen to be arrested while her husband and son escaped, rather than sacrifice her child's life for her own: the only choice the cards had granted her.

Lately, Blake had become concerned about some of the readings he had given, the arrays that had arisen from his shuffling and their manifest interpretations. In the preceding month, there had been an unusual increase in Knight cards, especially the ones with images of actual swords, and nearly all the Minister cards had been reversed. More ominously, there had been a preponderance of Cauldron, Pestilence, and Mantis levels in close conjunction, and the Stars and Planets had only occurred in reversal. When he had cast for himself, the Queen of Swans immediately followed by the King of the Road indicated that imminent flight would be wise, even though his mother's relatives told him he had nothing to worry about.

Last night he, in his guise of Madame Méduse, had told a prominent kimchee purveyor that there was a risk of corrosion (the Sword of Vengeance was immediately followed by a reversed Queen of Wastes). The fellow had taken it as a warning about his copper fermentation vessels and had angrily vowed retribution upon their maker—but Blake knew that the bribes paid by the purveyor to Comestibles Bureau representatives had encouraged their shake-downs of other businesses that were less inclined or able to pay, and there were rumblings of disquiet throughout the local provender manufacturers. Blake chose not to contradict him and had been given a lavish tip, accompanied by a large jar of extra-hot kimchee.

This evening's function was the aftermath of some government-department dinner. There were a surprising number of military uniforms, the wearers of which were drunker than Blake liked. Every now and then some sot would try to fondle him, despite his giving careful attention to projecting an impression of decrepitude. (Usually this enhanced his aura of expertise.) He had prudently removed both Zeros and Ones from the deck months earlier.

The man who approached him now, weaving slightly, bore not only insignias of high rank and a chestful of medals, but also an expression of deep hostility and a nearly full glass, which appeared to be his third, fourth, or possibly fifth. "So you think you can tell the future, granny, eh? Let's shee whether you know anything. How'sh the operation tomorrow going to pan out?"

An aide-de-camp at the officer's shoulder began a frantic muttering in his ear, but a heavily gold-braided uniform sleeve waved him away. "Let's shee what the cards say! Let her have at it!"

Blake smoothed out the plain gray linen cloth, shuffled, cut and began to lay out the cards, the Inner Circle first. The Significator was the King of Volcanoes; just as well, that would flatter the fellow. He began his spiel about rank, prestige, power, importance—but the man interrupted him angrily. "I know all that shtuff! Whatsh happening tomorrow, thatsh what we want to know!"

Blake continued to turn over cards, intending to be as conciliatory as possible. His mind was spinning: why the fixation on tomorrow? Why so many military officers, who seemed to be engaged in some incomprehensible debauch or celebration? He watched more carefully, placing the cards automatically, and saw a few of the officers flashing each other surreptitious but unmistakable finger-signs.

Zeroes.

Trembling slightly, he focused on the cards. Everything in the Inner Circle was a Fire sign: Cauldrons, Torches, and of course Volcanoes. Most were reversed. The Outer Ring was even more foreboding: Mantis, Mammoth, Raptor, Avalanche; Swords everywhere. The five Outer points were all Slave cards, all reversed: Flower, Well, Cottage, Field, Palfrey. All that would be lost first in whatever endeavor this array was attempting to reveal. He raised his head to meet the general's grinning face.

"Well, we don't need granny to explain thish one, do we, boysh? Sheen a few spreadsh in my time. We'll cut through them like butter!" There was a muted cheer from the other officers who had gathered around them in curiosity.

Blake noticed that not all the aristocrats seemed to be in on the joke. A number of them bore puzzled or dismayed expressions. A pretty young lady approached him, trailed by a lieutenant who had eyes for no one else (and didn't notice the general's meaningful glare). "Could you do mine next? Mamma doesn't like me to stay up past midnight. She says I need my beauty sleep!" The girl giggled as she took the querent's chair.

Blake shuffled again, murmuring platitudes. He cut, had her draw her own Significator. The Slave of Flowers. He was careful not to look at the general. Attempting to conceal his consternation, he cascaded the Deck back and forth from hand to hand a few times, then began laying out the other cards.

Next was the King of Volcanoes, reversed. He could not help seeing the general's predatory grin as the lieutenant let his hand trail down the girl's arm. The remaining Inner Circle was entirely Volcanoes. He set his jaw and laid out the equally unpleasant Outer Ring (Ruins, Mantis, Flood), then the Outer Points, all reversed, all Fire: north, south-south-west, south, south-east, east...

YOU, TOO, CAN DISGUISE A LACK OF EXPERTISE BY MAKING SHIT UP!

BY F. J. BERGMANN

There are very few fields in which I can claim to be an expert. My story "In the Cards" is largely focused on cartomancy—specifically, Tarot-card reading—and while I own a number of attractive decks and have even written several poems based on the Tarot, I am no expert in divination... and not exactly a believer either. But you don't have to know much of anything where speculative fiction is involved! And this is just one of its many advantages over mundane stories set in the real world, where those confusticators intent upon "fact-checking" seem to have set themselves a goal of harshing your squee. There's a certain kind of magic involved in deception that is inherently satisfying and, for me, one of the major pleasures in creative work. Writing takes a lot of energy that I prefer not to squander on specific research, world- or character-building; excessive detail and accuracy is not only inexpedient, but can actually put off some readers, who also have imaginations and may not enjoy having them constrained to the extent that those writers who feel the need to describe or explain every aspect of their work might envision.

Keeping facts a little fuzzy, setting a bit tenuous, characters somewhat undefined, will allow readers to connect their own varied and unique experiences with your narrative by *not* introducing excessively specific details that might trip up or put off a reader. (This is especially recommended with erotica, where what you consider hot may be perceived as squicky or dramatic by certain readers—and these tend to be vociferous and unkind in their reviews and start-numbering.) Vagueness is not only far simpler to research and write, but it allows for more individual interpretation. Regardless of how skilled a given writer may be, reading is a participatory event, and giving the reader just enough material for them to do a substantial amount of the imaginative labor themselves is not only an efficient use of writing time, but results in a mutually pleasurable interaction. As a reader, I find connecting the dots of an implied occurrence vastly satisfying; as a writer, this saves me a good deal of trouble. And if you are writing horror, uncertainty in the narrative is your friend, producing, as it does, uncertainty in the reader.

I attended the Viable Paradise workshop (far too many years ago); one tip I remember vividly was that if actual firearms of any sort were mentioned in one's work, it would be best to insert the word "modified" before naming any specific weapon. Apparently gun aficionados obsessively call out the smallest deviation from fact... but it's hard for them to assert that a *modified* Uzi, for example, can't be used in whatever manner you have described, especially if you avoid specifying exactly what those modifications are.

Therefore, to ward off the disparagement of purists, the Tarot deck in my story (I also did not use the word *Tarot* for the deck in question) is a *modified* deck, containing many suits, Court cards and Greater Trumps that do not exist in any Tarot decks with which I am familiar. The story itself is rather dark, so a plethora of the named but fictitious suits are equally unpleasant: Cauldron, Pestilence, Mantis, Vengeance, Wastes, Volcanoes. The imaginary layout of the cards is not fully described either, but parts of it are referred to as the Outer Ring and Outer Points, which are totally made up, but intended to add gravitas. It amused me, since an obviously non-computerized society is depicted, to use Zeros and Ones to represent violently opposed political ideologies—names as arbitrary as the Big-endians and Little-endians from *Gulliver's Travels.*

Vaguely implied décor is also a useful way to elicit a more elaborate and/or harmonious setting, both in terms of the physical surroundings as well as those who inhabit them, without having to go to the trouble of being nitpickingly specific. The initial metaphor of visualizing the card spread as a piece of depressingly Brutalistic architecture analogous to the exterior of a "luxurious spa or hotel," serves to suggest that the buildings in this world may be similarly lacking in coziness, as well as foreshadowing the ominous developments in the story, although the description is sufficiently spare to allow the reader to form their own mental image.

However, I assure you that the kimchee mentioned as incarnate in this world can be assumed to be precisely analogous to that of our own dear Earth.

A similar economy—that is, recycling existing ideas rather than having to go to all the trouble of inventing them from scratch—can be achieved by placing endearing but inaccurate or obsolete tropes on other other planets or in other universes. This, after all, is the basis of most alternate histories. Do you regret the debunking of Martian canals? Surely a planet exists elsewhere or elsewhen with lovely winding canals, their blood-red mossy banks overhung with the arching tendrils of lethal florifaunal predators, awaiting the arrival of jet-skiing humans or human-analogues, whose juicy brains are just sitting there atop their fragile bodies, waiting to be plucked and slurped from their eggshell skulls.

Borrowings and allusions to the real world serve to create a sense of depth in both a created world and the stories set within it. Distortions of reality can be improvements, or admonitory dystopias. For horror in particular, the Uncanny Valley effect is generated by what is only slightly removed from reality rather than utterly alien. We writers rarely (almost certainly never) generate narrative out of whole cloth; we are taking, like master artists throughout human history, inspiration from those who have gone before.

After all, we're all making it up out of used words.

. . .

Because the majority of my written (and, FYI, published, and award-winning) work is in the form of poetry rather than prose, I am perhaps a bit more sensitive to the appropriate use of cliché and lyricism—and letting the reader do the heavy lifting.

In SF and fantasy, we make good use of clichés and conventions, which we call tropes. FTL, unicorns, time-travel, dragons, teleportation, enchanted swords—the science behind some of these concepts burgeons and evaporates on a regular basis, but these warhorses remain as archetypes and genre indicators. However, these tropes also reflect current culture and change with it—stories from the "Golden Age" of pulp literature now seem sadly out of date or even offensive.

What's often most interesting to writers and readers is to take someone else's good idea (or, for that matter, bad, outdated, and/or offensive idea) and mess with it in an unexpected way. As an example of this sort of thing, I immensely admire Mat Johnson's *Pym,* which is a hilariously entertaining riff on both Lovecraft's Cthulhu mythos and Poe's *The Narrative of Arthur Gordon Pym of Nantucket*—and the racism endemic in those works.

I am not a fan of the excessively lyrical, but spending some time on details and descriptions, especially if you can use language and vocabulary in unexpected ways, will give a much richer effect than a bald recounting of what you are proposing as factual within your imagined world. Excessively mannered or elevated language, even in high fantasy, becomes wearisome—pay close attention to the level of diction you employ and consider lightening shit up from time to time.

I like events in a story, including conclusions, to be implied rather than heavy-handedly spelled out. Remember, creative omissions can save the writer a lot of unnecessary work! I hope it is obvious in my story that things are about to go very badly indeed for the One faction, without having to describe the morrow's outcome. While the longer the work, the more detail and exposition is expected (and, usually, needed), there is still a limit to how much elucidation is necessary. When Gollum falls into Mount Doom, clutching the One Ring to his bosom, we do not need to be told that Gollum dies and the Ring is destroyed. Not only that, but letting the reader make assumptions based on incomplete data can be useful once subsequent works are embarked upon. Should J. R. R. Tolkien himself ever be raised from the dead (or an AI equivalent of him be generated), it is hard to imagine that he could resist a series of sequels (especially considering what the screen rights would be worth!), and the resurrection of Gollum and/or the Ring would easily achieve an opportune impetus.

Think of writing speculative fiction in terms of a distorted mirror, showing us a twisted, bent and incomplete version of reality that in the furthest shadows of its reflections generates monsters and transforms ordinary entities dwelling on our side of the looking-glass into allies, mentors, or gods in a universe that can only be imagined.

TURTLESPEAR
BY C. WINSPEAR

Chris Winspear is an Australian author and Narrative Designer who won the Grand Prize in the *Writers of the Future* contest 2020, and is currently developing *Frostpunk 2* at 11-bit Studios. His spec-fic stories have also appeared in *Teleport Magazine* and the anthologies *Short and Twisted* and *Empty Sky*. He has a master's of creative writing from UTS, Sydney.

His *1001-Nights*-inspired saucy fantasy *Nights Under the Sun* will be released late 2023. Find out more at cwinspear.com.

I was eight the first time the great city on the back of a turtle stomped through the forest east of my tribelands. My father took me, his only son, to walk along with all the curious and the desperate to see its great steel towers and its thousand lights, one for every star in the dark western sky.

As we watched, four men approached the turtle with cliff-climbing spikes and rope. They ascended one scaly leg of the beast. The crowd whooped and cheered as they almost fell to their death again and again, and yet they continued to climb.

"Shouldn't we help them?" I asked.

In his excitement my father answered. "Unspeakables." Then he realised his mistake and hid his face from the elders beside us.

It was the first time I heard the word, but I knew the concept, ironically, without it having been explained: sinners who our elders had declared living dead. Worse! It is not a sin to speak of the dead.

The men ascended, miraculously, all the way to the low wall at the edge of the turtle's shell. Spearmen dressed in gold and black looked down from the parapet, and an official in blue heard their cases.

We could not hear what was spoken, but we saw the unspeakables stomp and wave their hands. When that failed, they huddled together to confer. Then they ascended the wall. The first reached the parapet only to meet the tip of an awaiting spear. The second hesitated, accepted his fate, and then followed onto the same bloodied blade. The third flung climbing-spikes at the spearman, to no avail, and the last leaped off the wall to bounce off the turtle's leg as he fell.

"They're gone," I said.

"Who's gone?" my father asked. His eyes told me: *do not speak of the unspeakable.*

Someone told him my sisters had come against his instructions and were watching from the back of the crowd. He ran off to catch them. I tried to follow, but lost sight of him amongst all the strangers in the same sheepskin jackets. Then I almost lost myself amongst all the strange bushes with purple poisonous fruit. Eventually I made it back to where he left me, alone now, and watched the turtle stomp on south.

A spearman peered back from the wall. He raised the bloodied end of his spear towards me, not as a warning, but as a salute.

And I knew, always had known, that someone had been taken from me, someone my sisters and my father and the elders never mentioned. The few times I asked about her were rewarded with a swift slap to my face. The void in my life had no name, but it did not stop me from wanting—even so young— to fill the emptiness, or from despising those who could have saved her.

I hated the spearman whenever I thought about that day over the coming years. I wanted to show the ghost of his black and gold armour that I, unlike my father, would never fear the elders and would show as much illicit kindness as I could to the unspeakables.

My sisters encouraged me with their own small successful circles of change. I began to say out loud that I would congeal my rage into a tower in the path of the turtle, a spear of my own, so the great city would have to avert its course. Then I would stand on the pinnacle and shout the names of the unspeakables down to both my tribe and the people of the so-called great city.

My father heard I had been saying these things. He came behind me at dinner, slung an arm around my neck and choked me unconscious. When I woke, I found my battered self tied to a barrel tree with cliff-climbing rope.

"The elders are afraid of our strength." My father was never good at explaining anything.

He whipped me with an occoro reed switch. I cried for him to stop and he whipped me some more. Trickles of blood flowed down my hands and legs and he whipped me some more. His arms cramped to the point he could barely raise the switch, but he whipped me some more until the sun set. I passed out.

In the morning he placed muni, a sort of salt-like sap, over the wounds, which hurt more than the original punishment. He left me in the sun without water, and in the cold without fire or blanket, for two days and two nights.

I grew feverish, hearing music when there was none. Four unspeakables came and tied more rope around my arms. A man in gold and black armour walked around me and sliced me with the end of his spear. An elder apologised, explaining this ritual would save me. Apparently it had saved him long ago, and he looked forward to the day I would come to understand the way of our world and become an elder myself.

"I don't know what's real and what's not, uncle," I mumbled. "But kindness is always kind."

"And pain is always humbling," the elder responded. "Even the strongest column cannot support a home if it's not in its right place."

I grew too thirsty for thoughts. The next morning, the fourth after choking me into the black, my father sliced my bonds, poured water on my lips, and embraced me. He had tears in his eyes when mine had all dried.

"I am so proud of you!" he cried.

Something in me broke as I realised the switch had hurt him twice as much as it had hurt me. My poor father loved me more than anything in the world. It was not his fault that the Maker Tree gave him an abundance of love in his heart, and yet—to express it—such poor tools in his hands.

I don't hate him, not anymore. He was strong, and strength was the one gift he could pass onto me. To hate him would be to hate myself, and I don't have time for that, not anymore.

I pretended piety, and the elder who'd overseen my cleansing had a vested interest in my improvement, so I sank deeper into sin than most before I had to leave, before I unspoke myself.

How could I not go? It was a sin to taste the sweet teki fruit reserved for the elders. It was a sin to dance after darkness in a clearing of trees by the light of the two moons. It was a sin for a man to kiss another. It was a sin to lie naked in the forest with a single lover, let alone two. It was a sin to speak with an unspeakable, let alone to marry one in the darkness with only the stars as our witness. It was a sin to bring yet another into the covenant, as if there were no knots to bind three ropes together as one.

Even as I sat with the elders and discussed the importance of order and survival, all I heard were the yearnings of my own soul. Later, I would meet many who struggled with this pressure to listen to the laws of the world without, rather than the truths of the world within. For me, there was no option, no hesitation.

It helped that my transgressions were more or less ignored. I brought in an extra quota of teki and tillagrain, and I hunted the most joyflicks out of anyone. The only person concerned was my father. He'd wounded himself hunting and now moved too slow to hit me, so instead he frowned and shook his head.

"No more," he moaned. "No more."

I scoffed. I was ashamed of him then. He had grown weak, a husk of himself, light and frail and ready for the winter breeze to take him away.

My debauchery could have carried on forever if someone hadn't spotted me taking our leftovers to feed the unspeakables.

I returned from hunting to find no one would greet me. I wasn't shooed out of town though, so I know this was the Rite of Penance, a warning. My sisters came to me in the morning.

"If you'd given them leftover tillagrain, or even meat, no one would have cared."

"But no, you had to give them teki."

"To unspeakables!"

"It doesn't matter," I answered them. "I'm leaving."

They glanced at each other, not seeming to understand, or maybe too afraid to accept what I'd said.

"I'm going to hunt and gather for the unspeakables and we're going to live in the forest under our own laws, created by love and reason alone." I smiled. "And one day you'll ask to join us."

They argued with me while I gathered a rucksack and a pallet and a spear and every useful item I could carry. Then they scattered as I stood before the elders' tent and shouted "Jui" and "Olp" and all the unspeakable names I knew. I walked out of the village and no one met my glance and no one called after me.

∽

I learned later my sisters dragged my father—too old now to resist them—before the elders so he could beg them to forgive my outburst. The elders made them wait a whole day outside their tent before they deigned to see him.

"You've come to beg forgiveness for your family?"

My sisters nodded and nudged my father forward.

The offended elder, who'd purged me and vouched for me, glanced down with eyes like daggers. "Then beg."

"Please forgive my daughters." My father fell to his knees. "And please forgive me. I have no son."

The love of my life was twofold.

Olp: tall, pale blue skin from his mother's winterside blood, built like a bear. His laugh echoed off the stone cliffs and filled the whole valley with joy. He would leave our favourite nuts and flowers by our pillows. Patient... Patient... Then he would fall into a deep rage and hit harder than my father. Afterwards he would have such an adorable sullen face neither of us could stay mad at him. At night we'd both lie in his arms and feel like the ground itself loved us.

Jui: skinny, sharp face, wide eyes, nimble like the joyflicks she hunted. Her smile could turn a winter breeze into a summer gale. Her jokes cut neater than steel and left us with teary eyes. Direct and bold, she demanded to know how we felt at all times, but she herself would disappear to be alone without a moment's notice. When she returned, she would lead us in songs of mending, in which we'd sing out our concerns and our love and together find the many paths to keep our love burning. Often—too often, perhaps—she would run her hands over us, and we knew this night's sleep would be sacrificed for that love.

I will not speak of the sins which brought their exile. Know they never harmed anyone. They were unspeakable because they had fallen for someone forbidden, or someone forbidden had fallen for them, and to the elders love is the signing of a contract—as if one were purchasing land or cattle—while we knew real love strikes between two people even at the most wild and inconvenient of times.

"A three-star system," a scholar from the great city later described us. "Rare, but not unseen."

When I think of joy, I remember lying on Olp's arms in a clearing under two full moons with a belly full of teki fruit. Jui runs her hands over us, and Olp's laugh bounces off the distant cliffs as we begin the three-partner dance we sculpted from ourselves.

Jui had to hunt often because the ice traders had been told not to deal with us, and muni preserves but ruins the taste. We knew our hunting would trouble the tribe, but we didn't understand quite how much until my sisters came into the forest one day and told us to move to new grounds, or there would be violence. I admired their courage, so much so I felt the need to best it.

"Tell the elders to speak with us themselves," I said.

"They didn't send us," the eldest said.

"Would it harm you so much, brother, to move a little east?" my middle sister said.

"We also have to tell you... father passed to last winter's wind," the youngest said.

Fury pulsed up my arms. How dare that man, who had beaten me to make me strong like iron in a forge, first discard my name and then discard his own body because of the opinion of a bunch of old fools! I wanted my father to stop this pathetic act and come out here, beat me senseless and drag me home—for one taboo I would never break was to raise my hand against him in return.

Now he was gone, and I felt I had to slam myself against something hard to make sure I did not follow him along that path of weakness and decay, to make sure I stayed strong, to make the ghost of him in my mind proud again.

I roared. "The only way we're moving is if we head west and start hunting elders instead!"

But before my sisters' frowning and tearing faces had left my sight, and even as I smashed the earth with my naked fists, I began to regret my words. No amount of pain would bring my father back, and no force in the world could change the decisions he had made—or that I had made.

~

It happened so fast. It was like I went to sleep and got stuck in a bad dream. I would spend the rest of my life in that nightmare.

I figured they would come for me, or Jui. We never considered they would sneak around our traps and routes and slay Olp while he was out collecting flowers and spice. We found his body face down in dead leaves.

Jui screamed at the occoro reeds and the western stars and the eastern sun and the Maker Tree and demanded they breathe life back into our lover. When they didn't answer, she took up her spear and began singing the songs of hunting with the names of elders as her quarry.

She expected me to pick up my own spear, but my fists were still bruised from uselessly smashing the earth when I heard of my father's death, and so instead I picked her up whole in my arms and embraced her.

"Please, Jui. Stop. I can't lose you, too."

She pushed me down and marched. I begged her the whole way to the village, and she didn't respond to me once. She didn't even face me, as if I'd become unspeakable amongst us unspoken.

It was unlike her to be so rash. She raged because this is how Olp would have raged. She raged on his behalf, because he could no longer do so.

She marched right into town and charged at the sentry by the elder's tent. His eyes went wide and dark blood spilled onto a pile of teki fruit. I couldn't watch. I turned around and ran as the sounds of raid bells and the screams of old men filled the valley.

I didn't look back. I could not be like those black and gold spearman who killed without qualm, and all this was my fault. Olp had died because of my arrogance. Jui had fallen into a rage because I was too weak to hold her back. What use would it be to kill some of my uncles and cousins? All this death, all these ends, all because I wanted to lie under the moons with my lovers and never have to get up, not for my father, not for the elders, not for the winter wind.

If only I'd learned to sway just a little in the breeze like the occoro reeds, then I could still be lying on Olp with Jui's hands on my chest.

I knew they would come for me, so I fled, hunting joyflick and harvesting tillagrain when I needed, following the river east and north. I went beyond the border of my tribelands and was shooed off by a party with whom I had no common language. I travelled east to the path of the great turtle, a swathe of ground no one dared declare, for every twelve years the great city would come and crush the soil, and all the plants growing there would wither in respect.

For about six months I moved north until I found a cliff very close to the turtle's path. A group of four armoured men camped at the precipice. I spied cliff-climbing spikes and rope.

Their chief only had to take one look at my face to know I would join him. I would become one of those unspeakables who threw themselves at the mercy of the city on top of the turtle, and I would die at last and see Olp and Jui in the Danceless Land.

But I didn't understand why these men put in so much effort and preparation just to die. We could leap off the cliff at any time.

"Fool," the chief said. "Don't you know? If you slay one of the black and gold who guard the walls, you may take their place."

I grew to know them: the chief with his foul moods, the father who could cook a feast out of barkscraps, the son who sang odd lovesongs to himself, and the smith who got drunk off one taste of bitterdrop and howled at the moons. After many months drilling in the art of shield and spear, which is very different to that of hunting, I came to know these men like brothers. They appreciated my strength, and even without knowing much of their tongue I enjoyed their company. But they never quite trusted me enough to lend me a set of armour, even though the chief had two of plate steel, stuff from the winter-lands practically invulnerable to any blade made here on the summerside.

When the turtle finally came blundering up from the north, I stood ready to conquer alongside them. The cliff stood just as tall as the wall on the turtle's shell, so we could toss our spikes and rope and then fall like birds of prey upon the spearmen on the wall.

The turtle approached. Its steel towers glistened in the sun, each with a hundred lights like little eyes. The cliff shook with each stomp of the turtle's huge legs, and for the first time I stared into the dark abyss of the beast's single eye. It did not seem to have a soul. Closer, I shivered as I made out the spearmen on the wall in their black and gold armour. Slay one to become one.

"Why should we let you in our great city?" the official in blue asked us, his voice carried on the wind by strange magic.

I answered, the only one willing to try conversation before violence. "I was exiled from my tribe, not for hateful sins, but simply because of the people—"

"That's not of import," the official interrupted. "What can you offer?"

I blinked. "Anything. I'll do any work you need. I'm strong. I am good with knots and hunting—"

"This is a waste of time," the chief cried. He prepared to throw his cliff-climbing spike.

"I see you are handsomely armed, and I grow tired of re-rostering the wall," the blue official responded. "So this is my offer: slay those next to you, and the last one standing shall join us in the city."

The chief dropped the cliff-climbing spike. We stood silent. We had been training for months now, as close as brothers. The turtle took a step. In a few minutes it would drift out of reach of our ropes. And I was the outsider...

I ducked as the tip of a spear shot over my head. I spun and stabbed down, hitting the son in the unarmoured flesh at the back of his ankle. I raised my shield and stepped back as the four of them turned to face me.

"How long will your alliance last?" I asked.

"We'll deal with you first, then–"

The son, wounded and probably thinking they'd go for him next, stabbed the chief through the back of the neck.

The smith, on the right, turned against the limping betrayer, charged his shield, and sent them both to the ground. The father on the left buffeted at my own shield, then turned to the others. He was too late. His son lay still with a gouge across his neck.

"That's my boy!" He charged the smith, bashed away his spear, bashed away his shield, bashed off his helmet, and bashed in his face. He would have kept bashing the smith's skull until there was nothing left, if I didn't seize my chance and kick him off the cliff edge.

I stood there, panting, unwounded, with four men dead at my feet.

"Now you are one of us," shouted the official, and to my surprise it was they who tossed over a rope.

I don't remember much of the first few weeks except for my duties patrolling the wall. I was surprised to find some female spearmen, and indeed I had some hope for my sisters when I heard there were more female council leaders in the city than men.

It occurred to me if Fate were feeling particularly cruel, my mother could be here. Over time, she might hear my name. She might check my eyes and know I was hers. But would she greet me, or would she despair to know her son had followed the same violent route through life as her? I for one hoped she had managed an honest life and death and wasn't like me up here defending the same plodding city I had once hated and vowed to destroy from below.

We passed my tribelands and I was glad to have the black and gold armour to disguise myself. I looked down at the crowd, noting a few less elders, the result of either Jui's vengeance or a bad winter breeze. I didn't see my sisters, which seemed odd. Indeed, many things about the crowd looked odd from up here: the way people stood in clumps, the way they seemed to cower away from the elders at the centre.

No unspeakables approached the turtle with cliff-climbing spikes or rope, and I breathed out a sigh of relief.

When the crowd below began to dissipate, I noticed a young girl alone staring up at me. I raised the end of my spear towards her in salute.

The city was an amazing place, by all means. Light at any time. Mechanical and magical wonders. I always felt alone there. I could not share the city folk's fascination with silly impractical things. I came to know that the spearmen guarding the wall were considered an undesired necessity. It seemed all tribes had their elders and their unspeakables, and people could not have paradise without a wall, complete with monsters without and scarred heroes within.

I took many lovers over the years, but they could not peer into my soul as deeply as Jui and Olp, because no matter how well I spoke the city tongue, and no matter how many times we made love, there still seemed to exist a chasm between them and me. They were of a world of paper and magic and science, and I was one of fire and lying under the moons with a belly full of teki and joyflick.

One lover took me to the tallest tower of the city. I looked to the east, into the neverending sun which blazes even when the nightfog comes, and saw the vegetation fade out to the blanched white of the summerlands. Then I looked to the west and saw the light fade away and the reeds turn to dark ice. At night the breeze brings the fog from the winterside and covers the earth with darkness, except up on the towers which soar higher than rain. The lover explained that the turtle marched perfectly between the two sides, and its feet harvested the earth to feed the city its cornucopia of delightful food. Like the others, this lover saw these things with a sense of wonder, and they took pride in teaching me the way of the world.

"I don't think we should see each other again," I said.

I fell into a routine; the years and the years slid past. I got a bit better at the city tongue, I made some real comrades along the wall, and after blooding my spear in a huge battle on the winterside I found myself promoted to captain. But I might as well have been a walking corpse. Even when I realised twelve years had almost passed and I would soon see my tribespeople again, I felt nothing but dread at the thought of killing someone I might have known.

Why should I feel any worse than normal? It was a sin, whether I knew my victims or not, and I slayed someone every other week. That was basically my gift to the world: swift death. I had become the black and gold monster I'd seen on the wall as a child, the black and gold ghost which had paced around my body as my father tortured me in a misguided and unsuccessful attempt to save my soul.

"Changing course!" the navigator shouted. Rare words. "Obstruction!"

I ascended the guard tower over the head of the turtle and glanced north.

A shadowy tower stood where my tribelands met the turtle's path. My heart stopped.

What other explanation was there? My congealed fury had at last risen to challenge the great city on top of the turtle, as I'd promised my sisters those many years ago. Soon I would face myself.

I prepared my men for battle, but I also told them violence would be the least effective of our weapons. When we were minutes away, I saw the tower was made of stones and the entire tribe waited at its base. I prepared cliff-climbing spikes and rope, for no logical reason. I received the command directly from my soul.

Only when we were very close did I make out figures of three women at the precipice of the tower, which stood even taller than our wall. The city's navigator had turned too late and the edge of the turtle's shell grinded against the rock, billowing smoke. Somehow the sound reminded me of Olp's laugh, and the smell reminded me of Jui's flint.

Despite the clamour, I made out the voices of the women above. I immediately plunged my cliff-climbing spike into the tower of stones and tossed a reel of rope over my shoulder.

"Brothers, if you've ever sought paradise, grab this rope and jump with me."

They stared at me as if I had transformed into an ice bear before their very eyes. My lieutenant took up the rope. Then my sergeant. Then a surprising number of the rank and file, who I never realised had come to look upon me as a father. We ran along the wall to keep our place against the cliff while the turtle continued its inexorable march. When we reached the edge of the shell I leaped off and rapidly plunged more spikes into the wall to hold the weight of the men behind me.

The turtle slid away beneath us. My men descended the rope, but I went the other way. I climbed the ragged pile of rocks knowing I would be fine, I would taste teki fruit, I would soon lie again naked in a clearing under the moons, and I would work in my homeland speaking for all those lost and all those found; for the women at the pinnacle were my sisters, and they were calling my name.

A NEW MYTHIC
BY C. WINSPEAR

Part I: Brave New Worlds

An author steps into a huge second-hand bookstore and smells a distinct miasma of timber, paper, and dust. They gaze on thousands upon thousands of weathered books.

"What can I possibly articulate that hasn't been said a thousand times before?" they think. Their fantasy & sci-fi passion drives them to question further: "What is the benefit of creating new worlds when there are so many already here in front of me?"

The books seem to glow as they offer points to consider.

Every Story is Written for the Present

In Philip K. Dick's *Ubik*, an apartment is a collection of individually coin-operated objects, where one must pay a dime to open a window and a quarter to use the dishwasher—to the point where an impecunious character finds themselves unable to open their front door and escape their own home. Delightful, and perhaps even relatable to the

1969 audience contending with the spread of vending machines, but an unlikely vision of the future from today's perspective.

In the recent *Cyberpunk: Edgerunners* anime, the protagonist cannot pay for the washing machine to finish its cycle and is almost locked out of the unit entirely for not paying the rent. The same story! Only now the tale rendered in the style of a Japanese anime and with an instantaneous digital payment system—all far easier to understand for the contemporary audience, and more likely to strike an emotional or intellectual response.

"Why is it important to be easily understood?" the ambitious author wonders. "Surely my next work will be a timeless classic, and readers will enjoy using their intellect to peer through the mists of anachronism and discover the full cathartic potential of my opus."

Perhaps. Or perhaps the only difference between a teacher and an author is one provides answers while the other provides questions: both find their work more effective if their audience can easily understand the message conveyed, and thus it helps to use elements familiar—if not contemporary—to the audience.

New Thoughts Become Thinkable

Fortunately for us artists, the world is constantly changing and providing new concepts to be explored.

Ann Leckie's *Ancillary Justice,* winner of the 2014 Hugo, Nebula and Arthur C. Clarke awards, includes what is essentially an out-of-sync error in a personality spread over multiple bodies/instances. Such a concept is somewhat difficult to fathom by today's audiences (fortunately sci-fi readers are the brightest minds around), but it would be near impossible to those unfamiliar with the internet, digital files, digital backups and the cloud.

We can understand one save file not matching another, and imagine if that save file was a personality, but such discussion would be fruitless thirty five years ago. This story is achieving the rare feat of exploring new conceptual territory.

As humanity acquires new ideas, it demands new myths.

Part II: Better Dreams

The author ponders this metaphysical experience of extracting wisdom directly from old glowing books, and they conclude their own subconscious genius must be projecting on the dusty tomes.

"Would it not be easier to base my story in the well-known milieus of Star Wars, Lord of the Rings or Harry Potter? What exactly makes one world greater or more appealing than another?"

A Story for the World, or A World for the Story?

Consider the success of 2020 novel *A Memory Called Empire* by Arkady Martine, another debut novel which won both the Hugo and Nebula awards.

Its worldbuilding is stellar: deep, fresh, and full of inspiration from non-Western history, but most importantly aligned to the novel's core discussion: the tension between personal, local and global cultures.

The world supplies a local traditional culture for the protagonist Mahit to be raised in, and also a contrasting invader culture which she cannot help but adore. Going further, it supplies technology for a different personality (a different self) to reside inside Mahit's mind. Her fragmented mental state mirrors her abstract connection and disconnection with her home culture, making these themes much more tangible to the reader. Likewise, the various power and status rituals of the dominant nation accentuate the complex relations between states, cultures, and the individuals who cross borders to seek peace and an overall greater good. It all fits together.

The story could not be so successful if it dressed itself in whatever world lay around in the author's mind. Instead, the world has been measured, cut and sown like a couture garment over the body of the novel. It has not been treated as a sacred idea carved in stone but rather edited as rigorously as any other element in the novel to explore the novel's core themes.

No Holes in this Cheese

Although the reader will only encounter the tip of the iceberg that is the story world, they will be able to infer much more than they can see and will take delight on finding a robust universe where all its elements adhere to the same inherent logic.

The creators of *Avatar: The Legend of Korra* were tasked with imagining the world of *Avatar: The Last Airbender* as it goes through an industrial revolution. The society invents electricity and mass education—but this is a world with magic. Ingenuously, the creators figure mass education meant the greater portion of "benders" could reach the ability of the masters in the previous series, and fire benders assist with electricity generation by flinging lightning into generators to earn extra coin. Only benders have this opportunity, and so the inequality of our real-world industrial era is exacerbated by the inherent inequality between benders and nonbenders, the latter conceiving technological marvels in order to rebel against the magically empowered ruling class.

Every element of the worldbuilding is coherent and consistent with the others, creating a convincing reality that invites the audience to imagine the sea of possibilities beneath what they've seen. Do water benders assist with naval trade? The reader is free to take delight in imagining their own answer.

Part III: The Mythmaker's Manual

"Ok, ok," says the author. "So how do I construct one of these beautiful worlds?"

On this note the books remain silent. The author runs their hand along the perfectly bound spines; their fingers are covered in dust.

The author goes home and washes their hands. Instead of writing, they play *Hades*. They've just started the game and they wonder if they'll ever leave the underworld. They also wonder if they'll ever finish their novel. Consumed with frustration, they put down the controller, open up Scrivener and create a blank document.

Designer Universes

The author glances at their trunk novels, which will never be published but do an excellent job of propping their monitor up to the ergonomically correct height. They realise, in a horrifying flash, the main mistake they made in those manuscripts.

Our first ideas are rarely our best ideas.

Yet we feel "this is the way the story goes." Once created, we believe the world is the way it's meant to be, unmalleable. This may be because as readers and residents of our own world, we cannot change what is written. It takes authors time to learn they can be the god of their universes.

Just as we edit prose, we can edit the world. Just as we plan out our plot, we can design our world to suit the story. Eventually, as with characters, the world will take on a life of its own—but by that point the author's work must be already done. This is the difference between growing an Eden and growing a garden of weeds.

The Iceberg Becomes Interesting When Viewed from the Titanic

An author never talks to the reader during the storytelling, but remains out of sight, like the cameraperson of a Hollywood production. The story is told by a narrator, who may be one of the characters —or who may slide their narration in and out of the point of view of the characters. For this reason, every word in the novel should reflect the voice of this characterised narration.

No modern-day person (and therefore no relatable modern narrator) watches someone save a phone number and thinks along these lines:

> "Electricity whirled through the device as the woman pressed the screen, which used the conductivity of her skin to locate her input to be processed as co-ordinates of a mouse click by the software, which then called the relevant functions to write the number in a 32-bit format on its drive."

No. We simply say, "Zoe saved his number."

And yet in sci-fi, writers often have their narrators remark upon the workings of the ship's engines, the nanobots which sew together wounded flesh, or the precise working of their beautiful weapons. As high-level concepts, these are cool, but to go down into the inner workings of each is to give a lecture no one asked for—especially if these details are not based on factual scientific theories.

"But what about hard sci-fi, like *The Martian* by Andy Weir?" the author ponders. In this case, the character is very much concerned with the technical details of their situation, as this is necessary for their survival. The Martian's success is it manages to add tension and humour to a scientific thought experiment about surviving on Mars.

Tell Me Something I Don't Know

The author considers *A Memory Called Empire* and *The Martian,* stories which enhance their appeal by educating the reader or inviting them to conceptualise a theme (and educate themselves).

"But how do I make my fantasy romance feel like it's teaching you something?" the author ponders.

Stories needn't be packed with facts in order to feel insightful but can also provoke your reader into creating their own opinions on the subject—even through the worldbuilding. For example, having some true botanical facts in this fantasy romance may prove educational, but the reader may be further entranced by a magic system based on flowers and smells—especially if the novel discusses seduction and attractiveness as a form of power.

Sometimes the novel's theme is known before writing the first page, sometimes it's only understood after the first draft. Once you know what you're writing, you can figure out how to write it.

Before that, do you dare ask yourself why you're writing at all?

ASH FALL
BY A. X. ANDER

There is a rumor that A. X. Ander has worked in more career fields than most people have fingers and toes. That probably is true. There is a rumor that Ander has lived longer than anyone living or dead. That probably is not true, but then no one has found the birth certificate. What is true is that Ander's work has won awards or been a finalist in the Writers of the Future and *Amazing Stories'* Hugo Gernsbeck contests, among others. Sadly, the rumor that you can ward Ander off with garlic has been proven untrue.

~

Cut 1: Day One

What's past is prologue, or maybe the prologue lies in the future, even if unwritten.

I, Yugl—the matriarch of our kin-tiger village and shaper of life through destruction—recall the prologue before now, and the prologue before that. Until now, we'd not questioned them.

Whenever the village birthed a new litter, we teated the cubs' milk. A week after, still blind yet able to crawl, they performed their first life test: the rapscallion-crawl.

Humans have questioned our ways before. They've always thought their ways superior and all beings must think as they do, but their design is not ours. Before our cubs' first kill, the cubs invariably asked, "Can we do this kill?"

And we replied, "You have completed a far more brave task: the rapscallion-crawl." This instilled the necessary fearlessness required among our kind.

Carrying our cubs down to the river in slings, we purred or growled about the weather as if what lay ahead were a frolic in the tall grass. We placed our cubs by the river lapping at its banks. The river's whistle reeds were melodic, reverberating low in the breeze, lulling listeners to sleep. However, during full-force gales, the reeds screamed. Whether lulling or screaming, they led many cubs astray.

Over the piping reeds, mothers called and their children crawled to the cacophonic voices. Some sang without ceasing, shifting keys from dulcet to *agitato, allegretto, animando, appassionato, furioso*, and *patetico* masking the plaintive tones from seeping through. Some only barked when their prodigies seemed to lose their way.

Some mothers moped, refusing to call. Their cubs tended not to live. Was their silence because we'd harried these mothers as cubs? Or did we harry because we knew they'd be unfit mothers? Either way, since they cared not for their young, it was best to drown the cubs—dodging a misery that might have lasted years had they survived. Crawling into the water, the rapscallions would enter the scaly maws of the Sbqsaq and integrate into their muscle, sinew and bone. If you can't become a predator, unite with one in the flesh.

In the midst of the rapscallion-crawl, we fell silent. Our ears pricked up, hearing muffled cries. Inside a sticky wine barrel by the river, a human cub—or whatever humans call their whelps—wailed, its face red as carrots. We named it Maximilian after our best guess of the marks scratched on the barrel. We suspected its family were victims of orc raids led by the Mad Queen, a creature that claimed to be human but bonded with goblins and orcs.

As long as she didn't attack us, we didn't question. We were, after all, animals. We raided rivers for fish, dens for bears, and prairies for goblins and their demon-dog herds. Unlike goblins and orcs, we ate our kills as all respectable predators do, honoring their victims with life after death. Study the Sbqsaq. They know.

Goblins and orcs wasted so much good meat, letting it leak blood and rot in fields, drawing disease-bearing insects and vermin. Their fires scorched life to useless carbon. Sometimes they maimed victims, letting them limp through life. There are no more disgusting beings.

Since Maximilian's parents had sealed their creature in a cask, it must have had great value, so we fed it until the new owners showed up to collect, and we would exact our fee.

The human creature grew. We fed it until it was clear its relatives weren't returning, and it was too late to throw it back into the river for the Sbqsaq to feast on. None of us had a taste for human flesh, so we could not improve his life that way, either.

Worse, most of us fell in love with Maximilian. The whelp seemed to care for all life. Even the cubs who died in the rapscallion-crawl. He would greet all woodland creatures and exchange information about hunting, battle, and one-on-one combat. This amused us because the tribe had all it needed to know of war. To us, he was like a rabbit armed with a splinter before a bear.

What else could we do? We raised Maximilian as one of us. He was wild, wilder than our cubs, dashing off gracelessly across dusty plains on two limbs to investigate everything. His favorite word was "Go, go, go!" and he ran, ran, ran.

The only thing that gave him pause were stories around village bonfires, lit in the fire-pit circled by our bamboo huts. That night, awaiting the council, I told the myth of the Great Tiger who judged all animals. His eyes fastened on me as if I might alter the tale. Well, I might, a little, depending on what the tribe needed to hear. It was only when the others spoke about their hunts against great bear today that he looked into the fire. The flames mesmerizing him, as did the smoke made fragrant by the bear thigh roasting on a spit for him.

My lover, Hedig, glared at me and shook his head. He thought I coddled Maximillian. I should have told the tale how the Great Tiger judged the first tiger for wanting the first bear to be a tiger.

Unlike kin-tigers, humans apparently cooked flesh. As a child, he spat out raw meat, so we assumed he was vegetarian until meat fell into the bonfire. After it cooled, we fed it to him on a lark and he gobbled it up.

The village council entered the gathering, one by one, avoiding Maximilian's gaze and nods. His eyes drifted, latched on to flecks of ash that drifted down like whirling bits of paper—a thing I must have gleaned from the words of a bard or a Mad-Queen survivor whom we chose not to eat. Any language we wanted to survive was kept on wood marked with claws. Humans had too many words they wanted to keep.

When the council formed a semi-circle before the bonfire, Hedig gestured to Maximilian and spoke to the council. "Purge the rapscallion from the village. He eats and defecates too much. He does not think like us, and he did not do the crawl. He is almost a man, but has not adopted our ways but the ways of every creature he meets. Destroy him before he infects us."

I sensed Hedig's jealousy for this creature whom I cared for as a son, but what could I do? I asked, "Any speaker for the cub?"

Around the bonfire, all ears went flat, all tails drooped except Hedig's, snapping to and fro. This surprised me. I thought most of us loved the beast, but I could not stand alone and disagree.

Maximilian stood. "Then let me do the crawl."

This made the whole village laugh. Of course, he could do it as an adult, but it was a good argument. He could pass the test now.

"Silence!" Hedig's snarl made the whole village go still except for the crackling, popping, and shifting of logs in the bonfire. His eyes were only on Maximilian, though.

"Don't I get to speak?"

Hedig pointed a claw at him. "Your people used to have all the words. Now only we get to have words."

Maximilian held back his frustration, but his brow furrowed, eyes narrowed. "What is this hypocrisy? All acts of silencing deserve the same reward."

Ears perked, tails snapped side to side, deep-throated growls arose, but no one would reply. The languages of the human body was not unknown.

Hedig replied, "I challenge you!" And he leaped without awaiting consent. To attack without consent was itself a death sentence, which Hedig must have known but did anyway.

I sighed, expecting the death of this son-like creature. Hedig was three times the size of Maximilian and probably four times as strong. But apparently Maximilian's long chats with the foreign woodland creatures transformed him. He moved swift as a demon-dog, limber as a fish twisting its body away from Hedig's outstretched claws.

Hedig stretched his limb to turn with Maximilian, but Maximilian used Hedig's momentum and awkward angle, to twist that limb behind Hedig and plant his face in the dust with a foot. After two minutes of grunting, whimpering, and trying to jerk his body free, Hedig surrendered.

However, Maximilian refused to let go until the council promised to not kill Hedig for his crime. A strange request, since Hedig's death by combat would save us from having to execute him.

We debated and granted life to Hedig and permanent guest status to Maximilian—neither a citizen nor a foreigner but something in between. This satisfied him.

Maximilian grew into a strapping young man, and he argued against the rapscallion-crawls, but what proud destroyer listens to people of peace? They are weak. Destruction carves strong citizens.

Even weak creatures get lucky. Away from the village, Maximilian was chopping trees into woodchips and firewood when the orcs crested our hill of golden wheat grass so near harvest. They set the wheat ablaze, stirring a strong headwind that made the whistle reeds scream.

As village matriarch, I herded the mewling young kin-tigers among the tall reeds by the river, to hide them from the orcs, thinking the reed screams would cover the cries of our cubs.

Unaware of the orcs already lurking in the reeds, I missed most of the village destruction as I was the first to get clubbed in the head. A short-lived mercy.

Cut 2: Rage / Hate

Ash fell like snow, drifting over the bamboo village. My senses returned, hazily. I was atop an overlook and I'd been locked in a bamboo cage for a night and a day, my paws chained to the earth like a frothing demon-dog. The Mad Queen, a human (sorceress?)—in her bejeweled crown stolen from some unfortunate monarch—towered in her golden palanquin over my prone form, delighted by reaction.

I was weak from fatigue and hunger, so her orcs held my eyelids open. My eyes watered until they became painfully dry. They stung as smoke rose from the huts of my kin.

The yips and howls of my kin-tigers haunted my ears. Hedig was weighted in chains. They humiliated him, stripped him of fur, yanked out his claws and fangs, plucked out his eyes, and castrated him.

I struggled against my bonds until I lay, panting. I'd bitten myself and supped my own blood, the only thing that sustained me.

The Mad Queen sat imperious in her palanquin except for the least crack of a smile, watching me as she called for more deaths and sipped chamomile tea, pinkie finger raised.

"Yugl, this may seem unfair." She sipped, laid one ankle atop another, and adjusted her tasseled silk pillow embroidered with the foreign word "Hammurabi." "But this is justice. Your great-great grandkin devoured my grandfather, leaving my mother fatherless. Now you get to feel the same pain and wander the world homeless and kinless."

I could have said that that was a blood debt that they owed, but instead vowed, "I will not only end your life, but every creature dear to you. One day, before I claw your throat to ribbons, I will match wound for wound on your kin three for one that you killed today, and you will whiff an inkling of what I feel."

The Mad Queen laughed and laughed. Without breath. The laughter seemed to last minutes as if she were a black disc on a rotary machine stuck in a groove. Where that image came from, I cannot say.

For the first time, I questioned: Maybe reality was an endless chain of pain: birds eating worms, kin-tigers eating birds, worms eating kin-tigers. We transform with each feeding, become other than we are. Why not? Are we not animals? Go on all-fours?

Was I even alive? Maybe I was dead and, despite being a good person, had tumbled to the land of the damned.

Finally, the Mad Queen broke from laughing and bade me to watch my village while goblins dumped scalding buckets of green, gooey stimulant on my fur, refusing my refuge in the escape of unconsciousness.

When the village fires were smoldering embers, the Mad Queen's orc minions came and went, beating my body with charred bamboo. Again and again. Pain broken only by lectures about how my kin caused all the trouble in the world.

Had Maximilian been right about peace? Or was our fear of weakness what made us vulnerable to attack?

My brain shuttered itself from agony and mapped its revenge.

Maximilian found me, delirious. I half-remembered his ax splintering and splicing the bamboo and vine that kept me pinned down. And he fed me as a child at the teat.

He built a new hut around me, salved my wounds, brought back kills and regaled me of their valiant struggles as once we'd done around the village bonfire.

Slowly, my body and mind healed. We debated whether it was

fair to avenge the death of my people. His answer was enigmatic:

"We are not here for murder, but to kill the Mad Queen and, through this, ourselves. As the pines that require fire to be reborn, sometimes death is necessary for rebirth. For the butterfly to be reborn, the caterpillar must die."

Perhaps that was answer enough. I trusted him. Sometimes we must trust to take the next step or remain forever entombed in the cocoon, lost in a smoky fog. The end would bear out whether what he said was true.

Together Maximilian and I trained our bodies and honed our minds in the ways of the warrior. One day we'd topple the Mad Queen, and the smoke would clear.

Sequence Breaking

Snow fell like ash, drifting, dusting the crinkly brown grass, occasionally dotted with carnations poking their heads out of the ground too soon. Scraggly pines patchworked the steep mountain slopes. We stood by the mouth of a cave that might prove a useful resting place, should we need to rest there for the night, though we never seemed to tire in our pursuit.

Mid-way in our journey toward the Mad Queen's castle, Maximilian produced a map. It crackled as he unrolled it across a tree stump. A tree stump meant a logger must have scoured the area to keep his family warm.

Maximilian's index finger traced out our position by the cave and the march through the mountains we still needed to make. There was the cabin of a former guard to the Mad Queen who had a key before being discovered a traitor. There was the locked gate that kept giant iron men from taking over the world. Further on was the village of witches. Nearby lay the city that had written us for our help.

"Here." He stabbed the map with a forefinger. "There be dragons."

As he rolled the map back up, I gazed into the gray sky. Snow fell steadily but never collected on my tawny forearms. Odd.

Even the arms themselves looked foreign to me. Why would something of mine feel foreign?

"Yugl," shouted Maximilian, "stop gazing at your arms and use them to claw the enemy." He thrust his scimitar at the cave.

From its mouth poured hordes of goblins on demon-dogs and orcs on armored elephants, screeching and bellowing.

In the heartbeat after I raked out a demon-dog's eyes and thrust the beast aside to skewer the leaping goblin with my spear, I glanced at my arms again. "Where did I get such massive limbs?"

"The better to slay our enemies," Max yelled, voice hoarse and scratchy.

A demon-dog, fur-less but for his coat of red flame, whooshed by and knocked Max under it. I whacked the demon's back with the base of my spear, its spine cracking like a walnut. Max disemboweled it with his scimitar.

With no chance to catch our breath, armored elephants with green-glowing eyes charged us. I leaped up a pine, and a tusk narrowly missed puncturing my ribs.

Maybe—an inner voice suggested, a voice mine and not mine— *you should give up this silly war and forgive this Mad Queen. Retire to a quiet Caribbean village.*

Caribbean?

My brain replied with images: the ash fall, the tiger howls, Hedig's dismemberment, and that damned pinkie finger.

"Never!" I fell upon an armored elephant and claw-raked the side as I slid down to spear its underbelly.

Maximilian shouted as if reading my mind: "Kill first. Question later."

Horde

Our wounds healed quickly. I suspected that there was magic just being in the presence of Maximilian.

For miles we jogged without a stumble or the stab of the rocky earth biting into my frost-numbed paws. We crossed one mountain and another. We jogged without toil over mountain grass, snow and the rich earth loam that filled our nostrils.

Everywhere we went, goblins riding packs of demon dogs attacked. Where did they come from? What were they guarding in the middle of nowhere? What did they live on? How did they get paid? What did they spend money on and where?

Maybe they were independent hunters and fur traders, who sicced themselves on passersby in case they might be poaching. But they attacked without seeing us carrying animal furs or carcasses.

En route, we retrieved a key from the dead guard's cabin that opened the cursed gate where giant iron men tried to crush us with their feet, fetched a prince from a coven of witches, saved a city in flames from hordes of dwarf orcs.

The boar-tusked dwarf orcs trapped us in an alley, surrounded by enemy and flame. I flashed my spear and claws, and Maximilian wielded that scimitar with the pearly handle. We dispatched all, but one gutted Maximilian, his intestines spooled on the paving stones like a warm white worm. Death was certain.

He stuffed the guts back in, hand holding the wound in place. In the next second, the blood stopped flowing the flesh sealed together. He was ready to hack zombies. I followed a powerful healer.

On the one hand, this all felt natural. On the other, my body hung off me like an ill-fitting cloak. My claws instinctively knew the best way to rip apart zombies. Part of me felt it all unnatural.

A hulking bear with teeth that curled like a boar's, growled from an outcropping at my shoulder. It leapt. Max decapitated it. How often had he saved me?

Why did we just kill a bear? Maybe it was lonely and wanted to play. Not everyone who is not us need be a blood-crazed enemy to be dispatched. All of this good meat, rotting in the fields.

Maximilian sheathed his blade, yanked out a bow, and notched an arrow as though plucking it from air.

Belatedly, I noted the great flapping sound like the snapping of tent canvas in the wind. Overhead, a dragon circled. It breathed fire, torched my fur to short, blackened ends.

Max fired off three arrows. Each hit their mark: the heart. The dragon tumbled, end over end, like a giant sack of potatoes, although I couldn't say where I'd seen a sack of potatoes. It thudded to the earth, shaking the ground beneath our feet.

Because Max's skin was shredded and bloody, I said, "We are weary. Let us rest our bones and build a campfire, cook these beasts over charcoal, eat, and talk of our loved ones and cubs."

He shifted his weight from one foot to another as he did whenever we spoke. Although his face merely flickered a change, I sensed anger, simmering, building steam. "Fine," he said.

He did not help me collect the wood, build the fire, skin the bear, or skewer the meat on the spit. He seemed surprised that I could. "What will you look for in your wife?" I asked.

He swayed, foot to foot. "Come. We are healed and must yet kill the queen."

I turned the spit, browning the meat evenly. "She can wait." My mouth watered. "What kinds of traits do you most admire in women?"

"I'm not marrying."

"Really? A handsome, strapping man like you?"

He yelled at the heavens. Into the fire I dropped the stick with which I prodded the meat. How had he misconstrued my compliment? He inhaled before articulating his yell into intelligible speech. "You're breaking the illusion!"

"Pardon?"

He hit a pine so hard that snow fell from the tree and hit me on the head. I felt the heaviness of it, the cold wetness of it. But when I went to paw off the snow, it was gone. No melting, no damp fur.

He slumped down the rough bark of a saw-tree as though the bark's serrated edges were nothing. "Why do you have to ruin everything, Ma?"

I glanced at my tawny fur and at his furless skin. *Ma?*

"How did you break the code?"

"Code?"

"Yes, yes, the programming."

The language he spoke was familiar yet foreign. I stared at the cooking meat. Why cook? Kin-tigers ate food raw. Was I evidence of reincarnation? "Help me understand, Max."

He turned so that I could not see his face. "You aren't awake."

I said nothing, waiting for him to continue. When he did, his voice shook. "In a coma." Idly, he sharpened his blade against the saw-tree's trunk. "I uploaded you, so you'd live forever and help me slay monsters in the game."

The word "game" triggered memory as a shout might trigger an avalanche. My tiger tongue formed forgotten but primal words, tumbling out before I could consider their meaning: "You'll rot your brain playing those stupid things."

"Gah!" He withdrew his blade from the pine and sliced at my chest.

The ancient tongue had motivated him to murder. I expected to breathe my last.

I touched my dry, intact chest and felt no wound. The blade passed through me as though I or it were a ghost. Was I already dead?

His gravelly voice spoke our ancient past, explaining events I'd missed, and stirred dormant memories like invisible ink activated by lemon on an old, familiar map. Where my map held dragons, he sketched them back in.

Real-Time Corruptor

A pregnant, meth-addled mother without family stood before me in the wood-paneled courtroom. She was a lean woman, supposedly in her twenties, but she looked over forty with blotchy red sores over her face, saggy bags hanging under her dull eyes. Every time she open her chapped and scabbed lips to speak, I winced, glimpsing a mouthful of missing and broken teeth.

Since I was not a tall judge, I sat on books—on top, a slender leather-bound copy of *The Code of Hammurabi*. They made me feel like I towered over adversaries.

The lawyers and I examined street cams of the addict living in abandoned houses. She claimed that wasn't her. The video's facial recognition software said otherwise. Not that anyone needed the software.

I sipped chamomile tea, pinkie finger raised, and stared at her over my specs, which scrolled a long list of past crimes. I waited for her to confess without using the list. Her lawyer feebly protested the videos could not be used due to privacy, but he was overruled. Only criminals required privacy.

The case was simple. I breathed deep through my nose to hide my sigh from the courtroom camera and whiffed the woman's body odor which explained the disarray of her apartment, the trash rotting in every room, the broken washing machine. The court cam captured my involuntary sneer. "My child, how have you allowed yourself to fall so low?"

She mumbled something vulgar I chose to ignore. I ruled the young woman an unfit mother. The state would raise the unborn child.

She begged, "Have a heart, Judge Kilborne. I was a foster child. I got no fambly. He don't got no fambly either."

I leaned over the podium, and leveled the gavel at her. "Young lady, were I you, I'd consider how I got myself into this mess and how I'd get myself out. Case closed." I pounded the gavel.

As they were cuffing her, she shouted, spittle flying, "I know how I got here. Human beings, that's how. Nobody cares about bodies who don't think like them. One day you will hurt, and I hope you got somebody on your side 'cause I ain't got nobody."

Clearly she had a baby, thinking that it would understand her like no one else. Babies aren't crutches, dear. Frowning, I slid off my tower of books to exit and eat some conscience-clearing éclairs.

That night in her cell, the cams recorded her: She scratched an itch. A mundane act. She seemed to pretend to hallucinate, going into labored breathing, which everyone thought must have been feigned because how could she have gotten drugs? Just a desperate cry by the weak for attention.

When this carried on for suspiciously too long, and the seizures looked too real, a guard opened her cell, checked her pulse, fetched another guard to rush her to a nurse who ordered the ambulance to send the woman to the hospital.

The forensic pathologist said she'd had enough methamphetamines tattooed into her skin to knock out a herd of stampeding elephants. Bruising the area released the drugs into her blood. The medics didn't save the mother and barely saved the premie.

Though past our prime, Pa Kilborne and I decided to raise the premie boy as our own. We were upstanding citizens doing a good deed. Pa was an owner of a local hardware store and a Lion's Club member. We got a write-up on page ten of the local e-news aggregator, but the fame was less than fifteen minutes.

Maximillian, afflicted by ADHD, challenged us more than our previous three children rolled into one. The kid, a pyromaniac and firecracker fiend, set fire to his bedroom three times, once almost disastrously. He moved faster than either of us could handle. I must admit we did not handle well the discipline for his storing firecrackers in the neighbor's grill. The neighbor yelled every time Max lost a ball, so we thought the firecrackers were payback. Sadly, we laughed with our son, when the neighbor lit up his grill. We failed to greet the irate phone call with the proper stoicism.

Max loved animals. The neighborhood dogs and cats followed him everywhere. It was how we found him when he hid himself in the closet, our corgi whining outside the door to be let in.

Although the rearing method has fallen out of style, we educated the boy "by the seat of his pants," just as generations of Kilbornes had done before us. Our own children had become a doctor, a state senator and a CEO under this method. Why change a good thing?

We loved Max as if he were our own, but he got wrapped up in video games. He didn't socialize enough except through the video games as if they were reality. Locking him in his room was no punishment.

Once we'd left to hardware convention and returned to find not a single chore done. Trash cans overflowed. Dogs and cats unfed except for their sniffing out the occasional soggy Cheetos stuck to the carpet. Bags of chips, crumbs, and moldy microwave dinner trays strewn across his bedroom. He was still playing some fantasy role-playing game with Conan or Tarzan avatars and tigers against an array of grotesque monsters when we arrived. How silly he looked in his VR gear—without one wit's sense of reality—madly waving arms at the imaginary monsters, shouting at invisible demons like a schizophrenic.

We exploded. He could have killed the pets from starvation or eating the wrong food, he could have brought disease-causing insects and pests, he was of age where he needed to be responsible.

More than anything, we feared the consumption of fantasies would distort his already scattered sense of how deal with the real world. We'd met a couple at the convention who talked about her teen who'd killed herself. She showed us a site that said the too much gaming led to depression, social anxiety, lack of motivation, poor emotional regulation, interpersonal conflict, suicidal ideation. All of which he'd done.

So, yes, when we got home, our belts came out. We lectured, whipped, and left, lectured, whipped, and left. We were so aggravated, we didn't know the other parent had already disciplined.

With his VR gear, he'd recorded our outrage. In three dimensions.

"I'd planned on uploading it to the world," Max said inside the VR world as cache after cache of memory opened. "But in the morning, I was just as ashamed of myself as I was of you all."

～

Ten years later, Max met an activist named Reed at a gay club; they went home, hanging on one another's shoulders, singing the remake to "Baby, I Was Born This Way."

Max showed Reed the VR. Reed wanted to destroy our lives by showing the world what hypocrites we were, putting people behind bars when we were just as flawed.

Max said no, but couldn't explain himself, so Reed uploaded the recording anyway.

Max spluttered, finger shaking in Reed's face. "You want to destroy lives after witnessing seven minutes of them at their worst? What if I showed the world you at your worst? Did you witness the lifetime of their love? The way I'd wake in the wee hours as a kid, bawling due to lightning, nightmares, monsters lurking in the cave of my closet, and they would take me to the living room rocker and hum to me until I fell asleep again? The way they kept me from poverty and homelessness, passed around to different foster homes? You want people to know you were born this way, but baby, they were born their way. Who appointed you judge? No one. You are exactly the thing you hate."

Reed trashed Max's apartment before leaving, not to mention trying to turn all of Max's friends against him.

Max wanted to ruin Reed's life too, after that, punching holes into his own apartment's plaster walls. He even consulted a lawyer to discuss lawsuits, but eventually stopped entertaining the notion, as he didn't want to be as slimy as Reed.

Ten million people watched the VR: seven minutes of corporal punishment gone wrong. The excess embarrassed me—not the whipping. At least, that's what I told myself.

To reporters waiting for me on the sun-blinding courthouse steps, I stated that that was long ago, and Pa and I had repented. I refused further questions.

Nonetheless, people online demanded that Pa's store be boycotted, name brands withdrew from selling to us, even friends quit buying at Pa's hardware store, lest they receive threats from their employers. Facing bankruptcy, he had a heart attack and a quadruple bypass. Friends and our own children distanced themselves to protect their careers. Voters didn't renew me as judge.

Years passed. Savings dwindled. We mortgaged our home to eat and pay taxes. People still discovered that nasty VR, and for them it was new. It displayed everything they hated about our "kind," so they loaded our email addresses and physical mailboxes with threats. We dreaded looking into either box, so we didn't. Bills piled up, ignored, unpaid. Collectors came knocking.

One writer who dubbed herself the "Mad Queen" wrote us to say when we'd been at the grocery store and what we bought. Our credit cards filled with charges we had to dispute.

One morning, after stumbling into the kitchen for a pot of chamomile tea, I found Pa Kilborne on the couch in his frayed pajamas. He stared unblinking at the ceiling.

The savings account emptied. I am ashamed to admit that I dabbled in drugs. I needed an escape as I had nothing and no one. Movies shared a gospel of hope that seemed a lie. It was either drugs or suicide—the latter seemed cowardly to me.

A documentarian and photographer briefly interviewed me inside an abandoned apartment building—the oldest user in residence. He photographed me as I warmed my hands on old law books flickering in the fireplace, paper flecking off and fluttering through the air. A broken window pane let snow drift in. I neglected to mention to the documentarian how I used to send users to prison.

Memory stopped there.

Secret Level

Glancing at my tawny arms, I asked, "Is this hell?"

Maximillian hugged me, audibly weeping, though his eyes were dry. "No, Ma. Because my VR killed Pa, I had to save you."

"Save?" The fur prickled at the back of my neck. Simultaneously, I lusted for the hunt, for my claws to rake deep gouges and my teeth to sink into the flesh of the Mad Queen's minions. My heart thumped faster. I fought back the urge. "How is this saving? What kind of life is this? Why would I waste my life as you waste yours on fantasies?"

His fists clenched and unclenched at his sides. "What do you think your TV shows are? What bearing do your soaps have on the reality of love? Dad's mysteries of everyday murders solved in forty-two minutes instead of the real-life crimes of passion where both parties often share some blame? Where's the realism in your news when every journalist selects, slants, and spins what to present? At least my fantasies don't pretend to lay claim on reality."

Kin-tigers don't weep, but my eyes seemed to have sprung a leak. "How do I know that I'm really me, not some bit of code?"

He braced my shoulders. "I don't know that you can. I will say that without your presence here, the kin-tigers are solitary creatures. Without your presence in my life, I'd have probably died as my birth mom did. You saved my life. You've done good in this world and the last."

I opened my mouth to reply, wanting to argue, but the words clogged. I cleared my throat. "How can anyone who causes pain claim to be good?"

He held me with his head on my chest. He spoke in my fur. "No one is good. All we can do is try."

I patted him on the back with one paw. That was part of the answer. Everyone is the Mad Queen.

As barbecued bear cooled in my paw, visions crept in: the bamboo village of my youth, the ash falling, my mother playing with me as a cub when I surprise-attacked her—even when she didn't want to.

Those visions mingled with my human father weary after work in his rumpled suit, sitting down to a tiny stool at a tiny table, drinking imaginary chamomile tea with his pinkie finger raised, playing dolls, and intently listening to me complain about my imaginary husband and our wee problem child.

I gently pushed Maximilian back, bit off some bear meat and spat out the tasteless, cooked flesh. I brushed off the endless snow fall from my furry arms. A growl rumbled at the back of my throat. "Time to unwrite the past and skewer the Mad Queen."

REWIRING THE WORLD: THE TRANSFORMATION STORY
BY A. X. ANDER

From *Harry Potter and the Philosopher's Stone* to *WandaVision*

I. Metamorphosis: A Personal Story

At the sage age of four, my best bud and I argued about which had the greater value: the nickel or the dime. As all brilliant logicians know, the larger the coin, the more the value. Ergo, the nickel has the greater value.

My friend, the poor fool, dared to believe otherwise. Seconds after his "Wanna bet?" we shook grubby hands and marched through the sliding glass door to ask the world-renowned experts: our parents.

After the erupting adult laughter subsided, to my red-faced shame, I had somehow lost. These supposed experts couldn't explain why. The ground shook beneath my feet.

Civilization is slapped together from Cracker-Jacks and gingerbread, mortared with mayo and a buttery lack of logic spread on a firm foundation of hard knocks. Hopefully, that bet didn't lose me much more than a nickel.

This seismic shift represented a tectonic transformation in thought.

2. The Transformation Story: A Definition

For our purposes, a transformation story is where a character moves from one state to another. Generally, the larger the transformation, the more powerful the story, so long as the characters evolve through a believable arc of change(s). The transformation could be as simple as an interior one. Think of all the interior transformations in Charles Dickens's *Great Expectations*. Sometimes the change is exterior as well, such as Pip's change in fortune.

But let's shift to more visible changes, such as transformations of bodies into plants, animals, birds, landscape, different genders, objects, etc. One will encounter these in Ovid's *Metamorphoses*.

The transformation of the body isn't the only kind. The world itself may change—or seem to. Examples include John Cheever's "The Swimmer," *WandaVision*, *The Matrix*, or J. K. Rowling's *Harry Potter and the Philosopher's Stone*. These may create greater seismic shifts in thinking. Often the change is in the eye of the beholder. The world may not change but one's perception of it may have.

3. Seismic Shifts: A Partial List

In an earlier draft of this essay, someone said that transformations don't occur in real life. *Au contraire*. This list is dedicated to the naysayers:

Humans have built industries and philosophies around people transforming themselves: self-help, religion, psychotherapy, etc. One late-night show I've listened to on the radio in the US and Honduras: *Unshackled*—a show listing transformations that are not only religious but often personal in nature, correcting behavioral and addiction problems. At present, they are nearing 3,800 true-life narratives, over the last eight decades.

Despite "epiphanies"—a term coined by James Joyce—to discuss non-religious character arcs, some like to argue against people changing. But it happens. Deathbeds, birthing rooms, jailhouses, school houses, foxholes, and steel street-sign poles which someone was talked into licking when the temperature dropped below zero.

Grander paradigm shifts affect whole populations: propaganda machines, coerced political or religious conversions, changes in climate, scientific knowledge, or technologies.

Metamorphic rock, anyone?

Alchemy and transmutation of metals is impossible!

Except if we're talking radioactivity.

In biology, the term "metamorphosis" accounts for critters that undergo large morphological changes during their life cycle—from eggs to tadpoles to frogs, from caterpillars to cocoons to butterflies.

What about steam engines, shortening travel time between distant geographies, enabling more to travel the globe; the end of spontaneous generation; aseptic techniques, extending life spans; and the revelation of the heliocentric universe wrought upon our lives and thoughts?

Imagine the invention of an Ansible-like thing called the "World Wide Web" that connects everyone on the planet almost instantly. Politics could be debated in real-time everywhere. People could monitor, scold, and shame each other from anywhere across the planet. Of course, that's just a silly science-fictional idea which would never change the world.

Right?

Perhaps the most common physical change, affecting two out of five people, is when part of one's own body decides to change, to lose its sense of self, and to threaten the rest of the body:

Cancer. That changes people, literally and psychologically.

Even more common than cancer is the act of reading. During the unfolding of narrative, the reader becomes the protagonist, despite presumed barriers of race, gender, religion, etc.

Any new converts to the power of the transformation tale, shout "Amen!"

4. The Transformation Story: A Short History

Ovid wasn't the first to metamorphose characters. He may be the most famous among the early transformers. Rather, Ovid borrowed from the Greek collectors of myths, Nicander of Colophon and Boios, who was probably knocking on door after door, asking neighbors for their tales of bird transformations. Sadly, Boios's work is largely lost.

Two other Latin writers of metamorphoses should be noted: Antoninus Liberalis and the North African, Lucius Apuleius Madaurensis, who wrote the only surviving Latin novel, *The Golden Ass* or *Metamorphoses*. The character Lucius accidentally uses magic to turn himself into an ass.

[Side bar: The writer Lucius was accused of using magic to seduce a wealthy widow.]

The above writers—Ovid, in particular—influenced most of the major writers of the next millennia, including Dante Alighieri, Geoffrey Chaucer, Christopher Marlowe, William Shakespeare, Miguel de Cervantes, Michel Montaigne, John Milton, Robert Louis Stevenson, Oscar Wilde, Bram Stoker, et al.—not to mention modern writers like Franz Kafka, Ted Hughes, Anne Sexton, and Angela Carter.

5. Why Transform?

In terms of narrative, compared to most metamorphoses today, Ovid's are simple. His may have been aimed at reminding people of religious symbols buried in nature: the origin of the seasons, of plants and trees like the anemone, larkspur, rose, grapevines, cypress, firs, and pines; of insects and animals like the stag, spider, and bear.

These stories may have also been morality tales, reminders to love others and care for strangers. Also, they may have reminded readers how steeped in history the landscape is, how generation after generation has fought the same battles we've fought. Other reasons may be lost now that once was immediately understood within the culture.

Today, the tales often compare two states: before and after the transformation. True, Ovid did as well—matching the color of blood to that of the flower, matching the nature of the man to the nature of the beast—his transformations either done simply or in a manner less obvious to today's readers.

6. The Transformation Story: The Parts of

A metamorphic transformation requires two parts: 1) a Before and 2) an After, or what I'll hereafter call two "worlds," referring to whatever is transformed.

Werewolves don't instantly switch from men to werewolves. They morph or go through stages—the truly fascinating part. Moreover, in nature, most transformations do go through transitions. Consider the frog and the butterfly. They are many things before they arrive at their final destination.

Besides, we readers crave the transition and a deeper understanding of it. A realistic rendering requires steps in between.

For simplicity, let's assume we know how to create the worlds before and after (if not, there are other articles on world-building). Instead, consider how to move your character from one state to the other—the two in-between stages of Doubt and Reconsideration.

6. Doubt

It isn't easy to change a person. When the second world penetrates the first, before one buys into a seismic shift, one likely doubts and denies, accepting only the first world—the world we are more familiar with—as real.

In *The Matrix*, Thomas Anderson is handed a strange phone. The caller, Morpheus, seems to know everything that is about to happen. Despite the confirmations, when Thomas is told to go out the window to the scaffold to get on the roof or he'd be arrested, his fear of falling causes him to turn himself in rather than buy into the reality Morpheus is presenting.

In *Harry Potter and the Philosopher's Stone*, Mr. Dursley reasons away the second world's appearance:

"It was on the corner of the street that he noticed the first sign of something peculiar—a cat reading a map. For a second Mr. Dursley didn't realize what he had seen—then he jerked his head around to look again. There was a tabby cat on the corner of Privet Drive, but there wasn't a map in sight. What could he have been thinking? It must have been a trick of the light."

My story "Ash Fall" takes a slightly different tack at the first intrusion: dismissal. The doubt is so strong that it turns the image that should be foreign into something she understands:

"The laughter seemed to last minutes as if she were a black disc on a rotary machine stuck in a groove. Where that image came from, I cannot say.

"For the first time, I questioned: Maybe reality was an endless chain..."

Depending how long and critical the transformation, repeat and escalate to taste.

In Kafka's *The Metamorphosis*, the second world is already present in the first sentence, but Gregor Samsa still doubts. The pre-transformation world is here—he wants to sleep on his side like a human being—but he cannot because the second world (that he's a bug) forces him to remain on his back.

7. Reconsideration

This step is a time to pause, a time to rewrite what the writer may have planned for the first or second worlds. What does it mean that the first world segues or gives way to the second? How does each world compare and contrast? The first world or state may persist but as a contrast, lending the transformation its power: the lingering palimpsest of two worlds occupying the same space.

The whole point of Kafka's tale is that these two beings—before and after—may not have been that far apart to begin with. This outcome is worse, of course, since it allows people to act out their disgust upon their fellow creature. That he is a bug suggests he understands their disgust, yet he wants what he wants, to be restored.

Wanda herself transformed the world in *WandaVision* to keep the memory of her loved ones alive.

In "Ash Fall," our protagonist is presented two worlds: 1) an opinion-driven world that permanently maims people and 2) one that destroys "lives," but in a manner that does have a real or permanent impact on the players. The world of brawn is preferred over permanent psychological damage. Destruction is destruction, of course, but one world is a fantasy. Two worlds invite comparison. That one might be preferable suggests the reader must mull them over.

The characters may do their own reconsideration, on or off the page. This is part of the transformation, if an interior change is to occur.

If this meaning—the reason why the world is changing from one to another—isn't present in the story, it can still be good but maybe not quite as potent as it might have been.

8. Closing the Curtains on One Tale, Only to Open Another

Years later, I learned why the dime was worth more than the nickel: the value of its composition. Dimes were made out of silver, nickels out of nickel, pennies (or "coppers") out of copper. Finally, we had a reason for this transition.

In reality, the answers may not readily be there for us when the next big paradigm shift arrives—people may sprout fur and snouts and howl at the full moon—but with more transformation stories, we'll be ready.

SHAKEN, NOT STIRRED
BY WULF MOON

Wulf Moon wrote his first science fiction story when he was fifteen. It won the national Scholastic Art & Writing Awards and became his first professional sale in *Science World*. He has won over forty writing awards since.

Moon's stories have appeared in numerous publications including *Writers of the Future 35*, *Best of Deep Magic 2*, *Star Trek: Strange New Worlds 2*, and *Galaxy's Edge*. His latest will be published in the *Game On!* anthology by Zombies Need Brains in the fall of 2023.

Moon writes a series on writing for *DreamForge* magazine. He teaches the award-winning Super Secrets of Writing Workshops and is the author of *The Illustrated Super Secrets of Writing* and *How To Write a Howling Good Story*. Visit TheSuperSecrets.com

As Cassie soared the galactic ether, she gathered up the mass from an unfortunate comet that crossed her path, spritzed herself in its emerald glow, and draped her body in radiant strands of cerulean

and magenta gossamer borrowed from a neighboring nebula. A girl had to dress for success, especially when you were called to a business luncheon with the chairman of the intergalactic Holistic Organization for Accumulation and Redistribution of Dynamics. Serving on the seven-member board of HOARD was Cassie's least favorite task since ascension, but someone had to protect the galaxies and solar systems that fell under the auspices of her delicately balanced constellation.

She fanned opalescent wings, riding a jet of subatomic particles like an eagle rising upon the thermals of her home world. As she vectored toward a dark matter nexus, she pondered the Law of Universal Gravitation. Why did this law seem to aid the reign of fat-cat ascendants and, in spite of their mass, always helped them float light as the ether to the peaks of celestial power?

Cassie could see only one equation to sum it up: density equals dense. And greed. So much illicit siphoning of mass from lighter galaxies into the heavier ones going on, hoarding in the name of HOARD, and no one calling the board out on it. So far, every "distribution" she had seen appeared to benefit the largest constellations, violating HOARD's charter.

Well, Cassie might be the "new kid," but she was no longer naive. She'd been around the universe a few times and she'd learned a thing or two. Cassie vowed she'd make her stand this time and call out the board's shenanigans at the upcoming millennial meeting. The lives of her sentients on the third planet from Sol depended on it.

But first, she had to comply with this invitation to a "private meeting before the meeting" from Chairman Hydra. *Just a friendly chat*, the invitation had chimed, *a little luncheon to discuss how we should vote on these starred agenda points.*

Cassie scowled. Board decisions might appear to be by majority vote, but Hydra knew all the slippery tricks to tip those votes in his favor. Weighty matters were decided long before anyone sat on their chairs at the spiral table to discuss them. And with her being the new ascendant and not knowing the ropes, she'd been pulled right into

Chairman Hydra's gravity well. If she wasn't careful, Cassie feared she might sink so deep she'd drown in it.

Cassie materialized at the specified location on the star chart in her shimmering nebulous form. She lowered inner eyelids, allowing her to add the dark matter spectrum to her sight. It appeared "lunch" would be spent relaxing in chaises longues, sipping dark-matter cocktails siphoned off the dense currents and strands emanating from the orbs that peppered the dwarf galaxy of Segue 2. The mass exchange was complex, but in the ascendant plane, actions mimicked your origin life, and hers had been on Earth.

Hydra had whipped up a hovering tiki hut over a pond of dark matter for the occasion, complete with neon palms—were those rope lights?—and pink plastic flamingos bobbing their heads into the surface that now glowed phosphorescent green in her enhanced vision. As she floated in and retracted her wings, Hydra rose off his lounge in a golden Budai form, the dark matter particles congealing under his bare feet as he stood. His lumbering mass swayed from side to side as he stepped forward and held out his hand.

"Ah, my dear Cassiopeia. You look radiant."

Cassie pretended she didn't see his hand and bowed instead. "Chairman Hydra. You are looking more massive than ever."

His sour look sweetened at the compliment. "Thank you, my dear. One's representative form should meet one's representative mass."

She cast her gaze down, taking in her slender self. Was that a cut?

"Please, my dear." He motioned to the lounge chair floating beside his. "Let's keep this informal."

"As you wish."

As they stepped within the tiki hut and eased into the cushions, Cassie had to admit the ancient chairman knew how to weave some mighty comfortable lounge chairs, and the glittering view of the Sagittarius Stream beyond stole her breath away... or at least the stellar gasses that sufficed for breath in ascendants.

Hydra winked coquettishly, but Cassie could see the snake eyes burning bright as quasars behind his pupils. "Thank you for agreeing to this little dalliance before the millennial board meeting, my child."

"Dalliance? You said this was to be a *business luncheon*. I expect you to keep it professional."

Hydra cleared his throat. "Of course, of course. Forgive me—still learning the nuances of your origin language."

Yeah, right.

He took a crystal shaker from a little table between them, scooped up ice cubes from a bucket, and poured colorful congealed gasses into it from a frost-rimed silver thermos. Hydra's jowls jiggled as he spoke. "A little concoction I brought from home. My *signature* recipe."

He shook the container vigorously, and although they were in a vacuum, Cassie's mind filled with the sound of rattling ice cubes. Hydra smiled as he worked; it was a bit disconcerting to see a Budai with ivory fangs.

"Shaken, not stirred," Hydra said. "Is that not the phrase of your people's mixologists?"

Whoa. What sharp eyes these ascendants kept on her world. "Correct. But it's become a bit cliche' these days."

"Pity. I admire a good metaphor. So much... opportunity when a galaxy gets *shaken*. The collision of the larger into the smaller, the resultant chaos as solar mass is exchanged, the subsequent appropriation of intact stars. So much to be... consumed."

"Stored for subsequent cosmological equilibrium, you mean."

Hydra coughed, sending tremors through his rolls of fat. "Yes, yes, for future needs of universal balance and all that, of course."

He sighed and looked heavenward, which could have been anywhere, but in this case was up. "Some of us, my dear, have the weighty responsibility of being the tent pins of this universe. Haste makes waste. Can't stack it all toward the hub or we'd all go down the proverbial toilet. Isn't that the phrase?"

Always the justification for hoarding mass with the massive. Never an atom for the new girl's systems. It was like they were intentionally trying to starve her out. *Whoa.* Were they trying to starve her out? If so, she could think of a few members on the board, present company included, that she wouldn't mind flushing down the toilet, proverbial or otherwise.

Hydra filled two martini glasses to the brim. He passed one to her, the little ice chips within flashing starlight. "A toast! To universal gravitation: may it ever bring us closer together."

Cassie clinked glasses. "To Hubble expansion!"

Hydra frowned, obviously unfamiliar with the term. Cassie hid a furtive smile by tilting her head down and placing her lips to the cool, tingling glass. She sipped from the ionized gasses swirling within. Sweet hydrogen, helium, and oxygen with a dash of raw carbon and a twist of spicy sulfur. Delicious.

Hydra smacked his fat lips, reached out, and patted her on the thigh. "You're our bright new star, Cassie. It's been a Gya since we've had a fresh Ascendant. Pity. Gargon the Lesser was not with us long. Unfortunate collision with Ursa Major." Hydra pointed. "You can still see bits of him over there."

Cassie pulled away from Hydra's touch. These meetings drained her; she suspected Hydra's touch acted as a conduit. He might have assigned himself her mentor, but she had come to recognize it wasn't her mind he was interested in. If he wasn't after her vote he was after her body—specifically, the mass her body represented.

Hydra stared at her with those sparking quasar eyes. "To business then. Point seven on the upcoming agenda."

"What about point thirty-seven? My request for a booster to Sol. I've done the calculations, and by the time that star expands, I don't believe human technolo—"

"Oh, I'm sorry, little one. No room for your request on this agenda. I moved it to Futures."

Cassie burned. Might as well have shoved it into a black hole. She bit her proverbial tongue.

"Now then, Ursa Major is going to call for a redistribution, a little charity project in the GN-z11 system, as your people call it. I've already spoken with Virgo, and we feel it's much too early to start donating from our reserves, there's plenty of expansion rate left in this universe before we have to start worrying about divestiture. No matter how compelling his case, I want you to vote *nay* on his proposal."

Cassie was fed up with being the mealy-mouthed apprentice. She took a deep breath. Nothing came in, but it made her feel stronger. "You want my vote, you have to put my point about Sol on the next agenda." She sat forward and put on her poker face. "*High* priority."

Hydra choked on his drink and raised a scaly brow. "My, my, my; my padawan learns fast." He weighed her in the scales of his eyes. "Alright. I'll deal. You make the chips fall my way, you've got your ticket in the big game." His eyes narrowed to serpent slits. "But be careful what you wish for."

In a galaxy far, far away from the primeval point of multiverse leakage, carefully positioned in the neutral zone beyond any constellation's territory, there floated an island fashioned from the densest material in the universe—the crust of a neutron star. As Cassie materialized upon its dark matter nexus, she chuckled. This wasn't a boardroom as one might describe on Earth—it looked like someone had scooped a chunk out of the Sedona desert and floated it in intergalactic space.

There was one peak on the island, oddly similar to Cathedral Rock back home—if the butte had been illuminated at its dome by a miniature swirling galaxy with a beam of radiation bursting out from its center. Cassie climbed a spiral path circling the butte to its plateau and expanded her proportions to match table and chairs the size of Seattle's Space Needle, all on a dais just ahead. Six of the board had already arrived, seated and ready for business. As the newest member, she was required to arrive last in respect to her elders. If the round table was a symbol of equality, why had Chairman Hydra fashioned himself a golden throne? Some questions you knew better than to ask.

None rose to greet her.

Cassie took a shuddering breath and stood tall. She had promised herself that she'd present herself as a *whole new you* at this board meeting. Things were going to change. They had to.

Chairman Hydra looked down upon her from his massive throne. His celestial presence was still housed in that behemoth form of the Budai. "Ah, here we are. Madam Cassiopeia. Please be seated."

Cassie sat upon the radiant blue chair, chiseled from the material of the glowing crust of this island. As her gaze circled the table, she burst out laughing.

Hydra frowned, toying with a golden gavel in his ham hands. "What's so funny, Cassie? Care to let us in on the joke?"

Cassie couldn't help herself. "All of you! Look at the forms you chose for today. They're all from my world! Back home, we'd call this cultural appropriation!"

Cetus, seated to Hydra's right, flapped the tentacles streaming from his mouth as he spoke. "It is so rare for the universe to bring forth a new sentient species. Your people have entered such an interesting time-phase. I for one find your mythos fascinating."

"But you're Cthulhu! Who would want to be—" She stopped. Of course. Why wouldn't Cetus the Squid identify with a creature mirroring his likeness? And Cassie had to admit, his cold and calculating eyes had always given her the chills. She felt naked before them, her wrappings of gossamer burned away, every atom in her constellation weighed in the balances of his keen and measured gaze. His gift, of course. Which was why he served as the board's chief financial officer. Which was also why Cassie didn't like him staring her up and down.

Cetus quoted Lovecraft. "'*They were not composed altogether of flesh and blood. They had shape... but that shape was not made of matter. When the stars were right, They could plunge from world to world through the sky; but when the stars were wrong, They could not live.*'" His tentacles vibrated in pulpy slaps as he sighed. "Pure poetry. It's as if he could see into our very souls."

"Uhmmm... ohh-kay." Cassie turned to Ursa Major on Hydra's left. "Ursa, is that you? What in the quacking quasar are you supposed to be?"

"I'm the Golden Ladle."

"Weren't you the Little Dipper last time we convened?"

"I was Ursa Minor, yes. I have since made acquisitions to my constellation and have accumulated mass to the level of Ursa Major now. Thus, my new form."

"So you're the Big Dipper."

"Golden Ladle, thank you very much."

"Oh, all right. And you, Virgo?" Cassie took in her augmentations. She was much more *top-heavy* than their last board meeting. *Bottom-heavy*, too. "Kim Kardashian? Really?"

"She has mass in all the right places." Virgo tossed her hair and gave Cassie *the look*. "*I buy myself a gift every year, so this year I bought myself everything I wanted.*"

Cassie was not about to get in a fight with her. Again. Don't feed the beast.

"And Hercules? Okay, you look the same. Keep rocking that Kevin Sorbo look, buddy."

He flashed his legendary hero smile, clicked his tongue, pointed at her, and winked. "I do it all for you, princess. Maybe after th—"

Cassie held up a hand. "No. Just *no*."

Hercules' chiseled chest deflated.

Cassie leveled on the creature in Orion's chair. "Godzilla? Really? How does he relate?"

Orion lifted his lizard maw and roared, coughed a few times on the smoke, and looked back at Cassie expectantly. Cassie shrugged and held both palms up, waiting.

Orion grinned. "Because he can *belt* it out. Get it? *Belt* it out?"

Celestial crickets.

Cassie shook her head, returned her gaze to the throne. Those quasar eyes of Hydra, burning down into hers. When her mentor looked at her like that she normally shriveled in fear. But she had promised herself today would be different. Poker face. Poker face.

"And you, Chairman Hydra. The Budai? Don't you think that form is a tad sacrilegious... and excessive?"

Hydra scowled. "What? At thirty trillion solar masses, I've got the bulk for it. A constellation of my stature should be represented proportionately. And as for religion, we are gods, we can do as we please."

Cassie raised a hand. "Excuse me, but we are not gods. We are ascendants, which means we came from—"

Hydra's eyes kindled. "Don't lecture me on origins, young lady. Know your place! Our races were here long before your race sprouted, and we will be here long after, ahem, well, we will all be here for a very long time, won't we."

Hydra rapped his gavel against the table, the sparks that ensued creating new comets in the galaxy currently represented. "Now then. As chairman of HOARD, I hereby call this board meeting to order. Secretary Virgo, please note in the minutes that we have a quorum."

Virgo plucked a gold hoop from her ear, rubbed it in her palms, and floated an amber sphere in front of her face. "Noted."

Hydra raised his voice. "All hail Theta, Sovereign of the Multiverse, who granted HOARD the oversight of balancing this universe..."

Cassie drifted off until they worked their way to the agenda points, barely discussed, decisions obviously made beforehand by deals done under the table. But one deal had not been made. Which was why Hydra needed her vote, of course.

Hydra cleared his throat. "Ahem. We come to point seven, proposed by Ursa Major. It would appear he'd like to keep this new acquisition of his even though jurisdiction is in question." Cassie heard the acquisition as if spoken in her tongue—the ancient galaxy GN-z11.

A face formed in the big ladle that was Ursa Major, propped upon his chair. He pointed his dipper handle straight at Hydra's face. "Damn straight! I expanded the borders of my constellation fair and square, and that galaxy is mine. I have big plans for reinvigorating it, big plans!"

Chairman Hydra rested his gavel on the table and folded his hands, the perfect picture of a caring Budai smiling on a supplicant... if that smile bore fangs. "Yes, yes, you've certainly done well for yourself. You have the full respect here of your colleagues. But this is an incredibly old galaxy, dating back to the universe's origin puncture. As he who was first awakened by the universe, I think it fitting that the galaxy should fall to its oldest member." Hydra leaned forward, leveling Ursa in his gaze. "And that would be me."

Ursa Major warped out of his golden ladle form and turned into a growling bear outlined in blazing stars. "You bastard! The sentients I rose from weren't far behind yours. Always grabbing up what isn't yours through seniority. Well I won't have it this time! GN-z11 is mine, I say! I have big plans for it. Big. Plans!"

Hydra nodded, jowls swaying. "Then we must put its possession to a vote."

Ursa Major roared, baring rows of shimmering teeth. "Yes! Have at it. Let's vote." He lowered his gaze hard and heavy on Orion and Hercules. And then he swiveled his bear head in Cassie's direction. She could see the question lurking in his depths. Pleading. He really wanted to win this one.

She looked down. This was the day she said she would stand up for herself, stand up for her people. And that meant on this point, she would have to stand down.

As the vote was called, Cassie watched the hands.

"All in favor of leaving GN-z11 in Ursa Major's control?"

Ursa Major raised a mighty paw. "Aye!"

Hercules raised a fist. "Aye!"

Orion hung his Godzilla shoulders and looked down; Ursa rumbled a deadly growl. Orion lifted his lizard head sheepishly and coughed out a weak atomic breath. "Aye?"

Three nays followed. All heads turned to Cassie. She would be the tie breaker. Chairman Hydra leaned forward.

"Nay," Cassie said, speaking without fear, without trembling. On the outside. For better or worse, a deal had been struck.

The gavel dropped. *Bang.*

The next motion was to decommission GN-z11 and transfer its mass to Hydra. Seconded by Virgo. Put to vote. A tie again. Cassie took a deep breath, voted in Hydra's favor. The deed was done.

More points were discussed, assignments given, motions passed, but it was all a blur to Cassie until Hydra's concluding statement jolted her from the haze. "Cetus, as our duly appointed CFO, is this quarter's Cosmic Census equitably balanced?"

An eldritch voice quavered through the tentacles. *"Ph'nglui mglw'-nafh Cthulhu R'lyeh wgah'nagl fhtagn."*

"What?"

Cetus gave a kick to something under the table, which Cassie found curious. "They are balanced," he said.

Hydra hissed. "As well they should be. For all our sakes. Please add the celestial accounts and cosmic census to the corporate minutes and transfer the sphere to Theta's accountants."

"As you wish."

Hydra rapped the gavel with finality. "This meeting is adjourned."

As the others headed one by one for the nexus, Cassie remained seated, watching the whorls in the table slowly turn. Shame flooded through her. If she truly had ascended, why did she feel so low?

A thousand Earth years she had waited—a thousand years Cassie had stewed and calculated, trying to see into the big game Hydra played. Cassie's people had moved from outposts on the Moon to cities on Mars. As mankind's first generation ship was on its way to Proxima Centauri, another HOARD board meeting was about to commence. The more she weighed the votes she had made in Hydra's favor, the more she calculated what the distribution had added to his expansion, the more sour the answer became.

In trying to get her people's everlasting future sealed, she had actually doomed their galaxy. She hadn't believed it possible, but she had done the math: Hydra's constellation was traveling inexorably toward hers. He was coming for her Milky Way!

Cassie ignored Hydra's latest invitation to another agenda luncheon. There was no way she could hide a last desperate gambit from his piercing eyes, especially while sipping exotic martinis.

Instead, she rolled the dice in a desperate throw: a secret missive sent to Cetus.

I have a proposition for you.

She had waited ninety-seven years. She had lost hope he would respond. And then, the missive chimed.

Your place, or mine?

Meet me in the Sol system on a moon orbiting Jupiter. Europa.

Cassie landed at the designated meeting place among the icy fifteen-meter spike formations at Europa's equator. Cetus loomed within the spike fields, still sporting his Cthulhu form, black smoke shrouding him, eyes as dark as the abyss that slept in silence below Europa's mantle of ice.

Cassie folded her wings, glowed bright for light, and took a deep breath of the thin atmosphere. Oxygen—it always smelled sweet to her, like apple blossoms on Earth's orchards. She drew power from that, savoring the scents of home. It might not warm a cold eldritch's heart, but it did wonders for hers.

Cetus gripped a spire with his claws and rose above her, fanning his wings, red eyes blazing like a blast furnace. Cassie expanded her form and spread her white wings out, matching him size for size.

"Look, we can do this all day," she said. "Let's cut the dominance crap and get down to business."

Cetus drew his mass in, standing within the ice spikes once again. He flapped his mouth tentacles; his voice grated like nails against a chalkboard. "As you wish. Why have you called?"

No poker face this time. Cassie laid her cards on the table.

"Look. I don't know what Hydra's got on you, and I don't care. My case for preserving Earth's sun with a hydrogen infusion is on the agenda, and I'm certain it will be voted down."

"And your question is?"

"I could do the manipulation of matter myself, rob Peter to pay Paul as we say in my world."

Cetus leaned against a spire and stroked his tentacles, his body shedding that eerie smoke. He said nothing.

"You'd report me to Theta for unlawful distribution of matter, wouldn't you? Lack of authorization by the board."

Cetus' breath rasped. He said nothing.

"Yet you Elder Ones do it all the time and cover up for one another, especially in regard to Hydra."

"I will neither confirm nor deny that accusation. Make your point."

Cassie folded in her wings, shrunk down to the size of her origin self. She was just a girl in a gossamer toga, laying it on the line. "The Celestial Census. It's always balanced. Proper distribution to maintain universal expansion. Come on, we both know that's not true." She pointed a finger at his elephantine head. "You're cooking the books!"

She expected a roar, feared a psychic scrambling of her ascendant mind. Instead, she got a pulpy chuckle.

"Of course. A little graft is tolerated. But if I sent Theta the real books under the table, there would be a *forensic* accounting. The last time Theta's entourage paid a visit, they stayed at what your people call Segue 2. It takes so much baryonic matter to maintain Theta's ascendants in this universe, they almost stripped that galaxy clean."

"Huh. I didn't know that about Segue 2, but as we say, it all adds up. So I'm guessing nobody wants a forensic accounting by Theta."

"No indeed. I believe your term is *about as pleasurable as a root canal*?"

"Nanobot nerve repair ended that one, but we still say *pain in the ass*. That one is timeless."

"Ah, your people's orifice of extrusion."

"Um, sure. Okay, riddle me this: Who would be bitten in the ass most of all if the secret accounts were revealed?"

Cetus' scaly brow rose over the crater of one of his sunken eye sockets. "Hydra. His violations would prove most excessive. He could not hide it, nor could he scatter that much mass fast enough. There would be a divestiture of his holdings. But all of us have dipped into the cookie jar. I fail to see—"

Cassie rested her hands on her hips. "On my world, the regulators can't penalize everyone, or their system would fail. So they find a prominent example to make their point, throw the book at him, and slap the others on the wrist. I'm betting the multiverse works the same. The wheels must keep turning, the show must go on and all that jazz. Am I right?"

The gleam in Cetus' eyes could cut through Europa's core. "Interesting. Many probabilities unfold. But probabilities also include uncertainties. The entire board could be disbanded. Yourself included."

"What? I've done nothing wrong!"

Cetus gaze ran up and down her form and stopped at the glowing pearls that graced her neck. Cassie touched them. She might have fashioned them from that comet on her last outing, and there was that illumination spritz the time before, and that dark matter she scooped—

"Oh."

The edge on Cetus' voice eased. "You see, my dear, we all have made infractions of HOARD's charter to one degree or another. If Theta's accountants apply the letter of the law, we all risk disbandment."

Cassie shook her head. "If we don't take risks, the handwriting is on the wall. Hydra's mass will grow. His power will know no bounds."

"My dear, the handwriting is already on the wall. This universe cannot expand forever. Gravity is grave. All matter will return to the source. Dust to dust. Ashes to ashes."

"I refuse to believe that. I will not surrender. And certainly not to Hydra! Won't you help me?"

Cetus waved a hand up and down his form. "You see my chosen representation. It is indicative of my spirit. Why in the sleeping salty depths should I help one so frail and young as you?"

Cassie smiled. Density made one dense. And greedy. "I don't know. Maybe because you're tired of being Hydra's yes man? Maybe you'd like *your* turn on the throne."

At that next board meeting, Cassie's agenda point was shot down by Hydra, just as she suspected it would be. Under the pallid light of the stars, Hydra drew the meeting to a close.

"Is there any final business before I declare this meeting adjourned?" He raised his gavel.

Cetus held up a prodigious claw. "Ahem. One last item."

Hydra lowered the gavel. "Proceed, but make it brief. It's been a long day."

Cetus unraveled a tentacle. Within shimmered a golden sphere, stamped with the imperial auditor's radiant glyph. Cassie actually heard Hydra gulp.

Cetus spoke with authority. "We have an official notice from Theta's accountants. I don't know how, the vault is sealed beneath this table, but somehow they've received some ledgers they find most disturbing. Like royal audit disturbing."

Hydra roared, shaking the foundations of the butte. "What? That's impossible. You're the only one with the access code!"

"I assure you, it was not I."

Cetus met Hydra stare for stare, absolute darkness to absorb quasar light.

"What is more," Cetus said, "Theta's entourage have requested housing within the Porpoise system."

"But that's my origin system! I'm involved in the takeover of another galaxy there right now!"

Cetus' voice arced with that chalkboard screech. "Then I suggest you get your house in order." His baleful gaze circled all in turn, but Cassie thought she caught a spark of light in those fathomless hollows as he passed over her. "All of you. They arrive tomorrow."

Hydra stood up from his throne, shook his gavel at Cassie. "You did this! I don't know how, but I know it's you. You've always been independent, a real pain in my ass!"

There was a day when Cassie would have quaked in fear if her mentor had bellowed like that. This day, she stood up, fanned her glorious wings to full spread, and spoke with all the power of the galaxies and suns behind her.

"You best get going, Hydra. I looked it up. It takes a super singularity for his ascendants to enter this realm. As they say in my world, Theta's about to rip you a new one."

Hydra's cheeks bulged and his face burned bright red as he slammed his gavel down. "This meeting is adjourned!"

The ascendants rushed for the nearest nexus. All but Cassie. And Cetus, who sat smoldering across from her in his chair, studying her.

After what seemed an eternity, his voice came up from the depths, but it was as calm as a frozen sea. "How did you figure out my combination?" he asked.

Cassie smiled. *"Ph'nglui mglw'nafh Cthulhu R'lyeh wgah'nagl fhtagn.* Took me a week to get your eldritch intonation down, but I finally got it right."

Cetus nodded, tentacles swaying in the brume clinging to his form.

Cassie slid a small wrapped package topped with a black bow across the table, the parcel protected by a containment field. "I had you all wrong. I might be mistaken, but I think there's just a *little* bit of starlight cloaked within all that smoldering cloud of darkness."

Cetus tapped the package with a claw. "What's this?"

"Present. Signed first edition. I think you'll like it."

"Ah."

Was that a smile? So hard to tell through all those tentacles.

"Thank you," Cassie said. "You could have told Hydra my plans."

Cetus raised a scaly brow. "Oh? I did this for you, did I?" He glanced at the chair to his left. "And who do you think is next in mass for the director's throne?" He winked. "See you at the next board meeting, Cassiopeia."

As Cassie flashed home upon the dark matter strands, moving from nexus to nexus, she wondered if she had played Cetus, or if he had played her. She decided it didn't matter. Because of her actions, that board had been shaken, not given the same old stir. Instead of taking her worlds over, Hydra would diminish... and her galaxies and people would survive. For billions of years to come.

And that, she decided, deserved a toast. She wondered what Hercules might be up to. She stopped at the nearest nexus and flashed out a sparkling missive.

Martinis?

BEHIND THE SCENES OF "SHAKEN, NOT STIRRED"

BY WULF MOON

So you want to learn a magic trick. The sleight of hand a magician does to make the audience believe they just saw a miracle that could not occur in their natural world. Well, that's what a good story is. Magic. Flourish your hands properly, pronounce the words of the incantation accurately, and you can levitate not only your assistant, but your audience as well. And not just over the stage. True magicians like Isaac Asimov, Arthur C. Clarke, and Frank Herbert were able to launch their audience across worlds, over galaxies, even... beyond constellations.

You sure you want to learn the steps to this one? Once a magician shows how it's done, the trick is never quite the same...

Okay, you're still here. You did read it first? Right. Now don't say I didn't warn you.

In the Beginning

In the beginning there was the void. Into the void came the spark. From the spark ignited the idea that became strands of matter that wound together and coalesced into a story. But first, there was the void.

Scot Noel asked me to write a story for the new *DreamForge Anvil* magazine. I told my buddy and fellow Writers of the Future winner Steve Pantazis about the commission, and that I hadn't decided what to write yet. He tossed out an idea. "How about a hobbyist who uses the energy spun off of black holes to create small worlds as charitable contributions to the less-fortunate interstellar races of the universe. Will the Blackhole Audit Committee shut him down or will he get to keep creating?"

There was the spark. That would have been a good story, but that was Steve's story. But what about a committee, black holes, and audits? How about a board of directors responsible for keeping all the matter in the universe balanced out? I had been itching for years to write a story about ascendant beings that could travel the universe at the speed of thought. They would be extremely rare, because intelligent life is rare—present company excluded, of course—and they would be the pinnacle of their species. Ascendants! What if the universe provided these ascendent beings, one for each intelligent race, to represent and protect them? Go bigger. What if each had dominion over a constellation? *Boom!* Now how, in dealing with godlike beings, do I make one of them vulnerable? Threatened? In danger of losing not only her life, but the very people she had arisen from to protect?

And that's how I made Cassiopeia. Call her Cassie, less formal, easier for readers to identify with. Let's make her the new kid on the block compared to her peers on the board. Insecurity. Now create a dominant power figure to face off against to amplify her vulnerability. Now make him bent on stripping everything from her while pretending to be her friend and mentor. Powerful opposing force. This is one of the Super Secrets in my upcoming books on the craft of writing. The basics are this: create a sympathetic character that readers can identify with, and then open your story with them already deep behind the eight ball. You have instant tension because your heroine is already in trouble. If your reader senses grave danger, they can't help but read on, because they will want to find out if this person they've become attached to is going to make it. Set your stakes high enough, and the reader's pulse will pound, wondering if someone like Cassie will live or die. Go bigger! How about making the reader worry if someone like sweet Cassie *and the human race* will live or die? Are the stakes high enough? What is the price of failure? I ramped up the problem so high in this story, the fate of the universe really does hang in the balance.

And that's how you hold a reader's attention. Sympathetic hero. High stakes. Powerful opposing force. Impossible odds. As *The Return of the King* scriptwriters had Gimli say when the company planned an assault on The Black Gate: "Certainty of death. Small chance of success. What are we waiting for?"

Remember that. That's the secret of a powerful page-turner.

The Opening Scene

So I have my ascendant being named Cassie. How do I tell my audience she's unique from the average female human? I open with her soaring across the galactic ether, absorbing a little power here and there for vanity's sake. This is worldbuilding, but in the same stroke I'm banking on the fact most readers will identify with the line 'a girl has to dress for success.' In the opening paragraph, I reveal her concern for the people she represents in her territory, and that the balance of power is delicate. The problem escalates in the second paragraph, as you discover Cassie serves on a board of power-hungry fat cat ascendants. In the third paragraph, you discover these board members are not only powerful, but they're also breaking the law. Cassie is in the process of deciding what she must do about it. Fourth paragraph, she's decided. Cassie, the new kid, is going to screw up her courage and call out these violations at the next board meeting. Why? *The lives of her sentients on the third planet from Sol depended on it.*

High stakes? You bet! In just a few paragraphs, I make you care about this young ascendant lady by giving you reasons to identify with her. She's new on the job. She's discovered the ascendants on the board are corrupt overlords. She cares deeply about the people she serves. And she has hero material within her—she's decided to take the bull by the horns and speak up against those more powerful than her, and call them out on their unlawful practices. Cassie is likeable character.

And then, *things get worse.* Cassie is heading to a luncheon with the chairman of the board, and she suspects he's been draining power from her. Worse, he's supposed to be her mentor, but he's violating the mentor/apprentice relationship. This is a hot topic in our culture right now, and I intentionally push these buttons to get you emotionally invested by having the chairman flirt with her, speak condescendingly, put his hand on her thigh, and even launch veiled threats in Cassie's direction. To top it all off, Cassie gets placed in a compromising situation where she is forced to make a dirty deal in order to get the important needs of her people even considered by the board.

At the end of the opening scene, Cassie has a choice. She can go on being the subservient apprentice, or she can choose to enter what is in effect a high stakes poker game where everything she cares about is placed on the line. I stood Cassie at the threshold and had her *choose* to play the board of directors' dangerous poker game. To enter the *journey*. All in a little over five double-spaced pages on my manuscript while building a unique science fiction universe with rules you could buy in to.

That's a magic trick.

The Journey

In the next scene, we come to the board meeting where Cassie is not going to let herself be pushed around anymore. The needs of her people demand that she figures out how to play the board members' game and find an advantage for her cause. We see more of how power is grabbed up, how deals are made under the table, and the moment of test comes to Cassie: will she vote with the chairman in an ends justifies the means moment? She feels she has no choice, makes her stand, and casts her vote to break a tie. Once again, the chairman has manipulated matters to his favor. New girl Cassie has grown in this scene—it's the first time she's figured out how the game is played—but she doesn't like what she's done. She is left with a haunting feeling of regret.

Shame flooded through her. If she truly had ascended, why did she feel so low?

Ever felt like that yourself? Ever wish you could take back a decision that might have benefited you but hurt someone else? I'm betting you have, and I'm betting you're emotionally invested enough in Cassie's feelings to read the next scene to find out how she's going to deal with it. That's called an emotional hook. I placed it at the end of the scene to weight it with drama and gravity. In my freelance editing business, I see too many writers failing to end their scenes dramatically. You get to the end of a powerful scene, and it's something like, "Tired from the long day, Cassie went to bed." That doesn't make me want to read on, it makes *me* want to go to bed!

A scene is like a mini story—it has a beginning, a middle, and an end. Make the endings on your scenes good endings. Give your readers drama, an unanswered question, a cliffhanger that forces them to read the next scene to find out what happens to their dear Cassie. Don't have your protagonist yawn and wander off the stage.

Because that's exactly what your readers will do as well.

In the next scene, a thousand years have passed and the next board meeting approaches. Cassie has calculated the results of her vote, and discovers she has made a terrible mistake: the additional mass the chairman picked up will give him the necessary gravitational force to destroy her. What is more, he is shifting mass in her direction to quicken the pace. Her galaxies and star systems and her people she has been fighting to protect are doomed.

Things get worse. To create escalating tension that rachets inexorably toward the do-or-die climax, even when your heroine appears to succeed, her actions must make things worse. Now, as a result of her deal, Cassie has a bigger problem on her hands. And she realizes even if the chairman keeps his word and gets her request placed on the board's agenda, Hydra will have worked out a deal to get it shot down. He's not going to help her; he's coming for her.

What's a girl to do? She comes up with a dangerous gambit, and she'll need to gain an ally to pull it off. Who does she choose? The one that might appear least likely to help—Cetus, the CFO that's taken a hankering to the eldritch Cthulhu mythos. But he's the guy that does the books, and if Cassie has guessed properly, the secret books, too. She figures he's either going to see the personal benefits of her plan, or he's going to scramble her ascendant brain. *High stakes.*

I also get to have some fun bringing details of Segue 2 back in that we saw in the opening scene. It's all researched, all of it has basis in astrophysics and astronomy. Please, go look it up and see how much about Segue 2 that I was able to weave into this tale. Everything in short stories should have a purpose, and when you add in real world details, it enhances the fiction and makes it feel real.

The scene ends with Cassie making her final appeal. Will Cetus back her when she plays her hand? We don't know. He's an unlikely ally, her gambit is just as dangerous for him as it is for her, and he could easily turn her in to curry favor with the chairman. The stakes are high, the outcome uncertain. And that's exactly where I want the curtain to fall. The questions compel the reader to find out what will happen next.

Shall we? After *you.*

The Climax

We come to the event everything in this tale has been ratcheting up toward. The do-or-die climax. New girl Cassie has been pitted against a mighty adversary with power and experience far beyond her own. She's had to grow up quickly, and she's had to face the fact that she can't beat Chairman Hydra on her own. She's also played a dangerous gambit by sending the board's secret ledgers to Theta's accountants. A royal audit from Theta can cost one dearly, depending on how the chips may fall.

Cassie banks on one fact about the board members she has stated from the very beginning: *Density made one dense. And greedy.* CFO Cetus has seen the advantages to himself, has made certain who the royal auditors will be staying with, and Chairman Hydra will be sufficiently weakened so as to no longer pose a threat to Cassie. Even cold and calculating Cetus gives her a nod of respect for her ingenuity, which is why I had him use her full name. *"See you at the next board meeting, Cassiopeia."*

But wait! There's more!

The Denouement

A story doesn't end at the climax. It's not fulfilling. Readers need a bit of validation that the heroine accomplished what she set out to achieve, grew from the experience, and will ride out for the cause of truth and justice once again should duty call. Hi-ho, Silver! Life goes on. The wheel of time goes round and round. But my favorite is this: *And they all lived happily ever after.* Why? Because it's been hardwired into us since we were kids, since our parents were kids, since our grandparents and great-great-grandparents were kids, all the way back into time immemorial. The story has ended, but it's not really over. And the world will be a better place, a *happier* place, because of what our heroine has done.

So what's the pretty bow I wrap the package of my story up with?

Cassie contemplates the loose ends. Perhaps Cetus played her, as he readily admits he's next in line for the chairman's throne. Cassie weighs it out and decides it doesn't matter, because she got what she desired—security for her realm and her people. And then, to show you she's no longer naive new girl Cassie from the opening of the story? She calls up a colleague and invites him to join her for drinks. This is a more confident Cassie, and we smile as we see not only that her life goes on, it's better, and she's the one asking the guy out for drinks.

Martinis actually. Which is where our story began.

THE WORK

BY JAMES A. OWEN

James A. Owen is founder and executive director of Coppervale International, an art and design studio that published the periodicals *International Studio* and *Argosy*, develops television and film projects, and is redesigning an entire town in Arizona, among other ventures. James has written and illustrated two dozen *StarChild* comics, the award-winning *MythWorld* series of novels (published in Germany and France), the bestselling series, *The Chronicles of the Imaginarium Geographica*, the inspirational nonfiction book *Drawing out the Dragons*, and more. More than a million copies of his publications are in print, and are sold all over the world.

The Work...

...is all that really matters.

Many years ago, I gave a lecture on craft to the art students at a local university. To the shock and dismay of the instructor who had invited me to speak, I told them that once they had comfortably learned how to use all the different tools available to them, they should drop out of school—because after that point, all they would be learning are the preferences and idiosyncrasies of their teachers.

This statement 1) does not necessarily apply to all art students; everyone's mileage varies; 2) was presented a bit less diplomatically than it might have been after I'd had a bit more experience teaching; 3) worked well for me and others I know, so...; 4) it's still my fundamental position about teaching craft.

This is why I decided to offer a three-hour workshop on cover design as my primary contribution to the craft day of the annual Superstars Writing Seminar. I don't teach how to *illustrate* covers; I teach how to try to effectively *design* a cover that will be attractive to readers and represent the work and the creator. That's it.

I have the skill set and experience to teach craft in art—I just have no interest in doing it. That goes double for teaching craft in writing. I just don't want to do it, full stop. And neither of those sentiments has anything at all to do with my commitment to encourage, assist, mentor, teach, and otherwise offer whatever support I can to both artists and authors in the pursuit of furthering their career goals.

I often share stories about how I pursued my own work and career, because while none of us ever walks the exact same path as anyone else, sometimes the paths are similar, and knowing how someone overcame their obstacles might help you in finding ways to overcome yours. I will, when asked, offer examples of my own creative process—I especially like sharing my combination of a short outline plus illustration thumbnails as a means of story development. If someone is trying to solve a specific artistic problem, I'm happy to talk technique, as others did with me when I was still figuring out how to create the things I envisioned.

Sharing technique is a different thing than teaching craft, I think. That may be a distinction without a difference, based entirely on personal experience. Maybe it's because sharing technique is about helping someone to solve a particular problem, whereas teaching craft feels more like imposing a creative viewpoint on someone who is still formulating their own. And maybe all of this has more to do with my own experiences of having craft pressed upon me by teachers who did not understand that what they were teaching did not apply in any useful way to the artistic goals I had.

I feel much the same about writing. And, again, when asked, I will tell someone that the most important thing they can do with a story is finish it, because something has to be completed to be evaluated and tuned up into something awesome.

I do not, however, have any opinion on *how* a writer gets to that point of completion. Everyone has to find what works for them, and then implement that process. Some are plotters, some are pantsers; some plow through the whole book in one draft; others write books in pieces over numerous drafts. And almost—*almost*—all authors could benefit from having some sort of editorial guidance in refining that work into the most publishable form.

If they want it.

If, because what I said to that art class holds true for writers as well: I think that once you have learned to use the tools necessary for creating new works, you should drop out of school/stop attending lectures/quit asking for someone else's opinion and just do the work. *The work* is all that matters, and nothing can teach you how to find and express your own voice better than just doing more *work*, as often as possible. Using the tools gives you greater facility with the tools, and the more you express, the more you are able to express, in the way you want to express it, until finally everything you write has the ring of confidence and authenticity.

Two caveats, here: first, if you are a beginning author, you may want or need the help of a developmental editor, to better find your path to your own authentic voice; and even seasoned authors can benefit from refresher courses on craft from someone who is truly inspired as a teacher, like my brother Kevin Ikenberry. And second, if you are selling your work to a publisher, they are going to want to have a strong editorial voice in the thing they are going to try to sell—and in that instance, it's part of the deal you signed up for, and part of the concession you make as part of that publishing relationship. But outside of those two examples, I don't think any writer anywhere, should be required to consult on anything with an editor or publisher or agent or really anyone in a position to request changes in the work...

...unless you *want* it.

I think that after all the seminars and lectures on craft, you have to take what you have learned that works for you and just start typing —because using the tools is how you become better at using them. There's really no other way. And there's only so much you can get from lectures by anyone else giving you the answers to a test that changes every time you sit down to write.

Some of the early genre writers stood by the assertion that volume improved quality: Robert Silverberg sometimes cranked out a novel a week; Ray Bradbury, my own mentor, was famous for having written short stories on pay-as-you-write typewriters that cost ten cents per hour to rent. There's no time to waste when you have to submit what you finish, and you only have six dimes in your pocket.

Those stories probably received little editing because of the compressed frequency of their publication schedules. These days, there are two groups who receive little to no editing: newer authors, who don't have the connections to find editors, or the means to hire them, but who want to publish anyway; and the super-successful mega-authors, who have been elevated by their commercial success past the point of needing actual editing.

I have friends who complained that Clive Barker's books had gotten too long, and would have been better if they'd been edited down. Maybe they could have been more streamlined; maybe not. But if the final form that was published is the one that was closest to Clive's vision of the ideal version of those books, then as far as I'm concerned, that's the only version that *needed* to be published.

Stephen King has, more and more frequently, inserted little stylistic bits into his novels that would have been stripped out by any editor editing anyone else—but he has, by any measure, earned the right to have his work released exactly as he wrote it.

When George R. R. Martin suggested that his next novel in the *Song of Ice and Fire* was imminent, his publisher went into overdrive to prepare to launch the book as fast as possible—including scheduling printing time and materials that would go into action as quickly as the book could be delivered and formatted. No mention of actual editing as necessary or important to the work.

And even Diana Gabaldon said, during a NasFic Koffeeklatsch, that she needed to finish a book before a cruise, so she was delivering a chapter at a time, which would then be recorded for the eventual audiobook release. Again, only talk of a streamlined process, with no real editing even hinted at, because the publisher knew the books were going to sell anyway.

And, in what is at once both my favorite example of creative freedom and my dreaded cautionary tale, I have had violent—relatively violent—disagreements with close friends about the fact that I really *liked* the movie *The Phantom Menace* and the two sequels that followed. They were of the opinion that the movies would have been better if someone had taken control away from George Lucas and revised the stories. I'm of the opinion that George had earned the right to tell his stories, his way, with no editing or interference in the telling. He paid for it—it was his magic to use.

Then again, when he sold the IP to Disney, and then expected them to follow his notes for new movies—which they absolutely didn't do—he learned, the hard way, that if you give up control of a story that you created, there's really no way to unring that bell. Others who did not have the same grasp of the story that its creator had told stories that did not resonate in as mythic a fashion and were not in harmony with his own vision.

Now, in that last example, George actually *sold* his story—it was a given that he had no formal influence on the direction of the story any longer—but to me, it's not really all that different from the latitude we authors give to publishers when we sign contracts to publish our books.

This all may sound like a great diatribe against editors—which, I will admit, it kind of is—but even *that* is rooted in my own experiences. I started out self-editing my creative works, because I was the one publishing those works. And then later, when I started writing novels for a German editor—a successful author himself, who had been a fan of my comics—he also did not offer any significant editorial suggestions about my manuscripts, but was mostly happy just to be reading new story material by *me*.

So, when I had my first real editing experience, with my book *Here, There Be Dragons*, it was a major awakening about just how much an editor can contribute to the finished version of a book.

I think a good editor can help to shape and improve work by even the most seasoned of novelists. I benefitted in huge ways from the quality of editing on my novels—especially with one book that a single editorial comment turned upside down. What had been the prologue was now the epilogue, and that one comment resulted in a complete rewrite of the book. It is a better book because of that comment and led to a better ending to for the series.

But I have also had editorial changes imposed that had nothing to do with the quality of the work, including being told I had to truncate a climactic scene and cut several chapters of a book, because the retail price had already been set, and including those chapters would increase the cost of producing the book. So, they were cut.

That's what I'm opposed to: changing a creator's work to serve other purposes.

I had agreed to accept those editorial requests as a part of my publishing contract, but I was not happy about it, because what I had envisioned for *The Shadow Dragons* had been much grander. Perhaps I'll have the opportunity to correct that choice sometime in the near future.

My rule of thumb about editing has always been that it has to be a situation of mutual trust: if an editor points out something they see as a problem, it's worth looking at more closely; but if the conclusion of the author is that nothing needs to be changed or added, the editor should be willing to accept that as the final creative word. Neil Gaiman says that when an editor says there's a problem with a specific passage, they are almost always right; and the suggestion they make to fix it is almost always wrong.

I think a lot of the value an editor brings to a creative work can largely be achieved through beta readers and peer reading groups.

Good readers can absolutely point out where a manuscript could have greater clarity and effectiveness, but I would never submit a work to the same readers more than once. It's been my experience that on the first pass, they are reading for clarity in communication, and are on high alert for instances where the book might be improved; but after that, they are reading to see how you incorporated the suggestions they made, which is not a good basis for making more changes to a manuscript.

As my experience grew, the actual editing became less frequent. The first book in my *Chronicles of the Imaginarium Geographica* came back with a twenty page edit letter, three hundred post-it notes, and numerous more written edits. The seventh book came back with a one page edit letter, consisting of five story questions and the note that "...apparently, after seven books, you have this thing down."

Using the tools makes you better at using the tools. The more words you write, the better those words will become—because an endless evaluation of a few words can perhaps make them a bit better; but learning through volume helps you learn and improve organically, without the need to have someone else try to decide what parts of the story are authentically in your voice, and what parts aren't. Doing the work makes creating the work easier—and the work is all that matters.

I am always and forever an absolute supporter of creative independence—and every time you begin a new story, you are in the same position as the noted authors I reverenced above: you have complete control of how that story is going to go, and complete control of how the final version will read. Along the way you may have the need or desire to submit that story for evaluation and feedback, and then you have the choice to implement that feedback or not depending on how you are positioning that work to be published.

I am a hybrid author who began my career as a true independent, found success as a traditionally published author, and then returned to my independent roots for many of the reasons I have mentioned in this essay. There's a point—more of an aesthetic one than an economic one—where you know how to use all the tools to say what you want to say. Any editorial comment that is solicited may be used at the discretion of the creator, but not imposed, unless you choose to submit to such direction. That's what it comes down to, in the end: how much of your voice is really authentic? And how much of that authenticity are you willing to change in the hopes it will somehow improve the clarity of the story you are striving to tell?

Those are the only questions that are relevant, I think. None of us are likely to be around in a hundred years, so what will remain are the stories we tell. That is how we pass on what is important to us. What we have to decide is how authentic those stories are—we always have the chance to change them, if we want to; or change them, if we must. But no matter how we decide, nothing moves forward until those stories are written, and finished, and then presented to the world, and how that is done is as individual and personal a choice as exists.

Get the words done in whatever way works for you. Because the work is all that really matters.

FLAVORLESS
BY ERIK LYND

Erik Lynd is an award-winning author who writes novels and short stories primarily in horror, dark fantasy, and urban fantasy genres. Currently, he is in the middle of two ongoing urban fantasy series; Silas Robb and The Hand of Perdition series. He also writes the occasional horror novel, such as *Asylum* and *The Collection*. He lives in the U.S. Pacific Northwest, where it does rain a lot, and no, he does not mind it. You can learn more about his writing at eriklynd.com.

It was all sparks and needles, like someone had shoved the mother of all hornets nests into Phil's nose. Fireworks against the back of his closed eyelids. Then the pain, sharp and all-consuming. He should have been standing, but his hands slid across gritty asphalt and through the thick build-up of dirt on the street. He landed on his shoulder in the gutter.

Rusty mucus slid into his mouth from the back of his throat. He wanted to spit but didn't have time before a hand clawed at his lapel and pulled him up. A fist slammed into his jaw. Then he did spit.

Blood splattered across that same gutter, one of his teeth bounced along the sidewalk.

Phil wished they had been on the Strip. Not that violence didn't happen there, hell, it was Vegas, there could be violence anywhere in this town. But at least on the Strip, there were too many witnesses to make this more than a severe beating. Here, on a dark side street, surrounded by warehouses and dilapidated buildings, Bobby's men could do anything they liked.

He had high hopes they would let him live, however, because dead men rarely pay off gambling debts. The question was, would he want to live after they were done with him?

He waited for another blow, but when none came, he opened his eyes slowly. He held up his hands in front of this face, an involuntary move to ward off any more blows, but it did not stop the boot from slamming into his stomach.

There hadn't been much in there, but what there had been—half a tuna sandwich, some chips, a not-insignificant amount of vodka— suddenly left the same way they had gone in. On the plus side, the blows stopped as he vomited into the conveniently placed gutter drain.

They gave him a moment, time to pull himself together before they continued the conversation. Phil knelt there suspended over the drain, spitting blood and bile in between poking at the empty spot of his gum line with his tongue. One tooth was gone for sure and two others wiggled in their sockets.

"Tonight, Phil. That's all you got," Raul said. "It's all Bobby's gonna give ya."

Raul wasn't the smartest guy on Bobby's payroll, but none of them were Rhodes scholars. Three others stood behind Raul. Phil didn't know their names; Raul always did the talking in these types of discussions.

"You be at the game by three a.m. It'll be at the Big House tonight. You know where that is, Phil?"

When Phil didn't immediately answer, Raul shoved his foot into his shoulder, knocking him off his knees and back into the gutter.

"I didn't hear you, Phil," Raul said. "I held back, so I know I didn't break your damn jaw."

"Yeah," Phil croaked, followed by a moan he had tried to hold in. "Big House tonight, I got it."

Raul was a big man, more muscle than many pro wrestlers. On the other hand, Phil was slim, slight some would say, and given to falling over in a strong wind. If Raul wanted him dead, he didn't need his three buddies.

Raul leaned over and pulled Phil up to get his face as close as possible.

"Be there, Phil, but more importantly, have the money. Cuz if you're not there and there is no money, then I got to hunt your ass down. I'm a lazy man, Phil, so if you don't show, I'll just pay a visit to your girl. She works at Stanley's, right, down the street? Shakes her ass by the name of Charity? When I'm done with her, ain't nobody gonna want a lap dance. Got it?"

Phil nodded. His blood turned cold. Despite the pain, this threat turned his stomach the most.

"I can't hear you, Phil. Got it?"

"Yeah, yeah. The Big House, three a.m. I'll have the money."

"Sure you will, Phil. It's a million dollars now. Look at you, where you got a million dollars? In one of those torn pockets? You ain't got shit, let alone a million dollars. Don't know why Bobby let it go this long, but it ends tonight. You're more valuable as a lesson now."

He heard them walk away chuckling. He didn't listen to the jokes, but Phil knew the gist.

Raul was right, though. A million dollars was impossible. This was Vegas. It sold dreams but rarely made good on them. It was like the whole city was some nasty drug. If you went all-in with the promise of a great high, you never truly got there and you never really got out again.

Phil needed a place to pull himself together, to think. Raul was right. Stanley's was right around the corner. He had been heading there before this unfortunate encounter. He would see Julie—Charity to the masses—she would know what to do. At the very least he would get some comfort from her.

~

"What the hell happened to you?"

Phil sat slumped on a curved sofa covered in a harsh neon pink. How she could even see what he looked like in the multicolored light swirling around him, he had no clue. He supposed his swollen face looked particularly gruesome in the black light, the dried blood on his face and collar a particularly deep black shade.

Julie stood in front of him, the blacklight setting her work outfit aglow. Normally, he would appreciate the way the radiant outfit showed off her curves and skin. But she stood hands on hips, glaring. There was concern too—at least he liked to think it was there under the frown. So much for the comfort, but even in her anger she was beautiful.

Then the frown broke and she sat down next to him. There was the concern. She still loved him.

"Did you get in another fight? Who was it this time?"

"Raul and the usuals. You should see how *they* look."

She didn't smile.

"Jesus, Phil, baby. Bobby's crew? Do you still owe him?"

He wanted to say *Don't worry about it, baby; I got it covered.* He wanted to reassure her, put her at ease, take her home, make love to her, forget about all of this. This is what he always did, and he always worked it out, always had a plan. He was a gambler. Schemes, getting out of jams, that was his superpower. God knows he'd had enough practice. But this was different. This might be too far, too big. A million dollars too big.

"I just need my luck to change, I need an upswing."

He let the words fade away. She wasn't buying it. She knew him too well. She gently reach out to touch his wounds. It was all in his head, but he thought maybe her touch did a little healing, made him feel a little better.

"I may have gone too far this time," he started again. "It's a deep hole."

"How deep?"

"A million dollars deep."

She stood up like he was suddenly on fire. "Holy shit, Phil. You asshole. How could you even—and with Bobby. My God, Phil, what —I mean, how can you fix this?"

He didn't know, but he had to somehow. "Like I said, I just need my luck to change. I feel it, it just needs to click and then—"

"And then? Christ, Phil, it's a million dollars,"

"Okay, so I need a lot of luck."

She sat back down and now it was her turn to slump, she leaned against him. He kept from wincing, it was the least he could do.

"It wasn't supposed to go this way. I love you. but you go off and do the stupidest shit."

Phil moved his arm, gingerly, so that it wrapped her shoulder. He pulled her close despite another surge of pain. "I'll fix it, I know I can. Just have to figure it out."

They sat for a moment. Rotating songs of rock and hip-hop blasted through the club's speakers. It smelled like perfume, whiskey and an unidentifiable scent that he liked to think of as desperation. Of course this was from his memory. Right now he couldn't smell anything through his broken nose.

"You really think some luck will help?"

He was a superstitious man. He supposed all hardcore gamblers were to some extent. He had his routines, his patterns, and deep down he knew it made a difference. Some games were skill games, like poker, some pure luck like roulette—though some would argue that assessment—but all games had that supernatural element of luck. It was a god they all prayed to. And in the end, the one they all turned to.

"Yeah, babe, some good luck."

"Then I'll get you some." She sat up and called out, "Sinnamon, hey Sinnamon."

The club was mostly empty, and her voice still cut through the bass heavy sound system. A woman he had never seen at the club before turned from the bar. She was graceful and radiant. Her lingerie caught the light and surrounded her in a soft aura. She smiled at Charity and glided over. Her feet touched the floor, but her body seemed to float gracefully. Like no earthly constraints could hold her down.

She was Asian, no, Pacific Islander, perhaps Filipino if he had to guess. She looked at Phil with eyes that held the promise of intense delights. He had no idea a look, a movement, could convey so much. He would never cheat on Charity, the love of his life, but if he had to, it would have been with this Sinnamon.

"Turn it off, Sinnamon. This is my man, not a customer."

Her shoulder slumped and the mystery disappeared, she was still the beautiful woman of a moment ago, but something had changed. He was no longer the target.

"So this is the Phil I hear so much about. Gotta tell you, Jules, you never described him as a beat-up piece of meat."

"Normally he's less bloody and swollen. That's why I have to ask a favor. Can you give him some of your luck?" Charity asked.

"Hey babe, I think I'm gonna need a plan and something stronger than blowing on a pair of dice," Phil said.

"Quiet, Lumpy. Trust me on this, she's got a gift."

"You sure about this? I mean, you know it can be a little double-edged," Sinnamon said.

Phil didn't like the sound of that. Charity looked at him as though trying to determine his worth through sight alone. Then she shrugged. "I think it's our only choice."

Phil said nothing, he had no idea what these women were talking about. For now, he just went with it. Charity always seemed to know best.

"Gimme a dollar," Sinnamon said and held out her hand. He looked pointedly down at the bills protruding from her panties, but she just raised one eyebrow and stretched her hand out further. "I don't have all day."

With a small grunt Phil pulled out his wallet. He had precious few bills in there, but a dollar wouldn't make much a difference in his case anyway.

With his dollar in hand Sinnamon walked to the vending machine in the dark back corner of the club. She didn't seem to float anymore. She walked like a mere mortal now.

Phil had never noticed this vending machine before. It was old, and while the place wasn't as recently remodeled as some of the clubs closer to the Strip, it was still newer than this beast of a machine. He watched as she fed his dollar into it and retrieved some small snack from the bottom bin.

"Funny time to have a snack craving."

"Shut up, Phil. This might save your ass."

Yours too, he thought but didn't have the strength to tell her.

Sinnamon returned to the couch and held up her prize. A pack of gum. She brought it to her lips and kissed it. For a moment Phil saw it again, the mystery, the ethereal beauty, the inhuman grace. Then it was gone and he saw Sinnamon the stripper once again.

"While the flavor lasts in this piece of gum you will have crazy good luck. You will win most games, things will just go your way, the dice will fall in your favor. Not just games: everything will work out for you, life will work out. But once the flavor fades so will your favor, your luck will turn sour. It might not exactly go bad, but nothing good will come of it."

Phil looked at the pack. It was called Fruit Stripe and had a multi-colored zebra on the front. He vaguely remembered it from when he was a kid.

"A pack of gum?" Phil asked.

The ladies nodded.

"Trust her, babe. It really works."

Yes, Phil was superstitious, but even he had his limits. "I don't see how gum can have such magic."

"Unlike the half-smoked cigarette you carry in the tin of yours, or those socks you wouldn't wash until I threatened to leave you?"

Good point, he thought.

"Just go try it out," Sinnamon said. "Go up the street and test it on some slots. But I wouldn't stick with just slots, the magic starts to fade on truly random-type games."

He stared at the pack, flipping it over and over in his fingers. This wasn't exactly what he was expecting when he set out to come up with a plan. But at this point he couldn't come up with a better option.

It was a small, off-the-strip affair—a baby casino basking in the shadows of its larger brethren. Probably owned by one of them, but small enough that he might be overlooked. He wasn't welcome in many of the larger ones. He hadn't always had the smoothest of gambling careers. So small and out-of-the-way worked perfect for this little test.

He stood before the machine with the largest payout in the room, twenty-five grand. And looked down at the handful of coins in his palm. It wasn't all the money he had left, but damn near.

In this other hand he held a stick of gum. Multicolored stripes ran down the length of it. It felt old, probably was going to be stale, but it was also full of chemicals and would probably still be safe long after he had faded to dust. He popped it into his mouth.

It was surprisingly good, refreshing really, but nothing special happened, no magic buzz, no blinding light, no sudden feeling of invincibility. He hadn't really known what to expect, but a part of him was expecting something.

He slipped the coin into the slot and pushed the spin button.

Phil found himself in front of the casino, a bag containing twenty-five thousand dollars clutched tightly in his hand. He wasn't sure exactly how it had happened, though, despite having just lived through it.

He had stood numb as the jackpot was hit, as the lights flashed, as the casino agent came over to congratulate him on hitting the jack-pot, though the man didn't seem too excited about it. He had stood quietly as the man ushered him over to the cage and had him fill out some paperwork. He had felt a little bemused as the teller counted out the stacks of bills and slipped them into the bag.

And now he was standing outside with a large sum of money in a black satchel dangling from his hands.

It had worked. The gum, that ancient stick of gum had worked. At some point, he was not sure when, the flavor had gone. He chewed now on a lifeless wad of nothing. Blandness.

But it didn't matter, he could spit it out, it was over. He looked down at the bag. Not over, no, just starting, he needed a million dollars. Hell, if this gum really was working he could get ten million, fifty million. He and Jules could have everything they could ever want.

The gum was pretty awful now, he was just about to spit it out when he was slammed into from behind. He went sprawling on the sidewalk, hitting the ground for a second time that night.

The bag, the precious bag flew from his hands, landing at the feet of a young man in shorts and tank top, dirty and stained. Not a tourist, a homeless man perhaps.

"Sorry, dude," someone said from above him. Phil turned to see a collection of tourists, the tallest seemed unsteady on his feet. "I usually hold my liquor way better than this."

His buddies laughed and they staggered off down the street, looking strangely out of place this far off the Strip.

Phil heard running and dread filled him. The homeless man was gone and so was the bag.

"Shit," Phil said.

The man was halfway down the block before Phil was able to get to his feet and run after him. After a dozen yards he knew it was fruitless. He had to stop. Even if his body hadn't been broken he doubted he could have caught the youthful runner.

He caught himself against the wall of a convenience store. What kind of screwed-up luck did he have? Then he noticed the gum had really gone bad, sour and foul. He spit it out immediately and slid down the wall until he was sitting on the ground.

The gum had turned bad like his luck. The girls had told him, but now he understood, now he knew. This was good, he told himself, he understood the rules. He could work with that.

He just had to find another casino; he had to be careful. A plan was forming slowly, but it was there.

It was midnight when he found himself standing in front of the small building known as the Big House. It was an older, unremarkable structure that received its nickname from the large bars covering the glass storefront on the bottom floor. Overkill for a deserted building, but then the building wasn't really abandoned.

It housed a moving card game. A game that kept itself far from the eyes of the gambling board and all its rules, hidden away from the reach of the IRS and other law enforcement agencies. A place where there were no limits, for those that liked to play with no limits.

Every few days the game moved to a different location, all owned by Bobby Corval, who also ran this particular game. The game wasn't running every single night, but close. It had an edge to it, this game; unlike the ones in the glittering palaces on the Strip, there was an element of danger here. Cheaters weren't escorted out or arrested. They were pulled out into the alley and shot. All bets were viable: cash, cars, even people, although Phil had never participated in that kind of tender.

He had another bag of cash in his hands, this one quite a bit larger. One hundred grand in cash was tucked away in it, plenty as buy-in money to the highest stakes game in town. He had collected it like he had the first twenty-five thousand, hitting a handful of smaller casinos, but this time carefully paying attention to the gum, spitting it out at the hint of flavor fading. It was quick, it turned faster than your standard Trident or Big Red.

He was careful also not to use too much of it. He needed as many sticks as possible for this, the next stage of his plan.

Slots were not going to be his ticket to a million dollars. The jackpots got smaller, his winnings thinning out as he progressed. Sinnamon had been right: such simple luck did not last. He had to switch to a different game.

Playing legit poker at one of the big rooms would have taken days to amass a million, too much paperwork, too many eyes. Even getting into the official big games at the last minute as a nobody would have been impossible.

His only option was this game. It was the only way to reach that million-dollar mark. The only way to pay off Bobby was to beat him. But luck was on his side

Phil knocked on the door.

"You have some balls," Raul said as he escorted Phil up the stairs.

The inside of the building was much better maintained than the exterior. While the outside was all graffiti and dirt-black stains and caked-on grime, the inside was marble floors and well-lit hallways. The wood paneling made him think of old-style gentleman's clubs he imagined might exist in London or some bygone era of New York. Crystal chandeliers completed the look.

"You think you can win the million from him. Lucky Bobby Corval? If he even lets you play, it'll be as a joke. Just a waste of the last hours of your life? You are an addict."

Raul shook his head and then opened the door to the game room. Ten tables, with a handful of players at each, filled the large room. Poker and blackjack were the primary games, but a few slots lined the walls. Nobody really played these; they were more for decoration or the hangout for a girlfriend while her man played at the table.

There was a bar, of course. You don't gamble without drinking. Air filters struggled to siphon off the cigar and cigarette smoke, but they weren't quite up to the task, and a haze hung over several of the tables, making it all look like a scene from an old James Bond movie.

Raul marched him over to Bobby's table, the only nearly full one in the room. Bobby himself was a big man, mid-forties, with a smile that flashed from jovial to *I'm gonna have to kill you* in one second flat. Phil was met with the second variety.

He leaned back when he saw Phil approaching the table. "I see you got a large bag there. Any chance you stuffed a million dollars in there? I have to say I would be impressed."

"Not quite. It's a hundred grand. I want in on tonight's game."

Bobby laughed and looked around at the other players. "What's to stop me from taking that bag right there, with only part of the money that you owe me, and throwing your corpse in the trash out back?"

Phil shrugged trying to appear casual, confident. He had the gum, but it wouldn't stop a bullet. "Your boy here said I had until three. I get a tiny chance, and you get a few hours to watch me squirm. Either way, you get all I have."

Bobby smiled big. "I like it. It's like out of a movie. It'll be a good story to warn people not to fuck me over."

Most of the others at the table chuckled, a few looked a little nervous. Not everyone in the room was a killer, some just had the money and influence to tour the edges. They didn't have to live there. They got a thrill from brushing this close to the criminal element, but they had money, and that was good enough for Bobby.

The game was Texas Hold 'em. They had all played it thousands of times. There was little talk as the cards began to slide around the table.

Phil had a strategy. He only had so much gum and he had to ration it. That meant he also had to rely on his skill, which was not inconsiderable, only leaning on the gum when he need a drastic change on his luck. The only problem was the clock: he had three hours. Any other night he would never have made it, but tonight he had the edge. That little pack of gum.

The first hour went well, and he was up a hundred grand when it started to turn. He was not going fast enough and made some risky bets. That did not go well. Before he dug a hole too deep, he slipped that pack of gum into his hands. Then slid out a piece below the table. It was just a stick of gum; they probably wouldn't even notice, but he was certain they would be able to tell he was cheating, that they would know it was magic gum. Somehow, they would know.

He kept it out of sight as he slipped the stick into his mouth. The first explosion of fruity goodness went off in his mouth, and he could feel his luck changing. He moved fast, trying to get as many hands in as he could, before the flavor was gone.

It worked. The cards turned his way, and Bobby's jovial smile faded to a grimace at the end of each hand.

Phil played it out. He'd slip a stick of gum into his mouth when needed, spit it out into his drink later when it went bad. He never made a show of it, covered it up like he was simply working on some chew.

It was shortly after two, the clock ticking. He was up three-quarters of a million and Phil was actually starting to think he might make it. He glanced at the pack. Only three left; he had to be careful, but he could make it. Maybe he could even get more than the million he owed. For the first time it felt like he could come out ahead.

Bobby glanced at the clock. He hadn't smiled for the last hour as the time ticked away and the money piled up in front of Phil. He leaned over and whispered something in Raul's ear. Who quickly left through a side door.

Perhaps, Phil thought, he should just plan on getting out of here with his life.

"A five-minute break, gentlemen," Bobby said. He said it to everyone, but he looked at Phil as though he was speaking only to him.

Bobby was nervous, Phil could tell—and he should be. Phil was going to win, and when he did, Bobby would have to let him walk out. There were too many people here to spread the word that Bobby's word meant nothing. Liars, thieves and thugs they might be, but reputation was everything in the circles Bobby hung out in.

Phil had to get more of this gum. This was crazy. He and Julie could live like kings on his winnings. He would have to still be careful, maybe even move out of Vegas for a little bit, hit Reno, Tahoe, little places, let Vegas cool for him. Maybe even take a trip to the casinos in Europe—talk about a James Bond movie.

"Hey, baby."

Phil recognized the voice and the woman plopping herself down in Bobby's lap. He had been so lost in his fantasy land that he never noticed Raul escorting the girl to the table.

"Here you go, Bobby. Your good luck charm." She handed him a pack of gum. Colorful stripes wound their way down the packaging.

In a daze Phil pulled out one of his few remaining pieces and began to unwrap it.

"You're my lucky charm, Sinnamon," Bobby said. His smile had returned in full force. "I want you to meet my business associate here: he's been playing the best game of his life, might have even beat me."

When she saw Phil, she gasped. Bobby, not a stupid man, noticed the look on her face and looked back at Phil, confused. Unfortunately, Phil was sometimes a stupid man. His pack of gum lay on the edge of the table. Stunned by Sinnamon's arrival, Phil hadn't been paying attention. Bobby's eyes widened in understanding. Then came the anger.

"Shit," Phil said. And slipped a piece into his mouth and snatched the last two remaining sticks from the table.

With a roar Bobby stood, hand darting under his jacket. Sinnamon squawked as she fell to the ground. Phil didn't need to be a genius to know he was going for a gun. The game was over, and so was Phil.

Juicy flavor filled his mouth as Bobby leveled the gun at him. Sinnamon's legs had become entangled with Bobby's and he stumbled as the gun went off with a loud crack. Shattering the corner of the wooden chair where Phil sat. The gun blast broke Phil's paralysis, and that's when all hell broke loose.

The tourists in the group panicked and bolted in every direction. Raul and Bobby's other minions seemed startled and most of them pulled their guns out of instinct. They might not know what was going on, but it was probably safer for them to have a weapon in hand. The sundry other criminal element not on Bobby's payroll stood back trying to get a read on the situation.

Phil rolled off the chair and onto the floor. He had no weapon. It was the best move he could make. Flavor swirled around his mouth, and a waitress tripped over his leg, stumbling into Raul, who fell back just as his gun was leaving its holster. Raul must have forgotten the safety, because it went off into the gut of one of his associates. The man dropped as Raul, off-balance, was dragged to the ground by the shrieking waitress.

Phil rolled and staggered to his feet, his body still a little broken from his earlier conversation with Raul and company. He moved slower than he wanted.

It was pure chaos now: two gunshots and the tourists broke, the ratio was off and there weren't enough cold-hearted thugs to keep things calm. Women screamed and cussed. Chairs and tables fell.

Across their table Bobby glared at him. Somehow he had lost his gun. But what really concerned him was that Bobby was chewing on something. Then the big man leaped onto the table and straight at Phil.

Phil could have easily dodged the charge, but he bounced off someone running by and staggered directly into Bobby's path. Bobby was upon him. But there was still flavor in Phil's mouth. What should have been an easy grab and tackle wasn't, and Bobby's hands missed his jacket. His body still carried through, and they both went down.

Bobby was on top, his fist flying toward a trapped Phil, but what should have been a final, maybe even fatal blow went askew as a stray foot caught Bobby in the side of the head. Phil brought his knee up to the man's groin. It was right there as Bobby knelt above Phil, an easy target. Somehow, though, his knee missed and drove into Bobby's thigh. Not anywhere near the level of pain he was going for, but enough to unbalance Bobby even more.

Phil was able to roll out from underneath him. It was the battle of luck versus luck, at least while the flavor lasted, but Phil could already taste the flavor leaving.

Speaking of which, it was time for him to leave too. In a room full of armed enemies and not-so-innocent bystanders, his luck would run out first. Trusting in the power of the gum, he had only one move. He got to his feet and ran at the nearest window. It shattered outward as he sailed through it.

He should have been cut to ribbons; moves like that only worked on TV. Luckily, he only experienced a few minor cuts from the glass shards that rained down around him when he landed in a dumpster. He didn't remember the dumpster being in that part of the alley. Usually it was at the other end so as not to bother the guests at the game.

A cry from above made him glance up. He saw Bobby sailing out the window. Diving like a madman straight at him. He felt his mouth go dry, but worse than that, the flavor was gone.

Bobby fell on him, driving him deep into the bags of filth. Phil tried to shift from under him. He needed to get out of the way of heavy punches he knew were coming.

"You son of a bitch. You try to cheat my game! MY GAME!"

He felt a punch, but it was a glancing blow, painful but not damaging, and now Phil knew Bobby's flavor was fading.

"And you slept with my girl, you son of bitch." Bobby continued, obviously not aware of his turn of luck. It also explained why he was so pissed: he thought Phil had slept with Sinnamon. How else would Phil have gotten the favor of her luck?

He couldn't set the record straight now. Bobby would never listen. Besides, he had other pressing matters. Phil spit out the flavorless luck and immediately the bags underneath him shifted. He sank out of Bobby's reach, and the big man flailed to keep his balance.

For a moment he was free, surrounded by rotting food and what he suspected were used diapers. Some nauseating combination of fluids ran across his forehead.

He ignored it all and popped his last piece of gum in his mouth. He thought he'd had more, but he must have lost some as his luck shifted. This was it. He had a horrible idea, but it was the only plan he could think of on the spot.

Phil clawed his way to the top of the pile and spotted Bobby a few feet away poking through the bags, looking for him. He had to keep him distracted.

"You know," Phil said. Bobby's head snapped around. "She did mention that I was way better than her 'tiny' boyfriend."

That did it. Bobby jumped or rather tried to, the bags mysterious shifted again and he fell deeper. Phil, mouth full of an unnaturally good taste, reached the edge easily. The bags beneath him were solid and did not shift around. Phil paused at the top, one leg out of the dumpster, one leg in. Bobby had recovered and had almost reached his dangling leg.

Phil didn't wait to see the gangster's next move; he swung his leg over the edge and dropped to the alley below. Bobby was right behind him, pulling himself over the lip.

Phil sprinted toward the main street. It was the middle of the night and deserted, but he had to trust in his fruity luck.

He made it to the curb and turned. Bobby was only a few feet away. He crouched, but did not launch himself at Phil. Bobby was pissed, but he knew that something else was at work here. He knew that care was called for. And that was exactly what Phil didn't want. A careful Bobby would screw up his plan.

Bobby's face twisted up as though he had just tasted something horrible. He had realized his luck had gone bad. He smiled a toothy grin at Phil, like an animal satisfied its prey was trapped.

Bobby pulled his full pack of gum from his pocket.

Phil didn't know what to do. He still had flavor, but it wouldn't matter if Bobby spit out his. He did the only thing he could think of: he lunged toward Bobby and punched him in the gut just as the thug was about to spit.

Although calling it a punch was giving it too much credit—he was never much a of fighter, nor that much of a lover despite what he had told Bobby in the dumpster. His fist was more of a flailing attempt at a punch.

But it connected, and it was enough of a surprise that Bobby stepped back. He didn't cry out because the punch didn't have that kind of force, and he didn't gasp as Phil often did when he received a gut punch.

Better than all that, however, Bobby swallowed. He looked at Phil in shock and confusion. He had swallowed his bad-luck gum. They looked at each other, neither one quite sure what it could mean, but they both understood it couldn't be good.

Bobby screamed in rage and charged. Phil put his arms up and scrunched up his face in anticipation of the devastating blow. But he held onto hope as the last little bit of flavor lingered in his mouth.

Neither had seen the rotten banana peel at edge of the curb. Perhaps Phil had dragged it there from the dumpster; he was covered with all sort of garbage and stains. Or maybe it had already been there. Either way, it was Bobby's bad luck that he stepped on it. That his momentum carried him past a cowering Phil and into the deserted street beyond. Where he tumbled to the asphalt face first, his impact much more painful than Phil's earlier experience.

Bobby rolled over, blood running down his face, and looked at Phil, a little stunned.

"Is that it?" Bobby said, as if they both had been expecting more.

Phil wasn't sure whose luck, bad or good had brought that banana peel to be there, right at that moment, but he liked to think it was his last little bit of good flavor that caused the large truck to decide to take a side street that night, and his luck that distracted the driver as it plowed into a surprised Bobby sitting in the street.

Phil grabbed Julie's hand and pulled her away from the bar at Stanley's. He pulled her toward a dark corner booth.

"Jesus, babe, you smell like, like..."

"A dumpster, yeah, I know. We gotta get out of here. End your shift early, we gotta go pack. We are getting out of this town."

"Wait, slow down, what happened? Did everything go well with Bobby? Did you get him the money?"

"Sort of. Bobby is dealt with, but we gotta get out of here. I will tell you everything once we're moving. Go change. I don't want to be here anymore. Things need to cool down."

She took in everything he said and instantly accepted it. As long as he eventually explained, he knew she was on board. Except for one thing.

"How are we going to live? I got a little money, but unless you got some more cash with that luck, it won't last long."

"Don't worry about that; I think we are going to be just fine."

In his pocket, Phil's hand clutched a blood-splattered, almost-full pack of multicolored gum.

HOW TO WRITE A STORY IN 24 HOURS

BY ERIK LYND

This seems like an odd title to me. On one hand it is obvious. Who needs an essay on how to write a short story in twenty-four hours? The math is easy, and perhaps that's the silver-bullet answer to this question, if it is a question. I estimate I write 1000 words per hour. Sometimes around 500 at the beginning and over 1000 as I reach the end, but 1000 is probably my conservative average throughout the story. So if a short story is, say, 3000 to 5000 words, I'm looking at three to five hours.

Done. Wrote a story in less than twenty-four hours.

But that's not the real issue, is it? Because on the other hand, the number of words really doesn't matter. The math doesn't really matter. Let's talk about what I think really matters, what I think is the real concern with writing a story so "quickly": time and ideas (beyond just the beginning premise). Let's start with time.

The story included in this anthology from me was written in about seven hours spread out over the course of twenty-four. I must say, however, I had it easy. It was an assignment given to us at the Writers of the Future writing workshop, and honestly, I had little else to do in those twenty-four hours, except dinner with my wife's family —and apparently, I missed a bunch of celebrity-watching in the lobby of the hotel we were staying at—but for the most part I had lots of dedicated time with no interruptions.

Usually when I write, as it is the case with most of you reading this essay, I have many other people, activities, and Netflix shows competing with my writing time. There's the day job that lasts until five p.m. Maybe I can squeeze out a half hour at lunch. There's the kids and spouse when I am done, dinner (eating or cooking or both), there's chores, there's the aforementioned Netflix shows (I call it "family time" as that sounds nicer than what I really do, more accurately described as my "lazy time").

Then there is music. Did I mention I play guitar (sort of) in a band? And, of course, video games, mustn't forget that (I play in obsessed bursts and then forget they exist for months at a time). I also must find some time to read; I mean, that was the reason I became a writer, after all.

I assume you have a similar full plate. There are two parts to finding the time to write: discipline and violence.

Start with the easier, less messy option: discipline. Identify the low-hanging fruit. That half hour at lunch, getting up an hour earlier while still having enough rest to function, the hour your spouse needs to find a good show on Netflix (yes, it is a running joke; we all know Amazon Prime Video is better). Maybe another hour at night after the kids are asleep. Preserve some reading time, however.

Great: you found three hours of split-up, disjointed time to commune with the muse and create genius. Could be more, or more likely less, but the principle is the same. Time to apply the discipline portion and sit down, fingers at keys or lips at recording device (but not pen to paper; that is for famous writers with way more than twenty-four hours). Assuming you are a newish writer, here is what is going to happen. During your first luxurious half hour of writing you are going to write one sentence and then stare at the wall knowing you only have a half hour and you haven't even had time for the coffee to soak in, or you need to envision many ways to slowly kill your boss because of the report/restocking/other inane non-writing task he has set upon you for the afternoon. You have only one sentence, and it is a shitty one, but maybe not; how the hell are you supposed to know? This writing thing is stupid.

But then, during your next writing break, you manage three more sentences. Unfortunately, they have nothing to do with the first, and you quickly delete two of them but keep one because you used a big, cool word you think sounds awesome. Your next writing period is a little better only because by this point you're too tired to think things through completely, and like a drunk you stumble along, putting words on paper.

My point is you won't get much work done when you start, and it might suck, but it might not; you won't really know. There is a good chance you will fail miserably at delivering a full story in twenty-four hours the first time you try (if you don't fail, then stop reading this essay and go write).

Now that I have you thoroughly depressed, let me let you in on the secret. The secret that is often overlooked by many writing instructors, famous novelists, and random "writers" on the internet.

You need to practice. A lot.

It is easy to believe that even the most revered writers did not start with a masterpiece, but it is not just quality that practice makes better; quantity also improves. Depth, amazing prose, show-not-tell, all those skills become better, faster the more you practice. The words come easier, the pacing more precise, the characters more defined, the story stronger the more you do it. You will also get better at fully utilizing those small windows of time you have found. You won't get a few thousand words done in a half hour, but you can get to a few hundred.

The real discipline isn't to make yourself write when you have your windows, it's to persevere when you fail repeatedly.

Eventually you might need more time than the short starts and stops you can cherry-pick throughout the day. It's time to get out the knife, it's time to carve. Cut some time away from the spouse, movies, video game time. Find compromises. Maybe you get takeout once or twice a week instead of cooking. Maybe your spouse takes on a few more chores so you can hit the page.

Talk to the family: let them know what you are trying to do. They should be supportive, and if not, ditch them. Okay, maybe not the kids—they're hard to get rid of—but if your significant other won't help or support you, time to get a new one. I'm serious about that: life is too short to hook up with someone who won't support your dreams.

I am not going to spend any more words on time management, as that is always unique to each person. You know better where to find the time than anybody. The important point to remember is that no matter how small a window you get, your efficiency increases the more you practice.

Let's turn to the second obstacle in writing a story in twenty-four hours. Ideas. Both the start of a story and the mid-point when you know the beginning and you might know the end, but have no idea to get from point A to point B.

Don't be that guy or woman who sits around waiting for "The Idea." They can't set fingers to the keyboard until they have the greatest idea ever thought up. Then they tweak it in their head, think about it, twist it around, and all the while the keyboard collects dust. I'm not talking about the writer kicking around an idea while he is working on something else. I'm talking about the person who must analyze each idea one at a time before even thinking about hitting the keys. Don't be that person.

Of course you can work out character and plot ahead of writing, but never let not knowing what to write stop you from writing. You are allowed to work it out while you write. You are allowed to go back and cycle through if you missed something. You are allowed to change the past if you realize you need to add a new scene or subplot. Writing need not be linear.

Once you have started the story, the next key is to have a sense of your characters. I find that if I let my characters lead me, ninety percent of the story is already written.

When the initial burst of idea is gone, when it is too soon for your thrilling climax, there is that mid-part. Some people call it the try/fails. I turn to my characters for guidance. The more you have their details captured in your mind the easier this will be. What are their likes and dislikes (as relevant to the story, no need to complete a hundred-page dossier after hours of Google research and image hunts)? Once you have the feel of your character, let them lead you around. Your job at that point is to just ignore the boring parts.

If they start to drift too far from the story, I might have to put up guardrails to guide them back. This is called plot. If they are going in direction that are not jiving with the story, then it is your job to create the situation that forces them to make the decisions you need them to make.

The point I am trying to make is that you can't wait until you have all the time you need or that you have all the answers for the story figured out before you begin to write. The more you practice at writing stories, at creating real characters, the easier it becomes to lean on the tools you are developing to guide you. Day by day it becomes more natural. The hardest part is sitting down and trusting the process.

THE BYGONE
BY ZACK BE

Zack Be is an author, obscure songwriter, psychotherapist, and PhD candidate long trapped in the Washington, DC-area gravity well. His fiction has appeared in *Analog Science Fiction and Fact*, *Asimov's Science Fiction*, and *Writers of the Future 36*. He was a finalist for the 2023 Jim Baen Memorial Science Fiction Award, and his band Pretty Bitter was the recipient of the 2023 Wammie Award for Best Pop Album and Best Pop Song for music from their album *Hinges*. More information about Zack's writing, music, and life can be found at zackbe.com.

"I'm done," I say, dropping the archaic game controller on our coffee table. "No one has the nerve to shoot me."

"Are you sure you don't want a few more minutes?" Erasmus probes.

All I want to do is sigh—and loudly—but that never lands as pleasantly as intended.

"I really wish everyone would stop asking me that," I mumble instead.

Erasmus rolls his eyes.

"*Especially* my husband," I continue. "Really, it's fine. I've had enough. What's the point of playing if they're all just going to let me win anyway?"

We lean together, our bodies blanketed beneath the blue glow of faux laser blasts strobing the *Doom* pause menu. Erasmus squeezes me like he always has, the stylized meat of his manicured hand grasping for whatever is left. I must feel like a handful of sand to him, slipping away the harder he hugs. But he knows there is nothing he or anyone else can do to stop me from aging-out of my own existence —the last person on earth to die from complications related to their old age, or more generally, the last person on Earth to age at all.

"Oh, come on, Aldo," he says, voice hovering just above the canned demonic chatter droning from the game. "It's like riding a bike. I bet you're winning because you've still got it."

"This is why I told you not to gamble anymore," I reply. "Seriously, you don't need to lie to me, or placate me. I think this isn't much like riding a bike at all."

"When was the last time you played?" he asks.

"I haven't even held one of these old controllers in probably 50 years, and the Ministry just had these servers rebooted for me. We still had wall warts and routers when this game came out, can you believe that?"

"I remember."

"God, the amount of work it must have taken to set this game up... I don't know why I asked for this."

"Don't worry about all that; this is *your* bucket list," Erasmus says. "And besides, other people are using it."

"They all just want to tell their friends that they played Old Aldo in some antique FPS."

"What's so wrong with that?"

"I heard one of the guards say they were selling tickets—*tickets*, Elmo—at the bars in the city. People are lined up around the block to let my avatar disembowel them."

"What else is there to do on a Tuesday night?" he asks.

We laugh and he pulls my head to his chest. I turn up my hearing aid and listen for the young heartbeat underneath.

"The whole scene is a little sad, that's all," I say.

"Well we don't want 'sad,' Aldo. If you're done, you're done."

"I'm done," I say, but Erasmus hesitates in turning off the screen, remote in hand.

"I just want you to be sure," he says. "I don't want you to feel like you're missing out on anything from your list. With so little time..."

"This freaking list," I say, poking his gut. "There's some deeply sophomoric irony in a man with no biological clock telling *me* he's worried about having 'so little time.' Cross my heart, Elmo, this just isn't the walk down memory lane I thought it would be. I'm sure."

The big monitor flicks back to an abstract screen saver and the lights come up to "mood" in our apartment. The city's tall ecolith towers loom outside our windows, their habitat spires spun to the heavens.

"What do you want to do now?" he asks.

"I want to stay here," I say. "Forget the list for tonight."

We snuggle in closer, and I try to ignore the posse of Ministry lackeys watching us from the edges of the room. Erasmus tries to ignore them as well, but I can tell by his fidgeting that he's feeling their glare.

"What is it?" I ask.

His eyes seem to dance, leaping between the guards and nurses and Ministry drone-cams recording my final weeks.

"I'm nervous," he starts, and I instantly recall how much I've learned to hate consoling him over my own imminent death.

"Everyone's nervous," I respond. "It's sort of a prerequisite for life."

"You know that's not what I mean," he says. "I want to know we're fulfilling everything you want. Playing games feels so inconsequential."

"Can we please not do this again?"

"I mean really, Aldo, are we doing enough? Is this really all you want to do before you go? You've got less than three weeks and all we do is play games and eat dinners and spend our nights in the same old penthouse."

"I'm 105, Elmo, I have limits."

"But the Ministry said we could do anything."

"Yes, they did."

"Then why aren't you asking for anything? This all just feels so... cursory."

"Not to me," I tell him. "I'm on my way out. Who do you think these events are for, exactly? Even this silly old game? I feel like I'm living this never-ending birthday party where I have to perpetually validate everyone else's charity. 'Please shoot me, Mr. Aldo, right in the kneecaps.'"

Erasmus leans back and frowns.

"Oh, Aldo," he says, "None of us know what you're going through."

"I can give you an idea," I say. "But you won't like hearing it."

"Go on," he whispers, eyes closed. "I can handle it."

I press a weathered thumb to his chin and nod.

"It's lonely," I say, "very lonely."

Erasmus hangs his head and I squeeze him back the best that I can manage. I know the embrace must feel superficial compared to how I used to hold him when we were both young. He's known this was going to happen since the day we met—that I would wither away and be gone, the last human with senescent cells. In all that time I never had the audacity to ask him to love me. He just did.

"Don't say that," Erasmus mutters. "I'm here with you."

I look around the room at the young nurses and publicists and armed Ministry personnel standing sentry, all of them prepared to keep me alive and safe until the bitter end.

"But it's true," I say, kissing his forehead with paper lips. "I am very alone indeed."

~

The skies above Oslo are bluer than I remember, and I think maybe the Ministry has done this for us.

Erasmus and I are walking arm and arm down the lanes of Frogner Park, our voices filling the air with empty commentary. My knees are burning, consorts of the crooked pain arching my antique spine, but my husband doesn't need to know. He convinced me to come up here on a whim, returning to the spot where we first made love out of a want for anything else to do. Neither of us can really believe we once joined the copper and granite bodies of Vigeland in their primal nudity. The pair of us, sewn into a pack of other fools, had romped around the pedestals under the cosmic pale of night. At some point we fell together, and decades passed.

Erasmus is gone on a full-blown nostalgia trip, detailing our adventure with fairy-tale insincerity. I feel a pang of inadequacy through him, his body not a day older than it was all those years ago, and his needs much the same. But sex, however loosely defined, hasn't been part of our equation for some time. The stiffest thing I have left is the wood cane propping me up. Our arrangement has always been open, though, and he's never had trouble bringing home new friends. Erasmus used to joke about the "boys lined up around the block" when I was in my forties and fifties and starting to look noticeably older than the average Post-Age man. I've been a global fetish ever since.

Things were still fine when I got too old to play, and it's only been in the past several months, as my date approached, that Erasmus started to withdraw from his own needs. I think the terminus became very real, very fast for him, and at times I've even felt some guilt. Someone should have warned him years ago what my special brand of love could do to a person.

As we walk, the Ministry's guards spread around us in one of their defensive postures, eyes wide and ears listening to the rubbernecking throng of people beyond. It's not easy to transport a sickly centenarian around the world, much less one that draws a crowd. I can't blame the gawkers, though—the Ministry has ensured the gawkers will never grow a day over thirty, but their hopeless primordial curiosity in the ravages of age has only grown more rabid as it has become more rarified. Even the petulant Ministry officials organizing my final days have asked for autographs when they thought their cohort wasn't looking.

"Wow," Erasmus says, pointing up. "I forgot how... gross it is."

His finger has landed on *Monolith*, the decidedly phallic center-piece of the park—a writhing mass of granite limbs climbing desperately toward salvation, or God, or whatever. I could confuse the delightfully wry look on his face for that of the boy I met seventy-eight years ago, when we were both still twenty seven. My sweet Dorian Gray—he still hates when I call him that. I've been told the reference is extraordinarily passé.

"We're closer than ever," I say.

"To what?"

"To whatever they're reaching for."

I take another step but my bastard knee gives out, forcing me to fall on Erasmus. Much sturdier than my cane, he holds me for a moment before guiding me to the nearest bench. Dr. Kathryn runs over with her medical bag already splayed open, its deep pockets clanking with the crisp crystal tones of various vials and instruments. The crowd is galvanized into a flurry by my sudden drop, a sea of handheld cams fighting for angles beneath the media drones.

Is this it? Is Old Aldo going to die?

These tourists would never forget their random decision to come here today, ending up as front-row spectators for a world-shaking event. Having lost the opportunity to control the pomp and circum-stance of my passing, I'm also fairly certain that the Ministry's PR department would spontaneously combust.

"What do you feel and where do you feel it?" Kathryn says, pressing two fingers to my jugular.

"I'm okay," I say, batting her off. "Just give me a second."

Kathryn taps her foot and then looks in the bag.

"Here," she says, holding up a palm with two smalls pills. "We're not taking any chances."

"I'm fine," I reiterate hoarsely.

"That is objectively not true," Kathryn says.

"Fair enough," I reply, and swallow the pills dry.

I've never asked what's in them, or bothered to read up on things like the efficacy of the cancer-busting treatments they give me at the state hospital. Many people distrust the Ministry—again, fair enough—but I've known since a very young age that they had an investment in keeping me alive and comfortable. My parents were apparently anti-Post-Age radicals, and among the last couples to be jailed for refusing to give their child genome therapy in utero, despite the Ministry's amendment to the Global Bill of Rights. Every new child had been guaranteed this treatment by law decades before me, never having to worry about genetic defects, disorders, diseases, or physically aging a day over thirty, give or take a few subjective years. Combined with the same modern medicines keeping me alive, people became highly unlikely to die of natural causes, able to live on interminably unless they managed to get into an accident or a fight. By letting me be born without the treatment, my ideologue parents were guilty of criminally negligent preemptive manslaughter, child abuse, and so forth.

When I was very young, before I can really remember, we lived in the woods and slept in tents, spending much of the day learning how to stay quiet and follow the moss. As we found out, the world wasn't really big enough anymore to hide from the Ministry, and I've been under their custodial care ever since my parents were taken away. I'm the so-called "last" of my kind, and boy, have they squeezed this utter dry for every last drop of propaganda. You could fill a museum with all the speeches, commercials, guest appearances, and posters I've been on in my life, and as a matter of fact, they probably will.

"My unfortunate nature is why the Ministry's genome therapy is so important," I would declare to the few people still hell-bent on having children. For everyone else, the rush to pass on their genes dissipated in light of their immortality, making my message to them even simpler:

"Isn't it great what the Ministry does for you? *Look how time has engulfed my body! All because the Ministry wasn't there to protect me...*"

Honest or not, I have a hard time complaining about all those years I spent parading my wrinkled brow for the world to see. I've been through my adolescent rage and midlife crises and existential nightmares. Overall? Life could have been worse.

"I'll get a wheelchair," Erasmus mumbles.

"The hell you will," I say.

"Well, that *would* play well with our pity-focused demographic," Yingpei, one of the Ministry publicists in my entourage, says. "Do we have one nearby?"

"No wheelchair," I reiterate, but the production team is too busy bickering back and forth about Yingpei's interpretation of the current social media stat report.

"He's my patient," Kathryn interjects, shoving a PA to the side. "It's my decision. Let me see that report..."

"No!" I shout, loud enough for the media drones to hear and zoom in. The group stops. "*No wheelchair.*"

They all look at me, and then down again at their devices, tracking responses to my outburst across the web.

"This is... interesting," Yingpei says, tablet outstretched like a divining rod. "5,502 hearts and climbing on @carter47657's comment, 'You got this, Aldo! 'No wheelchair!'"

"@realfakedylanthomas12 just tagged Aldo in a full repost of 'Do not go gentle into that good night,'" a PA says. "We're not clear if it's sarcasm or not, but it's got 2,095 upvotes already. We're trending."

"We're always trending," Yingpei grumbles. "But now he *has* to walk."

"Don't listen to them," Kathryn says. "Listen to your body."

"Help me up, Elmo," I say, putting out my elbow. Several guards move in to catch me if I fall.

"If I was just a little younger we could give them a real show," I say, and Erasmus starts coughing.

"Stop," he says, coughs turning to giggles, "you're gonna make me cry."

~

The goddam dog-thing is licking my hand and I can't believe we are having this fight again. When Erasmus pulls this type of shit I wonder if our little society could still weather the type of natural disaster needed to knock these idiotic ideas out his head. Before the Post-Age epoch, the Great Famine cut the world's population back to a quarter of its critical mass. It makes me marginally more comfortable to know that our ancestors didn't have time to figure out how to clone their dying husband's long-dead dog as a parting gift. There were too many bodies to burn.

"I asked you not to," I say, pulling my hand away. The dog-thing starts whining. "I've asked you not to do this so many times."

"I just thought..." Erasmus begins, then stops. "I don't know what I thought."

"Don't you know how this makes me feel? I mean really, can you guess? After all this time, do you really not understand why this upsets me?"

"Because you don't like thinking about the dog?"

"No, Erasmus, that's not it at all."

I roll off the chair and struggle toward our apartment's bar, my body creaking like a rusted automaton. I'm not allowed to drink anything one might think to keep in a bar, but I insisted the Ministry stock it with my electrolyte formula so I could retain some sense of normalcy. I pull one of my bottles out and pour a bit of the thick purple liquid into a short tumbler. I picked up this classy trick from Chinara Chukwu, the second-to-last oldest citizen of Earth. She passed a few years ago under similarly manufactured Ministry control. A weeks-long social media blitz had detailed her suddenly ailing health, leading rather conspicuously into one final grandmotherly address before the eyes of the world, finishing just as she slipped off. Like all of them before, it was a beautiful fake—Chinara was always going to die, but she hadn't exactly followed her own body's script. The Ministry's propaganda machine has a timeline, and when your time comes, that's it—they simply take you off whatever magic pills are marginally extending your stay and suddenly you can no longer "hold on." Everyone like me was going to die anyway, so why not get some political mileage out of us? The Ministry can be like that —a tribe of primitive fabulists who use every part of the political carcass for one need or another. Publicly, I'd describe the whole charade as an open secret met with blissful, voluntary ignorance. And it's that same ignorance—the type that pines for a round, theatrical ending—that probably led Erasmus to bring me a clone of sweet Plini.

"Explain it to me again," Erasmus begs. "I was trying to be helpful. Fix up the list…"

"Stop," Dr. Kathryn says from her spot at the edge of the room. "Stop riling him up, Erasmus. His heart can't take it."

"He's not riling me up," I say, and then point to the dog-thing. "That is."

"Can someone get this damn dog out of here?" Kathryn shouts.

"It just paints a picture," I continue, sucking down the goop. "In my opinion, not everything is replaceable. Evidently, you don't feel the same way."

"Aldo…" Erasmus starts.

"How will you do it, though? Will any other boy do? I mean, you can't clone me like the dog so you'll have to start fresh somewhere. It's quite a conundrum."

"What are you talking about?"

"Wait, I've got it—if you really miss me, you've got more than enough Ministry capital to convince a boy to go plastic for you. He can look just like me after a few months and you can brainstorm a new goddamn list to work out while he's recovering."

"What the hell is wrong with you?" Erasmus shouts, and the dog-thing starts barking. Two Ministry guards try to corner it unsuccessfully.

"I've asked you not to clone this dog a thousand times, to just let him be gone. Is nothing sacred, Erasmus? Will it be this easy for you to replace me? How long are you going to wait, really?"

"Wait? You want to talk about waiting?" Erasmus throws his head back and almost lets out a laugh. "Don't throw that word at me. You know exactly how much waiting I've done for you."

"Here we go," I say, taking another sip. I can't remember the last time we fought and his deferred appointment to the colony ship bound for Calliope's World didn't come up. "That decision was sixty years ago."

"Sixty years ago that I gave up my seat..."

"'...on the first jumpship to Luyten's Star,'" I parody, "'the promise of Calliope's World.' Yes, we know. You're a martyr, who gave up hundreds of years in a cryo-box to stay with me. Elmo, who will live *forever* knowing he could have had his name listed in the history books alongside all the other colonists instead of becoming a footnote under Old Aldo. My fault, right?"

"I stayed for you."

"And I told you to go, Erasmus; I told you not to waste your time on a bag of bones."

He suddenly churns out a growl, a taste of unmistakable angst I rarely get to see from him.

"Boys, stop it," Kathryn says again, jumping between us. She motions at the guards, who give up chasing the dog-thing and circle around us.

"Ever the victim," Erasmus yells. "'Poor me,' you say, 'don't waste your life on me...' Every time I hear that it's like a punch in the gut. Even after all these years, all the shit we've been through, do you really still think I could have just climbed aboard and left? That I *should* have climbed aboard and left?"

"You were afraid," I say, nothing left to loose in obfuscation. My knees are shaking; I'm over-exerting. "That's the truth, isn't it? You were afraid of taking the leap—saying goodbye to Earth and all of this—and you used me as an excuse."

Erasmus chews his lip and I watch the gears turning in that big bald head of his.

"You're an asshole," he says.

"Then tell me I'm wrong, Erasmus."

He stands there for a moment with his fists clenched and some new curse riding the tip of his tongue, but it never comes to pass.

Instead he lets out a sigh and marches into our bedroom, slamming the door behind him.

I slump against the bar in the resulting dust, anchoring myself between two stools. Rushing in, Kathryn and two of the guards help me back to my chair.

"I guess we can cross 'an old fashioned fight' off his list," I say. Kathryn gives me something to help me sleep while the faux-Plini runs circles around the room.

"This dog," I say, my breathing labored from the shouting "Please just get that thing out of here."

Kathryn nods, but the barking continues as I shuffle off into the deep.

I've been fighting with Dr. Kathryn this morning, trying to get her to cancel her script for counseling.

"I'm not spending the waning hours of my life bartering with a shrink," I say. "Right now, the only delusional person I see is you."

"Clever," she replies. "But like I said, the Ministry is insisting you both go after last night's squabble. They want you refreshed for the big day. They want you comfortable."

"That old chestnut," I say. "Don't you get tired of asking me if I'm comfortable? Or asking how to make me comfortable? Telling me to get comfortable? Has no one considered that, maybe, dying like this just *isn't* comfortable? There's really nothing anyone can do except wait until I'm gone to strip me for copper."

"Well, we haven't tried every pain reliever."

"Look, you can tell the Ministry they'll get their speech, okay? What I do until Sunday primetime is my business."

Kathryn jots down a note and then opens her bag.

"There's something else," she says, pulling out vials.

"What?"

"It's time to start lowering your doses, phasing things out."

"What does that mean?"

"We can't just take you off every medication you're on and poof, it's over. In order to let you down safely we have to phase you off your prescriptions over the next two weeks."

"Let me down 'safely?'" I ask. "Is that a joke?"

"No one wants you to suffer."

I feel a rattle in my spine, some dormant desire to fly from here. I've met my executioner.

"What do the next few days look like, then?" I ask.

"Well," Kathryn says, eyeing a vial. "It might get a bit uncomfortable."

I can see the downtown holotrons from my balcony, each one plastering different images of my face in the air above the city. Text trails underneath regurgitate the same question that's been on the world's mind for weeks: *How ill is Aldo? New video shows the ailing health of the last elder.*

I've been waking up early for weeks now, trying to catch as many sunrises as possible. They still let me drink tea, but it's a bitter remedy for the everlasting chill stalking my skin. Dr. Kathryn's medicinal reductions have started to let my innards break down, making it even harder to eat and sleep. In light of this I'm forced to sip gingerly, enjoying the aesthetic more than the taste. Watching the city hum to life and spark like a tesla coil will have to charge me for the whole day.

The glass doors behind me slide open and someone walks onto the balcony.

"'Thy drugs are quick,'" I say, assuming it's Dr. Kathryn. She likes Shakespeare, bless her heart. "The dementia is setting in, I think—I've already forgotten my manners. Would you like some tea?"

"It's me, Aldo," Erasmus says. He stands still at the doorway waiting for an invitation, as if we both don't own the condo.

"Well, do you want tea?" I ask.

Erasmus sits down on the chaise lounge next to mine and watches as I slowly lift the pot to pour.

"You know I've thought about just jumping over the edge," I say, nodding to the railing, "just to mess with them; just for the hell of it."

"I suspect they'd find some way to catch you."

"Maybe not," I say, sitting back. "I think they could spin a suicide well. 'He couldn't deal with the thought of his body giving up on him,' or some such nonsense."

We turn to watch the birds in silence, and for several minutes I can hear his mouth opening and closing as he tries to say what's on his mind. He never knows how to start.

"What is it, Elmo?"

"I'm sorry," he says, unexpectedly. "I'm sorry for the other night, but we can't do our normal routine. We don't have two weeks to avoid each other and come back fresh."

"You're right," I say, "but I need you to tell me why you thought that dog was a good idea. There's obviously something I'm missing, because you should know better than anyone I would've never put Plini on that list."

"It was a mistake, a misattribution," he says. "I didn't know how to ask you."

"Ask me what?"

Erasmus sighs and takes a sip of tea.

"What?" I ask again.

"Honestly, even I didn't know at first," he says. "I didn't know what I wanted. Then I talked to the counselor..."

"Lovely," I say.

"We worked through it, even came up with a plan for me to tell you what I want, but I've been struggling. I thought the dog might open the door to the discussion, but it was a stupid idea. I'm sorry for that."

"Okay. You realize this still feels highly indirect?"

He puts down the tea and holds out his hand. I put my hand in his and we lock eyes.

"This feels like a proposal," I say. "You know we're already married, right?"

"Yes, I know," he says. "But Aldo, this is about the future."

"Something I don't have much say in."

"On this, you do," he says, and closes his eyes. "Aldo, I want to have a child."

An "oh" comes out of me, and then I don't know what to say. We had had this discussion long ago and mutually decided it wasn't for us. Erasmus had never wanted to be tied down to Earth, and I didn't want to bring another person into the world who would just have to watch me die. It hadn't come up again.

"This is... new," I say.

"There's more," he continues. "The kicker, I guess... I want it to be your child, too."

"Mine?"

"Do you remember when we made cryobank deposits? Froze it, just in case?"

I nod and squeeze his hand.

"The child could be your descendant," he says, "not you, but a piece of you. So we won't be alone... I won't be alone..."

"Erasmus..."

"You're always asking me how I'll remember you," he continues, starting to tear up again, "or *if* I'll remember you, which is just silly. And I didn't have an answer before, but I do now. A child... a child could be the missing piece. And they'll never have to lose you because you'll already be gone."

I'm finding it hard to form words.

"But what... what about Calliope?"

"That actually sounds like a nice name," he says. "There'll always be time to see the stars, Aldo. Perhaps we'll go together one day, the three of us."

"The three of us..." I start to say, but my poise falls away, composure flat-lining as my decommissioned tear ducts well with water. Erasmus pulls me close and whispers in my ear.

"I don't want to let go," he says. "I've never wanted to let go."

The soundstage thrums on the pulse of the world, all hands on deck for the final chapter of my monumental plight. Set dressed, cameras cleaned, make-up applied—the only thing missing is the studio audience, itself replaced by the black void of empty bleachers beyond the ring of theater light. I've been wondering all morning which lowbrow comedy of errors the Ministry films here when they aren't filming mine.

The pain had gotten rather severe in the last two days, and last night I told Kathryn that I was losing confidence in my ability to give the final address. The Ministry mobilized so fast that I didn't even realize where we were going until it was too late.

Erasmus is here beside the bed, managing to stay collected with a little help from Kathryn's bag. He's mumbling, looking out of the set's fake windowpane onto the green screen backdrop and asking every technician who walks by why this couldn't be filmed in a proper hospital with proper windows.

The PAs drag in a teleprompter and help me test the sight line for my speech.

"I'll do my best," I say, and then start to fall asleep again, eyelids slipping like fingers from a cliff.

When I open them again a line has formed—a studio's worth of fresh young faces come to shake my scarecrow hand. One by one I let each of them grip me, their adulations a meal of empty praise. Kathryn is last, and she says the only words that matter.

"Goodbye, Aldo."

The set clears and everyone moves into position.

"Are you ready?" Erasmus asks.

"I love you," I say, and nod into the black.

My thoughts are with Calliope as the stage lights go up, their beams like bolts of laser light, and their heat like kisses from the sun.

ASKING AFTER DEATH
BY ZACK BE

Tragedy struck when I was fourteen years old. Someone had died—not the first person in my life, nor the last—but they had died young. Not in the canon of "middle-aged too-soons" such as, "should've got that colonoscopy at forty with that family history," or "should've worn sunscreen at twenty-two." I mean *young*, in the canon of, "what a shame they didn't make it to twenty-two," or even to twenty in this case. It's the kind of *young* that shatters families, if not whole communities, and challenges them to turn their back on any dreams they were holding on to.

I didn't, or couldn't, fully grasp the breadth of the devastation at fourteen. At the funeral, rows of teenage boys sat crying in pew after pew, not even attempting to hide their tears from one another. My uncle, who I'd never seen cry before—and not since—was deep in a handkerchief. Relative strangers embraced in long, unbroken hugs, and all of this is to say nothing of the despondency on display in the immediate family.

But there I was, dry-eyed and surrounded by people who seemed to be clued into something I was not—some detail that opened their floodgates to grief. I was experiencing something much more existential. Not numb, nor frozen; just questioning. Deeper beneath that was a shame that I might be actively engaging in some perverted, toxic stoicism, even though I knew this was not the case. As if on cue, my blank stare elicited this exact criticism from a passerby.

"Why aren't you crying?" the strange woman asked me. "Don't you understand what's happened here? Don't you understand this is a tragedy?"

Where does one even begin? Aren't all deaths a tragedy? Of course I knew this one was especially unexpected, but were tears a necessity? I stood silently in response, mouth open but no words coming out.

"Show some respect," she said, and pushed past me.

What little bit of shame I had been experiencing over my lack of tears was exacerbated by the attack. Even so, I couldn't help but sink deeper into the existentialism of it all. Don't all of these people see death every day on the news, or on their TV shows, or in their favorite books? I doubted they were reduced to tears at each one of those. And besides, death comes for us all, so why was this death so different, and what did it mean?

In life, questions about death and meaning don't necessarily have discrete answers. Beliefs differ between religions, cultures, contexts, and even over the individual's life course. Some deaths make us cry, but others make us laugh (see *The Darwin Awards*). Is there any rhyme or reason to it, or is it all the byproduct of our individual psychology? Your best bet might be to ask your preferred deity for an answer, but I suspect you might find their voice mailbox is full.

In fiction, however, we (the authors) *are* the deities. We move, seen or unseen, behind our creations and determine how they'll live or how they'll die. Fiction provides one of the best venues for us to explore the infinite possible meanings of death that life refuses to give us. When does death matter, and when does it not? Who needs to die? Who gets to die? How many will die? Does it hurt, and if so, who does it hurt most, the living or the dead? When a death occurs, what do we intend for it to mean?

Speculative fiction authors can take this power even further. We not only get to decide the fates of our characters, but the very nature of death itself. Is death the end, or just the beginning of a journey into uncharted lands per Richard Matheson's *What Dreams May Come*? Is death a place, a time, or perhaps even a character as in Neil Gaiman's *The Sandman*? Is death insurmountable or can it be conquered with science, magic, or will as in Richard K. Morgan's *Altered Carbon*? What are the intended and unintended consequences of conquering death?

Our powers here are great. You may not have previously thought there was so much philosophical weight hidden behind your decision to kill off a random bard in the pub fight scene. Your description of the "obsidian blade [entering] his throat in a shower of scarlet" was flashy enough, after all. But every move we make in our fiction sends a message whether we meant to or not, and that goes double for death. As a result, it is far too easy to wield death with reckless abandon and muddle the conversation between you and the reader. Leaving a topic as basic as death unconsidered in your writing process can lead to a story that is unbalanced and hollow.

Here are three interconnected questions to help you navigate death in your work:

1. In *Tuesdays with Morrie,* author Mitch Albom writes, "Maybe death is the great equalizer, the one big thing that can finally make strangers shed a tear for one another." We are all aware of the inevitability of our deaths, and thus it becomes one of the most direct ways we can connect with those around us, including our readers. At a primal level, death is the price all living things pay for their life, and thus its looming threat forms the backbone of all motivation. We eat because our evolutionary machinery wants us to fight another day (and procreate!). We run from Freddy, Jason, and Michael Myers for roughly the same reasons. In fact, the fear of death is a prerequisite propellant to most action scenes, regardless of context—we don't want to see Indiana Jones die, and even though we know he won't, we still grip the arms of chairs

during the mine cart chase in *Temple of Doom*, wondering how we might fare in his shoes. Authors can use the omnipresence of death to their advantage. If you know your audience's lizard brain is always on the lookout for danger and death, then consider the first question: how could you play off that basic instinct with intention?

2. While the awareness of death is ubiquitous, our relationship to it, and thus our motivations, can vary widely. Those who fear death are either pushed toward their goals by that fear, or held back from them; those who seek revenge or justice are often motivated by the promise that giving death to another will alleviate their pain, or at least end an evil; those who desire death for themselves seek an escape from the pain of the world, or to sacrifice themselves for a supposed good. Whatever the reason, we all intrinsically understand the nature of the final price, and as authors, we must consider whether the audience will buy what we are selling. There may be no greater crime in fiction than a meaningless death, the only exception being when the meaninglessness *is* the meaning, à la Erich Maria Remarque's *All Along the Western Front* and its portrayal of the senseless meat grinder of World War One. For each and every death, ask yourself: what are the perspectives of your characters on this death, and how does it feed their characterization?

3. Family therapist and communication theorist Paul Watzlawick determined in his Five Axioms of Communication that one "cannot not communicate." The idea here is that all of your words and actions communicate something, even when we try to use silence or avoidance to nullify the delivery of any message. Absence can boom like a megaphone, and not saying "it" can be as, or more, powerful than blurting "it" out—see Ernest Hemingway's "Hills Like White Elephants," in which the potential abortion at the center of the tale is

never directly addressed. As authors, we must understand that we also "cannot not communicate" a philosophy of death in our fiction. Per the previous point that death is the great equalizer, our readers are always on the lookout for death—to do so is a functional and evolutionarily adaptive state of nature. Thus, even a conscious attempt to avoid providing a philosophy about the meaning of death only reinforces an implicit message that you believe death is either unimportant, too terrifying to face, beyond comprehension, or something else. Now ask yourself: does this excess philosophy of death serve the themes of your story, or is it just an unattended leftover? For example, deaths in George R. R. Martin's *A Song of Ice and Fire* are often brutal and unexpected, regularly involving the execution of characters we assumed to be primary protagonists right alongside the copious anonymous violence of medieval war. Each death in the series serves to both invert fantasy tropes and reinforce the brutality, chaos, and hopelessness of a dark world descending into a long winter. So ask yourself: what themes does the treatment of death in your narrative reinforce?

In my story "The Bygone," death is a relative rarity in a future where humans no longer age past their peak physical condition. Thus, death from old age has become an anomalous event ripe for primetime viewing on a planet populated by bored and vapid eternal children. The insipid spectacle of Aldo's death reinforces themes of identity and the loss thereof via death. Aldo is poised to lose everything when he dies, but that loss of self makes him the only person left who truly understands what it means—or meant—to be human, so he embraces the desire to disappear. His cynicism and exhaustion with the fanfare is indicative of his struggle to accept that he lacks the privilege to be as nonchalant as everyone else, and his character turn comes when he realizes that he does, in fact, want his legacy to survive his death in the form of a child he'll never know.

Before I could explore the three questions with any sincerity in my fiction I needed to explore my own relationship with death. Why did that funeral generate feelings of grief and despair in the stranger, whereas for me it only created uncertainty? Naiveté, cynicism, realization all seemed to play a role in my response, and it didn't matter that this was my response upon reflection, and the reflection itself helped to garner deeper appreciation for our collective uncertainty around death and the ways that uncertainty makes us behave. As a technique, I suggest writing about a loss from your own life. This can be in the form of a journal entry, creative nonfiction piece, or even a social media post. Many of us do not fully understand our own thoughts about topics as complicated as death until we give ourselves a chance to process them on our own. The act of writing takes the amorphous cloud of thoughts you have about death and forces you to shape them into a coherent linear narrative. In the end, you are likely to discover something about your relationship with grief, loss, and eternity that you didn't have a grasp on before, and the result will be an author with a deeper well of feelings and perspectives to draw on in their work. Going through the process of better understanding yourself will greatly increase your ability to comprehend your characters, and answer the three questions about death above.

I am still working on understanding myself all the time. I didn't cry at that funeral, but I did the next time one of my dogs passed away. The autobiographical songs about death and family on the album *Carrie and Lowell* by Sufjan Stevens have stirred me, but I barely felt a thing when Chris Cornell, a musician I admired in my youth, committed suicide. These moments begin as mysteries, but through self-exploration some degree of truth can be revealed. As fiction writers we can determine the nature of tragedies, and offering a compelling meaning for those deaths is one of our greatest duties.

ACKNOWLEDGMENTS

And now, a very special thank you to all of the backers who made this project possible. We would not have been able to make *Inner Workings* come alive without them. We are grateful for all of the support!

A. Barre

Adam McDaniel

Akis Linardos

Alex

Alisa

Amy L

Andrew Kappas

Andrew Tontala

Anne Gaines

Benjamin Widmer

Bianca Elsensohn

Brandon Butler

Brian Beckwith

Brian Brandau

Brooks Moses

Bruce

Caitlin Campbell

Candice

Carol Elaine

Carolyn Rowland

carver rapp

Casey Humbert
Cherise Papa
Chris Ess
Chris Mandeville
Eric Christoffersen
Clark Newbold
Colleen Cruz
Colleen Feeney
Courtney Hagan
Craig
Cursed Dragon Ship
Dan
Darren Lipman
David Hankins
David Lawful
David 'slick' Sellers
Dean Berman
Dennis M. Martin
Dina Kraus
Dustin
Eric Honour
Eric Stallsworth
Erin Cyffka
fengypants
Fran Scannell
Fred Wehling
Gabriel Connor Salter
Garrett Pease
Greg Walti
Ian Chung
J.T. Evans
Jackie Wirsing
Jacob Perez
Jade Wildy
James Davies

James Riffle

Jared Nelson

Jennifer Perry

John Neal

Jon Gensler

Jonathan

Joshua McGinnis

Judy Goldsmith

K. Z. Richards

Kai Delmas

KANARI

Karen and Bob Cyffka

Karen Call

Ken Papai

Klikke Sietel

Kristie Humbert

LA Selby

Leah Ning

Lucinda Lawson

Lyn Krowe

M. Lang

Margaret St. John

Mark

Martha Pedersen

Martin Greening

Martyna Jermalonek

Meg Overman

Michael J Wyant Jr

Michael Madden

Moira

N. B. Littell

Natasha Chisdes

Nic & Mary Dibble

Nick A

Nina Goodman

Patrick Gunning

Peggy Kimbell

penguinonstrike

Peter Lead

Preston

reigheena

Richard and Nedra Fredrick

Robin D

Ron Carey

Ron Friedman

Ruth Ann Orlansky

Sarah Fisher

Scott Sands

Sean Quillen

shannon

Sherry Brandon

Space Cowboy Books

Steve Pantazis

Susan Lane

Susannah Campbell

Tanya Hales

The Creative Fund by BackerKit

Thorsten Daniel

Ticknor Tales

Tiffiny Felix

Tom Rawls

Tracy Hughes

Victor Gonzalez

Wilbur Smith

Will Sobel

William Call

Wulf Moon

www.ingramcontent.com/pod-product-compliance
Lightning Source LLC
Chambersburg PA
CBHW021339310726
48971CB00001B/197